THE NEXT BEST THING

By the author of THE BRAMBLE BUSH

Charles Mergendahl

THE NEXT
BEST THING

G. P. PUTNAM'S SONS New York

Part One

Chapter One

ANITA SLAYTON GATTONE—Mrs. Frank Gattone—sat in her dressing gown in her small dormitory apartment in Plimpton Academy's Slayton Hall and lifted a cup of coffee to her lips. The Swedish-modern chair in which she was sitting, like the sleek blond sofa and several other pieces of modern furniture in the room, struck her as particularly out of place in the old-fashioned, New England setting of the dormitory.

Fake old-fashioned, phony New England, she thought. After all, Slayton Hall was not really that old. It had been built in her own lifetime by her own father—well, paid for by her father, at any rate.

Our furnishings look like exiles from New York, she thought, grimacing at the bitter taste of coffee five hours old. Frank had brewed a pot of the stuff before leaving the house at seven that morning, while she was still asleep, to catch his train for New York. She hardly saw her husband at all these days. He was gone before she got up, and when he reached home at eight in the evening or later he was so tired he hardly wanted even to talk to her before going off to bed.

Remnants of our salad days, her thoughts continued as she eyed the furniture disapprovingly. Frank and she had bought the pieces on a shopping spree one afternoon at that Swedish shop on Fifth Avenue, when they were living on 72nd Street and he was beginning to make a name for himself in television.

They were so happy then; the world had seemed so full of possibilities. Why in God's name had she knocked herself out to tear him away from his promising career and get him a job back home teaching at the Academy? Securing the position was no problem, since her father was head of the Academy's board of trustees. But she'd practically had to drive herself into a nervous breakdown to get Frank to make the change.

Anita didn't have to ask herself why she had done it. She knew why. Because she was jealous. Because a wife can be just as jealous of her husband's career as she can be of another woman.

It was different in the old days when she was working as Frank's production assistant in radio and sharing all the excitement of the job with him. But then she had fallen in love with him and married him, and then Alan was born and Frank was in the army and when he came home from the war he was in television and he had no place for her in his work. She had stood it as long as she could, feeling her husband drawing farther and farther away from her as he became increasingly involved in his career. No wonder she had begun drinking—out of loneliness and frustration and boredom. It was enough to drive anyone to drink.

Anyway, she had won out in the end and brought Frank back with her to Plimpton Ridge. But did she think she could keep her husband safe under lock and key forever, teaching English to a bunch of kids? Well, she had for ten years—until that ridiculous offer came from Kingley Productions, and Frank was off for New York like a bat out of hell, eager to make a comeback as a director.

"Just this one chance," he had pleaded. "I've got to take it, Anita. If I don't there may never be another." And she had consented reluctantly, knowing that beyond this one chance he was already dreaming of Hollywood, because the movie people had their eye on the show he was directing. And if that ever happened, if he ever got to Hollywood . . . She knew her Frank, how impressionable he was, and the thought that she might some day lose him frightened her.

"Don't look so unhappy," he'd said, laughing at her fears, speaking to her as if she were a child. "After all, I'm not going to the moon. I'll be home every night."

Maybe. Not as she knew television he wouldn't. Once you got caught in that trap you no longer had a life of your own.

Anita studied the blue veins on the back of her hand. They said you could tell a woman's age by her hands. She was thirty-seven, but except for those telltale veins she could still pass for thirty. Anyway, it wasn't a matter of age; it was a matter of emotions. She happened to be the emotional type, that's all, and it showed in her hands.

I suppose I'm one of those dynamite women you read about, she thought. It was true; sometimes she felt so tense she wanted to blow the roof right off the place. She felt like that right now, as if nervous tension had been building up in her for days and would go right on building up to the explosion point and there was nothing she could do to stop it.

It's time I got out of this dressing gown, she said to herself, and went into the bedroom. An attractive woman with short yellow hair that she wore in the shaggy Italian style and tinted occasionally, she had the high cheekbones and blue eyes typical of all the Slaytons, and an erect, mettlesome body she let stoop when she was alone or tired, or when she simply didn't care.

Outside, she could hear the school bell tolling, and the boys' feet grinding in the gravel, their voices strident in the noon sunlight, and idly she brushed her hair and observed her high, full

13

breasts in the mirror where her dressing gown had fallen open, and thought: thank goodness, at least there hadn't been a single crisis during the days Frank had spent in New York.

"What kind of crisis could there be?" he asked impatiently when he'd first arranged for a three months' leave of absence from the Academy. "What are you talking about?"

"Things happen. That's why we're living in a dormitory, isn't it? Otherwise they'd let all the faculty members have homes of their own."

"What things?"

"Well, suppose a boy gets hurt."

"Send him to the infirmary."

"Suppose he becomes homesick, or has girl trouble of some kind."

"You're a mother. Alan's already sixteen, and if you can handle your own son you can handle any other boy."

Except that sometimes she seriously doubted her ability to handle her own son. Frank had sensed what she was thinking at the time. "I know, honey," he had said penitently, "I know I haven't been a very good father to Alan and too wrapped up in myself. But I'll make up for it, you'll see. If only I can make a go of this thing . . ."

Ah, yes, Anita sighed. *If* was such a big little word. If ever Alan needed a father it was now.

The bell had stopped tolling. Suddenly aware of the silence, Anita put down the brush and carefully applied lipstick to her mouth that was rather full for the narrow face, then went into the kitchen. She shook the coffeepot. It was empty. She decided to make fresh coffee, but changed her mind. She wandered back into the living room and paused to stare at the liquor cabinet.

If she wanted to she could open that cabinet and pour herself a drink. What difference would it make? Frank wouldn't care. If he cared he'd be with her now, instead of somewhere on Madison Avenue dreaming about his old TV comeback.

Only of course he did care. That was the reason he had quit television in the first place and taken the teaching job at Plimpton. Naturally he denied that was the reason. He was tired of the rat race, he said, glad to escape to the quiet, rewarding life of a teacher.

Rewarding! That was a laugh.

Admittedly, she had been drinking too much in the apartment on 72nd Street. Enough to bring her to the verge of a breakdown before Frank had taken her away. Well, she had kept her part of the bargain. She had not taken a single drop ever since. Frank knew he could trust her. That's why he wasn't afraid to leave the stuff in the house. "If you wanted a drink," he said, "you'd get it whether I tried to stop you or not. In fact, the more I tried to stop you, the more determined you'd be to get one."

The more anyone tried to stop her from doing something the more determined she was to do it. Like leaving home against her father's wishes back there in the early days of the war and getting a job in radio and setting herself up in her own apartment in New York. Like marrying young Frank Gattone in defiance of her father, who said Frank was only a common immigrant's son—which he was—and too far beneath her socially.

Her father! Insisting on *her* good behavior. Too bad he hadn't thought of his own. Then they wouldn't all be sitting on a powder keg the way they were. Some day, somebody was going to light the fuse and when that happened, Anita sighed, God help us. The old hypocrite! Every time she saw her father in church on Sunday with his handsome silver head bent in thought, she resented him all over again.

Yet here she was, a faculty wife, living in Slayton Hall donated by her father, named after her father. You could hardly turn around in Plimpton Ridge without bumping into the great Mitchel Slayton one way or another. Here she was, alone now,

15

a television widow again, waiting . . . waiting . . . waiting for what? For her son, Alan, to come back from his history class. For her husband to come back from New York. Waiting for the bell to toll again, stop again, toll again, day after day, while she grew older and lonelier, and Frank learned that you can't recapture your youth. Waiting for her brother Roy to come back to his insipid wife Mildred, on his next flight from Hawaii. Waiting for Alan to become nineteen, twenty, and elope some day with Paul Barker's daughter, Christina, who wasn't his daughter at all, actually, however ignorant Paul might still be of the fact.

No, she could never allow them to marry. Never! Anita clenched her hands fiercely. Whatever else happened, not that, ever. Poor Alan. Poor Christina. No wonder they were so bewildered by her insistence that they were seeing too much of each other. How could she ever explain to them why she was so set against their going steady? Could she spell it out for them, say the ugly word *incest*, tell them what would happen if they were ever to marry? The very thought of it made her feel weak, panicky. How could she ever tell her son that his own grandfather was Christina's father? No, she could not, any more than Roberta could tell her daughter the truth.

Dear old Daddy, she thought bitterly, you certainly fixed things up just dandy. Just dandy. Dammit! She would take a drink, she had to have a drink to stop her mind from racing around like a squirrel in a cage.

The telephone rang. Anita started guiltily, and jerked her eyes from the liquor cabinet. Going over to the phone she picked up the receiver.

It was Frank. He'd be a little late. Yes, things were going all right with the show, but they needed a rewrite man on the script. No, they hadn't got around yet to casting. June 23rd, the date of the show, was still a long way off, but if you wanted somebody good for the lead you signed her up right away before she was offered more money by somebody else. As a matter of fact, they'd have to fill the part right away. . . . Of course he would be home tonight.

As she listened to him, Anita could visualize her husband at the other end of the wire, sitting behind his desk at Kingley Productions, a slender, dark, virile-looking man with a shock of black hair that kept tumbling down over his forehead, still gesticulating with his hands, still speaking with the slight remnants of an Italian accent.

"Who do you have in mind?" she asked.

"What?"

"For the part."

"Oh . . ." The pause was noticeable. "I told you we hadn't got around to that yet. Why?"

"I don't know. . . . Not Edith Parkes, I hope. . . ." Frank's silence was provoking. "Don't tell me you're actually thinking of her!" Anita said.

"I'm not thinking of anybody," Frank said, but he didn't sound too convincing.

"What about your production girl?"

"What about her?"

"I mean, have you got one yet?"

"Of course. Why do you ask?"

Anita laughed nervously. "I was a production girl once myself. Remember?"

Again there was an uncomfortable silence at the other end of the wire.

"I hope you're not forgetting about Wednesday night," Anita said.

"Wednesday night?" Frank said vaguely. "What about it?"

"But I told you, Frank. I've told you several times. And you promised. It's Dr. Bullock's evening. You know. The whole faculty will be there."

"I'm on leave, Anita. I've got a leave of absence so I can be free to do this TV thing. Can't you understand? I can't be in two places at once. Besides, what's so damn important about old Batty-ass Bullock's evening?"

"You're still a member of the faculty even if you are on leave," Anita said, trying to sound reasonable, yet aware of the agitation in her voice. "Paul Barker will be there . . . I mean Dr. Bullock will probably make an announcement about Paul's promotion to head of the department . . . I mean, after all, you're Paul's best friend here. . . . Anyway, I want you to be there, and you promised, Frank, you promised!"

"All right . . . all right. Don't get so excited about it. I'll try."

"No, don't say you'll try. Say you'll be there."

"I'll be there," Frank said wearily.

Silence. "Then I'll see you about eight tonight," Anita said.

"That's right. Maybe next time I'll take the car and drive in. Unless you need it, that is."

"Next time?"

"Naturally, next time," Frank said, exasperated. "There'll be a lot of next times between now and June 23rd. You knew that when Lester offered me the job."

"I know. I know."

"Are you all right?" Frank said, and she said of course she was all right, good-by, then hung up and sat there staring at the telephone, wondering why she felt so depressed, and since when Dr. Bullock's evening had suddenly become so all-fired important to her, and what Frank had meant by asking if she was all right. Until she heard the outer door open, and Alan's voice in the vestibule, and Paul Barker's.

Alan nodded sullenly to his mother and went to his room.

"Hello, Anita," Paul said, standing uncertainly in the doorway as though waiting for her to ask him in.

"Come in, Paul," Anita said. "I'm sorry I'm not dressed, but you know how it is. With Frank away I never do seem able to get the day started properly."

Paul Barker sat down on the edge of the sofa, but soon got up again and walked slowly around the room, while she watched him from her chair by the telephone. He was tall, much taller than her husband with a strong, almost ascetic face, serious blue eyes and brown hair graying at the temples. Funny, thought Anita, I always liked tall men, but I married a short one. He was wearing a tweed sport coat that hung loosely from his shoulders, hiding the thin but strong body beneath. He was an excellent tennis player, coached the school team, and could outswim any boy on the Plimpton swimming team although he was more than twice the age of even the oldest senior. Paul Barker was, in fact, an extremely attractive man, and looking at him now admiringly, Anita could not help wondering what he would be like in bed.

An attractive man, and a balanced one, as well, she thought. The only dependable one among us. Not herself, not Frank, not Roy, and not Paul's wife, Roberta, either, although outwardly Roberta gave the appearance of extreme, almost frightening normalcy. But what lay beneath that appearance Anita knew better than anyone—certainly better than Paul himself.

"Anita," Paul was saying.

"Yes?"

"I don't quite know how to say this . . ."

"Maybe none of us knows how to say anything."

Paul had been busy feeding his pipe from his tobacco pouch. Now he paused to look at her sharply, frowning.

"Meaning what?" he said.

"I mean we've all known each other for so long, and yet we can't really communicate at all." Heaven help us if we ever do communicate, Anita added to herself. If I were ever to tell him that Christina is not really his daughter, as he thinks, but my own father's child. And observing him curiously, she wondered how he would react if the truth were revealed to him.

"I don't know what you're talking about," Paul said, suddenly aware of Anita's scrutiny. "It's about Alan I'm thinking. He's been acting . . . well, a little strangely in class. As though there's something bothering him."

"You mean his marks are not what they should be?"

"No, not that, although they have been falling off. It's easy to see that the boy's mind is not on his work."

"Maybe he's not interested in the facts of history. Just the romance."

Paul shook his head irritably. "It's more than that, Anita."

She lifted her eyebrows. "More?" You poor innocent, she thought, unable to meet his eyes. I'll say there's more. "Perhaps it's because his father is away so much these days. Perhaps he feels insecure. Frank has dreams of leaving Plimpton, you know, and going to Hollywood if his TV show makes a hit. Alan hopes it will be a flop so we won't have to go."

"I still think it's more than that." Paul was looking at her steadily as he held a lighted match to the bowl of his pipe, and she thought again, with a secret glow, how very attractive he was.

"You mean Christina," she said.

"That's right."

"Alan says I don't like them going steady. Is that it?"

"Yes. He can't understand. He's talked to me about it and I know it troubles him."

"Well, if you expect him to keep up in his studies . . ."

"But he hints it's something else. He says, ask my mother."

"Nonsense," Anita said emphatically, too emphatically. "What else could there possibly be? Except that it's not good for teen-agers to get too serious about one another. What else could there possibly be, considering you and Roberta are just about our closest friends? Actually, I should be delighted that

20

Alan is interested in your daughter, although I do think they're too young to be thinking of marriage, don't you? And . . . well . . ." Anita felt that her voice was becoming shrill, that she was talking too excitedly. She stopped, pulled her voice under control. "Paul, it's nothing, so don't worry about it. You've got enough on your mind."

"Oh, I don't know."

"But I do. And you don't have to worry about that, either."

"What do you mean?"

"I mean about Dr. Bullock's evening, when he'll announce the new head of the department."

"Well, what about it?"

"Just don't worry, that's all."

"Why shouldn't I? Or rather, why should I be worried about that?"

"Oh, come on, Paul. After all, my father *is* head of the board."

"You mean you could influence your father to persuade Dr. Bullock and the members of the board . . ."

"Not influence."

"I don't want that, Anita. I don't want you, or Roy, or anybody else to talk to your father on my behalf. I want to be head of the department as much as I've ever wanted anything in my life—the same way Frank wants that television show of his to be a success—but I want it honestly, on my own merits, with no outside help from anyone. You understand, Anita?"

"You needn't be so fierce about it."

"I feel fierce about a thing like that." Paul smiled apologetically. "So you see there is something for me to worry about, after all. . . . Anyway, to change the subject, I do wish you would talk to Alan. Take him into your confidence. He's a very unhappy boy."

Take him into my confidence! Anita thought, hardly able to suppress a nervous laugh. Oh my God! I hope I never have to.

21

Her lips parted, as if she were about to say something, but then closed again firmly.

"Well," Paul said, "I guess I'd better be getting along." He nodded good-by and walked out to the little vestibule.

Anita heard the door open and close behind him. She rose and walked over to the window and looked out at Paul's tall figure striding purposefully across the campus. "Oh no," she said softly, "you have nothing to worry about, nothing at all." And then, involuntarily, she started to laugh and could not stop herself, not even when Alan appeared in the doorway and asked her what the hell was the big joke and she told him not to swear. All the way back to her room she could not stop herself from laughing with mounting hysteria.

Chapter Two

SALVATORE FRANK GATTONE—he dropped the Salvatore on his mother's advice the day he entered school —was born on New York's First Avenue, between 7th and 8th streets. His father, Giovanni Gattone, an almost illiterate first-generation American who'd come over from Naples immediately after the first World War, had a bushy mustache, a violent temper, and a shaky job with the sanitation department. He was a short, heavy man, strong as a bull, and could drink more wine on a Saturday night than anyone else in the neighborhood.

22

Mrs. Gattone, a gentle, religious woman who had been born in America and spoke reasonably correct English, felt superior to her husband, and many of Frank's early memories were of violent arguments in two languages over his father's "low position," his father's "stink," his sloppy manners and drinking habits and his big, hairy belly—though Mrs. Gattone had found him attractive enough to have four children by him, all boys and three of them destined to follow close in the hard-drinking, hard-fighting footsteps of their father.

Frank was the youngest of the four, an intense, frail child, the despair of his father and favorite of his mother, who prayed each night on her rosary that at least one of her sons would amount to something, and thought quite rightly that Frank showed the most promise. From the time he could walk, he was given special lessons—violin lessons, singing lessons, dancing, public speaking—paid for with the nickels and dimes his mother saved in a preserve jar hidden behind a radiator in their shabby second-floor apartment. His father swore and drank and fretted. His schoolmates called him a sissy. Girls ignored him as being shy, queer, less attractive than the wild boys who roamed the block on early summer nights and often seduced them, hot and panting, standing upright in some empty hallway.

While his schoolboy friends were learning the rough facts of life, Frank participated in the school plays and was often the only boy in the class to do so. He liked acting because it gave him the chance to be someone outside his inferior self. Yet, paradoxically, he was always terribly embarrassed to show his feelings on the school stage.

After graduating from high school, through the efforts of a sympathetic sometime actor who hung around the corner bar, he got a behind-the-scenes job as a stagehand with one of the burlesque shows that were still common in New York in those days. During his three years in "the theatre," as his mother

23

called it, he played an accordion with the orchestra, played straight man to an old baggy-pants comedian, pulled up the curtain, sold boxes of cheap candy and dirty pictures to the patrons, and sometimes stood in the wings, catching the scanty clothing of the stripper as the pieces were tossed to him bit by bit, until the girl was down to the limit in nothing but a G-string, after which she'd leave the stage, say "Thanks, Frankie," and walk off to her dressing room, her breasts bouncing, her fanny wiggling, completely impervious to the men backstage, who couldn't have cared less anyway.

After his first weeks with burlesque, Frank too paid no attention to the girls. He was nineteen then, still a virgin, and though he had sexual urges he could not seem to attach them to the naked girls with whom he lived and joked and worked. For a time he worried that perhaps he was a homosexual, except that he did not attach his feelings to men either. The girls teased him because he had no girl friend, and the men made suggestive remarks (one oily-voiced, toupeed singer even made a deliberate proposition), until a Miss "Bubbles" LaVerne, nee Wanda Castersick of Astoria—billed as "The Mammary Marvel" because she could twirl a red tassel from each breast in the same or opposite direction by the gyration of her anatomy—decided that young Frankie Gattone should be initiated into the rites of sex.

Bubbles was twenty-four, a kind, open girl who'd been married to a tiger of a man, a "brute in bed," and in Frank she saw an opportunity to be generous and helpful, and perhaps receive a little gentleness herself.

Bubbles invited him to her hotel room, gave him a drink of cheap whisky, then spoke to him in a very motherly way. "Frankie, I know . . . all the girls know . . . you're still a virgin, and if you don't do something about it pretty soon, it's going to cause you real trouble for the rest of your life."

Frank admitted this was probably true.

24

Bubbles, who was a peroxide blonde, 38-26-37, said that he'd seen too many teats in his time, and "My God, I don't wonder you can't get it up, standing out there day after day watching me shake my breasts around. It must be repulsive as hell."

He said politely that it was not really repulsive.

"Don't you ever feel like touching them?" Bubbles asked curiously.

He said that at first he had, but now he didn't care any more.

Bubbles understood. She told him to take off his clothes, and when he hesitated, she took off her own to show him how easy it was without becoming embarrassed. She told him he had a nice, hard, well-built body—"wiry," she called it—and then she made love to him. "Don't look at me," she said, "because all you'll see is the same old Bubbles, and don't think about me because all you'll imagine is the twirling tassels. Close your eyes, honey, and think about something else . . . somebody else . . ."

He thought about someone he had never known. All his life his mother had wanted him not to marry beneath him— none of the tramps around First Avenue, none of those show girls where he worked. "The Lord help at least one Gattone to rise himself to a nice girl," she said. So he imagined a nice girl, like the kind he'd seen walking on Fifth Avenue, going to legitimate theatres, getting in and out of taxicabs, and the girl had blond hair (not dyed), and a thin, model's face, and high, firm breasts and narrow hips. She came from a good family, had a finishing school education, and would never do what Bubbles was doing because she'd be too much of a lady.

It was a great effort and he had to think very hard of the imagined girl. But it worked, and afterwards, as he lay panting beside Bubbles, all he could say was, "Oh God, oh God," because he had never before realized the ecstasy a man could experience.

Bubbles, her arms around him, keeping his face buried in her

25

talented breasts, said, "You're wonderful, Frankie . . . just wonderful . . ." And then, after a brief, aching pause, "Just for the fun of it— What were you thinking about?"

"You," Frank lied, because it seemed the least he could do for her unbounding generosity.

He never slept with Bubbles again, or any other girl for that matter, until he married Anita Slayton, whom he proposed to on a dare to himself and who, to his surprise, threw her arms around him and clung to him and said yes. It was in 1942, only a few weeks after she had been assigned to him as an assistant on a radio show. He had got into radio in the first place through a well-known burlesque comedian who had made the big leap in a single Broadway show, after which he was given a radio show of his own. He hired Frank to do odd chores, taught him everything he knew, bullied the network into making him an assistant director, finally the director of a soap opera, all in the course of three years.

Anita adored Frank, and he knew it, though sometimes he was annoyed, impatient with her demonstrative show of affection, and especially her possessiveness. But she fulfilled the image of the girl he had pictured that night in the arms of "The Mammary Marvel," physically, emotionally, socially, in every possible way. It did not matter a great deal that he was not madly in love with her, as he had thought himself to be, mistaking his idealization of her world for love of her person. Nor was he particularly upset by the objections of Anita's father, who told him flatly that he was "a couple of miles beneath my daughter." He took Anita on a visit to see his mother, who was very proud of his choice, though his father thought her "a frigid little piece of stick."

With Anita's tolerance of his background, her faith in his ability, he gained considerable confidence in himself as a rising young director. Following his stint in the army he developed even more confidence in his abilities as a fledgling television

26

director. He felt that he was in on the ground floor, and the ladder rose skyward, out of sight.

Frank had stopped climbing on the third rung. Not because he had lost his grip, and maybe not even—as he told himself at the time—because his marriage would go on the rocks if he didn't rescue his wife from her drinking and nervous tensions, but simply because life at Plimpton Ridge and at the Academy represented a social refinement he had never hoped to attain.

Well, he was through with such illusions now. He was back at his old stand where he belonged, all fired up to continue from where he had left off ten long years ago.

Frank shuffled together the pages of the script he had just finished reading, fastened them with a large paper clip, then stared out of the office window of Kingley Productions, down twelve stories to Madison Avenue.

Funny thing about Anita's mentioning Edith Parkes, he thought. Talk about feminine intuition! It was just like Anita to bring up Edith Parkes when the woman was so much on his mind.

All day the suspicion had been nagging him that Lester Garret, the producer, had not offered him the chance to make a comeback merely out of friendship. Les was too shrewd for that. It must have been as obvious to Les as it is to me, Frank thought, that Edith Parkes is the logical choice for the lead. But everybody knew Edith didn't want to have anything more to do with television; she had turned down better parts than this show had to offer. Still, he, Frank Gattone, had directed the last show she'd done on TV, and Les must have figured . . .

"Oh, to hell with it," Frank swore softly.

The door opened behind him, and Les Garret came in. "You finish it?" he asked.

"Yeah."

"So?"

"It needs a new ending, Les. No reason for the heroine and this jerk lawyer to get together. Maybe she goes back to the resort looking for the guy. But it's too late then, just like it was too late after that first love affair."

"I don't know," Les said. "She ought to come to realize . . ."

"*After* it's too late. So she goes back to being the school-teacher. And she dug her own grave anyway, considering she should have learned her lesson way back when her old man was still alive. How stupid can you get?"

"I know . . . but . . ."

"Les, listen to me. If this were an afternoon woman's show, then all right. But at nine o'clock at night—Jesus, Les!"

"Things are different," Les said. He sat on the edge of the desk, dangling his long legs, scratching his ear with a broken fingernail, while he stared bleakly out the window through his horn-rimmed glasses. "Back in '49, '50, you could do a lot of experimenting. There weren't many sets then, and people thought they were getting something for nothing. They'd take anything you gave 'em—even if it was good. But now they think we *owe* them something—even resent the advertising. Ask 'em who's supposed to pay for all this, and they don't know and don't care. They control the ratings, so *ipso facto* they own television, and they want what *they* want. Things have changed, Frank."

"Well, I haven't."

"Frank . . . Frank . . . you've got to be reasonable."

"Oh, I know. I've been away a long time—isolated myself directing a bunch of kids in *Charley's Aunt*. . ."

"I didn't say that."

"So letting me do this one show is a kind of special favor—for the sake of old times."

"Because I think you can do it, Frank. It's your kind of show."

28

"All right. I appreciate your remembering me. But look at it my way, Les. I've got a personal stake in this that makes me want to do the very best job I know how."

"I know that, Frank. That's why you're here."

"I had to fight the whole Plimpton faculty for the time off. I had to fight my own wife to get her to see the point."

"Anita?"

"Yes, Anita. She's not like in the old days, Les. She's changed. Scared of this whole business. Scared that I'll *be* a success, just like once she was scared I wouldn't be."

"You could make it," Les said. "On this one show, since it's already been sold to the movies. Naturally they'll consider the TV director for first crack at the film."

"So I *do* have a personal interest, and I say the script stinks. Let's get Peter Dunn in to give us a rewrite. Take out the soap opera and try to make a believable character study out of it. Actually, the woman is selfish—she *has* to be *needed*. But she's afraid of sex, so first she rejects it for the old man, then for the kids—even though subconsciously she knows it's all just rationalization."

"No sex," Les said.

"She's *afraid* of it. That's the whole point."

"Still it's got to be there for her to be afraid of it. Lay off the sex stuff."

"Oh my God," Frank groaned.

Les wanted another opinion. He called in the script editor, a small, stout, bouncy man named Arnold Schull. Arnold said he liked the script the way it was. He said that women made most of the decisions when it came to buying electrical appliances, and the sponsor was electrical appliances, and Frank had to remember that the ladies must not be offended in any way— especially those unpredictable housewives in the Midwest, who wrote all the letters demanding "true-to-life" stories, meaning stories about the way life ought to be rather than the way it is.

He said the sponsor had already approved the present script, and they couldn't call in Peter Dunn anyway, because according to the Guild contract the original author had to be offered the chance to do two rewrites before the script could be rewritten by someone else, except for minor production changes. So far, Curry had only done one rewrite.

Les scratched his ear. "Of course," he said finally, "we could get Curry in right now, put him to work on a kind of middle-of-the-road rewrite . . ."

"Except he's not up to it," Frank said. "His whole approach is strictly from Farmer Brown's cornfield."

"I know. I know. But we put him to work anyway. At the same time we get Peter Dunn to work it over too. We toss Curry's rewrite in the wastebasket and use Dunn's. Dunn doesn't know anything about Curry and Curry thinks Dunn was put on the script *after* he's completed the revision, and *after* we've rejected it."

"Something smells," Frank said.

"Okay. So we'll actually *read* Curry's script before we throw it out."

"It's quite within our contract rights," said the bouncy Mr. Schull.

"I'll say things have changed," Frank said.

Everyone laughed self-consciously. Then Arnold Schull went off to call the two writers. Frank looked out the window again. He wondered if Anita was still upset, the way she was when he got home late last night. The way she still was, obviously, when he'd talked to her on the phone a little while ago. Turning back into the room where Les still sat brooding on the edge of the desk, he reminded himself that if this was going to be the show that would shake him loose from Plimpton Academy he'd have to stop worrying about Anita. He couldn't afford to be troubled about her any more than about the ethics involved in Les's scheme to get around the Guild contract. The play

30

was the thing—or the production, rather—and the better it was the more good it would do for everyone concerned. Especially himself.

Arnold came back to say that Curry would be in to see him the next morning. Meanwhile he'd sent a copy of the script to Dunn. "I didn't tell either of them about the other. But they both know we've got to have a finished script in a hurry if we're going to get any decent kind of cast."

"What about casting?" Frank asked.

Les handed him a list. He recognized the names of some of the actors. Others he had never heard of. There was a blank space beside the name of the heroine.

"These are only suggestions," Les said. "I'd love to get Edith Parkes for the lead."

"Edith Parkes!" Frank exclaimed, feeling all his suspicions come home to roost. "Edith wouldn't consider it. Especially playing a woman of forty-five, even though she must be that old herself, older as a matter of fact, although she claims she's only thirty-four."

Les shrugged. "Who cares? So let her think she's still thirty-four. She'd make the show, that's all that matters."

There was no doubt about that, Frank had to admit.

"Of course," Les said, "she hasn't done any television since you used her yourself in *The Letter*."

Frank looked up slowly. Les was staring at him through his horn-rimmed glasses. "Maybe, Frank," Les said, "maybe if you talked to her."

"I'm not anxious to."

"But you handled her beautifully before, and I know, because I just saw the kine a few days ago when I was thinking of hiring you to direct this show."

"Yeah." Les's admission confirmed what he had been thinking. So it wasn't my talent, Frank thought, it wasn't even a matter of friendship. I'm just the bait to catch Edith Parkes.

"Maybe she was tough to handle during rehearsals," Les said, "but she sure gave one hell of a performance."

"Look," Frank said, "if there's someone else . . ."

"Like who, for instance?"

"Well . . ."

"Nobody else can touch her," said Arnold Schull.

No, there really wasn't anybody else. Edith would make the show, as Les said, and they were counting on him to get her. They'd had it figured that way from the start.

"Okay," Frank said. "Nothing to lose, I guess." And he promised to call Edith Parkes.

Les and Arnold left the room. The door closed behind them. Frank sat down behind the desk. He placed his elbows on the glass top and pushed his hands through the black mop of hair falling over his forehead. He didn't like this business with Curry and Dunn any more than he liked the Edith Parkes business. There was something wrong in making a fellow write for a wastebasket simply to get rid of him. On the other hand it was he who had suggested the changes in the first place, though he could still change his mind, he supposed, and accept the script as it was. The sponsor had approved it and Arnold liked it and Les would go along finally. But he'd staked his entire future on this one show, and he couldn't afford to be overly sensitive now. What was done was done, and he'd simply have to stop worrying about it, just as he'd have to stop worrying about Edith Parkes and whether he got the job merely because they wanted her for the show. One thing was pretty damn certain. If he was going to make a success of this thing he needed Edith Parkes and he needed her desperately.

He dialed Edith's number, and waiting, while the phone buzzed monotonously, he remembered that messy business the last time he'd worked with her. He'd been a lot younger then, of course, and not very tactful, so that when he'd told Anita about it even she'd felt he had acted a little too righteous, too oung husband. But hell, that was a

rkes' voice immediately, that won-
hat always sounded as if she had a
be it was the result of too much
king—anyway, it always seemed to

k Gattone."
elieving. "Not Frank Gattone!"
idea of his calling her somehow
can't believe it."
nk Gattone."
l my life?"
Edith. Up in Plimpton Ridge,
ool there—"
prep school! You?" Her laugh-
s so funny about his teaching
uored up even this early in the

old stand now. I'm doing the
. . . Not a permanent thing
. . . Well, you know what

es said, suddenly sober.
the weekend and he'd said
d spinster, and she loathed
loathed all spinsters, too.
," she remarked. "Not all

d, giving her a chance to
hole point, Edith. After

"After five husbands you should k
liness and disillusion—you, of all p

"Oh, I do, I do. But *forty-five!* M

"Thirty-four, Edith. Not forty-fiv
ten. I told Les. I said, 'How do you
forty-five? It would be like trying
like a cat.' So of course he agreed
script . . ."

Again she said that she loathe
it. Still, it had been fun doing *Th*
haps if he'd come to see her and
script . . .

"Just for you, Pumpkin," Ed

"Fine," Frank said, trying to
will be ready later this week an
we can talk about it."

"Wednesday night, Pumpkin
place. About nineish."

"But the script won't be re

"No, but I will be. . . . H

"Anita. She's fine."

"In town with you?"

"No, I'm commuting these
looking after the boys in the

"Well, that must be a refr
joying it."

"I don't know, Edith. I

She laughed. "Wednesda
See you, Pumpkin." And s

Frank sighed, and wiped
ing. If Edith Parkes took
get the "afraid of sex" bu
whole thing into a farce.
whole reputation on it. T

away from it; the woman was a first-class bitch, but she had plenty of talent. She didn't just make a show. She *was* the show.

And suddenly he remembered. Wednesday night! He'd promised Anita he'd be at Dr. Bullock's that night. Oh my God, he thought, how am I going to get out of this one? But then he thought Wednesday night was still two days off. He'd call Edith Parkes tomorrow and get her to change the date. There wasn't any point to his seeing her before she had a chance to read the script, anyway. Yes, he'd call her the first thing tomorrow morning. He made a note of it on his desk calendar.

Chapter Three

SOMETIMES it seemed to Roberta Barker that her French poodle Smokey was the only one she could talk to honestly. Even when she didn't say anything he seemed to understand her. He would look at her so soulfully with his great black luminous eyes—the way he was looking at her now as she drove back from cleaning the little cottage near the lake that she and Paul and Christina used as a weekend retreat from their dormitory existence at the Academy. As if he understood why she felt so emotionally keyed up this afternoon, that it was on just such a lovely spring afternoon that death had tripped her father and robbed her of her first and dearest love.

Roberta was only eight, a pretty, brown-haired, gray-eyed child, when she lost her mother. Her father had never married again. Roberta adored him, and he in turn felt that she was everything he would ever need of love, although as the years went by he came to feel a father's concern that his growing daughter should focus all her natural interest in the opposite sex upon himself. So they lived together in the small brick house, while Roberta matured into a young lady during the years of the Depression. The times were hard and her father, an engineer, could find only occasional jobs, although looking back on those years now they seemed to Roberta the happiest of her life. Then war came and he was offered a good post, working for the navy at the New London submarine base. Roberta was seventeen then, delighted with her father's new position, and she set up housekeeping in the small apartment with the enthusiasm of a young wife in the first place of her very own.

Every afternoon after the chores were finished she would walk the half mile to the base, where she sat silent and alone on a steel beam or a pile of lumber, watching her father as he discussed blueprints or gave orders and advice to the men who worked for him. Sometimes he would ride with the workmen to the top of the skeleton structure. It gained him the respect of the men, he said, and also, no doubt, he thought standing aloft on a naked steel beam was a fine way to impress his watching daughter, much as a small boy might look for admiration by walking a high fence in the presence of his girl. And sometimes he would pretend to slip, then laugh at Roberta's horrified face below. Or he'd wave a handkerchief to her, and might even let it go, so that it floated away and down on the ocean breeze.

That floating handkerchief must have been the last thing her father ever saw. He was alone that day on the rising girder, when to her terror Roberta saw the steel beam tip, saw her father grab for the cable, slip, and fall, his legs pumping futilely in the air as if he were riding a bicycle, before he crashed broken to the earth.

"Daddy! . . . Daddy! . . ." To this day, whenever she was greatly troubled the whole shattering episode would come back to her in her dreams, and she would awake screaming, "Daddy! . . . Daddy!" her whole body bathed in perspiration.

Roberta jerked her mind back to the present and to her driving. The car was entering the outskirts of the town. "Don't look at me like that, Smokey," she said, patting the dog's head. "Help me to forget."

Only there was so much that she could never forget. So many things that refused to be forgotten.

After the initial shock of her father's death had turned to unbearable loneliness, she had found a job in Plimpton Ridge, working for Slayton Firearms as secretary to Mitchel Slayton. He had been kind to the lonely young woman, treated her more as a friend or even as a father than as an employer, and she had responded to his kindness, like a drooping flower lifting its chalice to the reviving sun. She was too young, too inexperienced, to understand that her employer's need for her might match her own need for him, for someone to take the place of her father.

One quiet evening, when he was driving her slowly through the moonlit countryside in his comfortable big car, she had said impulsively—putting her hand on his arm—"Mr. Slayton, you're just like a father to me." And he had replied gravely, "Thank you, my dear, thank you for being my daughter." And for a while it had seemed that way, kindly, elderly employer, grateful young employee—father and daughter—until an inevitable evening in her small apartment over the supermarket when his expression of fatherly love, her own warm feeling of a daughter's gratitude, had taken another form, and then, in the height of her distorted passion, she had cried, "I love you, Daddy! Oh Daddy, I love you."

There were other evenings, and still others, of need and affection, desire and guilt, for in his own way Mitchel Slayton

37

was as lonely as she was, and in need of understanding. A year later Christina was born. But by that time Roberta was safely married to Paul Barker.

All that was so long ago, so many long years ago. It was all over and done with. "Oh, if it only were, Smokey," Roberta sighed, "if it only were over and done with," knowing in her heart that the past continued to live its own life along with the present, that it could never as long as she lived be over.

She passed the new brick building where Mitchel Slayton had once made army rifles and ammunition, and now built his own sportsmen's rifles and shotguns and pistols in a fast-growing, highly respected company. As she went by she saw in the rearview mirror the Slayton black Cadillac pulling out of the factory driveway, and felt once again the old confusion, the mixed feelings of awkwardness and affection, need and guilt. As always when meeting Mitchel Slayton unexpectedly, she did not know whether to stop or to run away. But he was honking for her to stop and she had no will of her own when he commanded.

The Cadillac pulled up behind her and Mitchel stepped out, Homburg in hand, his gray hair gleaming silver in the sunlight. He was a tall, well-set man, sixty years old now. He sported a gray mustache, wore a tailor-made English-cut black suit, a stiff-collared white shirt, a dark tie with thin regimental stripes. Everyone said Mitchel Slayton was a handsome man—"distinguished," they said—and his two children had both inherited some of his best physical qualities. Son Roy was broad-shouldered, though shorter and heavier, and daughter Anita had that same stubborn firmness of jaw, that same intransigence that made for conflict between them.

"Hello, Roberta." Mitchel smiled uncertainly. His hand played nervously with Smokey's ears. His eyes flicked to hers, away again, and as always she felt almost as embarrassed for him as for herself. He said, "I don't get home much these days

38

except for weekends . . . so . . . well, I haven't seen you for so long. How is everything going?"

"Fine . . . Everything's fine."

He looked at her searchingly. "That's good . . . And Paul?"

"Paul's very well," Roberta said, looking away, wishing he'd go, hoping he'd stay. "Except he's worried, of course, though he tries not to show it."

"What about?"

"Oh . . . you know."

"You mean about his promotion?"

"Oh, that! Well . . . yes," Roberta said, without much conviction.

Mitchel Slayton looked relieved. "I suppose the least I can do," he said, "considering I'm head of the board of trustees—"

"I don't think Paul would want any special favors."

"He wouldn't have to know. A word to Dr. Bullock would be sufficient."

"Mitchel," Roberta said carefully, looking ahead through the windshield, "you don't owe Paul anything."

"I think I do."

"Very well, if it helps your conscience." She started the motor. Mitchel Slayton stepped back and she put the car in gear, then stopped again and looked at him gravely. "There *is* something else. Why should I hide it from you?"

"Oh?"

"Christina. She's seeing quite a bit of Alan." Roberta saw the flicker of anxiety in Mitchel's steady eyes.

"What do you mean . . . quite a bit?"

"They're in love. I mean seriously. They talk of getting married."

"But that's preposterous. She's only fifteen and Alan's only a year older."

"I know. But still . . ."

Mitchel Slayton leaned heavily against the car door. Under

39

his tanned face Roberta could see the sudden pallor. "What about Anita?" he said. "Can't she put a stop to this nonsense?"

Roberta sighed. "It's not as simple as that."

"And Paul?"

"Put yourself in his place. He can't understand what all the fuss is about."

"Well, they mustn't get any marriage ideas. You know that," Mitchel said sharply.

Roberta didn't say anything. What was there to say? Except that of course a grandfather should have something to say about his grandson having eyes for his daughter. Only how could he say it, and how could she, without bringing her marriage to Paul tumbling down about their heads? And Christina . . .

With a sigh of despair she put the car in gear once more and drove off swiftly, her lips trembling, her hands damp on the wheel, until finally Mitchel Slayton, still standing bareheaded on the road, was lost in sight in the rearview mirror and she was driving slowly again, into town now, past the movie theatre and the supermarket and the upstairs apartment that once had been hers—Roberta averted her eyes; she did not want to think of that now—past Woolworth's and the Rexall drugstore, past the long rectangular green with its barren bandstand, past the Presbyterian Church and the fresh grass and the old brick buildings of Plimpton Academy, to the apartment——her apartment, and Paul's, and Christina's—at the far end of Slayton Hall.

Ivy grew high along the brick sides of the building, and rhododendrons and yellow blooming forsythia and evergreens lined the gravel walk to the doorway. As Roberta left the car and walked up the path with Smokey bounding ahead of her, the white door opened and Christina stepped out on the porch.

With her sweet, round face and gray eyes, Christina was the

image of her mother. Her brown hair was caught up in a pony tail, and her white sweater revealed her maturing figure. She was eating a sandwich, and she waved it like a glove while she called out with her mouth full, "Mother! Where in the world have you been, Mother?"

Roberta greeted her daughter with a quick, affectionate smile. She slipped an arm around the girl's waist, and they went into the living room with its comfortable oak floors and fireplace and shabby furniture that Paul had promised to replace some day, although that was years ago and now, of course, they probably never would bother to change.

"Where's your father?" Roberta asked.

"Search me," Christina said. "Seems like everyone's late today." She finished off her sandwich with a glass of milk she took from the mantel. Putting aside the glass, she ran over to the window and threw it open. "Hey Joan, Joanie!" she called outside to a girl on a bicycle. "Wait for me. Be right out." In another moment she was out of the house, with a slam of the door behind her.

Oh, to be her age again, Roberta thought. Without any past to regret, without the guilty remembrance of any past. She sank back on the couch and sat with forefinger curled across her upper lip, the way she had a habit of doing when she was trying to think something out. Only what was the use of thinking? Thinking wasn't going to change things any. Maybe she was too apprehensive. Time had a way of making things turn out different from what one supposed. Alan and Christina were still practically children. Maybe he would meet someone else, or she would, when he went away to college. Or if Paul would take a teaching post at some other school, maybe out in California, so they could be separated by a continent. But now Paul was up for a promotion; as head of the department he was not likely to leave Plimpton, not for some years, at any rate.

No, whichever way she looked at it, Roberta felt she was in a trap. It was no good telling herself she was too apprehensive. She could feel the whole thing hovering over her, like a palpable presence of doom.

She rose from the couch and began to pace the room nervously. Where was Paul? She needed him. They were so close in so many things . . . She loved him so. It was agonizing to have to hide from him, as she had all these years. And yet to tell him . . .

No! Roberta said passionately to herself. Let the anguish be mine, and mine only. Nothing matters but his happiness, and Christina's.

She turned sharply, suddenly aware of someone else in the room, and saw her husband smiling at her from the doorway.

"Paul! You frightened me."

"You looked like Lady Macbeth, pacing the floor that way."

He came over to her and she threw herself into his arms and clung to him as if she would hide in him from herself.

"Oh Paul, I miss you so when you're away."

"There, there," he said, caressing her hair. "Anyone would think I'd been away for years instead of a few hours."

"I know," she said, half laughing, half crying, as she tugged at the lapels of his jacket. "I'm just a silly goose."

He held her off at arm's length, his serious eyes fixed upon hers. "Has anything happened?"

"No, nothing." She forced a smile. "I've been down to the cottage, cleaning it up for Sunday. I'm tired, I guess."

Paul took off his coat. He patted the pockets, found his pipe and tobacco. "I had a few words with Alan after class today," he said.

"Oh?"

"Yes." He tamped tobacco into his pipe, lit it, and dropped the match in a glass ashtray.

"About his marks?" Roberta said, knowing the boy's marks had nothing to do with it.

42

"It's more than that. The boy is troubled because his mother says he's seeing too much of Christina."

"Anita!" Roberta could feel the blood freeze in her veins.

"Yes. I went along home with Alan and spoke to Anita."

"And what did she say?" Roberta tried to keep her voice casual, but it sounded false to her own ears.

Paul shrugged. "Oh, she went into some kind of rigmarole about none of us being able to communicate with one another. I don't know what she was talking about. She said the children were too young to be going steady. Maybe they are, I don't know. But it does seem to be a lot of fuss about nothing."

"But they *are*, Paul. They *are* too young. You know that."

He stared at the floor, a frown crinkling his forehead. "Sometimes," he said, "I wonder how much I really do know. Anita seemed to be hinting at something I couldn't fathom."

"Oh come, Paul," Roberta said with a show of laughter. "You know Anita. She always has to seem so mysterious."

"I suppose so," he said glumly. Then looking up, he fixed his gaze upon his wife. "Are you sure, Roberta," he said slowly, "are you sure you're not keeping something from me?"

Her panic took the form of defensive anger. "What do you mean?" she flared back at him. "I asked you to move to another school, didn't I. I asked you again and again."

"What?" Paul's frown deepened. "What in God's name has that got to do with Alan and Christina?"

"Then they wouldn't be going together, would they?" she cried lamely, and rushed in confusion from the room, up the short flight of stairs and into the bedroom, where she slammed the door shut and sat trembling on the bed until she heard Smokey scratching and whining at the door and she let him in.

"I can't go on forever, Smokey," she sobbed, leaning over the dog and embracing him, "I can't go on like this," while he looked up at her all compassion and darted his warm tongue against her chin.

43

Chapter Four

MITCHEL SLAYTON had bought the old Plimpton place in 1944, when the war had brought prosperity to Slayton Arms and he'd set up a New York office for the firm. The big square house of white-painted brick, with its chimney at each corner, faced the town's rectangular green, and was considered one of the show places of Plimpton Ridge. There was a time, when Mitchel and his wife Lottie were living in a modest frame house on Grover Street and the children were growing up —there was a time when the thought of possessing the grand old colonial house had seemed to him the pinnacle of his ambition. But these days he spent very little time at home, preferring to live in his New York apartment and coming home only on weekends or when urgent business at the factory demanded his presence.

Something had happened, the town knew, shortly after the Slaytons had moved into the old Plimpton place, although just what had happened remained a secret. Something *must* have happened, people figured, else why should Lottie Slayton who was, as everybody knew, so ambitious socially and had urged her husband to buy the big house, suddenly go into retirement? Until today she seemed to have escaped reality completely, and became rational only when she was talking to Mattykins, her yellow cat, about her faith in the Jehovah's Witnesses.

It was true that the decline began soon after her son Roy had gone off to the war with the naval air force, and Anita was living in New York, but everyone in the town knew that Lottie had always been more interested in herself than in her children. Then why should she become a recluse—now, it was said, she was suffering from heart trouble, too—just when everything was coming her way? The townspeople had gossiped, hinted at this and that, but the years had gone by and people had other things to think about and gossip about and Mitchel Slayton had become such an eminent citizen people forgot about his wife, who was seldom seen anyway and who, if they remembered her at all, they thought of only as the old lady in the big house who was slightly touched in the head.

Ever since they were married Mitchel had gone about doing the only constructive thing he knew—making money to buy the social position his wife thought her due and the Slayton family had always lacked, even though his father and grandfather before him were known as honest, hard-working men who struggled valiantly, if unimaginatively, with a dying firearms business. It was not until World War II that he really struck gold. Turning out rifles and ammunition for the government had given the company a boost that had carried over into the postwar years, so that now, quite late in life, Mitchel had more money than he would ever need.

With the purchase of the big white brick house fronting the green, he felt he had arrived, was able to give his wife what she so ardently desired. What seemed to appeal to Lottie especially was the fact that the house had once been the property of the town's founder, the creator of Plimpton Academy, who had killed two British soldiers with a coal shovel and buried them in his own back yard. Lottie wanted Mitchel to find these soldiers, make Plimpton Place into a sort of museum, as though it were the Slayton family's own homestead. He thought it was a pretty gruesome idea, if not downright silly, digging for those long-buried soldiers, and dismissed the matter from his mind.

Now that Lottie had long since retired to her personal world and still brought the subject up, he'd promise to search for the redcoats just to placate her.

"Soon, Lottie, soon," he would say, patting her shoulder. "Just be patient." And meanwhile his mind was set on gaining as much influence in the town as possible, as if now, when it was too late, he would bring his wife the social status she had always wanted so much.

He became president of the Chamber of Commerce, then donated fifty thousand dollars toward a dormitory for Plimpton Academy, to be called Slayton Hall. The following year he was made a member of the Academy's board of trustees, and two years later, after giving seventy-five thousand dollars for a new library, he became the institution's president.

There was little left for him to gain in life—only things to be forgotten or erased, or, more practically, to be tolerated. Mitchel Slayton, with all his money, was a lonely man who thought he had learned to live with his memories and regrets. But driving home after his brief encounter with Roberta Barker, he was not so sure. Let the past take care of the past, he thought gloomily. The main thing was to avoid any future tragedy.

He felt the old pang of guilt as he pulled his Cadillac into the driveway. No matter what others thought, he knew. He knew that he and only he was responsible for his wife's present condition. And for Roberta, trying to hide her worries from him. Of what use was it for him to say that those children, Alan and Christina, must not entertain any thought of marriage? Would mere saying so change matters any? he thought helplessly. His son Roy, a brooding, sensitive, often violent man— why had Roy refused to go into the family business, preferring instead to spend his time as an airlines co-pilot who would never be a captain. And even as he asked himself the question Mitchel knew why. And his daughter Anita? Everytime she looked into his eyes he felt that she was holding him at pistol point.

46

They knew, and Lottie, far back in that twilight world of hers, knew too.

But why? Of what in God's name did they accuse him? Was it a crime that he had once, for a brief time, been overwhelmed by love for a girl who needed him desperately? And what if he had practically commanded Roberta to marry the innocent, studious Paul Barker? Was she any the worse off for that? Here she was happily married to a splendid fellow, a perfect father for the child. She loved Paul and he loved her; you had only to see them together to know that. And Christina was a normal, happy child.

No, Mitchel Slayton told himself, he refused to feel guilty for an act of love. He refused, but he felt guilty anyway, guilty and troubled about the future.

Entering the house he squared his shoulders as if to throw off the weight that was oppressing him. Lottie was in the living room. She sat staring blankly at the book that lay open in her lap—the inevitable Bible—while mechanically, with one hand, she stroked the fur of Mattykins, the cat that was never far from her side.

"Hello, Lottie," Mitchel said, standing self-consciously befor her. "You've had your lunch, I expect." He took out his gold watch from his vest pocket, noted absently that it was almost two o'clock, and returned the timepiece to his pocket.

Lottie's eyes remained fixed on the Bible as she uttered a few meaningless words. He felt that he might just as well not be there, and impatiently he moved toward the door.

"June eighth," he heard his wife say abruptly behind him.

"I promised, didn't I?" he said over his shoulder, thinking hopefully she'd forget all about June eighth by the time that day came. Lottie and her Jehovah's Witnesses! He'd promised to take her to the big meeting in Danbury. "I'll even let them baptize me," he said, "if it will make you happy."

"What about the soldiers?"

47

"Soldiers?"

"You know, the soldiers sleeping in the yard. Have you found them yet, Mitchel? Have you raised them from their place of sleep?"

He groaned inwardly. "Making plans," he said, and left the room.

Going into the dining room he thought how all their brief, broken conversations these many years were always the same, like an old, cracked record that kept repeating and repeating itself. Would he take her to the Witness meeting on June eighth in Danbury? Would he become baptized, so that his sin might be washed away? Would he dig up those confounded redcoats? Of course he would do none of these things. The only thing that mattered was to say yes, to say yes to everything to satisfy Lottie for the moment. Eventually she would forget.

Lunch consisted of lobster salad, hot rolls and coffee. Mitchel sat alone in the paneled dining room with its massive colonial furniture. He had no appetite, and as he sat there poking at his food, his mind kept returning to his conversation with Roberta. Suddenly he got up and left the table and went into the library across the hall. Closing the door behind him, he sat down at the desk, picked up the telephone and dialed Anita's number.

The phone rang a long time before he heard his daughter saying, "Hello."

"Anita!" he said, trying to keep his voice casual.

"Well, what a surprise." Her voice was tinged with sarcasm.

"How is Frank coming along with his television show?"

"All right, I expect. I didn't know you were so interested."

"Is Alan there?"

"No. He has track this afternoon."

"And then he's seeing Christina Barker, I suppose."

"I wouldn't know about that. Maybe. Why?"

Mitchel could feel his hand sweating as he gripped the receiver. "I ran into Roberta on the road a little while ago . . ."

"Oh, did you really?"

Anita's ironical tone was not lost on her father. She always knew how to make him angry, confound her! Gritting his teeth, he pretended to be unaware.

"She's concerned about Christina's being with Alan too much."

"Well, so am I concerned," Anita said testily. "So what am I supposed to do about it?"

"You could speak to the boy. Get Frank to speak to him."

"Frank can't be bothered. He's too busy with his precious TV."

"But you're not, Anita, and you're the boy's mother. Do you want him to fail in his studies? How's he ever going to get into college?"

"Dear Papa, is that all that's worrying you . . . Alan's grades at school?"

"You know it's ridiculous for those youngsters even to be thinking of marriage."

"Yes, I know it, and you know it. But do *they* know it? That seems to be the question."

"Anita!" Mitchel said sharply. "Will you listen to me?"

But she had already hung up. The phone was dead. Exasperated, he flung the receiver back into its cradle and continued to sit there at the desk, staring at the wall, his face flushed with anger and frustration.

It was a terrible thing when father and daughter could not speak to one another except at sword's point. If Anita hadn't come back to live in Plimpton Ridge, all this worry about the children could have been avoided. Why the devil had he ever permitted it, even helped her to return by getting that immigrant Italian husband of hers a post at the Academy? Because he had felt guilty about her, that must have been why. Because he had felt he owed her something.

His mind went back to an evening fifteen—no, it must have been sixteen years ago, he thought unhappily. He was in Roberta's apartment and she was in his arms and they were bidding one another a fond good night when suddenly there was a knock at the door. Guiltily they had pulled apart from their embrace and stood for a long moment staring apprehensively at each other, hoping there would not be another knock at the door, hoping the caller would go away. But there was another knock, more impatient this time, and Roberta had gone to the door and unlocked it. And there was Anita, unexpectedly home from New York, standing in the doorway. The two girls had become firm friends the summer before.

"Oh!" exclaimed Anita, starting back in surprise to see her father there, her eyes taking in the unmade bed in the room beyond, the uneasy expression on the faces of the two people facing her. "I'm sorry . . ." She was blushing to the roots of her hair. "I'm sorry," she stammered, and turned away, and would have raced down the stairs if Roberta had not seized her hand and pulled her back into the room.

"Don't go, dear," Roberta said. "I haven't seen you for so long. Your father was just leaving anyway. I had some typing to finish up tonight—important papers that couldn't wait until tomorrow—and your father just stopped by to pick them up."

Naturally Anita hadn't believed a word of it. After all, she was his daughter, had inherited his own shrewdness. She had kept her eyes lowered, refused to look up even when he bade Roberta a courteous good night and said, "I'll see you later, daughter."

Nothing had ever been the same between them after that night.

Mitchel Slayton rose wearily from his chair and went over to the bookcase and pulled out a copy of Milton's *Paradise Lost*. He opened the book to the pages separated by a narrow gold silk ribbon. There was a certain quotation he remembered. But he didn't have to look for it. He knew it by heart.

"Govern well thy appetite, lest Sin surprise thee," he said softly. "Lest Sin surprise thee, and her black attendant Death."

Chapter Five

OLD MR. BEATTY, the father of Roy Slayton's wife Mildred, still made his postman's rounds at the age of sixty-six, shuffling along with his shoulders stooped under the weight of the mailbag, but his head held high because his daughter was married to a Slayton. What more could anyone ask in the town of Plimpton Ridge?

What more, indeed, it had seemed to Mildred when she married Roy after a whirlwind courtship. At the time, overwhelmed as she was by the sudden opening of doors on her narrow life, she thought she was head over heels in love with Roy. But later, those long nights when she lay awake beside her sleeping husband, feeling frustrated and still unsatisfied after enduring his passion, Mildred would sometimes wonder if she had ever really known what love was. People talked a lot about love, but she could not say truthfully that she had ever experienced it.

They had had a three-day honeymoon in New York. In a way it was wonderful—the luxurious hotel, the plush restaurants, the theatre—everything was exciting except the bed part; she hadn't really enjoyed one moment of that. In fact, she was relieved when Roy's leave was over and she could go back to live with her father for the duration of the war.

After the war, Roy had bought this eighteenth-century farmhouse on the outskirts of the town, with the beamed ceilings and the Dutch ovens and wide pine floors, and the huge buttonwood trees on either side of the door. She had tried so hard to make her husband happy, had even read all the books on ideal marriage she could find in the town library in her resolve to be a good wife. But no matter how much she tried, and pretended, and taught her husband the niceties of love-play the books talked about so that maybe she would become more willing, more excited, she continued to think of love-making with Roy as her wifely duty, something to be gotten over and done with, and there were times when she wanted to scream herself into oblivion.

Roy was a passionate man but he was also sensitive, too sensitive not to be aware of the unsatisfactory nature of their marital relationship. Perhaps that was why he had taken the job of piloting the longest flights he could find; it permitted him to get home only infrequently. Sometimes, when Roy mentioned a certain Hawaiian girl by the strange name of Luanai, Mildred wondered if he had not chosen the Hawaiian flight for reasons other than that it kept him away from home. But she could never tell from the way Roy talked of the girl if Luanai was a child or a woman, and she did not think much about it, not enough to feel jealous, at any rate. All she felt was lonely. She was fond of Roy in her own way and would have liked to have had him around the house more. If only he didn't want to make love every night he was home.

The maddening part of it was that with a man she liked and respected—her husband—she couldn't get a thrill. While with a good-for-nothing like Matt Barlow, a man she really despised . . . It was true. She had known Matt ever since she was a girl at school, and they were both about the same age whereas her husband was considerably older. But if Roy hadn't been away so much, if she hadn't been so lonely and bored, if Matt hadn't been so insistent, she would never . . .

Only Matt wasn't insistent. That wasn't his way. He was always very much at ease—the way he was now as he lounged massively in Roy's favorite armchair, his long legs crossed indolently, a glass of Scotch and water in his hand, looking at her in his lazy, grinning way as if he knew her better than she knew herself.

A pretty, red-haired woman with regular features and a pleasing, almost boyish body, there was something very proper and even prim about Mildred Slayton. Uppity, the townspeople said. They said she couldn't forget she was now a Slayton—or remember she was only Millie Beatty from the other side of the tracks. She was sitting rigidly on the edge of the couch, her fingers beating an angry tattoo on the armrest as she looked across the room at Matt Barlow.

"What's the matter, Millie?" Matt said. "You're all on edge today."

His knowing smile was insufferable. He had a way of looking at her slowly, from the tips of her feet to the top of her head, and then back again slowly, his eyes dwelling on her breasts, her hips, her thighs, her legs, as if he were undressing her at his leisure. It made her feel hot and cold all over. A shiver ran down her spine and she felt her face flushing.

"I want you to go, Matt," she said. "You've been here long enough."

"But I just got here, Millie," he laughed. "There's plenty of time. You said Roy was in Hawaii, and that's a long way off. What are you so nervous about?"

"I'm not talking about Roy and I'm not nervous. What do you suppose the neighbors must think when they see your car in the driveway? You might at least be a little considerate about my reputation."

53

"Your reputation!" Matt hooted with laughter. "You always were a great one for reputation, Millie. You even used to worry about it when we were kids and did it in the woods a million miles from nowhere. Besides, what can the neighbors think? Just an old school friend paying a social call. What's wrong about that?"

"What do you want?" Mildred cried in exasperation. "Why are you here?"

He did not answer. Instead he grinned, as if to say she knew why he was there as well as he did.

"But I told you, Matt, I told you I never wanted to see you again. I told you not to come."

"So you did, Millie, so you did."

His attitude was infuriating. "Look, Matt, I'm a married woman," she said, trying to sound patient, reasonable. "I'm not the Millie Beatty you used to know. I'm Roy Slayton's wife, you understand?"

Matt snorted derisively. "Big deal. So you're a Slayton. What have the Slaytons ever done for you?"

Mildred bit her lips. Big deal was right. She had never even met her mother-in-law. Maybe the old lady wasn't quite right in the head, but after all—her own mother-in-law! And she still called Roy's father Mister—Mister Slayton, as if he were some kind of stranger. They had never accepted her as one of the family. As for Roy's sister, that stuck-up Anita— Well, Mildred thought, I might just as well be dead for all she cares.

"Never mind what they've done for me," she said. "They're decent people. Not like you."

"And not like you, eh Millie? You know you belong to me more than you do to Roy Slayton."

She felt herself cringing under his words. "Don't say that," she hissed. "Don't ever say that again."

"Okay, Millie." Matt shrugged good-naturedly. "Don't get yourself all excited."

54

"I did what I did in a moment of weakness. You know that. Because I was lonely. . . ."

"Seems to me there's been more than one moment."

"Oh, damn you, Matt Barlow." Mildred stamped her foot in rage. "Will you please stop looking at me like that? I told you it was all over between us."

"You said it was. But I didn't."

"You've got to go. Now!"

But he made no move to go. Unhurried, he finished his drink and set the glass on the table. "Remember, Millie, how we used to go swimming in the moonlight in Beetlewood Lake? Ride down on our bicycles, and then you would act so surprised because you forgot your bathing suit and it was too late to ride back and get it. So . . ."

Mildred got up from the sofa and took the glass from the table and went into the kitchen, feeling Matt's eyes on her back.

"Just one more drink and then maybe I'll go," he called after her teasingly.

She slammed the door shut behind her and ran water into the sink to drown out his voice. She leaned heavily against the sink, tears of anger and helplessness coming to her eyes. "Oh God, don't let it happen again," she whispered. "Don't let me go on like this." She could feel her whole body trembling. Wanting Matt . . . hating him . . .

With the noise the water made coming from the faucet, she did not hear the door opening behind her. In another moment she felt Matt's arms around her from behind, his mouth at the nape of her neck, his hands caressing her breasts.

"Go away," she moaned, without turning to face him. "Please go away."

"Just one more, Millie," he said, his lips teasing her ear. "One more, and then I'll go."

"The whisky's in the cupboard," she said, knowing he wasn't talking about another drink. "Help yourself."

55

"I will," Matt laughed, turning her around to face him, enveloping her in his embrace in the slow, sure way he had of drawing all her body to him, until she felt herself yielding, clinging to him, and her knees turning to water, felt she would sink to the floor if he did not support her with his strong arms.

"No, Matt, no!" she cried, trying to thrust him away from her in a last hopeless burst of denial, then clinging to him again. "Oh my God, what am I doing?"

"You're not doing anything, Millie. I just appeal to the slut in you, that's all."

Incensed, she struck out at him, but laughing he parried her blow easily. In another moment his arm was under her knees and she was swept off her feet and he was carrying her, kicking and scratching at his face, up the stairs and into the bedroom. Once in the room, he kicked the door shut behind him and threw her like a bundle on the bed.

"Now take your clothes off," he commanded, not laughing any more, his pale blue eyes like two cruel slits of light as he looked down at her. And when she refused, and fought off his hands trying to undress her, he threw himself upon her.

"All right, if you want it this way," he said, lifting her skirt from under her and thrusting his knee between her thighs. "I can play rough, too." Savagely he tore at her panties.

His mouth was crushed against hers, his big body bearing down on her. For a moment she lay quiet under the weight of him, then suddenly caught his upper lip between her teeth and bit hard on it. With a howl of pain he pulled away from her and touched his fingers to his injured lip and saw there was blood on them.

"You bitch!" he cursed, slapping her face violently, so hard the tears came to her eyes. "Bite me, will you? I'll show you."

Yes, show me, she thought, show me . . . Oh God, yes, feeling his weight on her, his heat within her, hard, insistent, brutal . . . her arms pulling him closer to her . . . inside her. . . .

56

Glad to be slapped around, glad to be overpowered, glad. . . .
Oh, Matt! Matt! . . . Oh Roy, why do you treat me like a lady,
when I'm only a bitch, a bitch, a bitch. . . . Roy, help me . . .
help me. . . . Oh God! Oh my God! . . .

Mildred wiped the hair from her perspiring face and looked
up into the eyes of Matt Barlow, laughing at her, knowing, triumphant.

"Hello, Millie," he said. "Do you like me better now?"

"I hate you, Matt Barlow," she said, too weak to push him away
from her. "I despise you."

Chapter Six

FRANK GATTONE glanced at the clock on the
mantel in the living room. It was not even ten, yet he felt dog-
tired and ready for bed. The long day at the office, with its endless conferences and need for decisions, had been grueling, and
Anita provided no release from the day's tensions. She seemed
to be all keyed-up; he hadn't seen her quite this way for years.
He felt that her insistence on his being present at Dr. Bullock's
evening was becoming an obsession with her. And the fact
that he had thoughtlessly made an engagement with Edith
Parkes for that same evening didn't make things any easier. If
he even so much as mentioned the possibility to Anita, there
would be hell to pay.

"Please, Anita," he said. "Please be reasonable. How can I be
here for the graduation dance when the show's the same night?"

"You can't. So all I'm saying is at least you can be here

Wednesday for Dr. Bullock's get-together. It would look pretty silly for me to go alone. I mean, considering that Paul's promotion will probably be announced, and we're such good friends, and—"

"All right, all right," Frank said, trying to keep his voice down. "You said that before."

He crushed his cigarette stub in the Swedish-silver ashtray, and his hand jerked, spilling ashes on the coffee table. Irritably he brushed the ashes into his hand and dumped them back into the ashtray, and thought he'd like to burn every stick of furniture in the place. Anita still clung to these reminders of the past—because maybe she was afraid of the future—but he wanted new things and new people in a new place. He was going to get to Hollywood if it was the last thing he did.

He pushed his hand through his hair. "Why are you always so apprehensive, Anita? What are you afraid of? I didn't get it ten years ago and I don't get it now."

"I'm not afraid. I never was."

"Well, something's bothering you. That's obvious. What is it?"

"I'm jealous," she said quietly. "That's all. Just jealous."

"Of what?"

"You. Your job. Because I did exciting things once, too, you know. We did them together. And then Alan was born and I had to be a mother instead. I couldn't just sit in that apartment alone, all day, every day—"

"I offered to get a nurse. You didn't have to stay there all the time."

- "I didn't say I *had* to."

"Okay, let's forget it. To hell with the past. I'll try to make old Batty-ass Bullock's since it means so much to you. I promise, honey." He bent down and kissed her. She was sitting in an armchair and his lips only brushed her forehead. She did not raise her face, but kept staring at the carpet.

58

Frank sighed. "I'm tired. It's been a rough day. Guess I'll go to bed."

"Who's the production girl?" said Anita, still without looking up.

Frank looked at her, perplexed. "I don't have one yet. Why?"

"But you said you had when I talked to you on the phone today."

"All right, so I have," Frank said, wondering why he had lied, seeing in his mind's eye Joan Leonard, the black-haired, efficient girl he had hired the week before, with her figure of a young Diana that she took no trouble to display, and the blackest eyes he had ever seen. "What difference does it make?" he said, suddenly realizing how much Joan Leonard, despite her different coloring, had reminded him of his wife when he had first interviewed Anita for a similar job.

"I used to be a production girl."

"Oh, for God's sake, Anita."

"I did," she said, looking up at him challengingly. And then fiercely, "I did, I did, I did."

She rose abruptly and swung into his arms, clinging to him desperately as she buried her head in his shoulder. "I hope she's old and ugly. . . . I love you, Frank, and I miss you, even when you're away for a single day. . . . I'm jealous of her already even though I don't know who she is, and don't care, either. . . . Only please don't use that awful Edith Parkes for the lead. Anyone but her."

Frank's body stiffened in her embrace. Maybe I ought to tell her now, he thought. I'll have to, sooner or later, anyway. But not about Wednesday night. I'll get out of that, and besides it would only make her hysterical.

He took her by the shoulders and held her off at arm's length. "Look, Anita, you might as well know now that if I can get Edith Parkes I'm going to sign her up fast. In fact, I called her this afternoon."

She looked at him, stricken. "You called Edith Parkes?"

"Why shouldn't I go after her? Everybody agrees she'd make the show."

"That sexpot! After the way she behaved . . ." Anita started to cry. She pulled away and sat on the sofa and after a while she laughed a little, as if ashamed of her foolishness.

"I'm sorry," she said. "After all, why should I care who you get for the part?" When he did not say anything but continued to stand there looking at her, she said, "You go to bed, Frank. I'm all right now." When he still made no move, she reached out for his hand and pulled him close to her. "Do you want me to go with you?" she said softly. "Do you feel like sex tonight?"

He grimaced. He hated questions like that. Do you feel like sex tonight, for God's sake!

"Of course you don't," Anita cried, stung by the look of disapproval he tried to hide and mistakenly taking it as a rejection of herself. "You never do any more. You're too busy sublimating yourself—isn't that what's it's called?" She was crying again. "My God," she sobbed, hiding her face in her hands, "what's got into me, tonight? What's wrong with me?"

He put his hand on her shoulder. "Look, honey," he pleaded, genuinely moved by her unhappiness, "please don't cry. You're worrying yourself about nothing, believe me, nothing at all." He took her hands away from her face and put his fingers under her chin and lifted her face to him, murmuring endearments as if he were talking to a child. "Take it easy, honey . . . please, just take it easy."

She did not answer, but continued to sit there sobbing. Frank felt helpless. He had the sinking feeling that with each passing year their evenings were becoming more and more like this, that he was always either fighting her in her jealous possessiveness or comforting her in her dissatisfactions and fears.

"Well, I'm going to bed," he said with a sigh, and turned away from her and left the room.

60

"Go, go," Anita cried after him in a fury of imagined rejection. "Go to bed. I don't see you all day and then you come home late and all you think of is going to sleep so you won't have to be with me. You must think I'm stupid or something."

Frank closed the door of the bedroom to shut off his wife's accusing voice. He felt angry and hurt. He'd make that goddamn evening at old Doc Bullock's if it meant so much to her, although he couldn't for the life of him understand why it should mean so much. If he could just make that, and then if he could just get through this one lousy, so very important show and get that offer to do the picture—well, he'd grab it no matter what Anita thought or said about it. He was fed up with her hysterics, fed up with the whole damned prep school crap and his pompous father-in-law, wasting his time trying to teach a bunch of bored kids. Sometimes it was hard for him to believe that he loved his wife, the way she behaved, although he supposed he still did love her in his own way and needed her as much as she needed him. Maybe the way one sick person needs another, he thought bitterly.

Well, need or no need, nothing was going to stop him from making a success of that show. Anita could think what she wanted about his production girl, she could protest all she wanted about Edith Parkes. But by God! he needed Edith right now more than he needed a wife, and he was going to get her if it was humanly possible. In this television racket very few men ever got a second chance at all. If you did get it, and muffed it, you were cutting your own throat. He had no intention of cutting the throat of one Frank Gattone.

The apartment was quiet. Outside, a boy's feet crunched on the gravel. Maybe it wasn't a boy. Maybe it was Paul Barker, wanting to come into the house to see her yet hesitant because Frank might be home.

Only why, Anita wondered, should she be thinking of Paul

61

Barker now? Because she was bored, that must be it, jealous, bursting inside for reasons she could not explain to Frank or to herself, either, bored and jealous and yes, afraid, afraid of something terrible that was going to happen, something that she was going to make happen no matter how hard she would try not to. Feeling horribly tense, she rose to pull down the blinds.

Alan appeared in the doorway behind her. "Mother . . ."

She jerked about, frightened by the sudden, unexpected voice. She had completely forgotten the boy was in his room, studying.

"What's the matter, Mother?"

"Nothing. You startled me, that's all."

"That's not what I mean. I mean today, when you were talking to Mr. Barker. I wasn't in the room but I heard what you were saying."

"Now Alan . . . look, dear . . ."

"But *why*? Just tell me why. What's wrong with my seeing Christina?"

"Don't be silly. There's nothing wrong about your seeing her. But I'm older than you are and I just don't want you to get too serious, that's all."

"You mean you're afraid we might get married."

There it was again. No wonder she felt continuously upset. Every time Alan talked of marrying Christina the blood chilled in her veins. Poor innocent lamb! She wanted to hold him to her breast and tell him—tell him to get this foolish idea out of his head. But how could she? How could she ever tell him?

"Now, Alan, please," she said pleadingly. "I'm really very tired. Remember you're only sixteen. Surely you must realize—"

"Oh, I realize, all right. I realize that you're scared that some day if you don't stop interfering we might run off and get married anyway. Isn't that it? Tell me. I've got a right to know. Tell me what's eating you."

62

Anita felt numb. Her eyes fastened on the closed doors of the liquor cabinet while Alan talked on with growing hysteria and finally shouted that he was going to the Barkers' cottage Sunday no matter what she said. He'd been invited and he was going because Mr. Barker wanted him to. He was going to spend Sunday with the Barkers and that was that, and what was the matter with everybody anyway? What in hell was the matter?

The boy was almost in tears, and he turned away to hide his weakness from his mother.

"Don't swear, dear," she said softly, automatically, while Alan's footsteps sounded hard and angry in the hallway. "You mustn't swear," while his door banged shut angrily.

Footsteps outside the house . . . wind in the trees on the deep, dark campus . . . a trembling inside herself . . . the cabinet door feet away . . . inches away . . . her hand reaching out, sliding back the blond wood panel . . . noiseless because it was a well-built cabinet, expensive, from Jensen's on Fifth Avenue . . . full of bottles, gin and vermouth, Scotch and bourbon and rye . . . because Frank trusted her . . . trusted her . . .

"Frank!" She slammed the cabinet shut, ran wildly from the room, down the hall, into the bedroom, where Frank lay on his back on the bed, his dark hair tumbling down over his forehead in the dim light. "Frank, Frank . . . help me, Frank, please help me," she cried as she threw herself across his stirring, waking body and wept into the black hairs on his partly naked chest.

Chapter Seven

OUTSIDE Luanai's window, the sun shone bright on her window box. The evening would be rather cool though, she knew. She would take a blanket along for them to lie on. Roy would bring a car and they would have dinner somewhere and then drive up into the hills. With George on duty at the base all night, everything was working out as planned.

Yes, everything would be comfortable and natural. There was nothing for her to feel guilty about. And yet she was aware of nagging doubts. It was not because what she was planning to do was an unfaithful act to her husband. She loved George; she was doing it for him. It was true that she had never slept with anyone in her life but George, and by rights she supposed she ought to think about Roy in some sexual way—with anticipation or repugnance, with embarrassment or hysteria. But the fact was she felt nothing for herself, really. Roy Slayton was the oldest friend she had and the closest. Closer, actually, than her own husband. She was confident she would feel no strain at all with Roy.

It was not what she was going to do that worried her. It was her womanly fear that Roy might not after all find her attractive.

The phone rang. Luanai had already slipped off her robe to take a bath but now she put it on again, as if somehow she felt she should be clothed when talking to Roy.

"Luanai!"

"Hello, Flyer Roy."

She heard him cough nervously. "The flight was delayed. I just got in. So . . . well, I thought I'd better let you know."

"There's plenty of time," she said calmly, aware of the tenseness in Roy's voice.

"Yes . . . Well, I'll rent a car in Honolulu. I thought we might drive somewhere."

"That would be lovely."

"Well . . . then . . ."

"I'll see you, Flyer Roy."

She hung up, pursed her red-bowed lips, went into the bedroom and removed her kimono. She laid the garment on the bed and thought how considerate Roy was, because it would be very difficult for her to carry this through in George's bed. Even though she was doing it for George, it would be wrong to use their marriage bed.

In the bathroom she soaked for a long time in a tub of hot water filled with the fragrant suds of a bubble bath. The odor was that of pine. They had pine trees in Connecticut, where Roy lived, but not in Hawaii. That was the reason she had selected pine. To remind Roy of home. Yes, even to remind him of his wife, for she did not want him to feel compromised in any way.

She closed her eyes, half dozed, then sat up and bathed thoroughly with the pine-scented soap. She ran the bar over her shoulders and arms, her breasts and stomach and thighs and legs. Everything would smell of pine needles, so of course Roy would be able to . . .

Her hand stopped, carefully placed the soap in its rack. She remembered the stricken look on Roy's face when she'd asked him, begged him to do this for her. . . . The hoarse sound of his voice when she'd talked to him on the phone only a few minutes ago. Suppose old Flyer Roy didn't want her? She couldn't bear to feel ashamed with him.

She rinsed off, dried herself with a big towel, went back into the bedroom and studied her naked body in the full-length mirror. It was a good body. She knew that. Many men had chased after her before she'd decided on George Olger. But all men were not attracted to the same kind of woman. Roy, for instance, was married to a slender, red-haired, freckled girl. She, too, was slender. But black-haired, Oriental, dark-skinned. Perhaps Roy did not care for her type. Perhaps he would even be repulsed. More than that—maybe after all these years it would be impossible for him to see her as anything but the child he had always known, almost his daughter, almost his little sister, so that he would not be able to do anything at all.

Luanai shook her head sharply to rid herself of her doubts and sat down on the bed. She thought of George becoming more and more withdrawn every day, picking fights with her for no evident reason at all, beginning to feel unsure of his manhood simply because they did not have a child. He wanted a child more than anything on earth.

And she thought about Roy, and how he would do anything for her—*anything*— Except that she had no right to ask this. No right at all. But it was too late to think of that now. Roy was on his way, and if she did not go through with it, if it did not work, there would never be another chance.

I'll make it as easy for him as I can, she thought. I'll do everything possible to keep him from hating me or himself. And if possible, I'll do my very best to make him enjoy it.

She rose and began to dress. Panties, but no slip or brassière because they'd be awkward and unmanageable. She selected a simple white cotton dress, bare-shouldered. She would wear a scarf in case it was cold. A touch of French perfume behind her ears (though she prayed it would not clash with the odor of pine), a neutral spray deodorant under her smooth-shaven armpits, flat sandals for walking in the dark. She brushed out her hair and went back into the living room.

66

It was shortly after four. She lit a cigarette, remembered she'd forgotten to brush her teeth, and then, brushing them, wondered if Roy would kiss her or if she should kiss him, and decided to let Nature take care of things in her own way.

Quarter after four. She thought that perhaps they should have a cocktail in the house first, before going out. They'd often had cocktails here. It would help put Roy at ease. On the other hand, perhaps it would only make him see her as he always did. And tonight she wanted everything to seem different.

A car outside. For a moment she felt panic. Then, as the bell sounded, she rose, her calm self again, opened the door and kissed Roy cheerfully on the cheek.

"And how's my Flyer Roy today?" she said, leading him by the hand into the room.

Roy said yes, he would like a martini. He sat on the edge of his chair, pulled up his freshly pressed slacks at the knees, stared down at his highly polished loafers, then looked at Luanai through the kitchen doorway. Her back was turned to him as she went about preparing the cocktails. Her white dress had a zipper that ran the full length down the back, and he thought how beautifully the white set off her black hair and her golden skin. She bent forward over the sink and the dress tightened across her back, and he saw that she was not wearing a brassière. He said, "That a new dress?"

"No, you just haven't seen it before."

Luanai gave him a cocktail, sat down with hers in a chair facing him. He stared blankly at his shoes, finding it difficult to meet her eyes. Silence.

"You look very nice," she said softly, and he said, "You, too," thinking with a sudden pang of anguish, Does she really think so, or is she playing a game, pretending that she finds me attractive? Suppose what she really felt was repulsion for him and the entire idea of the evening ahead? If that were so, he couldn't bear it. She meant too much to him. Surely she must see through his pretense, the hypocrisy of his attitude, acting as if he was doing this for her when he wanted her, wanted her with every ounce of his being.

It was hard for them to find words to say to each other. He had a second cocktail, refused a third, knowing that a small amount of alcohol might stimulate the sexual drive, while too much thwarted it. But the way he felt there could never be too much to stop the aching tremble that would not leave him in peace.

"Where would you like to eat?" he asked.

"You decide, Flyer Roy."

"There's a new place along the beach. The Grass Hut, it's called; sort of like Trader Vic's, except they have a kind of Hawaiian *smörgåsbord*."

Luanai said yes, that would be lovely. She took the empty glasses to the kitchen, went into the bedroom and returned with a white knit shawl. "It might get cold," she explained. "Do you think I should bring the old beach blanket?"

"Yes, it might get cold," he said, and added, "in the car."

She went back to the bedroom, returned again with the blanket folded over one arm. She locked the doors and they went out together to the rented Chevrolet.

The sun was low. They drove past the "rainbow shower" trees and the tiny dooryards colored in purple and red bougainvillea and gold candlebrushes and yellow alamanda that sprawled over the little fences, and the endless rows of hibiscus hedges in every color of the rainbow. The still air was filled with the fruity fragrance of copa de oro and, strangely enough, Roy thought, in all these tropical odors he could detect the odd, familiar fragrance of pine.

He glanced in the mirror, met Luanai's almond eyes, and said, "I smell something like pine."

"Me," she laughed.

"Oh?"

"You like it?"

"Very much. I grew up with pine trees."

"I know. I wanted you to feel at home." Her hand touched his knee, rested there a moment, sending a shock that tingled all through his body, until they reached The Grass Hut. At last they were safe inside under the matted roof, sitting across from each other at the tiny table, a single candle between them.

The "Hawaiian *smörgåsbord*" was a commercial imitation of the famous luaus—pig and taro, bananas and chicken, fish and sweet potatoes, presumably baked in an earth oven; puddings of coconut and arrowroot, coconut and sweet potato, coconut and taro, and deep, cool bowls of lavender-pink poi.

They drank a legal *okolehau*, mild, with none of the deceiving kick of the old-time liquor which was now condemned and could be bought only from bootleggers.

Luanai said, "You know who invented *okolehau*?"

"No," Roy said vaguely, aware only of her smooth brown shoulders in the candlelight, and the ache in his hands to caress them.

"It was first made on Pitcairn Island by a man named McCoy. He was one of the mutineers on the *Bounty*. He distilled it from the root of the ti plant, the same plant they use for leaves to make the hula skirts."

"You're quite a historian."

"I've lived here all my life."

"Not so very long," Roy said, and he thought how he was old enough to be her father and soon, now, he would repeat the sin of his own father. Except this was different . . . not to harm anyone. Only himself, maybe. And suddenly the thought occurred to him, who was he to condemn his father? And he realized, for the first time, that his father might not have felt any

69

different than he felt, might have loved the girl just as much as he loved Luanai, and wanted only to give, not to take.

"You're not eating," Luanai said, breaking into his revery.

"I guess I'm not very hungry."

"Me either. It's beginning to get dark now. Do you want to go?"

"Unless you'd prefer to stay."

"No . . ." She reached across the little table for his hand and held it for a moment while she smiled at him reassuringly. "Let's go."

She took his arm as they walked to the car. He wondered if he should kiss her, touch her, indulge in any of the love-play that Millie thought was so very important. How did Luanai expect him to behave? Would she be pleased if he made violent love to her? Or shocked? He was her great friend, she said, but what he felt for her now was not friendship. Could she understand that? Did she sense that he was helplessly in love with her, and that this might be the most disastrous—or the most sublime—experience of his life? The thought that all the time she was in his arms she would be thinking of George made him groan inwardly.

There was a low moon, full in the bright, sweet-smelling night. Tormented by his thoughts, Roy drove slowly, up into the hills beyond Waikiki, past Diamond Head, down into the tiny valleys, along the moonlit beaches.

Luanai was silent, withdrawn. Until finally, as he made a sharp turn and dipped beneath a long row of coconut trees, she said, "Do you know the first thing I remember about you?"

Roy didn't say anything. He was thinking of how he had found Luanai that morning in hell at Pearl Harbor—a little girl, beautiful as only a Chinese-Hawaiian child can be, her large almond eyes filled with terror as she clung to the prostrate body of her dead mother. In an odd sort of way, because he had found the homeless little creature and saved her from death, she was associated in his mind with a secret of his childhood.

One day he had found a toy stuffed kangaroo abandoned on the village green and had taken it home and hidden it in a cardboard box under his bed. He'd wanted to name it Kanga, after the kangaroo in *Winnie the Pooh*. But it was a boy, he decided, whereas Kanga was a girl. Kanga's son was named Roo, but Roo was very little, according to the drawings in the book. So he'd finally settled on Big Roo, since it was quite a large stuffed animal.

He'd never told anyone about Big Roo, but had kept it hidden in the box for long childhood years, the object of a lonely boy's affection. At heart he was still that same lonely boy, Roy knew, just as Big Roo was still with him, hidden under his bed at home. . . .

"The first thing I remember about you," Luanai was saying, "was not when you found me that day. You've told me about that, but I can't remember Pearl Harbor clearly. It's all a jumble of terror and death. It was before that, and you've never told me about it."

"Oh?"

"I remember it was nighttime. I was sleeping behind a screen or something. You were talking to someone. I could see through the crack in the screen and there was a Chinese woman lying on a cot. She was naked, and she said, 'For you it's free,' or something like that, and you said, 'Thank you very much' and left. I remember the woman was very angry after you had gone. She came behind the screen to see if I was awake. I was, but I pretended to be asleep."

Roy was silent, remembering.

"The woman," Luanai said softly, "was my mother. She was a prostitute, wasn't she? She meant you wouldn't have to pay—"

"Look . . . Luanai . . ."

"Only you didn't want her, and later she was killed. . . ."

71

He took her hand affectionately. "Baby, that was years and years ago. Don't try to remember."

"But I do remember, and that's why I'm telling you about it now. I don't want you to think of me in the same way. It's not free to you, Flyer Roy. It's free to me."

He laughed. He could not stop laughing. He pulled the car under a row of trees along the mountain road and sat there behind the wheel laughing foolishly, intermittently, until finally the laughter ended in a sigh and there was silence, with the moon across the water far below, and the waves white as they made the long roll to the moonlit beach.

"It's so beautiful," Luanai whispered. And after a pause, "Why were you laughing?"

"The way you said it, I suppose." It would take all night for me to explain, Roy thought.

"Do you want to get out and sit on the grass?" Luanai suggested.

"All right." He opened the door. "I'd better get the blanket. It might be damp."

She walked beside him, under the stand of coconut trees, to a patch of grass that looked inviting. He did not look at her, did not dare look at her lest she see the hunger in his eyes. He took her arm, and she said, looking at him compassionately, "Oh my dear, you are trembling so."

He spread out the old blanket and she sat, hugging her knees. He sat beside her in silence, lit a cigarette, looked out over the far Pacific and the long path of the moon. He wished it were completely dark, was glad there was enough light for him to see Luanai plainly. She looked so beautiful. After a while he flipped away the half-finished cigarette. He could feel his heart pounding, a dampness in his hands. His mouth felt dry, and when at last he said "Luanai," it was almost a groan of despair.

"Don't say anything, Roy," she whispered. She touched his arm. "We can't ever explain how we feel about one another.

72

Not really. You're warm and comfortable, and I . . ." Her voice trailed away. She laid her head on his shoulder and he smelled the fragrance of pine. His arm enveloped her bare shoulders and he held her close, with the excitement mounting in him, until she turned her face to him. He kissed her then, felt her darting tongue in his mouth, and eased down beside her on the blanket. He tried to remember that the whole thing was planned, that it had nothing to do with their real emotions. But it was no good. His whole being yearned for her, and he crushed her to him and kissed her eyes, her throat, her shoulders. His impatient hands found the zipper, slipped the dress from her with her willing help. He caressed her firm and lovely breasts, kissed the upthrust nipples, ran his trembling hands over her smooth, cool belly, her taut thighs, until the passion within him flared into something wild, unbearable.

"I love you, I love you," he cried. "Oh my God, Luanai." And it seemed to him, in the full, uncompromising way she gave herself, that she loved him, too.

"Roy! My darling Flyer Roy."

"My kangaroo," he whispered, "my kangaroo." And the world exploded in red and black, in fire and storm, then settled itself once more, slowly, slowly, so there was the moon again and the sea again and the scent of pine and beautiful little Luanai lying naked beside him, her eyes closed while she breathed ever slower.

"Yes," she said finally. "It's happened. I could tell."

"Oh, Luanai . . ."

"I'll name him Roy. And if it's a girl, I'll name her Royale."

"My little Roo," he said, gathering her in his arms again, feeling his heart would break because she was no longer thinking of him but of the joyous gift of love she would be bringing to her husband.

73

Chapter Eight

THE first thing Frank Gattone did when he reached his office Tuesday morning was to call Edith Parkes to get her to change their date from Wednesday evening to the following day—or night—or any other time just so long as it didn't interfere with Anita's obsession about his having to put in an appearance at Dr. Bullock's.

But Miss Parkes was not at home, the maid who answered the phone said. No, she didn't know where Miss Parkes could be reached. Miss Parkes had left word that she would not be home until the following morning.

Now it was the following morning—Wednesday morning—and thank God! when he called Edith she was there, at the other end of the wire. Frank heaved a sigh of relief.

"Hello, darling," he said, trying to sound intimate, trying to sound casual. "I was thinking about tonight . . ."

"Yes, Pumpkin, so was I."

He wished she wouldn't all the time be calling him Pumpkin. It was a damn silly name for a grown man. "After all," he said, "the script's not ready yet, and I was thinking maybe by tomorrow night . . ."

"No, Pumpkin, not tomorrow night."

"Or maybe this afternoon."

"Tonight, Pumpkin, like we said."

"I mean there's this important function at the Academy tonight and I'm supposed to be there. I mean Anita expects me, and I promised her long ago, long before I called you on Monday."

The minute he mentioned Anita's name Frank knew he had made a mistake. He could tell from Edith's silence at the other end of the wire. For a woman like Edith Parkes all a man had to say was that his wife was expecting him. That was all she needed to know to make her absolutely determined to have her own way.

Perverse, stubborn bitch, Frank thought hopelessly. Now she'll never let me change the date.

"Of course, if you don't want me to do the part . . ." Edith said sweetly.

"But I do, Edith, I do want you. You know that."

"After all," she continued with a fake show of being oh, so reasonable, "after all, there must be many others . . ."

"There are no others, Edith. There's nobody like you."

"Then tonight, Pumpkin. Here. Nineish."

"But *why*, Edith? For God's sake, why does it have to be just this night?"

"You'll see, Pumpkin. . . . Good-by." She hung up before he could protest further.

Frank groaned. Now he had put his foot in it for fair. At least if he had told Anita there was just this chance that he would have to see Edith Parkes Wednesday night . . . of course she would have been upset, refused to understand . . . but at least it would have been there, on the record. Now he would have to call her, try to explain. He reached in his breast pocket for his handkerchief and mopped his forehead. Dammit! He had half a mind to call Edith again and tell her to go to hell. Only of course he couldn't do that. Without Edith Parkes the show would never make the grade. And she knew it.

All during the production meeting that day Frank kept one eye on the clock. Sooner or later he would have to call Anita.

75

Why not call her now and get it over with? Only he couldn't call her now. He was too busy. And so he kept putting it off, putting it off, while the day was getting older, and he had the growing, sickening feeling that somehow he was betraying Anita, that she was right in her fear that the job meant more to him than she did.

The production meeting had been going on for hours. Besides himself, there was Les Garret; the set designer, an obvious pansy named Dillon Sprague; the assistant director, Mike Purdue, a tall, snotty kid who'd graduated from the Yale Drama School; and Joan Leonard, his production assistant, with her black, black eyes and those slender, strong hands that made him think of Anita.

They were sitting around the big rectangular table while Frank studied the floor plan on which he'd worked for hours on his own. The garden set at the resort was out, he said. They had no use for it. The veranda was all right, but why all this outdoor stuff that always looked so phony anyway? Dillon Sprague looked as if his feelings were hurt. After all, Dillon said, the chief thing about a resort *was* the outdoors, wasn't it?

"All right," Frank conceded. "We'll use it for one establishing shot. That's all."

Mike Purdue protested.

"Look," Frank explained patiently, "I'm doing the whole thing in close-ups—"

The phone rang and Joan Leonard answered it.

"Yes, Mrs. Gattone," Frank heard her say as she looked across the table questioningly at him.

He shook his head. "I'm sorry, Mrs. Gattone. He's still in conference," Joan said, and hung up.

Oh my God! Frank groaned inwardly. That was the third time Anita had called. He looked at the clock. It was almost four. Let's break this thing up, he thought. I've got to call her. Now. Before it gets any later. Well, they were almost through.

No sense in getting all worked up about it, he told himself, trying to clear his mind of everything but the matter at hand.

"As I said, I'm doing the whole thing in close-ups," he continued to explain carefully to Mike Purdue. "A couple of establishing shots here and there. Maybe a couple of long shots so we won't waste the sets. But basically it's being done in close-ups."

"Sounds like ten years ago," Mike grumbled, "when there weren't any sets and there wasn't any budget. You just had to make the best of things then."

"That's right." Frank leaned across the table. "There weren't any sets and there wasn't any budget. You were still in knickers then, so maybe you don't remember. We did a lot of close-ups, and maybe some of the technical stuff was a little crude by today's standards. But at least people *saw* the actors—even on their seven-inch screens. At least there was some feeling of being *involved* with the action, not just looking at a stage from the last row in the balcony. I haven't directed a play in a long time. That's true. But I've watched plenty of them, and what with color and bigger screens they're beginning to get so weighted down with their sets and their tricks and their crowd scenes and special effects that the plays themselves are getting buried beneath the productions. Well, this is not a spectacular. It's a simple, straightforward story—a little corny here and there, maybe—and maybe we'll even come in *under* the budget. But with Edith Parkes playing the lead—"

"Edith Parkes!" Mike broke in.

"That's what I said."

"Nobody can get Edith Parkes."

"I'll get her." Frank looked at Mike and saw his contempt turn slowly to respect. He looked at Joan Leonard. Her eyes were bright with open admiration. "Okay?" he said. "So let's get on with the work."

They worked steadily for another hour, then the meeting

77

broke up. After the others had gone, Les Garret, who had remained in Frank's office, said, "You're worried about something?"

"No . . ."

"You think maybe you can't land Edith Parkes?"

"I said I'll try," Frank said irritably.

"You get us Edith, all your troubles are over."

"Ummm . . . maybe."

"What time you seeing her?"

"Nine. At her place."

Les Garret grinned knowingly. "Well, good luck."

"Thanks. I'll need it. . . . Anyway," Frank burst out suddenly, "it's not about Edith I'm worried. It's Anita."

Les blinked behind his horn-rimmed glasses. "You mean because of what happened between you and Edith that last time? Man, that was years ago, and—"

"No, it's not that." Frank sighed. "It's not that at all. It's just that I promised Anita I'd be with her tonight at some function of the Academy that means a lot to her. Now I'll have to tell her I can't make it."

"What's so terrible about that?"

"What's so terrible is that I lied to Anita. Said I'd be with her when I knew I'd made this date to see Edith Parkes."

"Call your wife, man, call her," Les said. "What the hell? That's the way things are, that's all. No use getting yourself in a stew about it. Anita'll understand."

Les left the room and went down the hall. Oh sure, Frank thought unhappily, Anita'll understand. She'll understand what a heel her husband can be.

Joan Leonard was standing in the doorway. "I thought I'd go now if you don't need me any more today," she said. "Is there anything else you'd like me to do?"

"Yes. Call my wife," Frank said. He was about to add, Tell her

78

I won't be able to make it tonight, but thought better of it. "Get her on the phone for me."

When the phone rang, Anita was pacing the floor of her living room. Three times she had called and each time that same girl, whoever she was, had told her she could not speak to her own husband because he was too busy. Of all the nerve! And no doubt Frank had told her to say just that. What was going on? What the hell was going on in that office of his? Anita felt herself being consumed with jealous rage.

She let the phone ring four times before she picked up the receiver.

"Yes?" she said curtly.

It was a young woman speaking, the same young woman who had answered her calls before.

"Mrs. Gattone? One minute, please. Your husband is calling."

"Hello, Anita," Frank said. "I'm terribly sorry I couldn't get through to you sooner. This confounded meeting had been going on all day and—"

"You mean you'll be very late and will I pick you up in Bridgeport on the twelve-thirty-two."

"Look, Anita, I—"

"Who was that girl who answered the phone?"

"My assistant, of course. Her name is—"

"I don't want to know her name."

"For God's sake, Anita. Her name is Joan Leonard."

"Oh, how charming. So it's Joan Leonard."

"I mean, she's only my assistant. Why get so disturbed about it?"

"Who said I was disturbed? It seems to me you're the one who's disturbed."

"Okay. Have it your way."

79

"Have you found your female lead yet?" Anita's voice was cool, and Frank knew she was making an effort to keep herself under control.

"The deal isn't closed yet," he said. "I told you we were trying to get Edith Parkes. That's what's holding me up. She's coming to the office tonight. Les and I are going to talk to her about it."

Now why did I say that? Frank thought guiltily. Another lie, for no purpose at all except to spare Anita's feelings. His heart sank. Once you told an untruth you had to keep on lying to back it up, and all the time you were getting in deeper and deeper.

"So you're going to see Edith Parkes," Anita said sarcastically. "Be sure and give her my love."

"Now you're not going to be jealous of *her,* are you?"

"God, no! That old bag? I give you credit for better taste, darling."

Frank was saying something else but she did not bother to listen. She felt completely collected now, calm, in absolute control of herself and her emotions. She said, "In other words, you won't be at Dr. Bullock's this evening."

"I fully expected to be," Frank explained lamely. "I did plan to make it. But then this thing came up, and there was no way of getting out of it, and—"

He heard the phone click and realized that Anita had hung up on him. He was just talking to himself.

Anita's hand was shaking as she replaced the receiver. So he wasn't coming home, she thought. It was just what she had expected would happen. He had never intended to make it at Dr. Bullock's in the first place, had only said he would be there to keep her quiet. Well, she'd show him how quiet she could be. Edith Parkes was coming to see him in his office. She didn't give a damn about Edith Parkes. But the production girl would be there too, and there was nothing on earth that brought two people closer together than the hectic madhouse of television. Every production girl was more than half in love with her director, who took out his anger, his worries, his ambitions, his frustrations—yes, even his love—on his Girl Friday. Wasn't that how she had met Frank herself? Oh, she knew his moods, wild one moment, small boy the next, intense, excitable, and very passionate, too, about everything. And everything included sex.

"Calm," she said aloud, jumping to her feet. "Keep calm," beginning to pace the floor again. Suddenly she went into the kitchen.

She took an Old-Fashioned glass from the cupboard, put some cubes of ice in it from the refrigerator, and took it back to the living room. Deliberately she opened the liquor cabinet and poured herself a large shot of bourbon. Nothing sneaky about it. She wouldn't care if Alan came back from the tennis court right now and saw her, not even if Frank walked in right this minute and found her with a glass in her hand. She'd say, "I'm having a drink, and what's it to you?"

After her long period of abstinence, Anita quickly felt the shock of the liquor. That was quite a drink, she said to herself, draining the last of her glass. Still, it wasn't too much. She never had drunk too much and she never would. She always knew when to stop. Everybody had made such a darn fool fuss about it just because she used to get bored in the 72nd Street apartment when Frank wasn't home, and have a couple of drinks before dinner—well, maybe one at lunch now and then, too. They had dragged her off to that wretched hospital for four days, and just because she'd been unhappy and upset they'd started calling it the D. T.'s, and made her go to Alcoholics Anonymous with all those drunks, as if she was a drunk herself or something.

Well, she wasn't, and if she had another drink right now,

she wouldn't be breaking her word to Frank any more than he'd already broken his word to her. She'd have another and be damned to everybody.

She did. She felt fine. Even a little superior, if anyone cared to ask her. She had never felt calmer, more sure of herself than she did right now. If Paul Barker should come into the room she would offer him a drink, too. She'd like just once to see Paul Barker lose that famous reserve of his. Now look, Paul, she would say. You thought I was talking a lot of nonsense the other day when I said we couldn't communicate. We're both two adult human beings. No reason why we can't communicate. Let me tell you what I was driving at. But first I'll take just one more drink, just a teeny little one.

I suppose I really ought to be getting dressed for old Batty-ass Bullock's affair, Anita thought. But there was plenty of time yet. Plenty of time for another drink, and even another if she felt like having another.

The glass of whisky in her hand, she made her way to a chair and sank down into it. Funny thing; her body felt shaky, but her mind was perfectly clear. Clear as a bell. I must have said that because I heard the school bell, she thought, counting the strokes to six. Six o'clock. Now let's see, what is it I have to explain to Paul Barker this evening?

In her troubled state of mind, it did not occur to Anita that she was confusing Frank and Paul, that it was Frank who was the object of her resentment, not Paul, and that somehow she was getting at Frank through Paul. It seemed to her, through the whisky haze that made everything clearer and at the same time more confusing, that she had a duty to tell Paul Barker he was living a lie, just as her father was, and Roberta, and she herself, and Frank—yes, Frank; he couldn't fool her about his production girl—they were all living a lie. Except those two innocents, Alan and Christina. Somebody had to keep them from

82

committing a dreadful sin. And if she was the one nominated to do it, by God she would accept the nomination.

Only of course she wouldn't say anything about it to Paul. The very thought of telling him the truth about Roberta and Christina panicked her. She wouldn't hurt Paul for the world. She loved Paul. Why should she want to hurt him? And in her fantasy she saw Paul coming to her for solace, and she held his head to her breast, and then she was kissing him, and his arms were around her, and she was swooning in his embrace—

"Better get hold of yourself, my girl," Anita said aloud as she got up unsteadily from the chair. "Keep your lips buttoned up or you'll bring the whole damn house tumbling down around our heads. Take a good cold shower to clear your head." Yes, that was the trick. A good cold shower. And maybe a good cup of black coffee. Meanwhile, one more drink wouldn't hurt, she thought as she weaved her way back to the liquor cabinet.

She was in a dangerous mood. She could feel it in her bones. Maybe I'd better not show up at Dr. Bullock's, either, she thought. Maybe I'll just stay home and go to bed. Then I won't be able to say anything I'll regret later. But in her heart she knew she was not going to stay home and that nothing was going to stop her from going to Dr. Bullock's, not even herself. The way she was feeling, anything could happen and probably would.

Well, let it, she thought vengefully, staring gloomily into her glass.

Chapter Nine

EDITH PARKES finished her drink, poured a last martini from a gold-leafed pitcher into her gold-leafed glass, then sat down on the gold sofa once more in her black lounging pajamas decorated with a huge, metallic gold dragon, and thought how black and gold were her favorite colors because they were so in tune with her personality. "Black for my wicked side, and gold for my innocent side." And she did have an innocent side, too, though no one had ever seen it, really, except perhaps Stewart Bolls, who'd been her first lover, then later her third husband. Dear Stu. She wondered whatever became of him. She curled her legs under her and sipped at the martini and wondered what had become of a lot of people she had known more or less intimately and why she was drinking so much when she hadn't eaten yet. She wondered why in hell she was even considering this ridiculous television play, although secretly she did know, of course, and that was part of her wicked side.

"Darling Frank Gattone," she said into the glass. "And how is your darling wife Anna, or Anita, or whatever her name is? Of course I'll do the show, Pumpkin, on conditions, of course, because of course there are always conditions about this sort of thing."

She wondered if Frank remembered "that dreadful night" as clearly as she did. Not that the memory was with her always. But it had a way of returning when she drank too much, and sometimes she felt rage in the memory, and sometimes hurt, and sometimes a cool, almost satisfying hatred. Tonight, though, on her seventh martini, she felt nothing but a wonderful sweetness—almost one of her gold feelings.

"That dreadful, humiliating night" had been many long years ago, right after *The Letter*, when she'd invited the entire cast to her apartment. Frank had been very young then, in his late twenties, married to that Anna or Anita girl with the dirty blond hair and the narrow face and those disgusting high breasts. It had been a gay party until somehow, during the party, she'd decided it would be marvelous fun to seduce Frank right under the nose of his wife. She could see that the girl was too excited, too madly in love, too happy over the success of the show to pay much attention to what she was drinking. It had been quite easy to make her drinks too strong and serve her a few too many, until she was quite obviously drunk and Frank was terribly embarrassed.

He'd apologized profusely. She'd touched his arm and said, "Now don't you worry about a thing, Pumpkin. Just take your little wife home, get her to bed, and then trot right back again."

"I don't understand," he had protested. "She's never been like this before."

"She's only a child, Pumpkin."

"I know, but still . . ."

"And I've been married five times. Think about that, Pumpkin. Five times. All those hundreds of experiences. You will come back, won't you, darling?"

"Sure." He'd looked at her slowly, beginning to understand then, and she'd thought how young and virile he was, how very attractive, how good he must be in bed, and what a pity it was for such a bright and attractive young man to be married to such an inexperienced young thing. "I'll be back," he said, and guided his ridiculous wife through the doorway.

She had soon gotten rid of the other guests. She'd dimmed

the lights, put soft music on the phonograph, changed into a sheer, black negligee, and doused herself with perfume. It made her feel quite young herself, almost like she'd felt on her first honeymoon, with Edgar White, almost like that first night on the beach at South Hampton with Stu Bolls. "Romantic"— that was the word for it. She'd felt deliciously romantic, giddy, a girl of eighteen again, when the buzzer sounded and Frank stepped into the twilit world of black and gold.

Precisely what happened after that had become blurred in her memory. Only the sense of shock and shame remained. He had come back to accuse her, called her a conniving old bitch. He'd ignored the soft lights and the romantic music and the expensive perfume, the lovely negligee, trampled on her wonderful young feeling, until she'd actually begged him, begged him on her knees. It was then, when he'd showed her nothing but contempt, that she'd felt the terrible rage coming on, that she'd screamed and hit out at him while he held her off, crying, "Want you? My God, I'm just sorry for you! Just plain sorry for you."

Then he'd gone, and she'd lain on the gold sofa in her rumpled black negligee and wept out her rage and frustration, swearing through her tears that the next time he rang her bell, the next time she came face to face with Frank Gattone . . .

The bell rang.

Frank was waiting in the hall, tugging nervously at the brim of his hat. When he'd talked to Edith on the phone, his hopes had been reasonably high that he could get her to do the show. But now, recalling so vividly that night long ago, he felt less sure of himself. Still, she had been pretty drunk that messy night. After all these years she had probably forgotten about the whole affair. Considering how many times this sort of thing must have happened to her, with her five husbands and countless lovers —well, she couldn't possibly still bear him any grudge.

The door swung in and there was Edith, putting out her hand, smiling with those hazy, gold-flecked eyes, saying, "Frank . . . it's so good to see you, Frank. . . . Come in, Pumpkin. Do come in."

He sat on the edge of the sofa while she made him a highball and mixed another martini for herself. He watched her slim back in the black pajamas, and thought that even at fifty-two, with proper lighting and make-up, she could still pass easily for thirty-four. She was probably tight now, but she was always sober when she worked. Everyone had been trying for years to get her on television again, they had offered her all kinds of inducements, and she'd always refused. There was no reason for her to accept now. He'd been a damn fool even to consider the possibility. What was he going to say to Les when she turned him down? Who were they going to get? And without her, what would become of the future that had looked so bright only hours before?

Edith turned, gave him the drink, and sat on the far end of the sofa, leaning back against a cushion. "So," she smiled, "the return of the native."

"Just for this one shot, Edith."

"But I understand it's been bought for a movie."

"Yes, it has."

"So if all goes well enough on TV, they'll be giving you first crack at the picture."

"Well . . . there's been no agreement . . . as yet."

She smiled at him over her glass. "It's all very important to you, isn't it, Pumpkin?"

"Yes. Yes, it is. Very important."

"The most important thing you've ever done in your entire life. You're all fed up with teaching little boys way out there yonder in the wilderness, and this is your way out, and I'm very important to your plans."

"Look, Edith . . ."

"I mean, if I don't do it, then who will?"

"Frankly, I don't know."

"Mr. Gattone signs up wonderful Edith Parkes, and that's his first big step toward the movie contract, so of course I'll simply *have* to accept, won't I, because if I refuse then what'll happen to little old Frank?"

"Edith." He put aside his glass, rose, and stood looking down at her amused face. "If you asked me over to play games . . . I mean, if you're going to say no, just say it, and I'll be on my way."

"Now don't get excited, Pumpkin. You always were so excitable."

"I admit we can't meet your price."

"Oh, I'm not so sure."

"I mean I was trying to approach you on a personal level."

"Yes, Pumpkin. Personal."

"So thanks anyway." He turned toward the door, but her voice stopped him. "Frank . . . I haven't seen the script yet, but if you say it's good I know it must be. If I like the part, I'll do it."

He came back to the sofa and stood there close to her, trying to fathom the depths of those teasing eyes. "On a personal level," Edith added as if it were an afterthought, lowering her eyes now as she sipped at her martini. He looked at the gold design on the glass, at the golden dragon with his open mouth by her breast, at her slim, pajama-clad legs, then sat down again slowly and said, "I don't get it, Edith."

"Don't you, Pumpkin? Let me ask you a question. Are you still in love with Anna?"

"Anita. Yes, of course I love her."

Edith laughed. "You say it so strenuously, I wonder. Well at any rate, you've never been unfaithful to her, have you, Pumpkin?"

88

Asked the question point-blank like that, Frank was taken by surprise. Come to think of it, he never had been unfaithful to Anita, although there had been plenty of opportunities and he had never thought of himself as the faithful type.

"I don't see . . ." he protested.

"Have you?"

"No," he said slowly. "As a matter of fact, I haven't."

"I thought not," Edith said. "You're the honorable kind." She took his glass and went over to the black teakwood bar and mixed them both another drink. "Well," she said, her back to him as she dropped ice cubes into his glass, "I haven't forgotten that night. I know you think I have—hope I have—but I haven't. All these years I've been thinking, How can I revenge myself on that noble, moral, upstanding little bastard?" She turned around to face him. "And now, you see, I've found a way."

"I don't understand," Frank said, although he was beginning to get the drift of her conversation all too clearly.

"You will." She gave him the drink, stood over him, looking down. "How much does your big future mean to you, Frank? Would you lie a little for it? I think you would. Cheat a little? Of course you would. But all that doesn't count, because you're such a moral man and such a fine, faithful husband. Aren't you, Pumpkin? As it happens, I don't believe it. I worked with you before, you know, and for my money you're on your last trip to market. You're off to buy yourself a big, fat pig, and it's going to have to last you the rest of your life."

"What are you driving at, Edith?"

"I said I would do the show and I will. I'll do the very best job I possibly can. Everything will be marvelous for everybody. You'll buy your pig, and it won't be in any poke, either. And then you can jiggety-jig home again to a nice big place in Beverly Hills. It's all up to you, Frank. If you meet my price."

"I told you we can't touch it," Frank said, wanting to believe she was talking about money but knowing well she wasn't.

"I said it was on a personal level."

"Meaning?"

"Meaning that some night after we start rehearsals—some night before the show—you will come up here to my apartment —just as you did ten years ago. Only this time *you* will get down on your knees to *me*. This time you will be deliberately unfaithful to your wife."

Frank was shocked and his face showed it. He had always thought of himself as a man of some sophistication, but now he was shocked—not merely at Edith's bald proposition, but also at the thought of being deliberately unfaithful to his wife. At bottom he was something of a Puritan, he supposed. At any rate, the thought of a married man sleeping with other women and then going home to his wife about it had always seemed to him dishonorable and he rejected it. Of course, anything could happen in a moment of thoughtless passion. He was no prude. But to be propositioned like this! It was unthinkable.

Edith laughed into his astonished face. She turned away, still laughing, then sat down on the sofa and sipped her martini. "You see, Frank, I'm just an old bitch. Married five times, lots of lovers—such a disgusting old hag. And you're so goddamn pure, and your little old wife is so goddamn innocent, and you're so happy and faithful to each other, and it's all so goddamn lovely. Only I'm ten years older now—even more of an old hag. . . ."

"You're drunk," he said softly, careful to hide the disgust he felt.

"Take it or leave it, Pumpkin."

"Edith, you can't be serious."

"Oh, can't I *just*."

"So you hate my guts. Is that what you're trying to tell me?"

90

"Yes, I hate you, Frank. You're right there. I lowered my pride for you, and now you'll have to lower your smug little standards for me. I know you fought your way up from the gutter to marry those phony New England standards. But you're going to dirty them for me."

"I suppose . . . afterwards . . . the idea is for you to tell Anita all about it."

"You would think something like that—you little crumb. But I've nothing against your wife. Maybe some day *you'll* tell her. And of course when you do, she'll understand. Just a business arrangement, with *so* much at stake. After all, I'm sure even she must be able to cheat just a little—if she can find the opportunity in that backwoods town you live in."

"You're drunk," he said again.

"Take it or leave it."

"And crazy besides."

Laughing at his discomfiture, she went over to the phonograph and switched on a light dance number. He watched her and thought that she was drunk all right, and that he ought to be getting the hell out of there. But he made no move to go. He sipped at his drink and thought that rehearsals wouldn't begin for some time, and she *would* make the show, and it would be the biggest casting coup of the TV year, and God he did want that movie job—that big, fat pig—and he was sure he could find a way out of this, get sick, get drunk, something that was an act of God, so that by June 23rd the show would be over and he wouldn't have to make good on his agreement. If he agreed to do anything, that is. There were a thousand ways to handle a situation like this; he could be just as clever about it as Edith Parkes any day. And afterwards, out in Hollywood, sitting by the swimming pool, it would make a wonderful story, and Anita would laugh with him about it. It wouldn't be unfair to Edith, either, because she'd be paid for her work. What she was proposing was only a form of ugly, almost ridiculous, blackmail. He had a perfect right to play it the way he wanted, get out of it any way he could.

"Take it or leave it, take it or leave it." She was swaying to the music, dancing about the room with amazing grace.

I ought to leave it, Frank thought. I ought to tell her to go to hell. But then he thought again how vital she was for his show, and beyond this one show, if he were ever to get to Hollywood. Besides, he couldn't let Les Garret down, even if Les was a sonofabitch to get him into a fix like this. They were all counting on him.

"I'll take it," he said quietly.

"I knew you would, Pumpkin."

She kept on dancing, sipping at her martini as she moved about, until finally she placed the glass on the phonograph as she whirled by. And then, still laughing, still dancing, she un-buttoned the loose black jacket and slid it slowly from her shoulders so that she was naked to the waist, and watching her, Frank had to admit that she did have a good body for a woman of her years. A slim waist and small pointed breasts that hardly sagged at all. By God! He felt his desire rising. If he couldn't get out of it . . . But he mustn't think that way, because he *would* get out of it, and he was reminding himself of this when she came over to him and bent and kissed him on the mouth. "I just wanted you to see what you'll be getting," she said. "Don't look so worried, Pumpkin. You'll love every minute of it."

"Then you'll sign the contract?" he asked, trying to sound casual, as if it was just an ordinary business deal they were talking about.

"I'll sign, Pumpkin." The music had stopped. She slipped into the jacket again but left it unbuttoned, and sat down on the sofa. "I'm so happy. It's so nice to know that other people can be just as rotten as I am."

92

"The script will be out of mimeo by tomorrow or the next day. I think we've taken care of the corny ending."

"Pumpkin, you've taken care of everything. Only remember, don't try to renege. Little old Edith has ways of coping."

He rose from the sofa, put down his drink. "See you then, Edith."

"I'll be seeing you, Pumpkin."

He felt her eyes on him, laughing at him, as he crossed to the door. Going down in the elevator he thought how in all the difficult years of his marriage to Anita he had been faithful to her. And now this—this cold-blooded deal with Edith Parkes! What am I doing? he thought. What the hell am I getting myself in for? He'd be damned if he ever went through with it the way Edith expected him to.

Stepping out into the spring night he reassured himself that he'd find a way out—after she'd signed the contract. Meanwhile there was no harm in promising her anything. Even Anita would understand that. He was on his way to market, and nothing could stop him now. Nothing at all.

Part Two

Chapter Ten

FOR the first time in her life Roberta Barker had the same anxiety dream twice in the same night.

The first one began whenever dreams begin and ended when she woke abruptly, heard the continuing rain, glanced at the luminous hands of the electric bedside clock pointing to 2:35, then dropped back into sleep.

And then the dream again. She was sitting on a pile of lumber, looking up at the steel structure that would add a needed building to the submarine base at New London. Her father was standing on a huge crosspiece that was being lifted skyward by a crane, his balding head shining in the afternoon sun. Now he was waving his handkerchief to her. And now, suddenly, the steel beam swung and tipped. Her father groped at the supporting cable, lost his balance, then plunged the more than one hundred feet to the ground. All the way down he kept running in the air, as though to climb back to safety.

She screamed. She was running toward the fallen man, but a guard tried to stop her. The guard was Paul. She fought him off, screaming over and over that she must get to her father. Her dress ripped as he tried to hold her. She scratched at his face, broke free, and ran wildly toward the man who lay face down on the concrete beneath the high-swinging steel beam. Paul was running after her, drawing his revolver, shouting for her to stop. She reached the fallen man and bent down, whimpering, "Daddy, Daddy," while the man moaned, and Paul said, "Out of his misery," and shot her father in the back of the head. But even as she watched the blood flow from the wound, she realized it was not a bald head at all. The man had thick hair, graying, blood on gray, and it was not her father as she had supposed. It was Mitchel Slayton.

Roberta felt herself crying as if her heart would break. She heard a siren screaming wildly, and then, waking with a start, realized it was the buzzer of the alarm clock. "Paul," she said weakly, "turn it off. Please turn it off." Paul did not answer. She opened her eyes, saw that he was not in the bed beside her, and turned the alarm off herself.

Everything was quiet. She lay still a moment, half in the dream, half in reality. Outside the window, water dripped from the rain-soaked trees, although the rain had gone away and the sky was radiantly clear. From the kitchen below she could hear bacon frying in the skillet. Christina's voice called, "Are you awake, Mother?" and she answered, "Yes," and sat up in bed and wondered why Paul had gotten up so early this morning.

The bathroom door was closed, but she did not hear the familiar stropping of his razor. (Paul had learned to shave with his father's straight razor, and he never used anything else.)

"Paul!"

No answer.

Roberta shook the dream and the sleep from her mind, went into the bathroom and doused her face in cold water. She noticed that Paul's razor was dry, untouched.

Something was wrong, very wrong . . . Paul was not home. Then he must not have come home at all last night. . . .

Feeling suddenly panicky, she hurried back into the bed-

98

room, pulled a dressing robe over her pajamas and went over to the window. The morning was lovely. The wet trees glistened in the early sun. But where was Paul? He was nowhere to be seen.

Something was very wrong, and she didn't know exactly what it was. Only how could anything have happened? Paul had seemed perfectly composed, even serene, when he went to Dr. Bullock's with her the evening before.

How happy she had been, how happy and proud, when Paul's promotion was announced and everybody was congratulating him. The only flaw in the evening was Anita's behavior. Anita was quite obviously drunk, although everyone pretended not to notice it. Except her father, who exchanged some sharp words with her and even told her to go home and sleep it off, only to have her laugh in his face contemptuously. It was embarrassing, actually shocking, even though everybody acted as if they hadn't noticed anything unusual, the way people will do on such occasions.

And then, Roberta recalled, she was talking to Mrs. Bullock about some indifferent matter when her attention was drawn to Anita and Paul in the far corner of the room. Anita was saying something to Paul in drunken earnestness, and Paul was biting his lips and his face looked pale and drawn. Then abruptly he had turned away from Anita and stalked out of the room.

Anxious, wondering what Anita had said to disturb him so, she had wanted to run after him, ask him what the trouble was. But then Mitchel Slayton had come over to talk to her and she couldn't break away. She had tried to assure herself that Paul had only gone out for a breath of fresh air, to walk by himself for a little while the way he liked to do when he grew tired of too many people and too much talk around him. He'll be back soon, she had told herself, furious with Anita for whatever it was she had said to upset him. But he had not come back.

Nor was he at home when she got there. She had prepared herself for bed, thinking to wait up for him, anxious yet not desperately so, for she knew her husband to be a man of many moods. But she must have fallen asleep in the meantime.

Where could Paul be? What had Anita said to him to make him leave so abruptly? Even when he decided to spend the night alone in the cottage, as he would sometimes when he was working on his book, he would always tell her beforehand, leave a note for her if she was not at home when he left.

She went over to the phone and picked up the receiver to call Anita, began to dial, then slowly replaced the instrument in its cradle. There was no use calling Anita, no use trying to delude herself any longer. She knew with a chilling, deadening certainty what Anita must have said to Paul. And what Anita said could never now be unsaid.

She had known it all along, however much she tried to reassure herself that nothing unusual had happened, had suspected it even. As she watched Paul's suddenly haggard face while Anita was talking to him. Now she knew the meaning of her terrible dream.

Heavy with despair, Roberta sank down on the bed. If it was what her heart told her it was . . . if what she had feared so long had come to pass. . . Sooner or later, she had always known, Paul would have to learn the truth about Christina, would have to learn that he was not the child's father, that her father was Mitchel Slayton. But Roberta had hoped to tell him the truth some day herself, some day when she felt in her heart the time was ripe and he was ready to understand and forgive.

And now Anita, in one drunken, dangerous moment, had ruined everything. Now Paul would never understand, never forgive her. His hurt was too sharp, too deep, the revelation too shattering. Roberta could feel what he must have gone through, what he must be enduring even now.

Suddenly frightened, she sat up, stricken by nameless fears.

100

Oh God, don't let anything happen to Paul, she prayed silently. Punish me, but don't punish Paul. Dear God, bring him back to me.

Downstairs, from the kitchen, she heard Christina calling, "Breakfast, everybody?" and she answered mechanically, too unhappy for tears, "I'm coming," wondering as she descended the stairs what she was going to say to her daughter.

"Where's Daddy?" Christina said, and when her mother did not reply she went into the hall and called, "Daddy! Breakfast!" and came back and said, "Darn. His breakfast'll get cold."

Roberta lifted her glass of orange juice to her lips, then put it down again without drinking. She picked up a piece of toast, but her hand shook so she could not butter it. She felt that in another moment she would burst into tears, and made an effort to control her emotions.

"Is something wrong?" Christina said, looking across the table at her, troubled.

She lifted the cup of coffee. Her hand was trembling so the coffee spilled on the yellow eye of the fried egg in her plate.

"Mother!" Christina said sharply.

"All right. I'm sorry." Roberta steadied her hand, took a long swallow of coffee, heard the milk truck stop outside, the clink of bottles, Smokey barking to announce the milkman's arrival.

"I'll get it," Christina said, and went to the back door. Roberta heard the milkman say "Hello, Christina," and Smokey barking again. She heard Christina say "Hello, Mr. Potts," and then, "Daddy! What in the world . . . !"

Roberta put down her cup of coffee and gripped the edge of the table so hard her knuckles showed white. She heard Paul saying dully, "Hello, honey," and then he was there before her, standing in the kitchen doorway, looking at her distantly as if she were a stranger to him. His suit was rumpled and he needed a shave. She sat there at the table staring at him, relieved that

101

he was unharmed and home again, yet filled with foreboding. His eyes looked tired and pained, and her heart went out to him in the strained silence between them.

Christina was putting the milk bottles in the refrigerator, talking all the while. "Where in the world have you been, Daddy? I'm so proud about your getting to be head of the department. Your breakfast is getting cold. Oh Daddy, I'm so happy for you!" She slammed the refrigerator door shut, swung abruptly in girlish enthusiasm into his arms and kissed him full on the mouth. Instinctively he embraced her and held her close to him for a long moment, until she broke away from him and looked at him as if she were puzzled and embarrassed. "Daddy," she whispered, sensing that something strange had happened between them.

"Don't ever call me that again," Paul said sharply. He turned away and avoiding Roberta's anxious eyes, strode from the room. Christina sat down, bewildered, frightened. She touched her lips with two fingers, as if she could still feel Paul's kiss. Mother and daughter looked across the table at one another, listening to his footsteps on the stairs. Then, in another moment, silence.

Roberta rose from the table. "Christina, stay here," she said. "Eat your breakfast."

"But I don't understand. What did he mean when—"

"Eat your breakfast," Roberta commanded harshly.

She left the kitchen and went up the stairs to the bedroom. A suitcase lay open on the bed. The bathroom door was open and inside, Paul was stropping his razor. He did not look at her. Mechanically he brushed lather on his face and started to shave. She watched him a moment, then turned to his dresser and selected clean shirts, socks and underwear, packed them carefully in the open suitcase.

"You don't have to pack for me," he said, coming out of the bathroom.

"Where are you going?" Roberta said.

102

"Home," he said. "Fremont."

"I suppose there's no need for me to ask you why."

"Hardly," he said dryly.

"I'll tell Christina that your mother is ill."

He shrugged. "Tell her what you want."

His curt remarks cut her to the quick. "I'd go myself, of course. Never come back. Except I have nowhere to go." She straightened, as if to throw off an intolerable burden, and turned to find him close, buttoning his shirt, looking at her with those strange, dead eyes. "Paul . . . Oh God, Paul!" she cried, holding out her arms to him, but he turned away, slipped on a tie and put on his coat. Picking up the bag, he started for the door. She stopped him in the doorway, her hand resting on his arm. "Think Paul, please. Think what you are doing."

"I can't think any more," he said. "I spent all night thinking."

"Please don't decide anything until you come back—not until we've at least had a chance to talk about it."

"I'm not coming back."

"No, not to this house maybe. But you will be back to finish the term?"

He did not answer. He looked her straight in the eyes and his face was not angry, only tired and sad and suddenly very thin. His eyes dropped to her hand on his arm. Then he pulled his arm away and went down the stairs, across the living room to his small study. He went in and closed the door.

Roberta went back into the kitchen, where Christina sat dumbly at the table, staring at her uneaten breakfast. "Aren't you going to eat, dear?"

"I'm not hungry," Christina said, without looking up.

"Try to understand, darling. Your Grandmother Dora is very ill, so Daddy has to go up to Fremont."

"He said not to call him Daddy."

"He's very upset, darling."

"When's he coming back?"

"Soon."

Christina bit into a piece of toast. It tasted like wood and she could hear it crunching between her teeth. Paul appeared in the doorway. In one hand he carried the suitcase, in the other a thin attaché case. "A couple of books," he said vaguely. Then, "Well, I'll be seeing you."

"Good-by," Christina mumbled into her plate.

Roberta said, "You'll take the car, of course."

"No, you'll need it to get to the cottage."

"Then I'll drive you to Bridgeport. I suppose you'll be taking the train there for Boston. You do have to change trains in Boston, don't you?"

"I'm not going to Boston."

"Oh?"

"Not yet, anyway.

"Well, I . . ."

"I'll walk to town. Pick up a taxi."

"Paul . . ."

"Good-by, then." He paused, as though there was something more to say that could not be said. "Good-by."

He left the kitchen and went through the living room, out the front door. They heard the door close behind him.

Roberta stared at the cold, uneaten eggs in his untouched plate. "He didn't even have any breakfast," Christina said.

Roberta went into the living room. Looking out of the window she saw Paul's tall body moving slowly down the street beneath the dripping leaves. Then, turning away from the window, she saw the open door to his study and went toward it. She leaned against the open door and tears came to her eyes as she looked at all the personal, dear odds and ends that stood for the man she loved as her husband and would never be able to think of as anyone else. She saw the tennis rackets and the ship models, the helter-skelter piles of books and papers, the gold trophy and the hi-fi. And there, in the half-open top drawer of his desk, the sharpened yellow pencils and paper clips and ball-point pens; the Silver Star medal he'd earned in the war; the automatic that Mitchel Slayton had given him for shooting tin cans behind the cottage. . . . Yes, the revolver should be there . . . only she couldn't see it from where she was standing.

Suddenly alarmed, she hurried over to the desk, rummaged through the drawer. The revolver was not there.

It must be at the cottage, she said to herself without confidence. Paul must have left it there last weekend.

But it was not at the cottage, she knew, and she also knew with a dreadful certainty where it must be, and why Paul was not going straight to Boston—not yet, anyway.

Chapter Eleven

THE campus seemed strangely quiet. The grass and trees had turned a bright green overnight, and there were puddles in the low spots of the uneven walk.

Paul stepped carefully around the pools of water. As a child, he had put on his boots and deliberately walked into every puddle he could find on his way to school. He was not a child any longer. He was pushing forty and he must not get his feet wet. At least Roberta hadn't said, "Don't forget your rubbers, dear," with that last wifely touch as her husband walked out on her. At least she had not cried and clung to him.

He wet his lips. But Christina had. She'd rushed into his arms and kissed him full on the mouth, and though at the time he did not understand his curious emotion, he did now, and it was a frightening, almost horrifying thing. For many years now he had accepted her affection in the healthy way that any father enjoys a doting daughter. But Christina was not his daughter. She was a mature, fifteen-year-old girl, no blood relation at all, and of course that had made all the peculiar difference.

He put down the bag, switched it to his left hand, walked on through the town along the rectangular green, past the bandstand and the big white home of Mitchel Slayton. The Cadillac was not in the drive. Mitchel Slayton had no doubt driven back to New York. He would be in his office, hardly expecting a visitor from Plimpton Ridge on such a lovely morning.

Paul felt the revolver heavy in his pocket. He touched it with his elbow, thought that if he killed Mitchel Slayton he would never go to Fremont or back to the Academy or anywhere at all except a prison cell or an electric chair. He would never sit on the cottage veranda again, never finish writing his book, never see Roberta or Christina again, never fulfill any of the small, pleasant ambitions of his life. He understood that perfectly. He was not insane with rage or jealousy or desire for revenge. Everything had been taken away from him. Now he would take everything away from Mitchel Slayton. The score would be even, and it made no difference what came after.

Pete, the local taxi driver, said, "Morning, Mr. Barker. It's a great day."

"Yes," Paul said. "Great."

He sat in the rear seat of Pete's old cab and stared out the window at the drying foliage as they drove on toward Bridgeport. Pete said his wife was pregnant again. He had four children already, was about to have a fifth. "Not that we try," he said. "But sometimes I have a few drinks, you know, and then

I forget all about taking any precautions, you know, and so does my wife, and every time—bang—she's pregnant again."

Paul did not say anything. Not that it mattered to Pete. He was used to having conversations with himself. "Oh, I like kids," he continued. "But in a way you're lucky, Mr. Barker. I mean one child—a girl—pretty and sweet, like Christina. Well, one's enough for any man."

"Depends on the man," Paul said.

"What?"

"Nothing," Paul said.

Silence, and the hum of tires on wet macadam. The early-morning traffic, the cars pulling into the Bridgeport station, the commuters spilling out, kissing their wives through the open car windows, rushing off in their gabardine coats, swinging their brief cases with that breezy attitude affected by men who earn a little more than they're worth and are slowly beginning to know it. Paul mounted the iron steps of the train, went into the smoking car. He found a seat, sat down and closed his tired eyes, only to open them when a familiar voice said, "Well, what the hell!"

Frank Gattone sat down beside him. He could feel Frank's eyes on him, curious to know why he looked so beaten and what he was doing on the New York train at this hour. The train lurched forward, began to pick up speed. Frank lit a cigarette. He looked at Paul's bag, then at Paul, questioningly.

"My mother became suddenly ill," Paul said.

"Oh, I'm sorry." Then, after a moment, "Well, bad news always comes with good."

"Good?"

"I mean about your being head of the department."

"Oh . . . Sure."

"Anita told me last night when she picked me up at the station."

"The twelve-thirty-two."

"Yeah. Sorry, I couldn't make it at Doc Bullock's. . . ." Silence, and then, embarrassed, "Was she very drunk, Paul?"

"No, not very . . . I guess."

"It's the first time she's slipped since we came to Plimpton. Of course it would have to be at the worst possible time, just when old Batty-ass—"

"Anita was all right," Paul said.

"All right? Soaking wet, shoes all covered with mud. She looked like hell. I started to get sore, but that never helps. . . . It never helps."

"No."

"Kept bragging about how she'd had a few, as if she wanted me to get sore. I didn't, so she changed her tactics. Acted hurt about my never being at home these days. I don't know . . . I get the feeling there was something else. Something happened . . . I don't know what. She wouldn't tell me."

"Don't worry about it," Paul said.

"Hell, I can't." Frank dropped his cigarette on the floor and crushed it under his shoe. "After June 23rd I'll pay her all the attention she wants. But until this show's over she's just going to have to make it pretty much on her own." He glanced at Paul, then away again. "I suppose you think that's cruel . . . selfish."

"No," Paul said, closing his eyes. His head was beginning to ache and he wished Frank would shut up and read his paper.

"Well," Frank said, "I've given my life to Anita. I'm only asking a couple of months for myself."

The train stopped to pick up passengers, moved on, stopped, moved on. The revolver felt bulky and heavy in Paul's pocket. He was going to kill Mitchel Slayton, but he did not quite believe it. Perhaps if he told Frank, then Frank would say, "You're crazy, fellow. You're absolutely nuts," and then he would believe it because someone else had talked about it.

108

"Paul, I want to ask you something," Frank was saying. "Confidential. Just between us, you understand."

When Paul did not say anything, he continued, "Well, hypothetically, can you think of any circumstance—any at all—when the end justifies the means. I mean, when a man could be unfaithful to his wife without it's being wrong. . . . Not because he's gone on the other woman, you understand . . . I mean for purely practical reasons. . . ."

"What are you talking about?" Paul's voice rose in sudden, inexplicable anger. "What the hell are you talking about?"

"All right, forget it," Frank said, astonished at the violence in Paul's voice. "For Christ's sake, Paul!"

And then the train plunged into the dark tunnel approaching Grand Central, and the anger was still there, growing deeper and deeper, directed not at Frank Gattone, as he supposed, but at Mitchel Slayton—the kind of rage Paul had wanted all last night, all this morning—a furious, unthinking rage that would carry him all the way to the end.

When the train stopped, Frank scuttled away in the crowd that streamed up the cement platform. Paul let the crowd carry him along, and he nursed the rage within him all the way, just as a man sometimes has to remotivate his own desire after a woman leaves the room to prepare herself for the final act. A man has to think about it, remember the excitement of the moment before, anticipate the moment coming later. In the same way Paul kept his mind fixed on Mitchel Slayton, kept the fury bottled up inside himself, his elbow pressed against the hard lump in his pocket, through Grand Central, where he checked his bag in a locker, all the way to the Seagram Building on Park Avenue at 52nd Street, with its great glass façade and the fountains playing out front, through the revolving doors, across the bare lobby, up the fifteen floors in the quiet-humming elevator, down the corridor to the glass door marked SLAYTON

109

FIREARMS, through the door to the middle-aged receptionist who sat behind spring flowers at the bare, polished desk.

The woman looked up at him, smiling. "Yes?"

"Mr. Slayton," Paul said.

"Do you have an appointment, Mr.—?"

"Barker, Paul Barker. He'll see me, whether he's busy or not."

"I see. It's . . . personal."

"Yes," Paul said. "Very personal."

The woman frowned, picked up her phone, said something he could not make out, then hung up and smiled again. "Mr. Slayton is expecting you."

"Expecting me?"

"The second door to your right."

He nodded, hesitated a moment, then followed her directions to the door marked MITCHEL SLAYTON and pushed it open. A young woman of perhaps twenty-four sat behind a desk in the anteroom, before a second, unmarked door. She was brown-haired, gray-eyed, with a soft, gentle face that was vaguely familiar from somewhere in the long ago. She said, "Mr. Barker?" and rose and opened the door. Then she smiled him in and closed the door behind him.

Mitchel Slayton stood at the window, looking down the fifteen floors to the fountains that fronted the building. He did not look around when Paul came in, but kept his back turned to his huge desk that was bare of everything but a glass case that contained the first revolver ever made by Slayton Firearms. On either side of the room the walls were lined with old rifles and revolvers, presumably collector's items.

Paul drew the automatic very carefully from his pocket. He had kept the fury all the way, and there was no reason to discuss anything with Mitchel Slayton. He would pull the trigger and leave—walk, not run, to the nearest exit.

110

Mitchel Slayton turned to face him. He looked at the revolver in Paul's steady hand. He said, "Hello, Paul," his face showing no emotion whatever. "Roberta called me after you left. She discovered the revolver was missing."

"You sonofabitch," Paul said. "You lousy sonofabitch."

"Sit down, Paul."

"You hypocritical bastard!"

"With that gun, Paul, it may take all nine shots to kill me."

Paul stared into Mitchel Slayton's lined, tired face, then raised the revolver and took careful aim, only to realize at the last fraction of a second that he could not shoot down an unarmed man, even a man he hated. Furious with himself, he shot at the pistol in the glass case. He pulled the trigger five times. Each shot smashed through the glass, ricocheted off the prized revolver, buried itself in the wall or the desk or the soundproofed ceiling.

"One shot would have been enough," he said. "Right between the eyes."

"Yes," Mitchel said. "You could have done it with one shot."

The door was flung open and the young secretary stood in the doorway, frightened, her hand to her mouth as if she would scream in another moment.

"It's all right, Miss Calhoun." Mitchel motioned the girl out, then sat down wearily behind his desk. He said, "You know something, Paul? I wasn't afraid of you at all. Even though I've got more to lose than you have. I'm older, and I've fought a hell of a distance for nothing at all. You haven't even started." He paused, drummed on the desk with his fingers. "You think I'm a monster, don't you? I've wrecked your life, you think— *your* life. Never mind about mine, or Roberta's, because we don't count. Christina doesn't count. Nobody counts except you, because you're the innocent party. Well, you may be the innocent. But you're not the only *hurt* party."

"*You're* hurt," Paul exclaimed. "You have a time with a young girl, get her pregnant and pass her off on me. And *you're* hurt."

Mitchel smiled. It was a crooked smile. He shook his head slightly, said, "Roberta's mother died before the child was old enough to know her."

"I know all about that," Paul said.

"For years she lived with her father, depended on him for everything, even rejected all other men in his favor. She would never marry until he died. Well, he died all right, while she was looking on. Fell off a swinging beam, right in front of her eyes."

"I know that, too."

"But you don't know how she felt about it. You don't know that she wandered to Plimpton on the verge of a breakdown. You don't know that I hired her out of pity."

"Pity!" Paul said scornfully.

"Yes . . . in the beginning that's what it was—pity. And then sympathy. We were both lonely people and I needed a daughter just as much as she needed a father. Anita was never very close to me."

"That's a good one. Father and daughter!"

"For Christ's sake, don't you know *anything*, Paul?" Mitchel Slayton rose, leaned over the desk, angry now, the words coming hard and clipped. "Of course you know *that* much—a father-daughter thing can become sexual, can *be* sexual. You know that much, and if that were all there was to it—just that I'd had an affair with Roberta when we were both a little sick, a little lost, a little younger—then you'd understand it, wouldn't you? You're no prig, no fool. A lot of people have a lot of sex in a lot of ways. Not very many men think or expect they're going to marry virgins these days. So it's all right if a girl's had a little indiscretion, but it's all wrong if she's been a little careless about it. It's no sin to sleep with anybody. The sin is in getting pregnant."

112

"Now look here, Mitchel—"

"No, you look, Paul. Sure there was an involvement between myself and Roberta. I loved her. I still love her. Very well, so I did urge her to marry you—not pan her off on you, as you think. For *her* sake, for the baby's sake, yes, for *your* sake too. Because you were in love with her, and if you'd just left town, gone somewhere else the way Roberta suggested, then you'd never have found this out and you'd still be a happy man. I'd have suffered. Roberta would have suffered because of her guilty memory. But you and Christina would have been happy, and that was exactly the way I wanted it."

Mitchel Slayton sat down again. He was breathing heavily. He said, "She could have had an abortion, you know. She refused." And after a moment's silence. "You don't get it, you can't reason it out, so you leave her because you feel wronged. Your goddamn pride's been hurt, so go ahead and leave her."

"I have," Paul said slowly, the fury all ebbed away now. "There's one thing you've overlooked, Mitchel. Love. She never loved me, and as of now I don't love her, either. You can't reason with that, Mitchel. There's nothing anyone can do about that."

"You're talking like a child," Mitchel said, throwing up his hands. "Roberta has always loved you and you know it. What's more, you can no more make yourself stop loving her than you could make yourself shoot me. You're not that kind of man."

Paul opened the door, looked back at the older man who sat now with his gray head between his hands, his elbows on the desk, his gold cuff links gleaming in the glow of the ceiling lights. He started to speak but felt too sick, deflated, too unsure of his own emotions. He went out and closed the door behind him.

Miss Calhoun looked up from her desk, trying to mask her curiosity. Pretty, brown-haired, gray-eyed Miss Calhoun. Remembered from somewhere. From sixteen years ago, to be exact. Here was Roberta all over again, sitting outside Mitchel Slayton's door. Only different, somehow. Shrewder, he thought.

He stared at the young woman, wondered if Mitchel had hired her because she reminded him of Roberta, wondered if she realized there was something special about her, and if Mitchel had ever made any advances.

"Something wrong?" Miss Calhoun said.

"No." He kept staring into her familiar gray eyes, then turned and went out, past the middle-aged receptionist and into the corridor to ring for the elevator. He felt frustrated, and exhausted, bitter at the thought that he had meant to kill Mitchel Slayton, that Mitchel Slayton ought to be dead now, except that it was he himself and not Mitchel who was dead.

For a long time Mitchel Slayton sat motionless behind his desk. He thought that if he had played it differently perhaps Paul would have shot him, and he'd be a lot better off if that had happened—a lot better dead. Only that was a selfish thought, too, wishing himself dead, selfish and self-pitying. It wouldn't be fair to Roberta or Christina or to Paul himself. He rose heavily and looked at the shattered glass case and the smashed old revolver, the first ever made by Slayton Firearms. That was back in 1877, when his grandfather was competing with Colt and Remington and Smith and Wesson to design the most popular of Western guns. It was a back-up gun, a reserve weapon for concealed use, where a full-bore side arm might not be indicated. A five-shot break-top, not a practical gun, and Slayton Firearms no longer made any single-system double-action guns, though they'd been popular enough in their day.

He brushed the pieces of glass into the wastebasket, put the wrecked gun in the desk drawer. He looked at all the American firearms that decorated his walls—the Hawken-type Kentucky, used by Kit Carson on the Frémont operation; a Sharps rifle

114

of the kind owned by Bill Tilghman, who'd killed 7,500 buffaloes with the same rifle; a New England flintlock; a Winchester '73—all the important, and a few of the rarer, guns that had made American history.

Personally, he did not care much for guns, had never shot anything in his life. An inherited business, luck, a drive to earn money, pretty good business sense. He liked to watch his stock rising steadily in the market, liked an occasional drink, a workout at the club, perhaps a little gambling now and then. What else? Things, but not people.

Once there had been Lottie and Roy and Anita. And once Roberta. But since then no one. Not anyone at all.

A knock at the door. Miss Calhoun entered and stared once more at the damage done by the little .22. "Are you sure," she said, "there's nothing wrong, Mr. Slayton?"

"Quite sure. An accident, that's all." Mitchel looked at the young woman curiously, perhaps for the first time seeing her more as a woman than a secretary. "Would you have cared, Miss Calhoun?" he said.

"Why of course, Mr. Slayton."

"Thank you." And then, as she was about to go, "Do you have a boy friend, Miss Calhoun?"

"No," she said, surprised by the question. "Not really."

"Then maybe sometime . . . in the next week or so . . . whenever it's convenient . . . would you like to have dinner with a very tired old man?"

Miss Calhoun hesitated. She bit her lip, then smiled suddenly, brightly, and said softly, "I'd love to, Mr. Slayton," and left the room.

Mitchel Slayton watched her go. He thought she had legs like Roberta's, a back like Roberta's. He knew now why he had hired her, and what would happen some day . . . next week . . . next month. . . . He was still a lonesome man, older, wiser, but still lonesome, still in need of a daughter or a wife or something . . . something to fill the emptiness he felt in himself.

Chapter Twelve

FREMONT had not changed. The wooden floor of the railroad station still smelled of oil; the cab driver was still Mr. Kilroney—white-haired, ageless, with a voice that rattled even more than the cab itself. He said "Welcome home, Mr. Barker," and rattled away through the small town, across the wooden bridge that scaled the river where the eels gathered in springtime, past the new brick post office and the little strip of stores—drygoods and cheap furniture, the barbershop with the red striped pole that was supposed to turn but was still out of commission, the hardware with its sidewalk boasting incinerators and wheelbarrows and lawn mowers, it's windows striped with fishing poles, the white Congregational church and the tall elms that were dying slowly of Dutch elm disease; a left turn, a right turn, and the old brown-shingled house, comfortably ugly, with its untended lawn, its overgrown grape arbor, the single apple tree, all very small now, a single plot in a very large world, that once had been the world itself.

Mr. Kilroney scowled, said, "I'm sorry, Mr. Barker."

"Sorry?"

"The best of luck, Mr. Barker."

"Thank you." He stared at the old man. How could he know

anything? How could anyone here know anything at all? The old man was saying something more, but Paul did not listen. He paid, nodded, carried his bag and attaché case up the cement walk to the porch, looked back at Mr. Kilroney, who was shaking his white head. Mr. Kilroney waved and the car rattled away.

The door was unlocked. Paul went into the hallway, on to the living room filled with Victorian furniture and potted plants, the neat, well-kept room of a widow living alone among all the physical reminders of the past. He called, "Mother!" But there was no answer. He called up the stairway, opened the back door and called out to the back yard where he had once built a tree-house, once kept rabbits, once practiced basketball with a homemade net above the garage door.

He went back to the living room, peered out the lace-curtained window as a car stopped out front and his sister came loping, almost running, up the walk. She pushed open the door, saw him there, and said, "Oh God, Paul, oh God!" Then she sat on the horsehair sofa and cried uncontrollably into her handkerchief.

Paul watched her. She was forty-two, with streaks of gray in her brown hair. She was tall and thin like himself, wearing a tailored suit that seemed a little formal for Fremont. "Lucille," he said. "What in the world—"

"At least you could have answered!" she wailed.

"Answered what? *What?*"

"My telegram, of course. I sent it last night and told you to come to *my* house, and instead you came here and Richard has to work and I'm going out of my mind."

He told her to calm down. He sat and spoke quietly, babying her, until finally she gained control of herself and explained that their mother had had a stroke, and was now in the local hospital. She was in a coma most of the time, on the critical list, not expected to live more than another day or two.

"Mother?" he said, and went into the kitchen and put hot

117

water on the old gas stove. In the living room, Lucille had started sobbing again. He thought how he had told everyone his mother was very ill, and it was true, and was it an odd coincidence, or had he somehow known it, sensed it all along? He was not shocked, not even upset really. His mother was seventy-five, hadn't been well for years. People grew old and died, and why was Lucille making such a damn fool of herself?

Back in the living room he forced her to drink the black instant coffee. She held the cup in both hands. The cup trembled and she said, "Everything's gone now. There's nothing left at all."

"Don't be foolish, Lucille."

"I just don't know what I'll do!"

It was a selfish remark. To Lucille, his mother had been a baby-sitter, a shoulder to cry on, a buffer against her husband, an emotional crutch because Lucille had never quite made anything on her own.

He said, "When were you at the hospital last?"

"This morning."

"What did they say?"

"They'll call me."

"But they don't know you're here."

"No . . ."

He phoned the hospital. Old Doctor Pearson said he'd been calling Lucille for the past twenty minutes. He was terribly sorry, but their mother had passed away a half-hour ago.

Paul said "Thank you" and hung up. Lucille looked at his face and cried all over again, on and on until he could no longer stand it, and he shouted, "Shut up! Lucille! Please shut up! Shut up!"

Paul made all the funeral arrangements himself, since Lucille was of no help whatsoever. Her husband, Richard, came over

118

that evening and tried to apologize. He was a big, bumbling man who'd moved from one job to another for twenty years, and had never succeeded at anything. He sat in the living room in dungarees and a torn shirt (he was now doing "temporary" work in the lumber yard), and shook his head and rubbed his calloused hands together.

"You got to understand, Paul. I know Lucille depended on your mother a lot. But it's more than that. She's having her 'change,' you know, so it's up one day and down the next. Forgets things, gets hysterical, won't sleep with me—hardly once in a year now. I've talked to Doc Pearson. He says she'll get over it. I don't know. He told her she *had* to sleep with me or I could get impotent, only she doesn't seem to care. Tells me if I can't wait, I can find someone else. She's not going to bed with me until *she* wants to. I don't know. Kids are grown up, have their own lives. So what's Lucille got any more? Me, I'm a failure, and now she can't even tell her mother about it. That's the point, you see. As long as she could *tell* someone about her troubles, then at least that was something."

"I understand," Paul said. He patted Richard's big shoulder. "It'll work out," he said, and knew that it wouldn't.

Richard left and the night was quiet, the room was quiet. The stairs creaked and Paul sat alone in the living room. He looked at all the familiar pieces of furniture, drank coffee from a familiar cup. Everything passed away. Towns and houses, things and people. Lucille was alone now, but not so alone as himself. Somehow God arranged things in patterns, all the good together, all the bad together. The point was to ride out the bad spots, and the catch was that you had no assurance that after the bad you'd always get the good. Sometimes you got nothing, only blankness, only empty time, and that was the worst of all.

The phone rang. It was Roberta, calling from Plimpton

Ridge. "I've been trying to get you all day, Paul. A telegram came from your sister." A pause, and, "How is your mother, Paul?"

"She died," he said. "This afternoon."

"Oh, Paul . . ."

"There's nothing to say, Roberta." He sat wearily on the horsehair sofa. Now, at this moment, he needed Roberta more than anyone on earth. You were betrayed by someone, you almost hated someone, and still you needed that person . . . you could never end the need, nor the desire. Some part of you died, but not all of you, and it would be so much easier if you could kill it all.

Roberta said, "I'll drive up immediately, bring Christina."

"No, I don't want you here."

"You mean you don't want *me*—there or anywhere."

"Yes. I guess that's what I mean."

"Well," Roberta said. And then, "Christina would like to speak to you."

Christina was half crying. She'd always loved her grandmother Dora. She said how sorry she was, and when would he be home? He said in a few days . . . he'd be back in Plimpton Ridge in a few days. Then Roberta again. She said that she knew this morning he had gone to Mitchel Slayton's. She'd been terribly afraid, and was so thankful he'd been sensible about it.

"I wasn't sensible," Paul said. "I simply realized that you can't just . . . kill a man."

Another long pause. Roberta's voice was faint, far away, slightly awed. "Paul . . . I told everyone your mother was sick. It's . . . odd, isn't it?"

"Yes."

"Paul . . . I'm with you. Christina's with you. Don't hate us now, Paul. Don't lose everything all at once."

120

"I already have. Good-by," he said and hung up slowly.

For a long time he sat motionless on the horsehair sofa. He listened to the sounds of spring outside the windows, then rose and looked for the whisky that his mother always kept for medicinal use in the wooden cupboard above the sink. He poured a large shot into a glass, sipped it slowly, then put out the lights and climbed the stairs to the room which had once been his. He undressed, put on pajamas and lay back on the strange bed, the old bed, the familiar bed. The bed was too small. The room was too small. He looked at the peeling wallpaper and remembered this and remembered that. Somehow, with his mother still alive, it had always seemed that there was somewhere to go —somewhere to write or call, to visit on a vacation, to live permanently, so the entire world could never crumble around him. Now the world lay in dust, and the last refuge lay in dust besides.

"Mother," he said aloud. "I wanted to tell you about Roberta. You'd have told me to live with it, and I'd have believed you and I'd have tried. Now you can't tell me. I can't live with it, and I can't even try."

He could not cry, either—only lie there awake, numb, thinking that Lucille was going through menopause and was no help at all, thinking that Richard was stupid and pathetic and defeated, and there must be someone who could understand something of what he felt but could not express. Not the minister, who'd tried to be kind; not the doctor or the soft-spoken men at the funeral parlor, who'd walked soundlessly on hardsoled shoes. Not the dimly remembered neighbors who'd called off and on during the afternoon, and sent over useless cakes and desserts wrapped in foil paper. But someone he loved, who loved him—or someone he *had* loved perhaps—yesterday or many years ago. Jean McElroy, for example—married now—but still remembered, though unseen for all these years.

121

Tomorrow he would look up Jean McElroy, his last remaining link to the town of Fremont, New Hampshire.

It was a small, one-story house, new with scraggly grass in front, no grass at all in the back. It was one of those thirteen-thousand-dollar development type houses that belonged in a long row of others exactly like it. Alone, in a large, treeless knoll on the outskirts of town, it had gained some identity at the cost of appearing too conspicuously cheap in a town that prided itself on its old houses. Sheets and pillowcases, slips and pajamas and children's clothes flopped on the clothesline in the back yard. A tricycle lay fallen on the walk, and large stones were piled in a heap along the rutted drive, as though someone had decided to line the drive with painted stones but had never quite gotten around to it.

Paul pushed the brass buzzer, heard the single chime, waited, nervous, apprehensive, depressed, until the door was pulled open by a small child with a runny nose.

"Hello there," Paul said, "is your mother at home?"

"Who is it?" from the kitchen, and then Jean Stutgard, nee Jean McElroy appeared, crossing the tiny, rugless living room. "I'm sorry, we don't want anything," she said.

"Not even a visit from an old friend?"

She studied him, her blue eyes puzzled, a hand brushing back the ends of black hair. She'd grown plump, middle-aged. Her breasts sagged under the pink cotton housedress. Her feet were veined and flat in open slippers.

"Paul!" she exclaimed, suddenly brightening. "Of course, Paul Barker! Come in, Paul, come in. . . . Lord, I look a mess. . . . I'm sorry about your mother. I just heard about it this morning. I'm terribly sorry."

He removed a picture puzzle box from the faded sofa, sat down, glanced quickly about, then back to her face. She was flustered.

122

"Just a minute," she said. "I . . . I'll only be gone a minute. . . . Go in your room and play," she said to the runny-nosed little girl, then disappeared into one of the two small bedrooms.

Paul remembered Jean as being slender and dark. She'd laughed a great deal. They'd gone everywhere together, made groping love together, sworn to wait out the war and marry as soon as he returned. He'd written her from San Diego that he was trying for a position at Plimpton Academy. They'd marry and she'd live there as a teacher's wife and it had all been a great dream.

Jean returned from the bedroom. She'd brushed her hair, applied lipstick, changed her dress to a skirt and blouse that managed to cover her bulging figure. "Well, now," she said, sitting down in a chair facing him. "Would you like a drink, Paul?"

"No, thank you."

"Of course you would." She laughed, too gaily, and went into the kitchen, returning with two tumblers of water and whisky, a single ice cube floating in each glass. "The refrigerator's pretty old, so . . . Well, here we go."

The whisky was strong, cheap. He groped for his pipe, tried to think of something to say. Last night he had thought he could talk, really talk to Jean McElroy. The truth was they could find nothing at all to say to one another.

"My husband," she said after a moment. "Chester. He'll be home for dinner—just a few minutes now."

"Fine."

"He's in selling, you know. Sometimes he . . . well, he gets delayed on the road, you see. But tonight he swore he'd be on time."

"What does he sell?" Paul asked.

"Oh, it's silly really. A disinfectant for the washrooms in gas stations. Odor-Out. Maybe you've heard of it."

"No, I'm afraid not."

"Well, it's a sort of local product, I guess." She sipped at the drink, glanced at the electric wall clock, which read 4:30. "He promised," she said, almost to herself.

"What?"

"He promised." She took another sip, laughed in that quick high way that was new, not easy as it had been those years ago. "And how's your wife, Paul?"

"Fine."

"You have one child, don't you?"

"Yes, a daughter."

"I have three. The girl you saw, and two boys. They're off somewhere now, though." She lit a cigarette. There was a long, empty moment. She put down the match, drew the smoke deep into her lungs. "What happened, Paul?"

"My mother's never been really well."

"No . . . after the war. You met your wife. It happened . . . so fast."

"Yes . . . I wrote you. I guess I've been embarrassed . . . I mean, actually avoiding you each time I came home to visit."

"I know." Then, "It's funny. I got your letter and I cried and cried, and then only a month later Chester came home from the war and I married him right away. I hardly knew him."

He said, "I hardly knew Roberta, either."

"I guess you never met Chester."

"No."

"Well, he's from Concord."

Paul looked into his drink. He said, "You have a nice little place here."

"Oh, we've been meaning to fix it up. But we just don't get around to it. New furniture and white stones along the drive and gravel the drive and a new refrigerator, but we've been . . . putting it off."

"Something to look forward to."

"Yes." Her eyes were becoming glassy. She leaned forward, looking at him and beyond him at the same time. She lowered her voice. "Are you happy, Paul?"

"Happy? . . . Yes, I . . . I've been made head of the department . . . Yes, I'm very happy."

"So am I. So am I." She rose abruptly, glanced at his half-full glass, then took her own to the kitchen. He heard the water running in the sink. He heard a small stifled sob. When she returned, he could see she had been crying. The refilled glass shook slightly in her hand. "I've often wondered," she said. "You know, just wondered . . . how it would have been if . . . well, if we *had* married, you and me. I mean I'm terribly happy and all, of course, but sometimes I just wonder, that's all."

"I don't know," he said.

"We were in love, though. I mean for *years* there, we really were in love."

"Yes . . ."

"So . . . sometimes I wonder."

He said, "So do I," and then the phone rang and she started and said, "He promised," and rose, swayed, and lifted the receiver. Her voice was low, intense in muffled hysteria. "Yes. . . . No, Chester, I don't understand. . . . No, I don't . . . You promised, Chester, and no, I don't believe you. . . . All right then, don't be on time for all I care. I've got company anyway. . . . Oh, wouldn't you like to know! Wouldn't you just like to know! . . . All right then, it's Paul Barker. . . . That's right, Paul Barker. Remember what I've told you about him. . . . Remember, Chester, just *remember!*" She slammed down the receiver, leaned against the telephone stand, then moved toward him once again. "He promised," she said dully, "but he's not coming after all."

"I'm sorry," Paul said.

"Someday . . . somehow I'll get back at him." Her eyes

125

lifted slowly, still hazy, and her tongue licked her full bright lips. "I'll get back at him," she said. Then, "I've told him about you . . . over and over . . . over and over . . ."

Paul rose. He said, "It was nice seeing you, Jean."

"I've even lied. . . . Said we had a regular affair, when of course we didn't."

"No, we didn't." He edged toward the door.

"Stay, if you like. Do you think *he'd* care?"

"No, I have to get along."

"The boys won't be home for a while. There's plenty of time."

"Good-by, Jean."

He went to the door, opened it, looked back at her. She was mumbling into the glass. "That sonofabitch! That unfaithful bastard. You could sleep with me on the front lawn, right in front of his goddamn face, and he wouldn't even notice!"

She was sobbing when he left. He closed the door carefully and breathed deeply of the late afternoon air, kept breathing in its freshness as he walked slowly, thoughtfully, back to town, as if the good Fremont air might wash away all the stale remnants of the past.

Chapter Thirteen

DR. PERRY C. BULLOCK sat at his desk in the Administration Building, beneath the faded oil portrait of Siras Plimpton painted by an unknown eighteenth-century painter, though Dr. Bullock sometimes hinted that it might very well have been done by Gilbert Stuart himself, who'd done the famous portrait of George Washington.

Siras Plimpton was a narrow-faced, hawk-nosed man with a mole on his cheek, a high collar, and mean little eyes beneath his wig. It had occurred to Dr. Bullock that he looked somewhat like a dishonest Abraham Lincoln, though he kept his little joke entirely to himself.

The chapel bell tolled, and outside his vine-framed window the boys were passing between classes. He was proud of the boys. He understood them, and he knew that his nickname of "Batty-ass" was affectionate really, that the boys liked him just as he was fond of them.

He noticed Alan Gattone walking alone as usual, brooding as usual, and seeing Alan, Dr. Bullock remembered that he had an appointment with Paul Barker this morning. Strange thing about his leaving Plimpton so suddenly, without arranging for someone to take his classes while he was away. But then, Paul's mother had died, he knew, and no doubt the shock had made him forget.

He rang the buzzer. His white-haired secretary opened the door. "Mr. Barker?" he said.

"You have an appointment with him in just two minutes."

"Very well. That will be all, Mrs. Hammond."

Dr. Bullock took off his rimless glasses and wiped them carefully with a piece of tissue. He ran a hand over his bald head, felt his belly pressing against his belt. For weeks now he'd been working like mad on his rowing machine. But he hadn't lost a pound, only ached from all the exertion.

What did Paul Barker want? His mother had died and the faculty had sent flowers. You became head of the department and the next day your mother died. That was life, thought Dr. Bullock. It all evened out in the end.

A knock at the door, and there was Paul, looking about the same as ever, his baggy clothes even more baggy than usual. The man seemed thinner, his face drawn, from grief of course, and it was too bad because a man as intelligent as Paul Barker ought to know that it all evened out in the end.

"Sit down, Paul."

"Thank you, sir," Paul said, but made no move to sit.

"I'm sorry it had to happen, naturally."

Paul seemed not to hear. He walked slowly around the room. Somewhere in the back of his mind he had been bothered by the thought that he owed his appointment as head of the department to Mitchel Slayton, and he wanted Dr. Bullock to know he knew it. He wasn't taking any favors from Mitchel Slayton. If Dr. Bullock hadn't wanted him for the job, now was the time for him to say so, even if he, Paul, had to force it out of him.

He touched an ashtray, looked at the portrait of Siras Plimpton, said, "You know, he looks like a dishonest Abe Lincoln."

Dr. Bullock was astonished. His own thought, finally spoken by someone else. He chuckled. "Yes, I've often thought so myself."

"As a matter of fact," Paul said, "he was."

"Now, I wouldn't go that far. . . ."

"Dishonest, I mean. . . ." And then abruptly, "And you're following directly in the old liar's footsteps."

Dr. Bullock half rose, then sat back slowly. He frowned, too shaken to be angry. "And just what does that mean, Mr. Barker?"

"It means that you didn't have the guts to stand up to Mitchel Slayton. He compromised you into making me head of the department. There were reasons for it that you don't understand. But that's not the point. The point is that you personally didn't want me for the job but Slayton did, and what Slayton wants he gets."

"I see."

"So I'm turning it down."

128

"I see. Paul, please sit down. You make me nervous, pacing about like that. Sit down and listen . . . listen to me."

Paul sank into a chair facing the desk, drew his pipe from his pocket and rubbed it absently between his hands. "Well," he said, "I'm listening."

"You showed a great deal of courage," Dr. Bullock said slowly, "saying that to me just now. What you don't understand is that it took a great deal of courage on *my* part to appoint you at all."

"Courage?"

"That's what I said. I'll admit, Paul . . . it's true . . . Mitchel Slayton did practically demand that you be given the position. He used every possible means to force me. His position on the board, his donations to Plimpton, future donations which might or might not be forthcoming. Well, I listened to him. And after he'd gone I spent a long time thinking about it. And you know what I decided, Paul? I decided that I wanted you for the job. Not because Mitchel did, but because *I* did. And that's where it took the most courage, Paul. I could have gone against Mitchel. I wanted to. I was tempted to. But I didn't, because then I'd have been using you as a pawn in a battle in which you're not involved. I wanted you, and I appointed you, and I have to live with the fact that Mitchel will never believe I did it on my own. He still thinks it was his doing; he'll never believe otherwise. That's all right. I can live with the fact that Mr. Slayton thinks he won a victory that he didn't win at all. Also with the fact that you don't believe me and probably never will."

The chapel bell had stopped tolling. The campus was empty, the room quiet except for the sound of Paul's pipe thumping against his open palm.

"I believe you," he said. "But it doesn't matter. I feel better, but still it doesn't matter."

"I don't understand."

129

"I can't accept the appointment."

"Can't?"

"No. I'm leaving Plimpton. Oh, I'll finish the term. It's in the contract, and only fair to you, anyway. But after this term, I'm leaving."

"I see."

"In the meantime, I'll be living in the cottage. I want to catch up on some research . . . find it hard to work at home. So I'll stay in the cottage until school ends. Then I'll be leaving for good."

Dr. Bullock drummed his stubby fingers on the desk. "Well," he said, "I can't stop you. I thought you were happy here. I presume your mother's death may have something to do with this. Or perhaps Mrs. Barker—"

"No," Paul said quickly. "It has nothing to do with my wife."

"She's very popular here. But I happen to know that ever since you started teaching she's wanted to leave Plimpton."

"It has nothing to do with my wife." Paul stood up, jammed the pipe back into his pocket, said, "Well, I want to get to the library before my eleven o'clock class," and left the room.

From where he was sitting, through the window Dr. Bullock could see Paul's tall figure crossing the campus. He thought it was not like Paul Barker to live alone in the cottage, without his wife and child. He wondered why Roberta had not gone to her own mother-in-law's funeral, and if she would go with her husband when he left Plimpton Ridge. And then, his attention turning back to the room, he saw the face of Siras Plimpton and wondered what Paul had meant by the man's actual dishonesty.

Hogarth's "Shrimp Girl" was gone from the classroom wall, replaced (as all classroom paintings were changed from time to time) by a large reproduction of John Constable's "Flatford Mill."

130

Alan Gattone eyed the painting absently. He knew, from the mimeographed sheet that had been passed around the class, that "Flatford Mill" had been painted at a time when fashionable opinion held that "a good picture, like a good fiddle, should be brown," and, since Constable dared to paint nature in her own true colors, that he was the pioneer of "natural" landscape painting. It was a nice picture, Alan decided. He liked the winding stream and the boats that were poled along; he liked the trees and the windy-looking sky. Sometimes he poled Mr. Barker's rowboat through the thick grass at the far end of Beetlewood Lake while Christina looked for frogs, then squealed each time she found one. Sometimes he sat with Christina under a big willow along the water's edge and they talked about very important things that nobody else would ever understand. Sometimes the sky was windy-looking, too, and the water ruffled up and the tree sighed over their heads—

"Alan!"

The boy jerked his eyes from the painting, pulled back to the reality of American History. Mr. Barker was looking at him from the far end of the room. "I asked you," said Mr. Barker, "on what hill the Battle of Bunker Hill was fought."

It was like asking who was buried in Grant's tomb. "Bunker Hill, of course," Alan said, and the other boys laughed, and Mr. Barker said, "I am not Groucho Marx, Alan. The actual name of the place was Breed's Hill. Do you think you can remember that?"

Alan thought that he could. Mr. Barker went on talking, and he forced his eyes to remain on the teacher's face, though his mind was on Mr. Barker himself rather than on anything he was saying.

Somehow Christina's father had changed, he thought. Mr. Barker was not at ease, not casual, the way he used to be. Alan could feel that something was eating Mr. Barker, and he wasn't the only one who noticed it either. Some of the other kids said he'd gotten real sore while coaching the tennis team yesterday, and smashed his racket to splinters on the net pole. And for another thing, he was living in the cottage now, alone, working on his book, supposedly, although Christina didn't seem to understand what it was all about.

"After he got back from Grandmother Dora's funeral," Christina said, "he just came into the house and packed some things in the car and drove down to the cottage. He's never even come back to see us, and it's been days now."

Yes, something was bothering Mr. Barker, and anything that bothered him was of great concern to Alan. Outside of Christina, Mr. Barker was the only real friend he had. All Mrs. Barker did was try to break up things between himself and Christina, just like his own mother. They said they weren't, but they were. It would be different if he could talk to his father about it, but these days his father didn't seem to have time for anything but his television show. . . . They were always having these television plays where the father doesn't understand his son, and then in the end he takes his boy fishing or something and they get all palsy-walsy. Only we don't go fishing and never get palsy-walsy, Alan thought. The sad part of it was— the awful sad part—he couldn't understand his father even if they were to go fishing together.

The bell tolled and Mr. Barker said, "All right, boys. You've got your assignment. Tomorrow we'll take up the actual significance of Bunker Hill, why it was what we call a Pyrrhic victory."

The boys filed out of the room, but Alan remained in his seat, his eyes fixed on his teacher's expressionless face.

"Yes, Alan?" Paul said without looking up, as he stuffed papers into his brief case.

"I'm sorry about Bunker Hill, Mr. Barker. I wasn't trying to be funny."

"I know you weren't, Alan."

"I mean I was thinking about something else."

"You do that a great deal too much, don't you think?"

"You know what I was thinking about?"

"I can guess."

"Not just Christina, Mr. Barker. About you, too. While you were away, Christina and Mrs. Barker spent a lot of time at the cottage. Christina invited me to come and visit, but Mrs. Barker never would let me."

"I see." The brief case closed with a snap. Paul lifted it from the desk, switched off the light, said, "Hadn't you better be getting along home, Alan?" He started for the door.

Alan moved after him. "Mr. Barker. You're the only one who seems to understand about how Christina and I feel about each other. I thought . . . maybe . . . well, maybe now that you're back . . . maybe you'd invite us to visit you at the lake. Go rowing again or something."

He could see that Mr. Barker wasn't looking at him, and he felt hurt.

"I'm afraid you'll have to discuss anything about Christina with Mrs. Barker. Or your own mother."

"But you're her *father*, Mr. Barker."

His remark only seemed to irritate Mr. Barker. "I've got to hurry, Alan," he said, and he walked fast through the doorway, down the hall, and out to the teachers' parking lot behind the building.

Alan walked home slowly, puzzled and disturbed by what he felt was Mr. Barker's unreasonable coldness to him. His mother was out. There was a note on the coffee table. *Am having lunch with Uncle Roy at the Inn*, the note said. *Sandwich in the refrigerator.* He went into the kitchen, took out the ham and cheese sandwich folded in a bread wrapper, and munched at it absently as he went back to the living room. He sat down in an easy chair and thought the cheese was too dry, and how he hated American history, even the exciting parts. It was after twelve now, and Christina should be home from school. He picked up the phone.

Christina answered, thank God, and not her mother. "Oh hello, Alan."

"How are you?"

"Fine. Just fine."

"I love you, Christy."

"Same here. You know I do, Alan."

"What's the matter? You sound as if you don't want to talk."

"Don't be silly. Of course I do . . . I mean . . . want to talk to you."

"It seems like we never can get to talk to each other, really, any more."

"I know."

"I talked to your father a little while ago. I asked if we could visit him at the cottage and he acted as if he didn't want to be bothered. He said it was up to your mother."

"Oh." The word very slow and drawn-out, the voice fading away as though she could not quite believe him. Then Mrs. Barker's voice calling in the background, and Christina said, "I have to have lunch now. Bye." And she hung up, too quickly.

"I love you," Alan said into the dead phone, then hung up, too, and sat there chewing glumly at the dry sandwich. They were all against him, now. Even Mr. Barker.

"To hell with them," he said softly. And then with sudden fury, flinging the remains of the sandwich across the room, "To hell with every goddamn one of them!"

Chapter Fourteen

THERE were times when Anita thought she must be going insane. Now, for instance, when she was sitting here alone, waiting for her brother Roy at the white-clothed table in the Plimpton Inn. A spoon touched a plate and the noise seemed to her almost deafening. A voice from behind her said, "Would you care for a cocktail, Mrs. Gattone?" and she started up so violently her cigarette fell to the floor. The waiter picked it up, carefully snubbed it into the ashtray.

"A martini," she said. "Very dry, with lemon peel."

She put her hands over her ears, but the spoons and forks and knives went on clicking against the plates, and she was sure she was going insane. Except that insane people never realized they were sick, so she was only neurotic really, or simply tired, or frantic, or worried—about Alan, about Frank, about Paul Barker. What a terrible thing to have done to him!

She stared at all the clubwomen with their ridiculous hats in the oh-so-fashionable, so chichi Plimpton Inn, with its little antiques on the little shelves and the oh-so-cute chintz curtains, and the waiters all dressed up in livery, and the whole business made her sick.

"Hullo, Anita." Again she started from her chair as if pulled by invisible strings. It was Roy. Roy with his tanned face but his Slayton mouth, his Slayton eyes, that didn't change just because a man spent as much time as he could as far away as he could get from Plimpton Ridge.

Roy sat down at the table, facing her, and the waiter brought her martini. "Something for you, Mr. Slayton?" he asked.

"No, thank you."

The waiter disappeared, and Anita noted the look of disapproval on her brother's face. He sat watching her sip the martini, acting so goddamn high and mighty because he wasn't having a drink himself.

"One," she said. "Exactly one."

"I didn't say anything."

"No, but you were thinking plenty. You heard I got looped at Batty-ass's that night and went running off in the rain."

"I didn't have to hear it," Roy said. "I was there. Remember? Or were you too blind to see?"

"Did anybody tell you why?"

He shrugged. "You mean why you got crocked?"

"No. I mean why I ran off like that."

"Listen, in the condition you were that night, you could have done anything."

"Roy," Anita said, and looked at him pleadingly, "please don't scold me. I hate myself enough as it is."

"You mean you pity yourself."

"Well, anyway, I thought I'd better be the one to tell you. That night at Dr. Bullock's I saw you say something to Paul that seemed to shock him."

"That's right. The death of a mutual friend."

Anita looked at him dubiously. "That's all you said? That's all you talked about?"

"Absolutely."

Anita's hand shook as she put down her martini glass. "I must have misunderstood," she said in hardly more than a whisper.

"What the devil are you talking about?"

"I thought you told him something else."

"Like what, for instance?" Roy's eyes were boring into her and she could feel her whole body trembling.

136

"Oh, Roy, I did something awful. Only four people knew who Christina's father really is—you, me, Roberta and you know who. . . . Now there are five."

"Paul!" Roy cried. "Oh no! Oh my God! It *would* be you who would tell him a thing like that. I might have known it." He closed his eyes, and elbows on table held his head between his hands. "The poor bastard!"

Silence. "I know," Anita said. "Believe me, I don't feel so good about it."

Roy opened his eyes to look at his sister wrathfully. "*You* don't feel so good," he said. "Who cares how *you* feel? Ever since we were kids—all your life, Anita—all you've ever done was get yourself or somebody else in trouble. If you didn't like something, you destroyed it. If you couldn't have something, neither could anyone else."

He looked at the tense, neurotic, unhappy woman seated across the table from him, and he thought, with a sudden pang of longing, of Luanai—Luanai who knew how to live and let live, love and let love—and he wished with all his heart that he was with her now.

"You never did understand me," Anita was saying.

"I tried."

"Older brothers are supposed to be so good for a girl. But you never had much to do with me. You were always concerned with yourself."

"I guess that goes for both of us. Two lost babes in the woods . . . With the richest father in town."

Anita threw up her hands. "Well, it doesn't matter now. Nothing seems to matter any more. No more Sunday dinners at the Slayton mansion. No more anything. Slayton is just a name, and as far back as I can remember it never was anything else."

The waiter took their order: lamb chops for her, a Swiss steak for Roy. They ate in silence, withdrawn from one another, only emptiness between them. Roy's fork clattered against his plate. The sound was shattering. She put down her own fork carefully, soundlessly, on the white linen, and put her hands to her ears.

"What's the matter, Anita?" Roy said, genuinely concerned. "Aren't you feeling well?"

"I don't know . . . Do you think, Roy . . ."

"What?"

"Do you think insanity runs in our family?"

"Don't talk nonsense."

"I mean Mother . . . and way back there was an idiot uncle or something. Do you think maybe I'm next?"

"That's ridiculous," Roy said. "If you'd stop drinking . . ."

"Do you call one martini drinking?"

"Yes, with you I call it drinking. It makes you even more destructive, more self-pitying, more everything that's not good. It's just not fair to Alan or Frank."

"Frank!" Anita scoffed.

"Please remember, your husband has a right to live his life just as much as you have to live yours. He came here because of you and he's stayed here because of you. If he gets a piece of sheer luck—unforeseen, not even asked for—you can't blame him for trying again at what he wanted from the beginning."

"He's getting on to forty, Roy. He's had it."

"Has he? Any more than I have? Or Paul has? We're all pushing forty. To you, I suppose, that means we're all supposed to give up."

"You might as well."

"Why? Why do you say that?"

"You think I can't see you're getting bored with Mildred? Even bored with flying. But what else can you do? You can't bear the thought of Slayton Firearms. So stay with Mildred. Stay with flying until they retire you. What else is there in the cards for you?"

138

"I'm afraid," Roy said quietly, "you don't know anything about my plans." He smiled, almost secretly, she thought, and rather sweetly, too, as if something quite happy had occurred to him. "Perhaps Frank will just pull off that show, perhaps he will go to Hollywood, whether you like it or not. And Paul— well, he'll have to start all over again. Sure, he's got it the toughest, except sometimes I think—"

"What do you think?" Anita asked eagerly, stirred by something mysterious in Roy's voice, something that was almost a promise of a brighter future.

"Maybe it's easier to have it all destroyed, and then start all over again, than to try to improve on the little good you already have." He pushed back his chair, got up from the table.

"You haven't finished your steak. Don't you want your coffee?" Anita asked. "Oh Roy," she said, reaching across the table for his hand, "I did so want for us to know each other . . . communicate . . . something."

"Did you?" He leaned across the table. "Believe me, Anita, it's not brother and sister who don't understand each other. It's men and women. The minute a man goes after something really good in his life—something he really wants, that may not entirely include his wife or sister or mother or daughter—then they all begin to pull him back. They try to gain some superiority over him. They try to castrate him. It's as simple as that."

"Oh no, not you!" Anita said, withdrawing her hand. "That castration stuff's a lot of crap."

"Okay, have it your way." Roy turned and walked across the dining room to the door.

Anita sat motionless, watching him go, resenting his going. He was talking nonsense, of course. She was not castrating Frank at all. Maybe Mildred wasn't handling Roy exactly right, and no doubt Roberta had deceived Paul. But good God! anything between herself and Frank could be solved so simply. All Frank had to do was give up his young man's lost illusions and come home for good. She'd forgive him, love him, comfort him. What more did a man want anyway?

Roy's Austin Healey purred through the streets of the town, along the green past his father's big, hollow house, and Roy thought, You bastard, you! and then, Poor bastard Paul! He stepped on the accelerator, raced over the macadam toward home, slowed down at the black and gold sign before his own house that he was beginning to hate more and more each day, then stepped on the accelerator again and drove on toward Beetlewood Lake.

Only yesterday Millie had said that Paul was living in the cottage. He hadn't thought much about it at the time. "Doing some research," Millie had said, believing it, of course, in that stupid way of hers. Just as she still believed his mother had suffered from nothing more than heart trouble. My God, in all these years, living right here in the same town, Millie had never even met his mother. It was incredible. But then, wasn't everything? People met and got enmeshed, entwined, their lives overlapping, each in some way affecting the other, never quite understanding what the effect of that was, never really wanting to understand, only feeling the need for one another for unhealthy reasons, making love without loving, taking without giving, going along, just going along in a big vacuum. . . . The stupid, unwitting rat race that ended in the same way for every single one of them.

What could he say to Paul? "Tough, old boy! Sorry you found out, old fellow! Matter of fact, I was interested in Roberta myself once. And wouldn't that have been a hot one!" He could say, "Look, Paul, we were very close friends during the war, though we haven't seen too much of each other lately. The way I see it is you ought to go ahead and . . ." And what? Paul ought to go ahead and what? What in hell could you say to a poor sonofabitch whose life had gone down the drain in a few simple words spoken by a drunken, neurotic blabber-mouth —especially when the blabber-mouth was your own sister, when the sin had been committed by your own father, and the poor bastard had come to Plimpton in the first place because you had sent him there?

Ahead, rounding a curve, was a young girl on a bicycle. Her pony tail, tied in a red ribbon, bobbed as she pedaled along in her faded blue jeans, a boy's shirt floating behind like a banner in the wind. She looked very pretty, Roy thought, riding gaily along under the green trees, and then in another moment he had pulled up beside her and recognized it was Christina Barker.

He stopped the car. Christina straddled the bicycle and smiled at him shyly. "Hello, Mr. Slayton," she said.

"Hello, Christina." Roy smiled. "I thought you were getting too old for bicycles."

"Too old?" Her still-childish, unlined brow puckered in a frown. "In Europe everybody bicycles, no matter how old they are. I've seen pictures of them. I'm going to see Daddy and there's no other way for me to get there. Except walking," she laughed.

"I see."

"I mean he has to keep the car to get back and forth from the cottage to his classes."

"Of course."

"He's doing some research, you know. Working on his book," Christina said, as if she were apologizing for her father's strange behavior.

"So I hear." You poor little kid, Roy thought, how in hell did my lousy father and that tramp Roberta ever produce such a really nice girl? Well, maybe she wasn't a tramp, he thought, feeling apologetic about Roberta.

"Mr. Slayton," Christina was saying, "have you seen my father since he got back from New Hampshire?"

"No, I just got back myself from Hawaii."

"Oh . . ."

"Why?"

"Nothing. I just thought maybe if you had, he might have said something to you . . ."

"About what, Christina?"

"Oh, I don't know . . . Just something . . . anything . . . She seemed about to cry. "Well, good-by," she said very quickly, and leaping on her bicycle she pedaled away swiftly. Her dungareed legs pumped hard, her pony tail bobbed, and then she was gone around the bend in the road.

Roy sighed. He made a U-turn and headed back for home, feeling sad and yet relieved, too, because there was nothing at all he could have said to Paul. He drove very slowly. It was a beautiful afternoon. The last time he had driven so slowly it had been a beautiful night in the hills and valleys of Oahu. Luanai had sat quietly, comfortably beside him, her face so very lovely and contented, perhaps because in her woman's way she knew he loved her even if he couldn't tell her. And then her shy, fleeting smile as they came down beneath the trees, as if she wanted to tell him that she loved him, too, and like himself would have to wait and think it through before she could say her love in words.

She'd said good night at the doorway, looking at him as if she would speak to him in silence that was more eloquent than words. And, "When will you be back again?"

"I don't know," he'd said. "Not for a while. I'm going to request a transfer."

"Because you can't face George after this?"

"No."

"Then why, Flyer Roy?"

"Well, yes, that's it. Because I can't face George after this."

They were both lying and they knew it. They were in love, but they needed time. They were both married, and it would be impossible for either of them to carry on an affair while faithful, trusting George still believed his wife was bearing his child.

"But you will come back," Luanai had said.

"Yes . . . some day . . . soon."

"Then good night, Flyer Roy." She'd kissed his cheek impulsively, in the old familiar way, then gone inside quickly and closed the door behind her.

"Good night," he'd breathed in the silent, moonlit darkness. *Good night, darling Luanai,* he'd said to himself, to the lovely night, after the door was closed, and driven off sad and yet exultant in the knowledge that he was committed to Luanai through an act of love.

The black and gold sign of his house again, the buttonwood trees again, Millie again opening the front door, dressed in a white shirt and black slacks, red hair put up so neatly, everything so neat and perfect—the quick kiss, the bright smile, the easy words. "How was lunch?"

"Fine. I really ought to see more of Anita than I do."

"Of course you should."

Into the living room, all neat and perfect as if nobody lived there—which he didn't, really. "You drove by a little while ago," Mildred was saying. "I saw you from the window. You went right on past the driveway."

"Yes, I was going to see Paul. But Christina was going down on her bicycle, so I didn't want to interfere."

"Such a sweet child," Mildred said.

Roy sat down in his favorite chair. "Umm," he said, and lit a cigarette. "Millie," he said, "when I got back to New York yesterday I put in for an immediate transfer. A European flight. Or maybe South America."

"Why?"

"Oh, I don't know. I'm getting tired of Hawaii, I guess."

"I don't wonder, after all these years. Wouldn't London be nice? I should think London would be perfect."

"Yes, perfect, perfect," Roy said. "Just perfect."

And as Mildred returned his gaze with a puzzled look he thought of how he had once been mad to go to bed with her, as if his very life depended on it, and he wondered how he could feel so indifferent now, so indifferent and cold and bored.

Chapter Fifteen

THERE was a slight breeze across the lake that May afternoon. It fluttered the young leaves in the stand of birch, filled the sails of the small catboat near the farther shore.

Paul Barker sat in a wicker chair in the sunlight on the tiny porch of his green cottage. Since his last class, at noon, he'd been working hard, steadily, his feet propped against the wobbly wooden rail, the chair tilted back dangerously as he made hasty notes with one of a half-dozen ball-point pens he carried in his pockets. Hard work, of course, was the easiest escape from all problems, the best anodyne. Better than travel, where your problems went along with you for the ride. Better than morose hiding inside yourself. Better than vain attempts to face up to problems that were insoluble in any case. Yes, work was best. Many men, seeking escape in work, had accomplished great things. Yet there was a catch to it. Working to escape was not the same thing as working to fulfill oneself.

He read over the page he had just written. It seemed to him dull and pedantic, utterly devoid of the light he had hoped to put into it. Disappointed, he tore the page from his notebook, crumpled it in his fist and threw it over the wooden rail.

There was a knock at the back door. He let the front legs of the chair drop to the porch floor, half rose, thought it might be Roberta, then heard a voice calling "Daddy!" and Christina appeared around the side of the cottage.

Paul sat down again and reached for his pipe. "It's you, Christina," he said, wondering at the sudden gladness in his own heart at the sight of her.

She edged up the steps, leaned embarrassed against the railing. "I just thought I'd . . . come to see you."

"I'm glad you did."

"How's the work coming?"

"Fine. It's coming along fine."

"You must be working terribly hard. I mean having to be all alone and all. Even all night."

"Yes, it's hard work," Paul said, striking a match to his pipe. The wind blew the match out. It played with Christina's hair, fluttered the red ribbon on her pony tail. Over the second match, cupped deep in his hands, Paul glanced up at the girl's face and caught himself searching for the Slayton look. Once, only weeks ago, he had thought Christina's modesty was overdone in front of her own father. Now, even thinking of such a thing as her breasts pressing against her boy's shirt left him uncomfortable and ashamed.

"Daddy . . ."

"Yes?" He threw the match away, stared out across the rippling lake.

"What's the matter, Daddy? I wish you'd tell me."

"Nothing's the matter, child. I'm just working, that's all. You know that."

She shook her head doubtfully. "No, there's something else. I know there must be. Ever since that night at Dr. Bullock's.

145

Mother cries a lot. Not outside where I can see. It's worse than that. It's all inside where it hurts the most."

"Your grandmother's death—"

"No, Daddy! No, no!" She knelt suddenly and dropped her head against his knee. Impulsively he touched her hair, then snatched his hand away. Something hurt in his throat and something ached in his chest, and it was love for his daughter, he supposed, except she was not his daughter, and in a strange, ugly way he resented her . . . he even hated her.

Christina spoke into his knees. "You and Mother . . . you're getting a divorce, aren't you?"

"Now, Christina . . ."

"You don't have to spare me, because even Mother admitted it. She said we were going away this summer and never coming back, and you were going somewhere else and you weren't coming back either." Then abruptly she stood up and shouted at him. "Why? What happened? Why can't you tell me? Why can't you just make up like other people do when they have fights?"

"It's not a fight, Christina," Paul said softly.

"Then what is it? Why do you act . . . I don't know . . . different toward me? You even act different toward Alan."

"Alan?"

"Yes. The last time we were all together here you took my side about seeing him as much as I wanted to. Now you're against him, just like Mother."

"Nobody's against you, Christina. Nor against Alan, either."

"You are, you are. I talked to Alan just today and he said you hedged about his seeing me. You never did before. You always liked Alan. You even said if we waited long enough, we might get married some day. Now you're just like Mother . . . and Anita . . . and I don't understand. I don't understand."

She began to cry. She sat heavily on the single step and put her face in her hands and sobbed uncontrollably, talking in choking gasps through her tears. "We used to be so happy when

146

I was little. . . . You loved me, and we were all so happy. Then when I got older you knew me better and we understood each other. I mean, we laughed a lot and everything, and I thought you were the most wonderful father. . . . All I wanted was to live with you and Mother and grow up and marry Alan and have a baby of my own. . . . And now everything is all crazy. Everybody hates everybody else, and—"

"Christina!" He wanted to go out to her, take her in his arms. "Christina, stop it!"

"They do, they do," she sobbed.

"Nobody hates you, Christina."

"Well, I hate everybody." The tears had stopped and now she rose and facing him, cried, "I hate you. And I hate Mother, too. The only person in the whole world I care for is Alan, and some day I'm going to marry him whether you like it or not."

Paul felt his blood run cold. Not that, he thought, dear God, not that, in any case!

"Christina," he said again gently. But she only turned away from him and rushed off around the side of the cottage. He rose and started after her. "Christina!" he called, but when he reached the rutted road she was already pedaling fast away, the red ribbon on her hair bobbing in the wind.

Disheartened, Paul went back to the porch. He stood by the rail, looking out across the water, and remembered how he had waited in the corridor of the hospital when Christina was being born. Afterwards he was so happy and proud he'd handed out cigars to everyone. He'd even given a cigar to Mr. Mitchel Slayton. And now that baby girl, that same innocent child, was talking about marrying the same Mr. Slayton's grandson.

He felt chilled. Inside, he put a kettle of water on the hot plate, turned on the portable television which he'd bought the day before to keep the nights noisy and busy. There was a Western on, and he tried hard to concentrate on the show. But who wanted to look at a horse opera now? He went into the

147

little kitchen. There was a drawing tacked on the wall—a drawing of the cottage, inscribed *To Daddy, from Christina*. And hanging on the door, a red apron, with white stitching spelling out the name *Roberta*. Impulsively, angrily, he ripped the apron from the nail, tore down the drawing, and threw them both in the fireplace and set a match to them.

He sat down in the living room again. The water steamed and bubbled in the kettle. The Western was coming to an end; apparently the Indians had lost again. The picture burned fast in the fireplace and the apron burned slowly. Soon they were nothing but ashes, and he thought, ashes to ashes. But without conviction, for he knew that nothing basic could ever really be burned away. Not experience, not memories, not happiness, and not love. I *did* love, I *was* happy, meaning you were not happy now, did not love any longer. Still, there had been a time; and still, hating Roberta, hating Christina, hating himself most of all, he did need them and did love them. He wanted them with the aching nostalgia of a man who has lost something precious through an act of fate—with the ferocity of a man who has himself destroyed what he wants the very most.

"You're sure?" It was Mitchel Slayton at the other end of the phone.

"Yes, I'm sure, Mitchel. I can bear up until Christina finishes the school year. It's only a few weeks now. And then I'm planning to move to the West Coast."

"Why the West Coast?"

"I don't know. Isn't that where everybody goes when they want to get away from the East Coast?"

"I suppose so. Then you don't think Paul will . . . forgive you . . . live with it . . . whatever it may take?"

"No, I'm sure he won't."

"Well . . ." There was a long pause at the other end of the

wire. "You realize, Roberta, if there's anything I can do . . . financially . . . anything."

"I'm a good secretary. Remember?"

"Please, my dear. I'm in no mood for that kind of talk. I want you to know that I've set up a fund for Christina's education. Also, now that there'll be no need for explaining to Paul, I'm including her generously in my will."

"Oh Mitchel, Mitchel, money can't turn back the clock."

"It can't. I know that. But it's money you'll need, nevertheless. You'll have to go to Nevada, or Mexico, then on to California if you like. That will cost money, and you might as well face it."

"Yes, I suppose it will." Roberta sighed. Money! Everything came down to money, eventually, with Mitchel. And suddenly the whole conversation struck her as absurd, and she began to laugh hysterically.

"Roberta!" she heard Mitchel Slayton say sharply. "What's got into you?"

"Nothing." She was crying now, and she didn't want Mitchel Slayton to know it. "Nothing," she said. "Good-by." And she hung up.

She sat down in the living room and stared at the French clock on the mantle. The clock ticked on monotonously, and now there was Smokey scratching at the back door. She got up and let the dog in. "Hello, Smokey," she said. "That was Mr. Slayton. The generous Mr. Slayton. I need him, Smokey. Isn't that funny? I still need him. For years I've been avoiding him, fearing that something might happen, and now it's happened and I need him again."

She returned to the living room, sat again, listening idly to the ticking of the clock. She thought of the ring in her jewelry box, one white pearl, one black pearl. Why had she kept it all these years, instead of returning it to Mitchel, when it was only a reminder of an ugly past? Because the past had not been ugly then, she supposed. It was only ugly now. Once she had needed Mitchel Slayton. He had been kind to her, given her emotional support when she needed that more than love. She'd sinned against Mitchel's wife, lied to Paul. For the sake of Christina? Herself? To protect Mitchel? His wife? Nature dealt you the cards and you played them the best you could.

She missed Paul. She loved Paul. Her heart ached for him. She knew that alone now, in the cottage, he needed her more than ever in his life. Yet though it was Paul she loved, it was Mitchel Slayton she needed, all over again, full circle. It was as if she was a fatherless young woman again and only Mitchel Slayton could give her security.

A bicycle banged against the porch rail. Christina came in, her face red from the sun, the wind, from crying.

"Where have you been, dear?" Roberta said.

"I went to see Daddy."

"Oh? How is he?"

"What do you care? I'm sure I don't."

"Christina! You mustn't speak like that about your father."

"All right." Christina paused on the stairs. "I don't love Daddy any more, but I need him, and that's something you could never understand."

She slammed the door behind her. The dog whined. The French clock on the mantle ticked on monotonously.

Youth is so cruel, Roberta thought, fighting back her tears. But age is crueler.

Chapter Sixteen

THIS was the first time that Frank Gattone had ever been in the offices of Slayton Firearms. After his marriage to Anita, he and Mitchel Slayton had entered into an unspoken agreement to keep out of each other's way, never to speak to one another except in emergencies. Such an arrangement was simple enough to observe while Frank was away during the war, and afterwards when he was living with Anita in the apartment on 72nd Street. But it was more difficult when he was living in Plimpton Ridge, right in Slayton Hall, and he often came across Mitchel on the street or campus, or met him at some faculty function. At such times they would nod, say a polite "hello Mitchel, hello Frank," and move on their separate ways.

Unless there was an emergency. Well, there was an emergency now, Frank thought as he pushed open the door marked SLAYTON FIREARMS, whether Mitchel agreed or not.

The elderly receptionist sent him along to Miss Calhoun, who in turn informed Mr. Slayton that a Mr. Gattone was here to see him. Miss Calhoun told Frank to wait, and eyed him suspiciously as he moved about the outer office, looking at the hunting prints that lined the walls. He was dressed in rumpled brown slacks, old tennis shoes, a sport shirt and elbow-patched sport coat. She obviously thought it was hardly the proper costume for the Seagram Building or Slayton Firearms, and Frank had to admit she had something there. But in another hour he'd be conducting a rehearsal, and if Mitchel Slayton didn't like the way he was dressed, he knew where he could stick it.

The buzzer sounded on Miss Calhoun's desk. She lifted a phone, said "Yes, sir," then, "You may go in now, Mr. Gattone."

Frank nodded and opened the door to the big, glass-fronted office. Mitchel was sitting at his huge desk. He stared at Frank's unconventional garb.

"I just broke away from the studio for a few moments," Frank explained. "I'm due for a rehearsal soon."

"No matter. It was rude of me. One gets unused to seeing people out of office uniform." Mitchel looked at him curiously, as if to say *What's on your mind?* "Sit down, Frank," he said.

Frank lit a cigarette, looked across the desk at the distant man who was after all his own father-in-law, observed his handsome, sun-tanned face (he probably uses a sun lamp, Frank thought), the full head of silver-gray hair that made him look quite distinguished. A handsome bastard, but still a bastard, Frank thought. A tough bastard with a couple of million bucks and no way to spend it except to buy himself a little prestige that doesn't mean a damn thing.

"Well, Frank?"

"It's Anita," he said. "She's . . . well, she's becoming a little difficult, Mitchel."

"Is that supposed to surprise me?"

"No."

"Then why talk about it? Anita's your problem, not mine."

"I don't know, I just thought . . . I'm afraid she's taken to drinking again. Has a snort now and then on the side."

"You can take it from me she gets loaded now and then. Not just a snort, as you call it. In fact, I saw her that way myself at Dr. Bullock's."

152

"But it's all my fault. She hadn't touched the stuff for years until this television thing came along."

"So that's it," Mitchel said. "You feel guilty about it, and it would make you feel less guilty—maybe—if you got old Daddy-in-Law's sympathy."

"Not exactly."

Frank felt himself getting angry. Maybe Mitchel was right, and maybe he wasn't, but he had no business talking that way in any case. He started to get up from his chair, then sank back again slowly as Mitchel Slayton leaned over the desk and thumped the words at him in a steady voice that neither rose nor fell, but kept the same harsh honesty in every sentence.

"I never wanted Anita to marry you, Frank. You know that. I didn't like what you came from and I didn't like what you were, and I told you so. But Anita insisted, and in the end I figured perhaps you might do her some good after all. She was always a problem to me. I thought maybe she'd settle down if she married you and had a baby, if that's what she really wanted.

"Well, it wasn't what she wanted, was it? At least not everything she wanted. She thought it was, until you began making something of yourself. Then she cracked up—sanitariums, psychiatrists, all that crap. I'll tell you this, Frank. As of this moment I have a hell of a lot more respect for you than I have for her."

"Now look, Mitchel," Frank protested, but the older man paid no attention to his interruption.

"Oh, I was on her side for a long time," he continued. "It was no easy job getting you a teaching post at Plimpton, considering your academic background, or rather your lack of it. But Anita asked me to get you the appointment and I did. And I give you credit—you worked hard at it, you've been doing all right. Except now you're fed up, aren't you, Frank?"

"No, Anita and I . . ."

153

Mitchel smiled sarcastically. "You protest too much, young man. Anyway, I wasn't referring to Anita. I mean you're fed up with Plimpton Academy and Plimpton Ridge and Slayton Hall and Dr. Bullock and all the stupid hours you've spent cramming useless information into the heads of stupid little boys. Isn't that true? So now you've got a second chance and you want to keep going with it after this one show, if it's at all possible. Except you're afraid it may send Anita off again and you don't know what in hell to do."

"Yes," Frank said, "that's about it."

"All right." Mitchel Slayton poured water from a brown carafe, took a brief drink, then banged the lid down on the carafe. "All right. I'll tell you what to do, Frank. Go ahead! If Anita gets in your way, brush her aside. If she goes on a bender, I'll see that Alan gets taken care of. Sure she's my daughter, but everybody has to make his own way in this world, and she's got no business dragging you down."

"That sounds kind of rough," Frank said.

"Certainly it's rough. But I'll tell you something, Frank. There's only one thing in this world that's worth having. Love. L-O-V-E. You love somebody, somebody loves you. That's all there is to it. But if you don't get that, you've got nothing. So you take the next best thing. You take power or money or fame or whatever little morsel you can pick up for yourself as second best."

"But I love Anita," Frank said. "I do love her."

"The hell you do," Mitchell Slayton said. "You've got a conscience, that's all. You don't even know what's going on with your own son, and you don't care too much. Why let your wife destroy you—why destroy yourself—when at least one of you's got a chance?"

Frank crushed his cigarette. His hand was shaking. He hadn't expected Mitchel to talk this way. He'd come for a lecture from his father-in-law, a reason to give up any plans that didn't include his wife, some moral support for avoiding Edith Parkes and remaining faithful to Anita. But Mitchel refused to condemn him. He was no help at all.

He got up from his chair. "One more thing," he said. "Suppose, in trying to get what I want . . . suppose I have to . . . well, do something unethical, immoral. Legal enough maybe, but not quite right, if you see what I mean."

Mitchel Slayton looked at his son-in-law with almost a trace of pity. "I see what you mean, all right. And my answer is: grow up! If you don't get love, get whatever else you can in any way you can. If a woman understood what a man really is, really wants, if she really loved him, she'd be with him all the way. But she never does. So he's on his own, except for a very small chosen few who are truly loved. The fortunate ones. Then there are a few lucky men who fight their way out from under. The rest just get sucked down and down until they're buried under this thing called 'the modern woman,' this efficient, neurotic, demanding, sex-wielding machine that'll cut you into little pieces and then blame you for not being a whole man."

If I wanted a lecture, Frank thought, I've got it.

The buzzer sounded. "Yes, Miss Calhoun," Mitchel said into the speaker. "I'll take it." He waved to Frank, lifted the phone. "Take it from there," he said, his hand over the mouthpiece, and then, into the phone, "How are you, Roger? . . . Yes, there's a sales meeting scheduled for Monday. . . ."

Frank went out and took a cab to the Central Plaza on lower Second Avenue, where the rehearsal was to take place. And all the way down he tried to tell himself that Mitchel Slayton was wrong—he was just a tough, mean, woman-hating bastard. How was it that with a wife and two children he had found no love with any of them? And he wondered if Mitchel Slayton had ever loved anyone in his entire life, if he had ever, even for a brief time, felt himself one of the "chosen few."

But what was the use of thinking about Mitchel Slayton?

155

It was Anita he was worried about, not her father. Anita—and himself. And Frank felt now that it was foolish of him to have run to Mitchel Slayton for advice. You could go to a hundred people for advice and it still wouldn't do any good. You still had to face up to your own problems.

Chapter Seventeen

WHEN Frank reached the ballroom on the second floor of the Central Plaza he found Joan Leonard there, meticulously laying white tape across the floor in preparation for the rehearsal. Joan straightened, brushed out her skirt, pushed back her hair, and stared ruefully at a broken fingernail. "You're early," she said.

"I haven't rehearsed here for a long time," Frank said. "I can't do any real blocking until I see how large the sets really are." He moved about, studying the lines of tape that marked the walls and doors, the entrances and exits, observing the straight-back chairs that were supposed to represent sofas and tables, desks and armchairs.

Joan lit a cigarette and watched him idly as she leaned against the green plaster wall, supporting her body on one flat-heeled shoe. She had worked for many directors in the two years since she'd graduated from college. Frank was new to her. He seemed pleasant enough, and he certainly had definite ideas about how to do the show, which was sometimes more valuable than talent. If a director took too many suggestions, if he didn't keep a tight rein on the actors all the time, then a show would have no quality at all—good or bad. Back of everything there had to be the unmistakable stamp of one man's conception of how to execute a lot of words on paper.

"The classroom's pretty small," Frank said.

"You're shooting from the rear, aren't you? Mike's only planning on seven students in the front row."

"We'll need at least twelve."

"But Mike said—"

"I don't care what Mike said."

He was not angry, she decided. Just firm. Then Mike Purdue arrived in person and Frank made it very clear to him that he was only the assistant director. He could pick out the music, take care of costuming, check the props and all that sort of thing. But all final decisions were to be made by the director, and if Mike didn't like it he could go back to Yale.

The actors straggled in, one by one—two students with speaking lines, the school principal, and Bramley Siddon, who was playing the indispensable lover of the indispensable heroine. They drank coffee, smoked cigarettes, read the newspapers, and waited for the appearance of Edith Parkes. Frank was getting nervous. He kept glancing at his watch. Finally he told Joan Leonard to call Miss Parkes' apartment, but nobody answered the phone.

"She must be on her way, Mr. Gattone," Joan said. She thought he looked unduly worried, and she wondered if he was anxious about Edith Parkes. She knew the woman drank a lot, was never entirely dependable. And yet she had taken the part, only the second she'd ever done in television and both times in connection with Frank Gattone. Something personal, Joan decided. They were old friends, apparently. And yet, during the reading the other day, they had seemed more like old enemies.

Finally, forty minutes late, Edith Parkes arrived, slim, flamboyant, wearing tight-fitting black slacks and a tight gold sweater and gold earrings. And falsies, Joan decided. She was reputed to be a real bitch. But the woman could act any other actress in New York right off the stage, and you could forgive her a lot for that.

Due to Miss Parkes' late arrival, the first-act blocking made little progress before the luncheon break. The actors moved about under Frank's direction. Joan made chalk marks on the wooden floor. Frank cupped his hands over his eyes to simulate a camera, spoke now and then to Mike Purdue, who seemed to be watching everything with a certain contempt. Edith Parkes slouched around in her tight slacks, called everyone "Pumpkin," and treated Frank with a deference that contained a touch of mockery. Then it was one o'clock, with an hour off for lunch.

When they had all left the room, Frank sank wearily into a chair and put his hands over his eyes. Joan Leonard came back and stood by the open door, observing him.

"Do you feel all right, Mr. Gattone?" she asked.

"Yes, thank you. And call me Frank."

"Can I get you some lunch?"

"No, I'll go downstairs to Ratner's." Frank got up and went toward her. "Want to join me?"

"Well . . . yes, I'd like to." Joan followed him down the single flight of stairs and walked with him into the clean, bright restaurant. They sat in a booth and looked at the menus.

"Maybe you don't like kosher food," Frank said.

"I was raised on bagels and lox."

"Oh."

"Yes, I'm half Jewish. On my father's side."

"Good. I'm all Italian on both sides."

They laughed, and she was aware of his eyes on her face. He frowned, and she thought he was most attractive. She decided she liked him and she wished him the best of luck.

"You know," he was saying, "my wife used to be my assist-

158

ant. It was radio in those days. In fact, that's how we met." He smiled briefly, and again she thought how attractive he was. "I should think, after all the shows you've done, some director would have caught you by now."

It was not a proposition. Joan knew that instantly. The man was warm, naturally friendly, with something on his mind. Like every director she'd ever known, he'd eventually tell her the problems that he could not discuss even with his wife. She said, "Don't you think every girl is always a little in love with the man she works for?"

"Yes, I suppose that's true. She probably gets to know him better than his own wife. . . . A little objectivity helps," he added with a wry smile.

"I guess I've been a little in love with twenty men. But I sleep with a doctor whom I don't really love at all. He's very clinical about it though, so it's clean and I won't get pregnant."

"I see." Frank was shocked and she knew it, and wondered if she'd been trying to shock him.

"You're a very modern young lady, aren't you?" he said, remembering Mitchel Slayton's remark about modern women.

She shrugged. "I suppose. Vassar and Freud, and I live in the Village and play the bongo drums, so that makes me a member of the beat generation, except I don't really feel beat at all. I just get bored and a little tired and wonder what it must be like to have a big ambition."

She felt his eyes on her mouth as she talked and knew that she was blushing, of all the ridiculous things to do. "I like you, Joan," he was saying. "I like your wide mouth and your black, black eyes."

She busied herself with her cottage cheese and black bread and tea and thought if he liked her, that made twenty-one men who felt a little something about her, twenty-one directors she was a little in love with. She wished she didn't have to work for so many men, become so close to them that romance was impossible. She wished she could be somewhere far away and alone where a man would have to reach out for her. Loving so many men a little and no man a lot, not even her efficient doctor who knew how to send her, was all quite modern, she supposed, but it was also a bore and she never stopped feeling miserable inside except when she was working. She would meet her doctor again at seven. She didn't care for cottage cheese. Something was bothering the very nice man sitting opposite her. He had a wife, and what did she look like? If he wants to sleep with me, Joan thought, maybe I'll let him. But he wouldn't want to. Even if he did, he wouldn't do it. He was that kind of man.

She felt that in another moment she was going to cry. She was being silly. She reached in her bag for her handkerchief and blew her nose.

"What's the matter?"

"Nothing. Can't a girl blow her nose? It's a free country."

Frank laughed. "What time's it getting to be?"

Joan looked at her wrist watch. "Quarter of two. We'd better be getting back."

The afternoon rehearsal began in earnest. Each time he gave her the slightest suggestion, a bit of new business, a different meaning or inflection in her lines, Frank could tell that Edith Parkes was having a ball. "Yes, Pumpkin," she would say. Or, "How right you are, darling," with never the hint of an argument, none of the temperamental arrogance for which she was famous. Even Mike Purdue was impressed. "You really know how to handle her," he whispered to Frank. "You've got a good show and if she keeps working like this for the next week, you're in."

"Thanks, Mike." Frank glanced at the clock, unbelieving. They had been working four hours, it was already six o'clock, and it seemed hardly more than a few minutes.

160

"All right, everybody," he called out. "Tomorrow we'll block Act Two. Start learning your lines right away. I'd like everybody perfect in his lines by the time we finish blocking. Good night, and see you all at ten tomorrow."

He turned away, began stuffing papers into his brief case— a badly marked-up script, pages of notes on lined yellow paper, a copy of the floor plan, rough sketches of the set. He heard footsteps and voices as the actors left, and noticed that Edith's voice was not among them. He looked around, curious, a little tense, and found her standing directly behind him. She was smiling at him faintly through her well-applied make-up. He cleared his throat. "Edith . . . I want to thank you."

"For what, Pumpkin?"

"You could have . . . well, you could have loused me up. Considering the way you feel about me. I mean, knowing how important this show is to me after ten years. . . Well, you could have made it difficult."

"Oh, but I won't, Pumpkin."

"I appreciate it."

"At least, not until June 22nd."

"The 22nd?" Frank said, puzzled.

"The night before the show, darling. Have you forgotten our sentimental little date?"

"Edith, I thought perhaps . . ."

"Unless you want to get it over with right now. Tonight."

"No, I've got to work tonight. And I'm dead tired." He was embarrassed. He thought of Bubbles from the years ago, and somehow it was almost exactly the same.

Edith laughed. "Oh, I do want you at your best, darling," she drawled. Then, turning to go, she said much more incisively, "The 22nd's the very latest. And don't try to renege. . . . I can get very sick overnight, darling. I hardly think you could replace me in a single day." She waved to him. "Good-by, Pumpkin, and my very best to your lovely wife."

Frank watched her go, her hips swinging in the tight black slacks, her hands turned slightly outward in that peculiar way of hers. He turned back to his brief case, closed it, and started to leave the room when he caught sight of Joan Leonard. She was sitting at a table behind a huge column, copying changes in the script. For a moment he watched her in silence. Then, "Good night," he said. "Good night, Joan."

"Oh . . ." She glanced up, as if startled, but he had the feeling she was only pretending to be surprised. "Good night, Mr. Gattone . . . Frank."

Her eyes remained fixed on his. She stuck a pencil between her lips. He hesitated, then came over to her and took the pencil from her mouth and threw it on the desk. "Nasty pencil." He smiled. "I thought you'd left."

"No, I had some things to do."

"Then you heard?"

"Yes."

"You understood?"

"It's none of my business."

"I asked if you understood."

"I'm thinking," Joan said. "That's all . . . just thinking."

"Then stop thinking. Let's go."

"Where?"

"A drink. Dinner, if they'll serve us in these clothes."

"But why? I mean so suddenly."

"Because you're thinking and I don't know why I should care, but I'd rather you got it completely straight, regardless of what you may think of me."

Joan hesitated. "I forgot," Frank said. "You have a date with your doctor."

"I can break it."

"Do, please, just this once."

Frank walked toward the door, feeling suddenly jealous of the unknown doctor. He waited, watching Joan through the

162

ballroom doorway as she switched off the lights, then walked toward him in her flat shoes, straight bare legs. Her plaid skirt was rumpled, her boy's shirt open at the throat, the sleeves rolled up. She was holding her shabby brief case against her breast the way a girl carries her schoolbooks, and he noticed a pencil smudge on her cheek and that her lipstick was smeared.

They came out of the air-conditioned building into the sudden warmth of Second Avenue.

"I know a place on Lexington," Frank said, and stepped into the street, waving at a stream of empty cabs that paid him no mind at all.

"They're going off duty," Joan explained. "All heading for Brooklyn. Let's go somewhere nearby."

"You know, Joan, I have a funny feeling standing here on Second Avenue. I was born only a few blocks away and it just occurred to me that I haven't been down this way for God knows how long. There's a bar on the corner where my father always used to have drinks after work. I wouldn't be surprised if he's still there, the old so-and-so. I'm curious. Shall we take a look and see?"

Joan clapped her hands. "It's an adventure," she cried happily. "I'd love to."

They walked slowly through the Polish neighborhood, east to First Avenue, then the short way to the remembered block where he'd been born and lived an even half of his life. The delicatessen, the plumbing supply store, the Chinese laundry, the cheap clothing store and the barbershop with the fading nude Scotch-taped to the wall, the children playing stickball in the streets, the pawnshop, the young couples sitting on steps and the old ladies looking out of upper windows. It was all the same. Nothing had changed at all.

"You're very quiet," Frank said as they stepped around a little girl playing hopscotch in the lovely spring evening.

"I thought you might be remembering. . . . I might be intruding."

"No, there's not much I want to remember. My mother's dead now. My brothers live in different neighborhoods, and I never really knew them anyway."

They had reached the corner bar—TONY'S, the window said in cracked gold letters. Inside, a row of men stood drinking beer along the faded bar. At a table, alone, Frank saw his father—white-haired, his face lined and veined, his big hand shaking as he raised a glass of beer to his lips. When he had taken a long drink, he wiped his big mustache with the back of his hand.

Frank took Joan's arm and led her toward the table, until they stood directly in front of the old man. "Papa," he said softly, "Papa . . ."

The old man looked up with hazy eyes.

"Papa . . . it's Frank."

"Salvatore?" He looked at Joan.

"And this is Miss Leonard. She's working on a show with me."

"A show?"

"Yes. I'm back in television, Papa."

The old man shook his head and spoke to Joan. "This boy," he said. "This Salvatore. I try all my life to make a man of him. Instead he prances on a stage. He marries a little stick. His brothers—all big, all tough, work hard—one a mechanic, one truck driver, one stevedore. Work hard for a living. But Salvatore? He ashamed of name. Frank instead. His mama's idea, rest her soul. My other boys, they do *my* work, man's work. But Salvatore—Frankie—he does woman's work. His wife's work now. Maybe yours now, too."

"No, not mine," Joan said.

The old man shook his head.

"How are you doing, Papa?" Frank said.

"Fine. On city pension. Collect from government, too."

"That's fine. And you speak English now, too."

"Sometimes English." Then, glaring at him, "You forget Italian?"

"No, I still remember."

The old man grunted, drained his beer glass, wiped his mustache. He did not ask them to join him. He waved to a crony and began talking to him in Italian. It was as though he had dismissed his two visitors.

Frank touched Joan's arm. She nodded, and they walked out to the street once more. They walked several blocks in silence before Joan said, "I forgot to make my call."

"He won't mind if you're late."

"I told you I don't want to go."

"All right." He felt tired. Depressed. They were in the Village now, going down 8th Street toward Waverly Place. "I'm sorry I took you to meet my old man," he said. "I don't know why I did it."

Joan shrugged. "Why be sorry?"

"I mean you'd think a father and son ought to have more to say to each other. . . ."

She smiled at him affectionately, understanding, and put her hand under his arm and pressed his arm close to her so that he could feel her breast brushing against him. "You really are a dear man," she said. "If only you'd stop worrying about everything."

"You mean about Edith Parkes? I said I'd tell you about Edith Parkes."

"Don't. I don't care about her. Let's just talk about ourselves tonight. You're a very nice person, Mr. Gattone."

"And you're a very nice girl, Miss Leonard," Frank said, feeling suddenly happier than he had for a long, long time.

Chapter Eighteen

MISS CALHOUN was taking dictation. She sat in a leather chair to one side of Mitchel Slayton's desk, her beautiful legs crossed, the spiral notebook propped on her knee as she wrote swiftly in shorthand.

Usually Mitchel dictated quickly and surely, rarely correcting his own words regardless of how important the letter might be. And always Miss Calhoun read back each word without having made a single mistake, without a moment's hesitation. Today, though, Mitchel could not concentrate. He corrected himself. He discarded entire sentences. He was angry with himself, and he did not know why. It seemed to him that there was something he ought to be remembering about this day, something special, but he could not for the life of him think what it was. He glanced at the calendar—June 8—but it didn't at the moment mean anything to him. It was just another day.

As always, when aware of his own failings, he took his anger out on his secretary. "That was not what I said, Miss Calhoun!" And, "What's the matter with you today, Miss Calhoun?"

"I'm sorry, Mr. Slayton."

"All right. Don't apologize." He rose, looked out of the large window, his hands propped on the sill. What was I supposed to do today? he thought. But maybe it wasn't anything. Maybe it was just that visit from his son-in-law that had upset him. The way he was always upset when he talked about Anita.

Behind him he heard Miss Calhoun rise and move toward the door. "Please stay," he said, turning to her.

"Aren't we through, Mr. Slayton?" she said.

"Yes."

"But you want me to stay?"

"Please sit down." He looked at her crossed legs, the brown hair piled neatly on her head, the gray eyes, the conservative tweed suit. "How old are you, Miss Calhoun?"

"Twenty-five."

"Rhoda."

"Yes, sir."

"There's no reason why I shouldn't call you Rhoda?"

"No, sir."

"You're a good secretary, Rhoda. I'm sorry I spoke crossly to you."

"That's all right, Mr. Slayton." She looked at him, curious, trying to guess what was in his mind.

"Do you remember, Rhoda, a few weeks ago?" Mitchel Slayton said. "I asked if you'd give an old man the pleasure of your company some evening."

"Yes. I remember."

"I'd like it to be tonight. Unless you're otherwise engaged."

"No, I'm free tonight," she said, masking her surprise.

"I want you to get all dressed up. An evening dress. The works."

"I'm afraid I . . ."

"You may leave the office early. As soon as you finish these letters. I have an account at Bonwit's. Go there and buy a dress, shoes, a fur stole—whatever you need. I'll pick you up at seven-thirty, and we'll have dinner some place. All right?"

Miss Calhoun seemed hesitant. "I don't think . . . Well," she said demurely, "letting you buy my clothes . . ."

"I want to buy them. No strings attached. I'll call Bonwit's immediately, tell them you're coming in. For some reason, tonight I want to go out. I want you to go with me. That's all."

"But . . . I mean . . ."

"No need to be conventional about it. After all, I'm old enough to be your father."

"Oh, I wasn't thinking of that, Mr. Slayton."

"I have your address," he said crisply. "Go along now and finish your letters. I'll see you at seven-thirty."

When she had left the office, Mitchel continued to sit behind his desk. He stared vacantly at the antique guns that lined the walls. He'd acted on impulse and was not certain why. Frank Gattone's visit, perhaps. But why? And why Miss Calhoun? Rhoda. This ridiculous business of going out with a young, beautiful girl, showing her off, showing himself off, making a fool of himself. What was the matter with him, anyway? Ever since Roberta, those long years ago, he'd had nothing to do with a woman. Nothing serious, at any rate. Now that he was older, and presumably wiser, there should be less reason, less desire. Except the same loneliness, of course, deeper than ever. Maybe it would be better if he called the whole thing off. Now, before it went any further. Nothing good could come of his impulse.

Hesitant, he was about to reach for the buzzer when the phone rang. It was a Mrs. Mauldin, Miss Calhoun said, calling from Plimpton Ridge.

"Yes?

Mrs. Mauldin's voice came shouting over the wire. Like many people who are hard of hearing, she thought she had to shout to make herself heard. "Mr. Slayton! . . . It's about Mrs. Slayton, sir! . . . She says you promised to take her to the Jehovah's Witness meeting tonight in Danbury. . . . She's fit to be tied because you haven't been home all week or called or anything."

"Tonight?" Mitchel Slayton looked at his calendar. June 8!

168

Of course! That was why he had felt all along there was something special about the day he ought to be remembering.

"Yes, sir, tonight!" Mrs. Mauldin's voice clamored in his ear. "She's fit to be tied."

"Mrs. Mauldin!" He was shouting himself now. "Mrs. Slayton can't go to Danbury. You know that as well as I do."

"What?"

Exasperated, he repeated what he had said. Mrs. Mauldin shrilled back that she knew it was ridiculous, but Mrs. Slayton was insisting. He had promised, and why did he promise in the first place?

I thought she'd forget, he excused himself lamely. And then aloud, into the phone, "Never mind. Just tell her I'm busy. I'll see her on Sunday."

"Well, I can't be responsible."

"Responsible for what, Mrs. Mauldin?"

"I don't know. Except she's raising Cain, and I just want you to know . . . whatever happens, I ain't responsible."

Mitchel warned her that he was counting on her, then hung up and sat there wondering what, exactly, Mrs. Mauldin had meant about not being responsible. What possibly could happen to a disturbed old woman who spent all her time in a rocking chair, talking to her cat, and seemed perfectly content in her own strange world? So she wouldn't get to Danbury tonight. The world wouldn't fall to pieces because of that.

It was true he had promised, and he supposed he could still make it if he left the office right away. But he had no intention of doing so. It was strange, how the mind worked. A few minutes ago he had been on the point of calling off his dinner date with Miss Calhoun. Now, finding that date threatened, he was stubbornly determined to keep it, regardless of any promise he might have made his wife. After all, when you got right down to it, what did he still owe her, after all these years?

169

Once, long ago, she'd been young and quite pretty. Forty-two years ago now. Nineteen-eighteen with the war just over, himself quite a hero in his Captain's khakis, considering he was only nineteen. He'd gone into his father's business after graduating from Yale. He'd sowed his wild oats in the roaring twenties, and married a flapper from New Haven—Lottie Trexler, whom he'd taken to many a house party, young, gay, of a good family, a promising wife for a promising young man.

What had gone wrong to change the picture so? Nothing he could put his finger on, although he supposed there must have been a definite point when he realized he was disappointed in his marriage. Lottie never seemed to be interested in the business, or, what was more important, in her children. She always had to be the belle of the ball, as if the twenties had fixed their mark of wayward youth on her forever. Only she was not getting any younger, that was plain, while for his own part he had lost interest in his home and family. For him, the business had become paramount. Until Roberta came on the scene, and he had felt his emotional life born anew. Everything seemed so fresh, so possible, with the brown-haired, gray-eyed girl who believed in him, trusted him, and clung to him with an honest affection that his wife, his children, never displayed.

Love? How could you tell? A man in his mid-forties, a girl in her early twenties. Need? Desire? Whatever it was, it was good, even right, in its own way. Perhaps Roberta had kept him from leaving his wife in a restless search that would have led him nowhere.

And yet, in the end, what seemed right at the time was not right at all. In the end there was nothing but shame, and fear, and disgrace. Roberta deserted by her husband; Christina fatherless, bewildered, bound to pay all her life for a sin that was none of her doing. Himself in this restless, lonely state, unable to recapture the past, knowing only and always a sense of loss.

170

And Lottie, sick in mind and body, holding his sin against him, keeping the knowledge inside herself all those years.

There was a knock at the door, and Miss Calhoun looked in through the doorway. "I'm leaving now." She smiled. "Unless you've changed your mind."

"No, I haven't changed my mind."

"Seven-thirty, then."

"Seven-thirty."

The door closed. Mitchel Slayton took up the phone and made his call to Bonwit Teller's.

"Mrs. Mauldin is in the kitchen, Mattykins. . . . If I listen very carefully, I can hear her clattering about. . . . Mitchel is not going to take me to Danbury. No, not taking me to Danbury . . . not keeping his promise. . . . Now be quiet, Mattykins. No mewing, no meowing. . . . We'll have no nonsense, shall we? There now . . . softly, softly . . . on little cat's feet. That's very good, little cat's feet, Mattykins. . . . Down the stairs . . . hold tight to the bannister. Not you, silly. Cats can't hold on to bannisters. . . . Now then, my coat. *Ssh* . . . Mrs. Mauldin has stopped banging the pans. . . . But the water's running, so she can't hear us, Mattykins. No she can't. . . . So out the door we go . . . except you'll have to stay behind. Not that I wouldn't like you to go, Mattykins . . . but don't you worry. God looks after his cats, too. You'll rise again, Mattykins . . . one of the chosen . . . and I'll put in a good word for you. . . . I simply can't for Mitchel, and of course I can't for that Roberta Farnham, either. You'll take their place, my lovely Mattykins. . . . Good-by, now . . . Good-by. . . .

"How lovely the night is. A new moon in the dark trees. It's been so long . . . I can't remember. . . . But there's the bandstand on the green, and the taxi is down the way, of course. Old Pete. . . . He has that atrocious rattling old cab, it'll be a terribly uncomfortable ride. . . . Thank the Lord it's only a few miles to Danbury . . . to my Savior . . . to my promise to rise again. . . . How do you do, Mrs. Brummer. Don't you recognize me, Lottie Slayton? Why, you were at my tea only last week . . . or the week before . . . it was so long ago, I suppose. . . . And you walk by without a glance. . . . Heavens, the manners of some people. Manners? Hah! Morals is more like it. Imagine Mitchel galivanting around with that young secretary of his. Oh, he doesn't know I know but I know all right. . . . Fooling me, are you, Mitchel? . . . Well, my eyes are open. Nobody's fooling Lottie Slayton. . . .

"It's all over, Mitchel . . . everything's ruined. . . . Now you won't even take me to Danbury, because you're out with that Roberta Farnham again. . . . Oh Mitchel, Mitchel, you've destroyed us all. Mitchel, my deceiving husband, my sinful husband, you've destroyed us all. . . . For that you shall rot in Hell, while all we others, we band of sisters and brothers, we faithful who are chosen in the eyes of our Lord . . . we shall all rise in singing and rejoicing. While you, Mitchel, you and your paramour shall wallow in lust in the great hot fires below. . . . And I shall sing and sing, and Mattykins will rejoice, purring beside me. . . ."

All evening Mitchel had brooded, oppressed by his thoughts, by his sense of wrongdoing, not toward the pretty girl who was his companion and tried to cheer him, but toward his wife. In the cab, at the Harwyn for cocktails, at 21 for dinner, all the way back to his apartment on Park Avenue, under his suave and mannered poise he felt ill at ease.

"I like to come back here some day for lunch," he said to Rhoda Calhoun as they were going up in the elevator. He paid no attention to her conventional protestations. Foolish girl! he thought. As if at my age I am likely to rob her of her virtue —if she still has it, that is, which is doubtful.

172

They had talked little, laughed little, at dinner or on the way back to the apartment. "You have wonderful taste, Rhoda. I like the dress. . . . So you come from Chicago, do you? . . . You're really a very beautiful girl. . . . Oh, so you went to Wellesley. . . . Why didn't you get yourself a stole?"

She explained that she did not like any ostentation. Actually, she knew it was not wise to seem too greedy on her first shopping tour. Let things take their course and the stole would become a coat. Play it smart enough, and the secretary could become an executive. Not that she was the gold-digging type, she told herself self-righteously. But if Mitchel Slayton really liked her . . .

Rhoda Calhoun sat with a Scotch highball balanced on her knee, and watched her employer as he moved back and forth across the long living room of his very modern and very cold-looking, expensive apartment.

"Something bothering you, Mitchel?" she said. He'd insisted she call him by his first name after their first three drinks together at the Harwyn, after his leg touched hers under the table and he'd observed the cleavage revealed by her carefully selected dress.

"No, I'm all right," he answered vaguely. "Nothing important."

"Have another drink, Mitchel. Forget your troubles tonight. I've had such a good time."

"Yes . . . of course."

He went to the bar, mixed himself a highball. He'd had quite a bit already, Rhoda thought, though at least he carried it well. As a matter of fact, he was quite handsome with his silvery hair and his tall, slender body under the beautifully tailored tuxedo. No sign of a pot belly. He was probably still as virile as he'd been twenty years ago.

Highball in hand, he came over and sat beside her on the sofa. He observed her profile—so young, so pleasing, he thought, yet without that innocence he had mistakenly believed to be there—let his eyes drop to the half-exposed, inviting breasts, then rose and moved to a chair some distance away. He stared into his glass, silent, brooding again.

"Mitchel . . ."

He looked up at her. "Yes?"

"Do you want me to leave?"

"No. I'm sorry, my dear. I don't know what's the matter with me tonight." Only I do know, he thought. Why am I lying to myself?

"You're lonesome. At least, that's what you said."

When he did not say anything, she added, "And you still are . . . lonesome. That's not very flattering to me, is it?"

"No, I don't suppose it is." He twirled the ice in his glass. "I'm afraid I'm not much company for a young woman like yourself. I thought . . . well, I thought maybe I still could be. I've made quite a fool of myself."

"But, Mitchel," Rhoda said, all sympathy as she leaned toward him. "You mustn't say that."

"No matter. At least you were kind enough to have dinner with me."

"Kind?" She smiled faintly. "I'm afraid you don't really understand me at all."

He looked at her piercingly, aroused by a certain suggestiveness in her voice. "No, I suppose not," he said vaguely, looking away.

"You're just a little, lost boy, aren't you, Mitchel?" It sounded corny, of course, Rhoda had to admit to herself. But if he wanted sympathy, if he wanted his youth again, it didn't matter much what she said. "You're afraid you're not attractive any more, isn't that it? But really, you are, you know. Terribly attractive." And after a pause, "To me, anyway."

Mitchel smiled wryly. "Please don't flatter me."

174

"But I meant every word of it." She gave him a slow, sidelong smile, unmistakably flirtatious, and he thought, I'd better send her home, now, before it's too late. Instead, he put down his glass and went over to her. She rose to meet him.

Her mouth was soft, warm, and his hands moved restlessly across her back. She pressed all her body against him, ran her tongue along his lips, caressed the small of his back, until she could feel the passion rising in him, then laughed nervously and pulled back out of his arms. "Rhoda," he said, his voice parched with desire, and she touched his lips with her fingers and whispered, "Don't say anything, dear," and then, "Lord, my make-up must be a mess. Do you mind if I fix up a little?"

"Off the hallway," he said. "And there's another bath in the bedroom."

She chose the bedroom, as she felt sure he wanted her to, and standing before the long mirror above the dresser, applied fresh lipstick and brushed out her hair, trying to make up her mind what she should do and what he expected. The telephone rang in the living room. "Oh damn!" she swore softly. She could hear snatches of what Mitchel was saying. He sounded so anxious. "Yes? . . . You're sure? . . . When? . . ." Small questions, excited exclamations.

Rhoda pursed her lips, looked at the big bed reflected in the mirror. Should she or shouldn't she? It was all very perplexing . . . especially with an old man who was, after all, her employer. If Mitchel were less preoccupied, she could play it differently, more subtly. The way things stood, however, she would have to play it all the way or risk losing out completely.

She undressed quickly, hung her clothes in the closet, then pulled back the covers and slipped into the large double bed. Mitchel was still talking on the phone. "All right now . . . listen very carefully. . . . Mrs. Mauldin, are you listening? . . . Telephone Mrs. Barker. . . . That's right, Mrs. Paul Barker

175

. . . Roberta Barker!" He was shouting as though Mrs. Mauldin were deaf, whoever Mrs. Mauldin was, going on about notifying Roberta Barker, whoever she might be.

The phone was slammed down. Rhoda squirmed under the covers. For a moment she felt a twinge of panic, then, remembering the way he had kissed her, the feel of his passion rising, pressing against her, she felt reassured. She would say, "I know you're lonely, Mitchel. I know you want me. You can have me, tonight and any night you like." Once she got him to bed, the rest would be simple. You could get anything out of an old man, once his passions were aroused. It could all be so much worth her while.

The silence in the other room worried her. She sat up, propped a pillow behind her and pulled up the sheet so that it half covered her breasts, leaving her arms and shoulders bare in the soft light shed by the lamp on the night table. She wet her lips. "Mitchel," she called. "Where are you, Mitchel?" She heard his footsteps approaching, and then he was standing in the doorway.

He was looking at her, but he did not seem to see her. He seemed distraught, suddenly haggard. "My wife," he said. "I promised . . . She went to Danbury alone . . . I should have kept my promise . . ." He was not talking to her. She might just as well not be there. He turned away to go back to the living room.

"Mitchel . . . for God's sake!"

He turned back slowly, and now, for the first time, he seemed to notice her. His eyes moved over her hair and shoulders, and she lowered the sheet so her breasts were exposed, and he stared at them, too, then laughed harshly. "You really thought," he said, "that's all I wanted."

Then she heard the outer door close and she knew he was gone.

Rhoda sat motionless in the bed. She felt numb, bewil-

176

dered, humiliated, until finally, dressing, bewilderment and humiliation turned to rage. She stormed into the living room, picked up an ashtray, and flung it against the row of bottles lining the bar. One of the bottles broke, spilling glass and liquor on the thick carpet.

"You stupid old man!" she screamed. "You've made me sick, you old bastard."

It was not until some minutes later, on her way down in the elevator, that Rhoda Calhoun wondered whether or not she should report for work tomorrow morning. She decided she would. Just for spite, if nothing else.

Chapter Nineteen

ROBERTA awoke from a fitful sleep to hear the telephone ringing insistently. She groped for the switch on the bed lamp, then came fully conscious and swung out of bed.

Christina called, "Mother!"

"I'll get it, dear." She padded downstairs in her bare feet, picked up the phone and listened to a hysterically shouting woman she had heard of, but never actually seen in her life.

"It's Mrs. Mauldin, ma'am. Mr. Slayton—he said to call you. He said young Mr. Slayton's in Paris and Miss Anita wouldn't know what to do, so he said to call you . . ." on and on, until finally it became clear exactly what happened.

"How long ago?" Roberta asked.

"When I was doing the dishes, I guess. About seven-thirty.

After that I sat in the living room and watched the television. Mr. Slayton doesn't mind when he's not here. I could see the stairs from the living room, and suddenly I saw Mattykins . . . that's her cat, and he's never loose around the house, I mean you never see him without her . . ."

Roberta said she'd do what she could. "No, don't call the police. If Mr. Slayton's on his way from New York, I'll meet him in Danbury. It will take him a couple of hours. Don't worry and don't blame yourself, Mrs. Mauldin. Good-by."

It was ten minutes before eleven. Christina appeared on the stairs in her pajamas to ask what had happened.

"Nothing . . . an old friend of your father's, sick in Danbury. I'll take a cab to the cottage, then we'll both go together in the car." She rushed back up the stairs to dress. All the time Christina kept asking questions Roberta could not answer honestly. And all the time she wondered why Mitchel had asked her, why her of all people. She was the last person on earth who'd be able to handle Lottie Slayton.

Christina called for a cab, and ten minutes later old Pete rattled up in his shivering Ford.

"Danbury," Roberta told him. "There's a meeting there of the Jehovah's Witnesses."

"Now ain't that a coincidence for you?" Pete said. "You're the second person I've taken there tonight. Except you're kind of late, ain't you?"

"The second? Who was the first?"

"An old lady. Couldn't be sure who she was. Something about her reminded me of Mrs. Slayton, except of course it couldn't have been her. She hasn't been out of the house for years."

"No," Roberta said. "It couldn't have been Mrs. Slayton."

The cab rattled on along the country roads under the black trees and the sky that was beginning to show cloud banks to the west and occasional far-away flashes of lightning, eight miles to

178

Danbury, on through the lighted town, north another five miles, and then a turn down a long, graveled road to a large picnic area on the edge of a lake.

Lights streamed down on rows of benches that faced a high platform near the lake's edge. The benches were filled with men and women of all ages. They leaned forward, listening intently to the words of the fiery speaker echoing, reverberating, through a temporary P.A. system.

"Shall I wait for you, Mrs. Barker?"

"No, thank you, Pete."

"I never figured you for a Jehovah's Witness."

She gave him a generous tip, then stepped out and moved slowly along the rows of people, searching for someone she hadn't seen for at least fifteen years—a white-haired woman with glasses, wearing a plain black dress according to the meager description given by the hysterical Mrs. Mauldin.

The speaker's voice roared in the night air. "Many of us were alive in 1914, when the spirit of Christ returned to this earth. . . . We are now in a period of transition, and the end must come before many of us here shall leave this earth."

The people leaned forward, as if drawn by invisible chords toward the speaker—an old man, twisted, bearded, hunched over his gnarled cane; a fat woman with widespread legs, who mumbled incessantly; a teen-age girl with her eyes large and bright and wild beneath the glaring lights.

"How many of you, how many can prove that you will be among the 144,000 to reign in Heaven? How many of you will remain on earth, the other sheep, destined to rule the risen dead for one thousand years, offering them one final chance to become a Witness? And after that—the second Armageddon, when Satan will be permanently vanquished, when all the faithful, including the risen dead who become good Witnesses— they shall then inherit the earth. And those who failed to become Witnesses, they shall return to everlasting death."

A small boy was eating popcorn from a soggy bag. A middle-aged woman was nursing her child under the protection of a torn raincoat.

"God's kingdom rules—is the world's end near?"

"Yes!" from the exulting crowd. "Yes, the world's end is near."

"Very near?"

"Yes, very near . . . very near. . . . The world's end is near, very near, very near," the crowd answered in a singsong chant which ended abruptly when the speaker raised his hand, lowered his voice, and spoke calmly to the hushed throng. "So now, fellow Witnesses, God will be near you. Go back to your churches, your Kingdom Halls, where you alone, of all peoples on this earth, shall find everlasting shelter when Armageddon strikes."

The faithful rose. They sang to the recorded sound of an organ, their voices high, off-key, making up in enthusiasm what they lacked in tone. Then they moved off toward their waiting cars at the edge of the park—the old man crawling, his beard touching the hand that held the cane; the young boy still eating popcorn; the fat woman waddling, still mumbling; the mother sheltering her child under the torn raincoat; the teen-age girl still singing as though unaware that the meeting was over.

Roberta stood at the narrow gate through which they jostled and pushed as they streamed toward their cars. She scanned every face, started a dozen times toward one elderly woman or another, becoming more and more unsure. A black dress . . . glasses . . . white hair. But there were so many old women in black, many wearing glasses. . . . Cars started up, drove away, their tires crunching on the gravel. The speaker had gone, the benches were empty; only the litter remained, paper bags and spilled popcorn, old newspapers and copies of *Watchtower* and *Awake*. Then, in another moment, the lights went out, the last car crunched away, and there was only darkness, lit by intermittent flashes of lightning.

Roberta groped her way to the nearest bench and sank into it, exhausted, uncertain of what to do next. She should have told the taxi to wait. She should have stopped the speaker and asked if he'd seen anyone who resembled Mrs. Slayton. The papers rustled around her in the darkness. A tree frog set up a far-off, croaking sound, and somewhere down the lake a loon screamed. She gripped the edge of the bench, suddenly afraid, and tried to tell herself there was no reason for fear. Now that her eyes had become accustomed to the darkness, she could make out the shadowy forms around her.

She saw something move near the speaker's platform. She straightened up, waited, heard the sound again, and called out in a frightened voice, "Mrs. Slayton! . . . Is that you, Mrs. Slayton?"

No answer, yet the sounds continued. Metal against metal, a scratching sound, and then abruptly, swelling forth into the night, an organ playing "Rock of Ages," and faintly, over the long-held chords, a woman singing.

"Mrs. Slayton!" She rushed toward the speaker's stand, stumbling against benches, bruising her shins, groping in the dark until she reached the large metal box that held the recording machine. A woman sat on the ground beside it. She was white-haired; she wore a black dress and rimless glasses.

The woman did not move. Roberta could feel her eyes fixed upon her, could hear her singing even after the record had come to an end. She groped her way to the metal box and turned off the machine. "Mrs. Slayton," she said gently.

"That's my favorite hymn," the old woman said.

"I've come to take you home, Mrs. Slayton. Your husband will be along shortly, and he'll drive us both home."

"I shall be among the chosen."

"Yes. . . . Please get up, Mrs. Slayton." Roberta saw her

face plainly in a sudden flash of lightning, the eyes staring blankly as if seeing something beyond the night. And she realized that Mrs. Slayton must have seen her face just as plainly, for now the old lady said, "Not you . . . not Mitchel."

"Please, Mrs. Slayton."

"Because you're sinning with my husband."

For a moment Roberta was too shocked, too taken aback, to say anything. "No, you've never seen me, Mrs. Slayton," she said at last firmly. "I'm Mrs. Barker. My husband teaches at the Academy."

"I know you, Roberta Farnham . . . I saw you. You didn't know about all the little things I found in Mitchel's pockets. Oh, I know, I know. You're both sinners, and you shall return to everlasting death."

Roberta touched the woman's arm. She did not resist, but rose slowly to her feet and brushed out her clothes.

"Mrs. Slayton . . . we can sit on a bench. . . . It won't be long now. Just a few minutes more before your husband arrives."

But the older woman was not listening. She peered into Roberta's face, gripped her arm. "You're young, my child," her voice squeaked with excitement. "The Lord says to forgive, and I forgive you, because you're only a child and cannot see the error of your ways." Her voice rose, inspired by her intentions. "There's still time . . . still time. You must become a Witness!" Another flash of lightning, followed by a long rumble of thunder. "Yes, God has spoken. You must become a Witness now, before it is too late. You must wash away your sins. . . . Baptized in holy water . . . and then cleansed of soul and body, you can face your God on the last day of this earth. . . ."

The woman's grip on Roberta's arm was surprisingly strong as she pulled her, stumbling, toward the lake, talking all the while, pleading, begging her to save herself. Roberta protested, tried to pull back but then gave in, frightened, until they reached the dark lapping water of the lake. Mrs. Slayton waded in, her hand still firm on Roberta's arm.

The water was cold against her legs, her thighs, the small of her back. "No, Mrs. Slayton, please, no!" she cried, and then she felt the strong arms pushing her down and under, heard as she raised her head above the surface again the woman's intoning voice. Blindly she stumbled toward the shore.

Mrs. Slayton remained waist-deep in the murky water. She stood motionless, facing out toward the far shore and the fast-gathering clouds in the black sky. "It's coming," she said, and then, as the lightning flashed and thunder rumbled in the hills across the lake, she cried out, "It's here . . . Armageddon is here!" in a last exultant burst of triumph before she swayed, faltered, and fell face downward in the water.

She was a heavy woman, and Roberta, slight and never very strong, had to exert all her strength to drag the inert body to the shore. Now the old lady lay with the upper half of her body on the muddy bank. She was still conscious, but her face was twisted in pain and she clawed at her breast with one dripping hand. A flash of lightning illuminated her face, her eyes bright, ecstatic in pain. Her white hair lay flat and wet in the mud, and now, in the increasingly frequent flashes of lightning, Roberta could see that she was smiling through her pain, as if she were seeing a vision of her God in the thunderous sky above her.

She tried to drag the woman further onto dry land, but could not budge her. "Oh God!" she cried, then shouted "Mitchel! . . . Mitchel! . . . Someone, help!" and ran frantically toward the speaker's stand, then turned and rushed back to the stricken woman. "Just lie still, Mrs. Slayton," she whispered as she knelt close to her. "Don't move, Mrs. Slayton."

The wrinkled lips moved. "You are saved, Roberta . . . on the day of Armageddon. . . . Baptized and saved on this very day when the earth is coming to an end."

183

"Mrs. Slayton!" Roberta wailed. "Oh God, why doesn't Mitchel come?"

"And poor Mitchel shall return to everlasting death. . . . Poor Mitchel . . . he would not be baptized, and I can't forgive him. I shall rise to Heaven, and I shall look down upon his dead soul, and I shall never forgive him." Her eyes closed wearily. She coughed, gasped for breath, said, " 'Rock of Ages' . . . play 'Rock of Ages . . .' "

Roberta stared distraught at the woman, then rose and stumbled wildly to the metal box beside the speaker's platform. She lifted the lid, fumbled blindly with the unseen knobs until after a moment she felt the turntable moving under her hand, found the arm of the instrument, and placed the needle on the record's edge.

The thunder rumbled and crashed like Rip Van Winkle's bowling balls; the lightning flashed almost continuously and close among the trees; and over all the organ swelled and swelled, the music defying the menace of the skies. . . . "Rock of Ages cleft for me . . . Let me hide myself in Thee . . ."

Awed, terrified, Roberta stood riveted to the spot. And then, all at once, the rain fell, torrentially, and she rushed madly back to the stricken woman lying at the lake's edge.

The woman who had been Mrs. Slayton lay with her eyes wide open, staring unseeing at the riven skies, the relentless rain. Her hands were folded carefully over her breast, and on her mouth a contented smile seemed fixed for all eternity. She had taken her place on Mount Zion, called to reign in heaven among "the hundred forty and four thousand," at peace forever in the lap of God.

Roberta knelt weeping in the mud. "You're dead," she cried to the rain-soaked, infinitely removed face, as if she might order it back to life. "You're dead . . . you're dead." And then suddenly the dead woman, the dark, the storm, the continuing rain thundering in the trees, struck terror to her heart. She stumbled up the bank, across the rain-soaked picnic grounds, not knowing where she was going, only running away, away from terror and death . . . until she saw the lights of a car shining through the rods of rain, saw Mitchel striding toward her, and "Daddy! Daddy!" she screamed, flinging herself into the big comfort of his arms.

By three o'clock it was all over. Mitchel had driven his wife's body to the hospital, where Lottie was pronounced dead. Roberta had called Christina to say that she might not be back until morning. A nurse had insisted she get out of her wet clothing, take a hot bath at the hospital, and had lent her a white uniform. It was all over, and the rain had stopped, too, and she was sitting beside Mitchel as the car drove slowly over the wet macadam road toward Plimpton Ridge.

Mitchel looked old and tired and sad as he sat disheveled behind the wheel in his damp and crumpled tuxedo, his black tie undone, hanging loose against his mud-spattered shirt. He tried to light a cigarette with the car's lighter, but his hand shook so Roberta had to help him. He said, "Thank you," and then, after a long pause, "How strange it is. For years Lottie and I hardly ever spoke. Half the time she didn't even recognize me. Under the circumstances, if I were being realistic about this, I suppose I should feel relieved. But I'm not. I feel lost. I don't know . . . perhaps I needed her sickness. But something I didn't want is gone, and now I shall miss it. I'll miss the simple knowledge that she's upstairs in her rocking chair . . . just the knowledge that she's there."

Roberta did not say anything as they drove on, until suddenly she blurted out, "She knew who I was, Mitchel. She forgave me."

"Oh?" He stared straight ahead along the winding road, the unspoken question hanging there between them.

"She forgave you, too," Roberta lied.

He drove on in silence. Roberta smoothed the white uniform across her lap. She felt sorry for Mitchel, and wished there was something she could do to help him. Hours before, in a moment of wild terror, she had called him "Daddy," and only now it occurred to her how strange it was that she should call him that after all these years.

After a while Mitchel said, "What are you thinking?"

"That finally . . . I like you again. For years now, no matter what I told myself, no matter how much I loved Paul, I was always trying to find you in Paul. I knew it and I hated myself for it. I loved Paul for himself, and yet always, there in the background—there you were. Someone to run to if things ever got bad enough. Maybe that's why I never really insisted that Paul leave Plimpton, even when I talked to him about it. I wanted you near me. I felt safe with you near."

"But now," he said, "now you're free of me, so you can honestly like me. What makes you feel so sure?"

"I suppose because I'm stronger than I thought."

Mitchel smiled faintly. "Or because I'm weaker than you thought." He drove on another mile or so, the smile still on his lips, until suddenly he braked the car at the side of the road and hid his face in his arms on the wheel and sobbed out his grief and weariness of soul.

"All right . . . all right," he said at last, straightening in his seat and starting the motor again. "I'm sorry. I'll take you home now."

"I'd rather you took me to the cottage," Roberta said, trying to sound matter-of-fact. It was a terrible experience to see a strong man break down and cry like a little child, and she pretended that nothing unusual had happened.

"Why the cottage?" Mitchel said. "Paul?"

"Yes."

"At this hour? It's going on to four o'clock."

"It doesn't matter. I must see Paul."

186

"Yes. I understand. You need him. Now and forever—more than anything. I die and he lives, and we both know it, and that's exactly the way it ought to be." He stepped hard on the accelerator, and the big black Cadillac hummed over the macadam, made a sharp turn, and bumped and splashed down the muddy road that led to the cottage on the lake's edge.

"Good night, my dear," he said, taking her hand. "And thank you for all you have done for me this night."

She leaned to him and kissed his cheek. "Good-by, Mitchel." She got out of the car and closed the door and stood there as the car lurched back up the road and out of sight, before she turned hopefully toward the dark little cottage.

Paul Barker was awakened from sleep by someone knocking at the door. He looked at the luminous hands of the loud-ticking alarm clock, noted it was quarter of four, and wondered who could be at the door at this hour.

He slipped from the bunk, groped for the light switch, and opened the door to find Roberta standing there in her white nurse's uniform. He had never seen her look so tired. She leaned against the doorway, said, "Paul . . . I had to see you."

He pulled the door wide, and she came in and slumped in the old wicker chair.

"Why the nurse's uniform?" he said. "How did you get here?"

"I'll explain . . . Mitchel . . ."

"Sure. Mitchel!"

"Listen to me, Paul. Please listen."

"I'm listening." He sat down on the edge of the bunk and waited for her to speak, and then she told him what had happened, the whole ghastly experience. When she had finished telling him, she was in tears. "God, I need you, Paul," she sobbed. "I want to stay here tonight. . . . I want you to come home with me tomorrow."

"You need me," he said, with a touch of sarcasm.

"I love you, Paul. Can't you understand?"

"Am I supposed to believe that?"

"You must believe it. It's true, it's true."

"I doubt it."

"All right, Paul," Roberta said, drying her tears. "But can I stay, and will you come home tomorrow? If not for my sake, at least for Christina's, at least for a few weeks. Then school will be over and you can do anything you like."

"I've already found another job."

She looked at him questioningly, wondering how he could speak of a job now when her heart was breaking.

"In Pennsylvania. A very good school near Harrisburg. I'll teach summer classes, then become a regular instructor in the fall."

She remained silent for some time, looking down at her hands folded in her lap. Then very softly, as though she realized only now that her husband was really leaving her, she said, "It's all over with us, isn't it, Paul?"

"Yes."

"You're happy about it?"

"No, I'm miserable about it."

"Than you won't mind if I stay tonight?"

Paul shrugged.

"And you'll come home tomorrow? Stay until school ends . . . until you go to Pennsylvania?"

"As you like."

She rose from her chair, said, "I have no pajamas," and he said, "You can use a pair of mine," and took a green pair from the cupboard he'd fashioned so proudly two summers ago. She undressed before him, and he thought how odd it was that all the intimate things in marriage could continue like this, everything personal, open, exactly the same as it was before, except you said different words and you did not touch each other.

188

He wondered if she were deliberately teasing him, standing before him like that, wearing only the pajama bottom while she brushed out her hair, her breasts full and soft and her body achingly familiar to him, infinitely desirable. Then she slipped into the pajama coat and climbed the ladder to the top bunk. Paul switched off the light and got back into bed in the lower bunk.

Lying there in the darkness that seemed to him to quiver with Roberta's presence above him, he thought how, in the past, with Christina sharing the cottage, they'd made a wonderful game of being together. Since they could not share the same bunk, they would often lie awake, listening to Christina's breathing. Then Roberta would whisper, "Are you awake, darling?" and he'd say, "Yes," and she'd sigh, "It's a lovely night," and he'd answer, "I know," and they'd creep from the cabin, carrying a blanket with them, and make love under the stand of birch, and it was young and secret, and some of the finest moments of all.

Tonight, Christina was not here. Tonight they could make love in the cottage. Only they would never make love again, here or anywhere else.

Outside, he could hear the crickets and the tree toads, the rain dripping from the trees. Something stirred in the bushes. Roberta shifted position and the bunk creaked. Then her voice, soft, intimate, "Are you awake, Paul?"

"Yes, I'm awake."

"Do you know what I was thinking?"

"No."

"Yes, you do. And isn't it a rotten shame?"

He turned over with his face in the pillow, pressing his body hard against the mattress. Now, after all this time alone in the cottage, he wanted her so his whole body ached, and he knew he wouldn't sleep again this night. But he would not touch her . . . her body, so warm and soft and inviting . . . he would not touch her . . . could never touch her again.

Part Three

Part Three

Chapter Twenty

IT WAS about four o'clock that morning when Anita
was awakened by a phone call from her father, informing her
that her mother had died that night in Danbury. She asked
what her mother had been doing in Danbury, who had found
her there, exactly what had taken place, and when her father
told her, she said, "So you called Roberta instead of me."

Mitchel said, "Yes," wearily, with no attempt at an explana-
tion. He said the funeral would be the day after tomorrow—
the next day, really, since it was already almost daybreak—and
he'd appreciate it if Anita would help handle the details. He'd
already sent a cable to Roy in Paris.

Anita said she would do what she could, then hung up, and
thought that of course he had called Roberta because Roberta
was more his daughter than his own daughter was. She
wanted to tell Frank, only Frank wasn't home. He was staying
in New York, too busy to come home to his wife. God only
knew what Frank and his production girl were up to.

She wanted a drink, but she ought not to be drinking at this
time of night, and besides it was hardly the occasion. She sat on
the sofa in the living room and tried to remember something

good, something sentimental about her mother. She remembered how, when she was a child, her mother was always scolding her for not brushing her teeth, not brushing her hair properly. She'd been a tomboy, not training herself rightly to be the daughter of a clever, social woman. Nor had Roy suited his mother, either. He was too withdrawn, too blunt, with no promise of becoming the charming, witty gentleman Lottie could introduce to her guests, while she held her son's arm and he called her "Mater." So out with Roy, and out with herself, the gangling tomboy, a disgrace to her mother because of her refusal to parade her good breeding.

Well, at fifteen she'd grown these high, firm breasts, and at sixteen, after her mother had made her leave a living room full of ladies having tea and scones because she was not properly dressed for the occasion, she'd gone over to the Academy and sneaked into the dormitory room of a boy she'd often played tennis with. He'd said, "For Pete's sake, Nita, you can't come in here," scared, because if they were caught he'd be expelled. But she'd taken off her clothes anyway, and slept with him under Plimpton Academy sheets, beneath a Plimpton Academy banner, and after that they had never played tennis again, which was the part she'd regretted most.

"Poor Mother," Anita sighed. "Poor, ridiculous, dead Mother." She ought to tell Frank. This morning she'd help out with the funeral arrangements, and then in the afternoon she'd take Frank his clothes and have a good look at the people who worked with him. She'd stay with him overnight in a hotel and bring him back with her for the funeral. That was one thing he couldn't avoid, no matter how busy he claimed to be.

The telephone number Frank had given her was still scribbled there on the pad by the phone. She dialed, listened to the phone ring endlessly before Frank's sleepy voice said "Hello." She told him what had happened and he was very sympathetic. He sounded more disturbed than she was, Anita thought. Yes, he still expected her, and she mustn't forget his clothes. "Don't break down, honey," he said. "Death comes to everyone." What a lot of crap! That's the way they talked on TV. "I miss you, Frank," she said, and he said, "Me, too, honey."

"Good night, darling."

"Good night, honey." There was nothing like death to make two people feel close to each other. She held on to the receiver, and it seemed to her, in the second before the phone clicked down, that she heard a woman's voice saying, "Your wife?" though she may just have imagined it. Frank had really been very sweet, and she loved him, and she ought to control her jealous suspicions that never did her any credit anyway.

Mildred Slayton did not hear of her mother-in-law's death until nine o'clock that morning, when Anita called to say that she was in a great rush, what with the funeral arrangements and everything. Her father had cabled Roy, Anita said; there was nothing for Mildred to do except to be at the Dodd and Duncan Funeral Home at two o'clock the following afternoon.

The news affected Mildred deeply, and when she hung up after Anita's call she burst into tears, although it was not so much out of pity for the dead that she wept as pity for herself. She had never set eyes on her mother-in-law, would only see her now, for the first and last time, lying dead in her coffin. She had never been accepted as a Slayton and never would be. Her father-in-law would go on being Mr. Slayton to her; her own sister-in-law had not even bothered to tell her what had happened until hours later. An afterthought. To the Slaytons she could never be anything more than Millie Beatty, the letter carrier's daughter, who had somehow "trapped" Roy Slayton into marriage.

Mildred paced the empty house. The wide pine floors creaked beneath her feet. The stairs creaked weirdly by themselves. Lord, she hated this house. Roy had liked it, and she'd said yes, she liked it, too, because it was proper for the Slaytons to have an old house filled with genuine antiques. Well, she was sick of dusting antiques, sick of waxing floors with wide cracks that filled with dust. Why couldn't they have bought a nice, clean, split-level with everything new and shiny and modern? Why had she ever married Roy Slayton in the first place? Suddenly she decided she would go to her father's house, the only place where she ever felt really at home.

Her father, as usual, was in the garden, making preparations to grow the monstrous tomatoes he was so proud of, his prize-winning string beans, his strawberries the size of golf balls. He was still in his gray-blue postman's uniform, and was slightly embarrassed at being caught in his "working clothes."

"Just having a look," he explained, and led her through the fenced-in yard, up the steps and through the back door into the small frame house.

"Like some cold lemonade?" he asked. "Always did like it, didn't you, Millie?" He poured two large glasses from a pitcher, then led her through the shabbily furnished "parlor" to the front porch, where they sat in rocking chairs, side by side, looking out at the cars moving by, the shoppers on their way to market. As a child she had loved this porch, and she could still sit there alone, or with her father, for hours on end, just "watching the world go by," as he called it. Very closely, too, since the house was only two doors down from the main row of stores in the center of town, and the front yard had disappeared entirely when the new sidewalk had been put in, so that now they sat directly above the heads of those who passed and nodded, said, "Hello, Mr. Beatty. . . . How are you, Mildred?"

Her father sipped at his lemonade. He was small, a wisp of a man, with thin reddish hair and freckles on the top of his head, and a great ability to laugh at himself and his mundane job. "Walking may be the best exercise in the world," he said, "but I never met a postman yet who looked like he could lick a truck driver." He tilted back his hair, put his heavy black shoes against the rail, then lowered them again. The chair legs hit the floor with a sharp crack.

"Delivered mail at Mitchel Slayton's this morning," he said carefully. "Housekeeper told me what happened. . . . Guess you'll be going to the funeral."

"Yes, I guess so."

"Funny thing. The way I hear, Mr. Slayton called Mrs. Barker to go after his wife. Don't make sense to me."

"Well, Roy's in Paris, and perhaps Anita wasn't home. Anyway, he wouldn't call *me*," Mildred said bitterly.

Her father glanced up, then out at the street once more. "But why Mrs. Barker?"

"I don't know, and I don't care."

"Far as I know, Mrs. Barker'd never even seen Lottie Slayton. Lived in that place over the supermarket, worked for the old man, sure . . ." He shook his head. "Beats me."

Mildred propped her slacks-covered legs on the rail. "I've never seen Mrs. Slayton either. At least, not since I married Roy." She remembered a tall, rather haughty woman who always wore a hat and carried a funny little umbrella whether it was raining or not. "Guess I wasn't special enough."

"What's the matter, Millie?" her father said.

"Nothing."

"You seem all upset about something."

"Sometimes I wish I'd married Matt Barlow."

Her father groped in his pockets for a small pouch of tobacco, began rolling his own cigarette as he'd been doing for years.

"You got a nice house," he said finally.

"I hate it."

Her father lit his cigarette. The paper flared; the tobacco burned unevenly. "You got a good husband."

"I know."

"Matt Barlow's a bum. One job after another."

"I know. Roy's kind, decent, not like Matt. I know that. Maybe things would be different if we had children. You know, during the war Roy took care of a little Chinese-Hawaian girl— sort of adopted her. She's married now, Roy says, but he still sees her once in a while. I mean he's that kind—generous, loyal."

"So don't hurt him."

Mildred didn't say anything. She was examining her fingernails. I need a manicure, she thought.

"Matt Barlow's just a no-good bum."

"Matt's twenty-seven and I'm twenty-six and Roy's thirty-nine," Mildred said. "Only it's not a matter of age. There are other things. Matt's father ran a candy store and . . ." She'd been going to say, "And my father's a postman." But she could not say it, could not possibly explain that she still felt out of Roy's class, had never felt she really belonged in a class with the Slaytons. She'd thought that after she married Roy things would be different, but they weren't. She was only playing a game, pretending to be Roy's faithful wife, when way down deep she was still the same old Millie Beatty. Matt had her number. Matt knew everything about her.

Her father said, "After Roy's back—after the funeral—you'll feel different."

"I suppose," though she knew she wouldn't. "Well, I guess I'll be going along home," and dropped her feet to the floor and patted her father's thin shoulder and went down the steps to her car parked at the curb.

It was almost noon, and the day was very warm. The black slacks clung to her legs; the red sweater was too heavy for June. Yes, Matt Barlow was a bum, she thought as she drove slowly out of town. Her father was right; one job after another. She had not seen Matt for days and she wondered where he was working now.

The car needed gasoline. She turned around, headed back

198

through town, and pulled into the gas station. No need for her to wonder where Matt was working now. He wasn't. He was there by the gas station, his face hidden behind the open hood of his old Chevrolet as he tinkered with the motor.

"Fill her up?" a boy said.

"Yes," Mildred said, her voice huskier than usual, "fill her up," watching Matt's body stretched over the fender.

The gas meter clicked, and her heart seemed to tick with it, louder and louder, until suddenly Matt straightened up and saw her, and the bell rang as Matt looked at her.

"Hear your mother-in-law died," he called out, giving her his slow, lazy grin.

"Yes . . . last night."

"How come you're not at the Slaytons' place?"

Furious, she started the motor. Hands on hips, Matt stood watching her as she drove out of the station. Then he slammed down the hood of his car, got in, and drove off in the same direction.

It was not until she was a mile out of town that Mildred glanced in the mirror and noticed the Chevrolet behind her. She was not surprised, she'd rather expected it, though of course it might not be Matt's car at all. Most of the cars looked about the same anyway, except that some were old and some were new. She turned off on a side road. The Chevrolet followed. Yes, she thought, and Oh, God! and her heart began pounding again. Her slacks were hot and sticky, and she was glad that at least she hadn't worn a girdle. Stop that now! she thought, and she stepped hard on the accelerator.

The Chevrolet dropped behind, and then, when she had rounded another curve in the road, it was nowhere to be seen. So it hadn't been Matt, after all. It was just her imagination . . . wanting Matt to follow her . . . afraid of him.

Mildred drove toward home, felt quick relief as she turned in the drive past the black sign with the gold letters, went around the house and through the open doorway of the old barn that now served as a garage. The motor stopped. A bird fluttered under the glass cupola high above. It was hot in the barn. The place still smelled of old hay. She put her arms on the wheel and accidentally sounded the horn. The noise startled her. Carefully, she put her arms back on the wheel and rested her head on them. She could hear the beating of her heart.

It seemed a long time before she heard the car crunch into the drive, then the slow footsteps and the harsh grating sound of the overhead door as it was pulled shut. Darkness, with only a long stream of dusty light from the cupola . . . the chirping bird, trapped under the cobwebbed glass . . . the smell of hay . . . footsteps . . . while she waited, her heart thumping, her bosom heaving . . . waited in the stifling heat for Matt Barlow to take her again.

Chapter Twenty-One

THE girls of Paris . . . the Michelles and Babettes . . . the Simones and Colettes . . . the Giselles and Gabrielles . . . all beautiful, and all—it seemed to Roy—beautifully available for a modest fee. Those along the Champs-Élysées, the prettiest street in the world, and those on all the little side streets—the rue de Berri, the rue Marbeuf, the rue Pierre Charron. . . . Those who sat waiting, gay, lovely, confident, in the tiny, unnamed bistros around the Opéra or the Madeleine—the rue Bordereau, the rue Halvey, the rue Danielle Casanova. . . .

200

Those in the luxury apartments of the Champs-Élysées, where you were served champagne and hors d'oeuvres, and the girls were dressed by Dior and Balenciaga and Lanvin. . . . The girls on the Boulevard de Sebastopol, who stood in doorways, laughing with crimson lips, swinging their legs in their tight apache skirts, not so pretty as the uptown girls, the expensive girls who wore mink and drove Citroens, but more sentimental, more volatile, more full of life, full of love, so that you, knowing how untrue it was, were still quite certain you were the very first of all. . . . And the Left Bank girls, the teen-age, semi-pros who hung around the jazz joints near the Café Les Deux Magots. . . . The arty girls with pony tails, wearing slacks and men's shirts and sneakers, the girls without bras or panties, who sometimes took money, sometimes didn't, would prefer a weekend in the South, perhaps a meal, perhaps nothing at all but a new place to live and a few moments of new adventure. All the girls in Paris . . . and Paris in the spring. . . .

It was ridiculous of course, Roy knew. Nearly a week of wandering, searching. Fellow pilots said it happened on everyone's first run. They said, "You can't have 'em all, but try anyway. They're all the same, and in the end you'll sit with us in a hotel room and play poker and get drunk, and you won't even notice if you find a girl in your bed that night."

They didn't understand. Roy didn't quite understand himself. He did not want them all. He didn't want even one. Yet he took quite a number in those few, short days, and none was Hawaian-Chinese and none was Luanai, and none of it was wonderful. They were all the same in their professional approach that reminded him sometimes of his wife—all except Luanai, and she was the only woman on earth who was beautiful and lovely and different from the rest.

He'd known this on his first night in Paris, yet had moved on and on, trying to erase Luanai, trying to erase love, he supposed, trying to degrade himself, defile himself, trying desperately to make Luanai disappear into a dozen faces and arms and legs and breasts. But in the end, on the last night, she was still there inside his mind, his heart, while he sat in the ridiculous quarters of one Marie Juliette.

Marie owned a white bakery truck with twin doors that opened at the rear. On the side of the truck, she had painted *Vive Marie* in large red letters, completely unafraid of the police, because though the law stated that a "residence" could not be used for "immoral purposes," it said nothing about vehicles. So the police could do nothing but stand by helplessly, secretly amused, even pleased, while Marie chose her man, drove him to a side street, tumbled with him into the mattressed rear through a window above the driver's seat, and then, a suitable while later, let him exit ceremoniously, with dignity, through the two larger doors at the back of the truck.

It was dark inside. Marie said, "You are very sad, monsieur," and Roy said yes, he was, and Marie said that he could brood and she would talk and talk, and soon he would not be sad any longer, and then he would rather do something else than brood.

She talked about the old days, thirteen years ago now, when her mother had been the most popular girl in all Paris. The girls were licensed then, and they had legal houses with dance bands and little theatres for showing intimate little movies, and long bars with an accordianist singing "Boum!" or "Valentina" or "Madelon" while the girls mingled easily with prospective clients, wearing tight slacks or apache skirts or Grecian-style skirts, but always completely naked above the waist. "The lovely days," she sighed, "before Marie was old enough to enjoy it all." She sighed again and turned on the tiny overhead light. "And now, a bakery truck."

Now, for the first time, Roy saw the bar inside of the truck, with the single glossy photo of Gregory Peck, his stenciled signature in the right-hand corner. Under the photo was Marie, quite pretty, with chestnut hair, quite young, sentimental, with

202

imagination and a fine sense of humor. She kicked off her shoes, started to unbutton her dress, then stopped and looked at him severely. "Monsieur, I have talked. For talk, it is six thousand francs. For business, also six thousand francs. But I guess— you are not interested in business, monsieur?"

"Please don't feel insulted."

"No insult, monsieur. Many gentlemen—they only talk. But sometimes—what makes Marie angry—they do not say they want only talk until I have taken off all my clothes, and then I must dress again, you see. And monsieur, that is the hardest work of all in this business, undressing, dressing, undressing, dressing— that is the most annoying of all."

"Well," Roy said, "I suppose I'd better leave."

"No." She looked at her tiny wrist watch. "Marie will tell you when your time is up."

He had never been to a psychiatrist. But now it suddenly occurred to him that this was exactly the way it would be. He would lie on the couch as he lay now on the army mattress and the doctor would sit above him as Marie sat now, cross-legged beneath the smiling, handsome face of Gregory Peck, looking down at him, and the doctor would say, "I'll tell you when your time is up."

"May I smoke?" he asked.

"Careful of the mattress."

So he would smoke, as now, while the hand put a tin can ashtray beside his elbow, and finally he would talk. He would talk as now, about Luanai. He loved Luanai. Luanai loved him. In the beginning, she had felt loyalty toward her husband, had intended only to give him a child. But then, that night in the Hawaiian hills, they had known they loved each other.

"She tell you this?"

"No . . . but I knew. So I got transferred to Paris."

"Now—you transfer back to Hawaii."

"Yes."

203

"You tell Luanai you love her. She tell you, she love you. She tell her husband; you tell your wife. Divorce, marry, for love, monsieur, is the greatest of all things." Marie smiled. "I know, monsieur. I am in love with Monsieur Gregory Peck. Sometimes I think, Someday—someday—he will be walking along the street, and I will slow down and he will wave, and—well . . ." She sighed deep, glanced at her watch once more. "Well, I am sorry, monsieur." She slipped on her shoes. He rose to his knees, adjusted his tie.

"*Bon soir*," he said in high school French.

"*Bon soir*, monsieur." And then she said gaily, and also a little sadly, he thought, "When you get back to United States, you say hello for Marie to Gregory Peck."

"I won't forget," he said. "Next time I run into Greg."

Then she opened the door and he stepped out to the narrow little street. A small group stood waiting at the rear of the truck. They gave a small cheer as he pushed through and began walking fast up the street. As he rounded the corner the bakery truck passed, squealing on the curve. Marie waved and he waved back. Two blocks farther on along the Champs-Élysées, he saw the truck stop, saw a tall man lean in the window. The door opened; the man got in. The truck swung right down another little side street, and the last he saw were the letters *Vive Marie*, painted in bright red on the side.

He felt rather sad, a little jealous as he strode on toward his hotel. But then, psychiatrists had many patients too, didn't they? And six thousand francs was only fourteen dollars, whereas a good psychiatrist charged twenty-five, so he had no complaints at all.

In his hotel room, Roy found the cable slipped under the door. MOTHER DIED LAST NIGHT FUNERAL TWO FRIDAY. It was signed DAD.

He sat on the bed with the message in his hand, and he thought, Dad. He never called his father "Dad." He never felt close enough to the old man to call him that. And poor Mother! The worst part of all was that he could not summon any warmth to his heart, could not feel any genuine grief for her passing. His own mother was dead, gone to meet her God, and he could not feel it, no matter how hard he tried. Unless he wanted to be sentimental, and he was not used to fooling himself. Poor Mother, he thought; you must have died for me long ago, and now I can't even grieve for you. He just felt terribly sad and alone.

He would make the funeral on Friday. After that, he would get an immediate transfer back to Hawaii. He would talk the whole matter over with Luanai, then return home and ask Mildred for a divorce. That would be the hardest part of all— asking his wife for a divorce. But without Luanai his life was a lie, and he could not go on any longer living a lie.

Chapter Twenty-Two

FRANK'S suitcase had been heavy and she was tired from lack of sleep, and all that running around making funeral arrangements during the morning while her father moved about absently, of no use whatsoever, and Mrs. Mauldin bawled hysterically. Now, sitting on this straight-backed chair at five o'clock in the afternoon, Anita was bored, completely, thoroughly bored.

After all, she'd seen many a television rehearsal in her time. The same scene played over and over again; the actors giving out so little, stumbling over their lines, lying down on the haphazard furniture or reading newspapers while they waited for their cues. Empty cartons of coffee all over the place. Dull, dull. No one excited yet—not yet—because the show was still some days off, and the excitement didn't come until the very end.

Les Garret was there. She knew Les from the years back. He said that Frank was doing a good job. "It'll be a great show," he said. "You wait, you'll see Frank in Hollywood yet."

"Not me," Anita said, and Les scowled, puckered his lips and moved away.

A snotty kid named Mike Purdue was there, and a real pansy set designer, and a bouncy little script editor they called Arnold, who kept studying the script and making little suggestions which everyone listened to politely, and then politely ignored.

Edith Parkes was there, too, acting rather superior, Anita thought, considering how the incident of years ago had been an insult to Edith, rather than herself. Yet here Edith was acting almost possessive about Frank, which was so completely ridiculous that Anita felt like laughing outright every time the old bag looked at her.

And Joan Leonard. A real phony, Anita decided. Jewish, of course, with unkempt hair, lipstick smeared, old tennis sneakers and unpressed slacks and a man's shirt with the sleeves rolled up. But she was young and she had gorgeous black eyes, and beneath the shabby clothes, probably a very good figure. Yes, here was the girl to watch. The way she acted so distant with Frank, calling him Mr. Gattone, the polite way she offered to get her some coffee, cigarettes, explain what was going on.

Well, she didn't care what was going on with the show, and she'd already made a pretty good guess as to what was going on with little old Joan and Frank. Hadn't she been in the exact same position once herself? And wasn't Frank just a little too polite to her, and just a little too much the detached boss to Joan? Oh, you bastards! Anita thought. You bastards, you!

The rehearsal ended at six. There were still major problems to be discussed, and Frank suggested they do it over dinner. Les and Arnold Schull and Joan—oh, and his wife, of course. But where could they go with Frank dressed like that, in old clothes, and Joan Leonard, too? And why did they have to discuss *anything* tonight? Frank had promised to take her to dinner, and if this was his idea of taking her to dinner, then he'd better start thinking—about this and a lot of things.

They went to an Italian place on Third Avenue. "I remember it from when I was a kid," Frank explained, and she thought, That's right, tell them about your lousy background. Tell them you were in burlesque and your father was a garbage man.

He didn't, though. He led them all to a long rectangular table, where she found herself sitting on Frank's right, next to Joan Leonard, while Les and Arnold Schull were on Frank's left. All during the meal of baked clams and lasagne, which she hated, as she hated the cheap Chianti wine and the stupid bottles all covered with wax—so damn cute, being used as candlesticks—all during the entire disappointing affair, Frank rattled on exclusively with Les and little Mr. Schull, while Joan Leonard tried oh, so hard, to be polite and keep everything hidden, as if she was fooling somebody. Who in hell did she think she was fooling?

"He's really a marvelous director," Joan said, "though of course I've never worked with him before."

"Oh, but I'm sure you're making up for lost time."

The girl stared at her, started to speak, stopped, said, "I'm terribly sorry about your mother."

"Thank you," Anita said sweetly, very sweetly. Then, remembering that low voice in the background last night—"Your wife?"—she looked straight at Joan and said, "Poor Frank—he couldn't come home last night."

"I know."

"He stayed with some—friend."

"Oh—I didn't know."

The little liar. Although, of course, she could not be sure. Not absolutely, anyway.

Finally, mercifully, it was over. All the good nights had been said and she was alone with Frank in a cab, driving toward the Plaza.

Frank sighed, leaned back wearily. "I'm really sorry, honey. But there was a lot to discuss." He sighed again, looked out the window at the lighted shops along Fifth Avenue. "She's nice, isn't she?"

"Who?"

"Miss Leonard."

"Oh, very nice." She glanced at his face. "Did she know you stayed with a friend last night?"

"Why should she?"

"I don't know." Then, "Who was it, anyway?"

"The TD. That's the technical director."

"I know what a TD is." But why fight? Why bicker? Why be jealous and suspicious and difficult, when they were finally alone? They had reached the Plaza then, and there were the carriages lined up near the leafy park, with the old waiting horses, and the old waiting men in their black top hats and long-tailed coats. Once she and Frank had taken a ride through the park together. It had been spring then, too, and they'd held hands and afterwards he'd said, "We'll do it again sometime."

"Frank," as he tipped the cab driver and lifted out the suitcase, "let's take a ride through the park in a hansom cab."

"I don't know."

"Remember the last time?"

"Yes."

"It was spring."

"Yes."

"Please, Frank."

"I'm tired, honey. Beat."

"Please, Frank. *Please*."

"Look, honey, I—" Then he seemed to sag beneath the weight of the bag. "All right, if you insist."

"If I *insist*." She turned into the hotel, spoke the last words over her shoulder. "Forget it. Please just *forget* it."

"No," Frank said. "It's absolutely impossible. In fact, I won't be able to get home again until the night after the show." He ran water into the basin, stood there in his pajama bottoms and began brushing his teeth furiously to drown out Anita's words as she called through the closed bathroom door of their room in the Plaza.

"My own mother's funeral! And this ridiculous play is *more* important."

He thought the second-act blocking was still not right.

"What will everybody think?"

He could tell already that the script was short, and padding was a hell of a lot tougher than cutting.

"It's an absolute insult to my whole family!"

Of course, if the love scenes were played slower, it would take up a minute or two . . .

"Frank!"

. . . though perhaps they wouldn't hold up.

"You're not listening, Frank!"

Or maybe extend the schoolroom scenes. Use all those extras, even give a couple of them some under-five-line speaking parts, and to hell with the added expense!

"Do you hear me, Frank? . . . My father is also the father of Christina Barker!"

Les Garret would kick, of course, but . . . He turned off the water, hung his toothbrush very carefully on the rack. He unwrapped the tiny cake of Ivory soap, washed his hands and face, then dried them with a clean towel. He noticed the word PLAZA on the towel. He shook his head, aware that he was pulling a Lou Costello, one of those long-delayed takes.

"Frank!"

He opened the door, picked up his pajama top from one of the twin beds. Anita sat on the other. She wore a black, filmy nightgown that he hadn't seen in months.

"Frank . . ." with a slight tremor in her voice.

"What did you say about your father and Christina Barker?"

"I don't know. I just wanted your attention, I guess."

"Then it's not true."

"All afternoon you haven't even noticed me—"

"Is it true?"

"Yes."

He sat carefully on the edge of the bed. "My God!" he said, and lit a cigarette, and thought about it for some moments. "Alan! That's why you didn't want Alan to see Christina." She nodded, and he thought about Mitchel Slayton, only yesterday, giving him the long, violent speech about love being everything, and if you couldn't get that, grab whatever else came second. He thought about a talk he'd had once with Roy, while they were driving up to Plimpton Ridge from New York. He'd said something about Paul having no real problems, just living a detached life in a secure little world, and Roy had said "maybe" rather skeptically and refused to say any more.

"Well, if Paul doesn't realize—" Frank said.

"He does."

Frank stared at her. "How? . . . When?"

"That night at Dr. Bullock's, when you didn't come with me and I got drunk."

"My God!" he said again. "How could you?"

"Of course you haven't been home enough to notice anything."

"Then why did you tell me? Why?"

210

"Just to . . . get your attention for a change."

"You got it," he said, then snubbed the cigarette and lay back on the bed. Anita sat watching him a moment. She'd brought that black nightie on purpose, he knew, and was disappointed that they had twin beds. She wanted him to show her some kind of affection, make some bridge across the widening gap.

"All right," she said finally, switched out the light, and lay back on the matching bed.

Frank stared up at the dark ceiling. He did not want to think about Paul Barker. He did not even want to think about the show any longer—not until tomorrow, anyway. He wanted to think about Anita and himself and where they were going, and why, as each day passed, they seemed to understand each other less and less.

"Honey," he said finally to the ceiling.

"Yes?"

"There's nothing going on between me and Joan Leonard."

"If you say so."

"I know you and I have both been on edge lately. And now your mother's death, and all my worries, and besides . . . you hate what I'm trying to do."

"No, I don't hate it, Frank. I'm afraid of it. And you should be able to understand that. I don't want to be second to your work, and least of all, I don't want to be a Hollywood wife. I don't want to sit alone all day by a heated pool, waiting for you to come home—waiting, waiting— Because I know what would happen, and so do you. I'd drink myself to death in six months."

"You wouldn't have to."

"Yes, I'd *have* to."

"If you loved me, honey—if we kept faith with each other."

"How many people in Hollywood keep faith with each other?"

"I don't know. But I want you to know this—I've *never* been unfaithful to you. Not once in all these years." Saying the words, he remembered Edith Parkes; these same words could be said tonight, but a few days from now, the very next time he saw Anita alone, they could never be said honestly again.

Anita said, "I've never been unfaithful to you either." Then, in the long silence, "What are you thinking, darling?"

"That I love you." But he was thinking that he loved success really, that if only Anita were like Joan Leonard he could tell her the whole story and she'd laugh and say, "As long as you don't *enjoy* it."

"Darling . . ."

"Yes?"

"I love you, too. And no matter how angry I get, no matter how much I ever resent you, I'll be faithful for as long as I live."

He said nothing for a long, aching time. Then finally he sat up, stumbled the few feet to her bed, and knelt on the floor beside it. She held his head against the filmy black across her breasts, and breathing the fragrance of her body he caressed her leg under the gown, her thigh, her hip, and for the first time in months he felt a real, honest, passionate desire for his wife.

Afterward, lying close, breathing slow in the sleepy dark, her head nestled on his shoulder, Anita whispered that there was always something exciting and wonderful about strange beds in strange hotels. "Yes, honey," he said, and held her closer, and felt her hair against his cheek and knew again a peace and a closeness he thought had gone out of his life forever.

Chapter Twenty-Three

AT TWO O'CLOCK in the afternoon, three cars drew up in front of the Dodd and Duncan Funeral Home, and a few darkly dressed, sober-faced people moved into one of the three rooms designed for small funeral services, each like a tiny chapel, with permanent oak benches facing the casket, buried deep among flowers.

Lottie's casket was open. Her white hair was combed neatly to cover a thinning spot, and her hands were folded across her breast. Without glasses she looked strange to Mitchel, who thought on the whole, however, she seemed more at peace in death than she had ever been in life. He nodded to Anita, noted with some annoyance that her husband was not with her, shook hands solemnly with Roy, who had arrived from Paris only an hour before, stared glumly at Mildred, who had had the ill grace to mention she had never seen Lottie before this day.

Mr. Dodd funereally said they were ready to begin any time. "I mean we're all here, aren't we?" he said.

Mrs. Mauldin and the Bullocks were not "family," neither was Mr. Dodd, for that matter, so why did he keep saying "we"? Mitchel thought irritably. "All right," he said. "Any time." He sat down between Roy and Anita.

The Presbyterian minister had stepped up beside the mahogany casket and was starting a prayer. Mitchel lowered his head, but he did not hear the words. He wished Roberta were there. He wished he had taken Lottie to Danbury that night the way he had promised. He wondered what he ought to say, what he would say, to Miss Calhoun when he returned to the New York office tomorrow. He thought that it would be lonesome as hell in the big house now. No reason at all to keep it except that it was the oldest, the finest house in Plimpton Ridge, and as head of the Academy's board he supposed he ought to keep a residence in town. He knew that he ought to be feeling some kind of grief for the loss of his wife, but the truth was he did not feel anything. Only a certain sadness, an awareness that some day he would be lying quietly up there where Lottie lay so quietly now, while the minister droned on and on . . .

The minister had stopped talking. A man sang to the accompaniment of an organ. Mitchel raised his head and saw Lottie's peaceful face in the casket. It was hot. He felt ill. And then the tears came, only he did not know for whom he was crying, Lottie or himself.

Following Mitchel's Cadillac and Mildred Slayton's Oldsmobile behind the hearse, Dr. Bullock decided that there was really no reason at all why he and his wife should have been forced to attend the funeral.

"You weren't forced," his wife said. "It's only common courtesy."

"Everyone else is family," Dr. Bullock said.

"Then consider it an honor that Mitchel wanted us."

"I consider," said Dr. Bullock, "that once again Mr. Slayton has compromised me into undergoing an unpleasant experience."

"Don't be silly," his wife said.

He didn't say anything. His wife would never understand. The reason Mitchel had wanted it all family was because if the funeral had been open, held in the Presbyterian Church, there'd be less than a dozen people who remembered Lottie well enough, or cared enough, to attend. That would have embarrassed Mitchel. This was his way out—something small and intimate, something simple and in good taste. A family affair, with only old Mrs. Mauldin and himself and Mrs. Bullock forced to attend. Simply because it pleased Mitchel's ego to think he ran the school and its headmaster in all matters, including whom to mourn and how to demonstrate a grief he did not feel at all.

The mound of earth was covered with some kind of green material that was supposed to look like grass, and it was this phony grass that finally broke Anita. All during the ceremony she had been able to stare at her mother's face, listen to the minister's words, without feeling any emotion at all. Now the imitation grass triggered whatever emotions had been accumulating in her, and she burst out into a long, sobbing wail. She tried desperately to stop it, aware as she was that it had little to do with her mother's death, that it was somehow involved with Frank's not being with her. She missed him terribly. She wanted him—wanted him to make love to her again, like last night. And now he wouldn't be home for days. Lord, Lord, how she missed him in this time of supposed sorrow.

Alan felt uncomfortable in his "best blue suit." He kept shuffling his feet in the grass while the minister intoned the final words over the open grave. He wondered how deep the hole really was, how long it had taken to dig a hole like that, and how they were going to get the casket down into it—lower it on ropes or what?

He had met his grandmother only once, as a small boy, on Christmas, when his grandfather had led him into that upstairs room with all the religious pictures around the walls. His grandmother had said, "You're a nice, legitimate boy," and patted his head. Afterwards he'd asked his grandfather what "legitimate" meant, and he'd explained that it meant "real." He was a "real" boy. After that, though, his grandfather had never taken him to the room again. Alan wondered why. What in the world was wrong with being a "real" boy, even if his grandmother had used such an odd word to express it?

It was all over. The baskets of flowers stood in a great pile around the grave. The minister shook hands with everyone. Roy remembered him vaguely from rare church attendances on Easter and Christmas. He was an old man, a pious old hypocrite, Roy had always thought. And that little speech he'd given in the funeral chapel about how Lottie Slayton had dedicated her life to being a good wife and mother, how she had done so much for the community—it was strictly for the birds.

"Come on, Mildred," he said, and took his wife's arm and walked toward their car. Alan and Anita were already seated in the rear. Alan stared down at the floor. Roy nodded briefly to his father, who was helping Mrs. Mauldin into the Cadillac, then drove out of the shady little cemetery.

"Isn't it a shame," Mildred said. "I mean all those flowers going to waste like that."

Roy said, "For God's sake, Anita," to his sister, who was still crying behind him.

"If Grandfather asked Dr. Bullock to come, why didn't he ask the Barkers?" Alan said.

"Never mind," Roy said irritably. "You were just hoping to see Christina, that's all."

Roy drummed his fingers on the wheel, and swung to the curb before Slayton Hall. Anita said, "Thanks, Roy," and he nodded as she got out, started to close the door, then leaned over to pick up two little objects from the back seat, which she handed to Roy through the window. One was the handle of a zipper, the other a cheap tie clip. Roy dropped them in his pocket without bothering to look at them and drove out toward home.

Mildred watched him in the mirror. "What was that Anita gave you just now?"

"I don't know. Something she found on the floor." He reached in his pocket, among his loose change, and came up with the zipper tab. "Big deal," Roy said.

"Why, it's mine," Mildred said. "It belongs on my black slacks. I remember the other day while I was driving home from visiting my father—well, it was hot, and I tried to loosen the slacks around my waist and the zipper broke."

"All right, so it's yours," Roy said, and dropped the shiny object in her hand.

"It must have fallen through the seat or something."

"All right."

"I mean I just don't see how else it could possibly have gotten in the back of the car."

"For God's sake!" Roy said, exasperated. "What difference does it make how it got there?"

"None, of course." She was silent.

"I'm sorry I got irritated," he said. "The funeral . . . things like that get on my nerves."

"I know, dear."

"Yeah." Only it wasn't the funeral. It was Millie's damn simple-mindedness, her trust in him, that made him angry. He was going to hurt her badly, and because he felt guilty and wrong he was taking it out on her. But he didn't seem to have a mind of his own any more. Every moment since that night in Hawaii he'd been consumed with nothing but thoughts of Luanai. Fair to Millie or not, it was impossible for him to go on living with her.

When they reached the house he went upstairs to change from his dark suit into sport clothes. Emptying his pockets, he found the tie clip that Anita had picked up in the car. He tossed it into the small box that held his cuff links, and all the other odds and ends he'd accumulated over the years. Then he went downstairs and made himself a stiff drink and sat down in the dead room in the dead house and thought that in a few days now he would see Luanai again, and she would understand, and he would come back and ask Millie for a divorce.

When Roy went upstairs, Millie had hurried into the garage where she frantically examined every inch of the floor and seats in the rear of the car. She found nothing, but God, she should have had sense enough to look before. Now Roy had found the zipper to her slacks, and like a big fool she'd made so much of it. But there must have been something else. "Them," Anita had said, "I found them," as she handed whatever "them" was through the window to Roy. The zipper and what else? . . . Something of hers? Something of Matt's? How much did Roy know—or guess? Why, why had she ever let it happen?

When she returned to the living room, she found Roy sitting there with a glass of whisky in his hand. "Well, I'll go change, I guess." When he did not say anything she went up the stairs and put on a skirt and light sweater. She sat on the bed and looked at the shelf of books, among them the books on sex that she had read, trying to find out about herself and Roy. She thought of Matt, hot and eager, and her own hot eagerness that had nothing to do with what she had learned in the books and practiced so carefully in her "sex in marriage."

She opened the closet door, groped through the pockets of Roy's dark suit, but found nothing. He'd hidden it, whatever it was, or thrown it away perhaps, depending . . . She went downstairs, walking very carefully, trying to compose her face so that it would not reveal the uncertainty and guilt she felt.

Roy was still in his chair with his drink, still brooding, and he did not even bother to look up when she came into the room.

She went into the kitchen, noticed that the bottle was down more than two inches. Roy must have had more than one drink, which was unusual with him unless he was quite disturbed about something. His mother, perhaps, Mildred thought hopefully. No, it wouldn't be his mother. He must be thinking about the zipper Anita had found, and that other unknown, damning little object she had picked up.

She made herself a drink and carried it back to the living room, where Roy still sat motionless, as if frozen to his chair.

"Roy!" She felt that in another moment she would scream.

"Hmm?"

"What are you . . . thinking?"

"Oh, I don't know. . . . About us, I guess."

Mildred felt her heart skip a beat. Then he must know. "Roy," she said, "look, Roy . . ."

"I mean we've been married, what—fifteen, sixteen years now? Tell me, have you been really happy, Millie?"

"Oh, yes!"

"I mean really happy."

"Of course, darling, of course!" She went over to him and knelt by his chair and put her face in his lap. "And I've been faithful, too. No matter what you think . . . I have . . . I have . . ." And she cried with her own lie, wishing to God it could be the truth.

Roy was too lost in his own thoughts to wonder about her protestations. He stroked her red hair, caressed the back of her neck with his strong, stubby fingers. Yes, she was faithful, and that was what made it all so goddamn difficult. If only she were unfaithful. If only Millie didn't care for him so goddamn much.

Chapter Twenty-Four

FROM behind the closed doors of his study, over the clattering of his typewriter, Paul could hear the French clock on the mantel in the living room chime its musical half-hour. He glanced at his watch: 10:30. Outside his window the trees stirred faintly in the balmy June night. Inside the room was dim, because he preferred working in a dark, small room with only a spot of light on his desk, surrounded by his ship models and tennis trophies, his books that stood in ragged piles on tables and chairs, all the meaningful clutter that Roberta was not allowed to disturb.

A knock at the door, and Roberta's voice. "Paul . . . it's ten-thirty."

"Yes, I know." He rose, opened the door, and in one of those rare moments during the past few days, he looked directly into his wife's gray eyes before turning back to switch out the lights.

"I didn't mean to disturb you," Roberta said.

"That's all right. It wasn't going very well, anyway."

"Oh, I'm sorry."

Polite. Always polite, as he'd been treating her, too, with the greatest politeness ever since he'd moved back from the cottage. They said little to each other and what they did say was either meaningless or carefully thought out, so that no direct reference was ever made to the glass wall that stood between them, no attempt was ever made to shatter it. Sometimes he wanted to smash his fist into that wall, shout, become violent—anything but be polite. Sometimes he wished that Roberta would try to smash the glass herself, though it was too late for that now, he realized. She responded quickly to everything he said, every suggestion he made. But so far he had rejected each one of her subtlest advances, and he knew it was all up to himself. Another three days of this, a cool parting, and perhaps a lifetime of never meeting again. Or he could smash his fist through the glass. He could, except that he would not. He wanted to, but could not do it.

Roberta stood by the window, the curtain pulled back, her face against the pane. He saw her reflection in the yellow lamplight, noticed the sweep of her back and her rounded thighs, and thought that she had not yet attained any middle-aged spread.

She turned away from the window. "I wonder what's making Christina so late," she said, troubled.

"Didn't that club meeting last until ten?"

"But it's only a five-minute walk."

"Well, you know how young people like to linger on a lovely night like this. Don't worry," Paul said, thinking how such words should be spoken with one's arm around one's wife.

"I'm not worried. In fact I think I'll go along up to bed." She walked halfway up the stairs. "Are you coming, Paul?"

"Yes . . ."

"You don't have to."

Paul watched her in silence as she disappeared up the stairs. He lit his pipe, heard the dog barking at the back door, went through the kitchen to let him in. He thought how he would be eating exactly three more breakfasts in this kitchen. After that he would eat alone in diners and tearooms, unless they had a special faculty dining room in Kenbrook. Even so, he would be eating all his meals alone.

Back in the living room he looked out the window at the

221

empty street, told himself not to worry, Christina would be all right, switched on the porch light and climbed the stairs.

Roberta was sitting at her vanity. She wore a blue dressing robe over her nightgown and was carefully rubbing night cream over her forehead. He took his pajamas from the closet and went into the bathroom to undress. Silly, perhaps. Even childish. But the line had been drawn, the glass wall erected from the moment he had first re-entered the house. For Christina's sake, to save themselves any embarrassment among the faculty, they would live in the same house, even sleep in the same bed. Everything would seem exactly as before, and everything was entirely different.

He returned from the bathroom in his pajamas, hung up his clothes, and looked once more at the slowly stirring trees beyond the window. Roberta said, "The laundry will be back tomorrow," and he said, "Fine." She asked, "You don't want any of the things in your study, personal things?" and he said, "No, I won't be needing them."

"But you'll want them after you get settled . . . when you find an apartment."

"I expect to live in a single room."

"Well, perhaps I'd better put them in storage anyway."

"If you like." He sat on the edge of the bed and removed his slippers. His back was turned to her now, and it was easier to say certain things without their eyes having to meet. "You still don't know where you're going?"

"California."

"But where?"

"San Diego, I think; a hotel, probably, until I find a small house or apartment."

"I was discharged in San Diego. You'll like La Jolla, I think."

"I'll store the furniture. I've already listed the house with three agencies. They think we're going to be with you in Pennsylvania, of course. Everyone thinks that."

222

"Except Mitchel Slayton, and Anita, and Roy."

"Yes," Roberta said with a long, weary sigh. "I'm not accepting money from Mitchel, Paul. I'll get a job and make out by myself. The fact that I'm letting him establish a trust fund for Christina's education has nothing to do with me personally. I mean, I suppose he does owe her that much."

"A father," Paul said pointedly, "owes *something* to his daughter."

Roberta sighed again and got into bed. "You can find a lawyer in Pennsylvania. I'll find one in California, then take a six weeks' residence in Nevada. Since we won't be fighting over who gets Christina, I think it can all be very amicable."

"Very," he said, and slipped under the covers and switched off the bed lamp. He could hear Roberta's slow breathing, feel the warmth of her body only inches away. If he were to move ever so slightly his hip would be touching hers, and if that happened she would not move. She would remain still, breathing evenly, waiting for him to edge closer, touch her, finally reach for her in passion and so end this stalemate, possess him once again, and make a mockery of his withdrawal from her.

A car sounded outside. Roberta said, "Christina. Where can she be so late?" and he said again, "Don't worry." But the truth was he was worried himself—about someone else's daughter, as though she was his very own. Then silence, with the faint rustling of the leaves outside the open window. Darkness, with the luminous hands of the bedside clock showing 10:50, 11:00. Roberta's body so near, so near, so wanted . . . it was torture to lie inert beside her like this— And then suddenly the loud ringing of the telephone downstairs.

"Christina," Roberta said, sitting up and turning on the lamp, and Paul said, "I'll get it," and rushed for the hallway, down the stairs.

"Hello," he said anxiously into the phone. From where he stood he could see Roberta at the top of the stairs, soft in her

223

negligee, her body silhouetted in the light from the hallway behind her.

"Hello," he said again, and then, "No, I'm afraid you have the wrong number." He dropped the receiver back in its cradle. "Just some idiot who doesn't know how to dial properly," he said looking up at Roberta, who was still standing at the head of the stairs. She might just as well be in the nude, he thought, seeing all her rounded, mature body through the thin nightgown, so infinitely desirable, so familiar in remembrance that he could not bear to look upon it now as something forbidden to him. He turned away, said harshly, "Go back to bed. I'm going to sit up a while."

She hesitated. "I won't be able to sleep."

"And I can't sleep, so there you are. . . . Go back to bed, I say," he said with a show of boredom and weariness he did not feel.

He heard the slap of her bare feet in the hallway, the closing of a door, then swung sharply and stared at the spot where she had stood. Stairs . . . a dimly lighted hallway . . . silence . . . the ghost of things past, gone now from sight.

The clock ticked on, chimed the quarter-hour. He sat in the dark front room and waited, waited with his heart aching . . . for the woman who lay sleepless in bed, unsatisfied . . . for the girl out there somewhere in the dark, the child who was not his, and that God, oh God—he wept silently in the darkness—he wished somehow, some way, he could make his own.

To the right the lights of the town winked sleepily, while to the left the buildings of Plimpton Academy boasted only an occasional light or two, like fireflies in the summer night. Here in the bandstand, though, it was completely dark and quiet, with the rustling trees forming a second leafy roof over the wooden roof above.

Alan's cigarette glowed bright, then dimmed, and the smoke

drifted away on the gentle wind. He said, "Would you like a cigarette?" and Christina said, "You know I don't smoke. I promised Daddy I'd wait till I was eighteen."

Silence, and the glow of Alan's cigarette, Alan's arm slipping slow and easy around her waist; the wooden bench uncomfortable against her shoulder; her head inclining toward Alan, coming to rest on his shoulder. There was no moon tonight, but it was nice anyway. Nicer here than anywhere. At least understandable, because Alan was simple and direct, which was more than she could say for anyone else.

In three days now, Christina thought, she and her mother would be on their way to California, while her father was going to some place called Kenbrook Academy in Pennsylvania. She didn't know why, what had gone wrong; why, following that night at Dr. Bullock's, her Grandmother Dora's death, everything had gone so completely, inexplicably, horribly wrong. Her father and mother were always so polite now, so damn polite it made you want to scream, so protective, so secretive. All they said was, "We've decided to separate, dear . . . when you're older . . . when you're older . . ."

"That's what people always say," Christina said aloud.

"What?"

"When you're older. You'll understand when you're older."

"And when it's too late," Alan said, with that bitterness she'd noticed in him so frequently of late.

"Your family, too?" Christina said.

"Aah, what's the use of talking about it," Alan said in disgust, flipping away his cigarette. His arm tightened about her waist and he drew her closer to him. "When I think that after three more days I won't be seeing you any more . . ."

Her hand clutched his knee. "Don't let's talk about that tonight," she whispered. "It makes me so sad."

"That stupid graduation dance, and then nothing. Nothing at all." His hand slipped along her cheek, her throat, slid down

225

across her breast and stayed there while she waited, feeling his fingers fumbling with the buttons of her blouse, reaching hotly under her brassière for her . . .

She sat up, tense, rigid, removed his hand from her breast. "Please, Alan, don't."

"All right," he said, taking his arm from around her. "God-damn it, what are you afraid of?"

"It's not you, Alan," she said softly.

"Then who the hell is it?"

"It's me . . . I'm all mixed up. I want you to touch me, but I know I shouldn't want you to, and yet I still do, you see, and I don't know . . . I don't know . . ." Then suddenly, brightly, as if she wanted to forget the whole thing, "I guess I'll have a cigarette after all."

He lit it for her. His face was anguished above the match flame and everything that was woman in her felt for him. She took a few puffs, coughed, and decided she didn't like to smoke at all, except it was one way of paying back her father for the hurt he was giving her.

"We could run away," Alan said. "Right now. Just get on a bus or something, and not even get married if nobody'll marry us. We could both work and we'd make out all right. Our parents wouldn't care anyway."

"No, Alan. I can't do that."

"I love you, Christy. I want you. Don't you understand?"

"I do, I do, Alan." She took his hand, stroked it tenderly.

"Goddamnit!" he swore, tearing away from her. He rose, paced the wooden floor of the bandstand. "What are they try-ing to do to us? What are you trying to do to me?"

"I'm not trying to do anything. I love you, Alan. You know that."

"Oh, sure," he said sarcastically.

"Just because I won't run away with you? Just because I won't let you touch me? I mean if I let you touch me then you wouldn't want to run away with me, would you?"

He did not answer, and she knew there was some truth in what she said. The chapel bell tolled eleven; it was getting terribly late. She said, "All right, don't answer. But I've got to go now."

He walked apart from her, his hands in his pockets. Occasionally she glanced at his brooding face, hurt, lonely, as she too felt lonely and hurt. Until finally, at the last street corner, she could not bear it any longer, and she turned hard into his arms and cried, "I love you, Alan. Please don't be mad. I'll run away with you if you like. Right now. This very minute."

"It's too late now," Alan said, knowing it had been too late all along.

"I know, darling, I know. But we still have tomorrow night. And the night of the dance. We'll get away from the dance. I promise we will. And I'll let you touch me. I want you to touch me . . . I mean everything . . . if you could get one of those things . . ."

"Darling, Christie, darling," he said, all his body pressing hard against her. She wished she had not said "one of those things" because there was something ugly about the very idea, and there was nothing ugly about Alan, nothing disgusting, nothing she did not love and want.

He kissed her, holding her close, pressed back against the lamp post. His tongue felt along her lips, probing, forcing her lips apart, until she could feel his tongue inside her mouth, and she was panting, trembling, frightened. She pulled away abruptly, almost pushing him from her, and said, "Good night, Alan" in a hoarse whisper; then feeling she wanted to be kissed again like that she turned and ran for home under the dark trees gossiping in the wind.

Roberta heard the front door open and close, and sitting up in bed heard Paul saying, "Where have you been?" angrily, though she knew his anger was only to hide his anxiety and relief. And then Christina saying, "I'm sorry, Daddy."

227

"That doesn't answer my question."

"I've been smoking."

Roberta could sense the defiance in her voice, and she knew from Paul's silence that Christina's tone had hurt him. Footsteps on the stairs, going down the hall to her room. Then, after a long time, Paul's footsteps, too. He entered the room, stood by the bed, looking tense, hurt, defeated. "She's been smoking," he said. "That's all. She's been smoking."

"I doubt if she'll talk to me, either," Roberta said.

"Goddamnit," he swore softly under his breath.

"I'll try, anyway," she said, and went down the hall to Christina's room. The door was shut. She knocked lightly, then pushed the door open.

Christina was undressing. She glanced over her shoulder, reached for her pajamas, put them on, her body half turned away, as much in defiance as in modesty. Her body was lovely, no longer a girl's, not quite a woman's, and looking at her daughter Roberta wondered in sudden panic whether this was the time for that long talk. Not about the facts of life, which Christina had known for years, but about how to handle boys, about keeping herself clean and virtuous, never giving way to sudden passions born of frustration and loneliness, never making the irreparable mistake of her own mother. "Christina . . ."

"I'm sorry, Mother. I mean about it's being so late. I went to the club meeting. And then afterward I met Alan and we sat in the bandstand talking for a while."

"Your father was so worried . . ."

Christina looked at her mother as if she didn't believe her, and was about to say so, then changed her mind. She said, "I didn't tell you I was going to meet Alan because I knew you wouldn't like it. But I didn't lie, and now that I'm home there's no sense in lying now." She spoke in a cool, detached way, as though to say, "Punish me if you like, because I don't care, and there's nothing you can say or do that will ever make me care again." Then she slipped under the covers, turned her back, and said, "Good night, Mother."

Roberta thought of a dozen things to say, but none was right. She put out the light, went over to the bed and kissed her daughter. "I love you," she whispered. "And Daddy loves you, and please don't go away from us."

"I'm going to San Diego with you, aren't I?" muffled into the pillow.

"You know what I mean, Christina." She bent again to kiss the girl's smooth cheek, then started to leave the room.

Christina rolled over and sat up. "Mother!" she cried anxiously, her voice choked.

"Yes, dear?"

"Nothing. . . . Just nothing." She rolled over again to face the wall. There was so much to say she didn't know where to begin.

Back in their bedroom, Roberta found Paul lying on his back in bed, staring up at the ceiling. "Well?" he said, and she said, "Nothing."

"She senses something," he said. "Something more than just the fact we're separating. She senses the truth about us."

"The truth," Roberta said wearily. "What is the truth, Paul?"

"That I'm not her father, of course." Only that was not the most important truth at all. The real honest truth, which he could not bring himself to admit, was that he loved his wife, loved Christina, no matter how hard he tried to hide it from them—and from himself.

Roberta slipped under the covers. His body, only inches away, was tense, rigid, as though every muscle was fighting against her. If he'd let her touch him, let her seduce him . . . If he'd only cry out, strike her, make love to her, rape her—anything but this unnatural, this forced rejection that was not the truth of his being. She moved slightly so that her hip was warm against his, let her hand fall lightly on his thigh. He was aching, bursting with desire, she knew, and she whispered, "Paul . . . just use me, if you like. You don't have to care. Use me and then reject me, and it will still be better than nothing."

He pulled away from her, lay motionless on his side, and she knew that he would not sleep, could not sleep for being near her. Tears came to her eyes. Only a few more nights, she thought, and then the last chance will be gone forever.

Chapter Twenty-Five

AT TWO O'CLOCK that afternoon, on the island of Oahu, the temperature stood at one hundred and eight degrees, combined with a humidity of ninety-two per cent. The heat steamed up from the sidewalks, and the white buildings along Kalakaua Avenue ricocheted the bright sunlight into the eyes of the slow-strolling pedestrians, who sought the shelter of the coconut trees that drooped tiredly in the relentless heat.

The taxi seemed to crawl, as though fighting its way through the heat. Sweat rolled down the back of the Hawaiian driver's neck and Roy felt his own perspiration running in driblets under his shirt. He said, "God, it's hot," and the driver nodded a weary assent before pulling up to the curb an even block from the Royal Hawaiian. "I'll walk," Roy told him, and went over to an open refreshment stand, where he drank two large paper cupfuls of Hawaiian punch. The stuff was warm, pineapple juice with red artificial coloring; it reminded Roy of the drinks they sold in corner stands along Times Square. Afterward, he walked slowly up the avenue, his eyes searching the group of sunbathers and swimmers who lined the beach as he tried to locate a slim brown girl in a bright red bathing suit.

He could not find her. Maybe she was not out there in the water. Maybe she was home. It was a simple matter to walk the two blocks to her house, knock at the door, wait for her to open for him. But he was stalling, he knew, walking in this heat, drinking that cruddy punch, searching the crowded beach, all in a strange effort to put off a meeting he had looked forward to now for agonizing weeks. I love her, he thought, and she loves me. What am I waiting for? I'll simply tell her how I feel, and she'll understand. *Then* we can worry about George, worry about Millie. First we worry about ourselves, so what the hell am I waiting for?

He turned the corner, and now, seeing her little stucco house looming larger as he moved down the street, he forgot the sun and the heat, forgot about George and Millie, forgot everything but the way she would look, the way she would kiss him, saying, "Hello, Flyer Roy," only different now, with love now and passion, not on the cheek but on the mouth, with her lips moist and moving and her arms pressed tight around him. His mouth felt parched, and "Luanai, Luanai," he whispered her name, and then he was hurrying along the pavement, past the hedges and blooming flowers, up the short walk to the door. He knocked once, twice, and then the door opened and there she was, flinging herself against him, saying happily, "Hello, Flyer Roy." And there behind her was George.

George said, "It's been a hell of a long time, Roy."

"I was transferred to Paris for a while," Roy said, his eyes fixed on George, afraid to look into Luanai's upturned face, until she moved away from him and he could not help but see her. She was wearing red shorts and a white shirt, the loose tails tied about her waist, exposing a small strip of bare skin. She was smiling at him, with love, of course, in that secret way women have, to be understood across candlelit tables and empty rooms and crowded rooms, through total darkness, and even sometimes through solid walls.

Trembling, he sat down in the nearest chair.

"You're late, Roy," George said.

"What?"

Luanai was still smiling that secret smile.

"By exactly three days."

"Three days? I don't get it."

"We've been celebrating, man. But that's okay. Now we'll celebrate all over again."

"Celebrate?" Roy felt hot, and slightly dizzy. George was talking in a loud voice. Too cheerful. Luanai kept smiling. "All over again?" Roy said, puzzled.

"Hold on," George said. "Hold on, man, and hear this . . . now hear this. The Olgers . . . Mr. and Mrs. George Olger . . . are about to become the parents of a bouncy baby boy or girl, whichever the case may be."

"About?" Roy said stupidly. "About when?"

"About eight months from now, you jerk." And George laughed, and Roy felt a cigar thrust in his hand, and George was saying, "Must get some gin. Be back in five minutes," and the door opened and closed, and then there was silence in the room, with Luanai still smiling mysteriously in the silence.

"Well," Roy said, "well . . ." slumping down in his chair, staring vacantly at the unlit cigar he was holding between his fingers.

"Isn't it wonderful, Flyer Roy?" Luanai said softly.

"Wonderful?"

"I told you I knew, I knew right away. Didn't I tell you what a difference it would make in George?"

"Luanai . . ."

232

"He's been a wild man, wild with happiness, for days."

"Luanai . . ." Roy's voice was hoarse, imploring.

"Oh, I'm absolutely positive it's true. I mean, I had a test and the doctor said there was no question about it. Don't I show, Flyer Roy? Can't you see?" She patted her brown bare stomach, then laughed and danced in small, happy steps about the room. "I'm going to take very good care of myself, too . . . read lots of books about it. The doctor said . . ."

She chattered and danced, danced and chattered in her happiness. George would be back any minute now. Suddenly Roy leaped to his feet and shouted, "For Christ's sake, Luanai, stop pretending!"

She stopped dancing abruptly, far away from him on the other side of the room. She looked at him, puzzled, said, "Roy . . . what's the matter, Roy?"

"My God," he said, "there isn't any *time*."

"Time?"

"Luanai . . . listen . . . listen to me . . ." He moved toward her. She was backing away from him, shaking her head, bewildered. And then the door opened and George burst in, waving a bottle of gin like a banner.

"To Roy," George shouted, pouring the drinks in the kitchenette. "Because that's what we're going to call him. Roy. And if it's a girl, Royale. All in your honor, man, because Luanai insists . . ."

The drink in his hand. His own voice saying, "I'm not supposed to drink twelve hours before a flight . . ." And George saying, "On this occasion . . ." The bitter taste, thinking, *This* occasion, the quick dizziness, the choking smoke from George's cigar . . . Roy felt he might be ill. He felt his whole body bathed in perspiration, and he groped for his chair and sat down again.

George was sitting beside Luanai on the sofa, his long arm

around her. That secret look in Luanai's eyes, only she was looking at George now, as if the baby was *his*, for God's sake. . . .

"You'll be Uncle Roy," George said.

"What?"

"Uncle Flyer Roy," Luanai said.

"What?"

"You crazy, man?"

She was gone behind the smoke, emerging, disappearing. Her head was on George's shoulder, her hand on his arm. George was grinning, the big man George, the virile man George, the great lover, the expectant father, all happy as hell. Why was Luanai disappearing, disappearing farther and farther away? Not his love, not even his child, nothing of his at all, but only an expectant mother, a proud woman, a happy woman, secure and at peace in the arms of her loving husband.

He was on the outside, looking in through frosted glass, through dark, rushing water. The girl wore a white cotton dress. He could tell that she was not wearing a bra, and he was very nervous, because in a moment they would put down their drinks and go out into the night. They would eat Hawaiian *smörgåsbord* at a place called The Grass Hut, and they would drive into the hills and make love on a torn green blanket spread carefully over a patch of grass beneath the coconut trees that smelled of pine. They would discover their love in that one ecstatic moment, and they would keep it secret, precious, until in time, when they could no longer live without each other, he would return, and somehow—somehow—they would live their lives together.

George was saying, "You sick, Roy?"

"What . . . ? What did you say . . . ?"

George emerged from the dark water. Blond, tall, young, the father-to-be, an arm around his wife who wore red shorts and

234

a white shirt and was not going into the hills any more, had never been in the hills at all, had forgotten . . . forgotten . . .

"Another drink?" George said, all concern. Dumb, stupid concern . . .

"Thanks, no . . . Thanks." Roy stood up, waited dizzily for the room to steady itself. "Congratulations," he said. "So happy for you . . . The best of everything . . ." He stumbled to the door. Luanai got up from the sofa and moved toward him, stood on tiptoe, kissed his cheek. "Good-by, Flyer Roy." She was four years old, six, eight, twelve years old, a button-eyed girl saying good-by to sweet old, nice old, comfortable old Flyer Roy.

"Good-by. Good-by." He was out in the sun. Behind him the loving couple stood waving from the doorway, their arms around each other's waist, their bodies touching, a little world unto themselves, a world from which he was excluded forever.

Roy walked on. And on. It was hot. God, it was certainly a bastard of a hot day.

Captain Norman Karpitch had been a pilot with Skyway Airlines for twenty-eight years, and in that time he had had nearly half a hundred different co-pilots in the bucket seat beside his own. Some had been good men and bad pilots. Some had been bad men and good pilots. Very few had been both.

Roy Slayton had been both. Captain Karpitch had made the strongest recommendation that Roy be promoted to the post of test pilot. But that was once and this was now, and the now had been going on, worsening in fact, over nearly half a year, reaching a small climax in the spring, followed by Roy's temporary transfer to the Paris run, and hitting the final climax now, on his reassigned run to Hawaii and return. It was most inconvenient because Roy had to hitch a ride across the country every time he wanted to go home.

Roy had been drinking. What's more, he didn't even deny it. "Yeah, Norm, I had a couple of drinks," he said. "So what? So report me."

"I'm not interested in reporting you," Captain Karpitch said. "I'm interested in flying this plane to San Francisco with a co-pilot who won't make a single mistake." The engines were turning over then, drowning Roy's answer. Engines one, two, three, four. He slipped on his headpiece, received instructions from the tower, and tolled the big DC-7 out to the runway, where he roared the engines and waited once more for the signal to take off.

Roy sat beside him, silent, staring straight ahead at the long, lighted runway.

"All right?" said Captain Karpitch.

"All right."

The signal came. The engines roared, and the plane gathered speed, then lifted slowly, ponderously into the early-morning sky. Roy made the routine checks. No mistakes. He was doing everything automatically, as a person dresses, or shaves, or drives a car. He would make no mistakes in the routine work. But he knew he would be incapable of handling the plane himself if anything should happen to its captain. And considering that old Karpitch was fifty-eight, due to retire in another two years, he could not afford to overlook any such possibility.

Roy leaned forward, staring down at the strip of beach at Waikiki as they swung past Diamond Head. "Good-by," he said, "you Waikiki bastard, you," then sat up straight again.

"You can flip off the no-smoking," said Karpitch.

"Off," Roy said, flipping the switch.

"Leave the safety belt on."

"On."

"It'll get smoother in a few minutes."

"It won't get any smoother," Roy said.

Captain Karpitch didn't say anything. He looked straight

236

ahead and listened with trained ears to the smoothly running engines. He buzzed the stewardess and ordered black coffee for Roy, waited until his co-pilot had finished it, then spoke very carefully to the low-hanging clouds beyond the bulb of glass. "You want to say anything, Roy?"

"Like what?"

"Like anything. Like why you didn't go to bed last night. Didn't even shave this morning."

"So I sat up."

"Like what's been eating you for so long. Like why you always took off for Waikiki alone."

"I knew a little girl," Roy said.

"You've told me."

"Well, she's dead."

"Oh? I'm sorry to hear that."

"I mean she's married and she's having a baby and she's dead."

Captain Karpitch started to say something, then thought better of it and remained silent. Always before, Roy had talked as though the girl were really a child. Now, for the first time, he was saying that she was grown up, married, having a baby. It didn't make much sense.

"All right, Roy," he said. "It's your business."

"Oh no it's not. It's none of my business," Roy said bitterly.

Captain Karpitch felt sorry for his co-pilot. The fellow was hurt, and pretty badly, too. That much was obvious. He'd always liked Roy Slayton. The man was extremely sensitive, despite his deceptively square, hard looks, thoroughly honest, a very good guy all around who was now going through some emotional problem that was on the verge of destroying him. He was unfit to fly, and the doctors would have to know about it. For Roy's own good. For the good of Skyway and the passengers.

"You need a rest, fella," he said.

"Yeah," Roy said. "I'm tired."

"I mean a long rest."

"So do I."

"I mean maybe even a few months."

"Maybe years," Roy said. "Maybe forever."

Captain Karpitch glanced at the set, blank face, the dull, staring eyes. Roy worried him, the way he was talking. It was no way for a man to talk. He wet his lips, turned his eyes to the clouds once more, and thought that in two years he would retire. Two years was a short time. After that, he might never be above the clouds again.

Now, in the low red sun at the day's end, Roy was driving along the Cross Island Parkway toward home. He was so tired he was past feeling tired. The traffic moved slowly, but an Austin Healey was built for coping with slow traffic. Low, fast, with direct steering and a smart getaway, it could be maneuvered from one lane to the next with an ease impossible in American cars, even at the inevitable bottleneck at the entrance to the Bronx Whitestone Bridge.

"Yes, I love you," Roy said to the car. "Yes, I love you, you little bastard." Riding free of heavy traffic now, over the long high bridge, along the Hutchinson River Parkway to the Merritt Parkway, with its dips and curves and long running hills, the trees flashing by on either side, the summer air whistling warm over the topless car. Speed was what he wanted. Roaring speed, purring speed, breathless, reckless speed, for going home or going to hell for that matter. Home or hell, hell or highwater. He was sober now, after sleeping most of the way from San Francisco. He needed speed and he wanted a drink, a hundred drinks, more than he'd ever had in his entire life. He would go home and get the liquor. He would go somewhere and have the drinks. He would get hold of Paul Barker tonight . . . well, maybe not tonight, he was too goddamned tired tonight . . . tomorrow night, then . . . he would get hold of Paul Barker and the two of them would get drunk together. Why Paul Barker? Because Paul would understand how he felt. Paul had been shafted himself, and if anyone knew what it was like to have the rug pulled out from under you it would certainly be good old, shafted old, cuckolded old Paul Barker.

Mildred's Oldsmobile was in the barn. There were lights in the living room window. Roy sat motionless in his little car, staring at the lights through the big shadows of the buttonwood trees.

Millie, he thought. Oh God, Millie. I can't face you. I can't live with you, Millie. I'm sorry, because I know you're the kind that makes a fuss. You're not so happy yourself being married to me, but you pretend you are, you pretend so goddamn hard you've almost come to believe it yourself. But it's a lie, and you know it, and I know it.

He was leaning against the wheel and his head sank wearily into his arms. "I can't go on, Millie, I can't, I just can't," he said. "What in the hell am I going to do?"

Chapter Twenty-Six

IN THE control room overlooking NBC's Studio 8 H Frank Gattone was speaking into the microphone. "All right, folks. That does it for today. Three-thirty tomorrow for notes, cleanup, run-through and dress." He turned to Joan Leonard, who was sitting beside him, notebook in hand. "They all have their schedules?"

Joan nodded.

"Fit in your make-up when you're not on camera," he said into the microphone. He released the switch, ran a hand through his tousled hair, stared at the soggy cigarette butts in the empty coffee carton, then rose and put on his coat.

Les Garret left the control room. Mike Purdue and the engineer followed. A monitor was still on; children's voices laughing in an early-evening participation show.

Joan said, "Anything else, Frank?"

"Nothing that can't wait until tomorrow."

"Everything can't wait till tomorrow," Joan said.

He looked at her, frowning. "Meaning what?"

Joan shrugged.

"Come on. Out with it."

"I'm just jealous, I guess." She made a pretense of laughing, stuffed papers into a Manila envelope, and started for the iron stairs that led down to the studio floor. Halfway down she stopped and looked up at him. "Well, enjoy yourself." Then the sound of her shoes clicking on metal, and then silence in the booth.

Sure, enjoy myself, Frank thought. It's not every night I get a chance to play the call girl—or should I say, call man?

He sat at the long table before the black monitors. The single monitor, high in the corner, still carried the laughter of the children as they played organized games. Everything was highly organized. Edith had said nine o'clock, which gave her plenty of time to make whatever womanly preparations were necessary. The whole thing was incredible. He had not quite believed it in the beginning, and he still did not believe it, although Edith had delivered her ultimatum less than two hours ago. "Nine, Pumpkin, or I shall be sick all day tomorrow."

Frank closed his attaché case, went down the iron stairs, and picked his way through the ropes and folding chairs littered with paper plates bearing half-eaten sandwiches; through the canvas sets, where tomorrow evening at nine o'clock his show would unfold before millions of viewers. The sets, as always, looked faded and shabby, though none of this would show on camera. He decided to ask for more shrubbery along the resort veranda. He reminded himself to tell the sound man to keep the crickets down. He'd like to eliminate them entirely, they sounded so phony, but in this kind of show—a summer night on the veranda of a resort hotel—the woman waiting, the man approaching, the calculated small talk that was supposed to hold double meanings, except it never did—well, what the hell could you use in place of those phony crickets?

He went out through the swinging double doors, past the tiny canteen, on down to the elevators. In the lobby a long line of tourists stood waiting patiently behind ropes for a chance to show themselves off to friends back home on an audience participation show. Another group stood close to a blue-suited girl guide who was explaining the details of the huge murals that lined the walls and ceilings. All the visitors seemed to have cameras. All the women seemed to be wearing hats. They all listened intently as though the girl were about to say something so profound they must not miss a word of it, and then they could go back to Utah or Idaho, Washington or Wisconsin, and tell all their friends, and live changed lives forever after.

Outside, the air was warm. Frank leaned over the wall of the skating rink, looked at the people in the English Grill, others sitting under umbrellas where the young, red-legged girls skated in the wintertime, and he wondered what percentage of all these people—the eaters, the drinkers, the tourists with their cameras, those who waited in the line inside and those who waited in that other long line outside that started at Radio City Music Hall and wrapped itself all the way around the

241

Associated Press Building—how many of them would be home tomorrow night at nine, their eyes glued to their television sets, making or breaking the entire future of a certain Frank Gattone.

What a lot of crap! He hailed a cab, drove the few blocks to the Plaza and took the message at the desk. Mrs. Gattone had called. Would he please call her back?

Up in his room Frank smoked a cigarette, drank two glasses of ice water before calling his wife.

Anita was lonesome. She could not forget their night together at the Plaza. It was the closest they'd been in years. "So what I thought, darling, I could drive in tonight, right now. Then we'd be together again tonight, and we could drive home together tomorrow night after the show."

"Well, it's kind of late to be driving in now," Frank said. "Besides, I'm afraid I have to do a little extra work with Edith Parkes tonight." He could feel Anita freezing up at the other end of the wire.

"Edith! I thought you said she was perfect."

"Her lines. If I don't drill her, no one else will."

"Well . . . I thought you would be glad if I came in."

"I would, honey. But not tonight. Come in tomorrow. You can watch the dress, see the show from the control room or the sponsor's booth, whichever you like. Les Garret's wife'll probably be here, and afterwards we'll take that hansom ride through the park."

"Really?"

"Absolutely. After this rat race, there's nothing I'd like better."

"I love you, darling."

"I love you, too," Frank said, and wondered why it was always so difficult for him to say those words, whether he meant them or not.

He hung up, took a shower, changed into a dark suit. It was

242

only quarter after eight. There was still time to call Edith and try bluffing it out. Except that it wouldn't work. Well anyway, there was still time to have something to eat, to breathe some fresh air before he choked on her heady perfume. He wondered if there could possibly be any tangible gain from this ridiculous and repulsive night, if the end could possibly justify the means. He thought that perhaps he should buy a contraceptive. Or was Edith prepared? Or was she so old it didn't matter anyway?

Alan was listening to an English mystery show on the radio. The voices were loud. Gunshots, somebody grunting, knocking over a chair, a vase shattering on the floor. He wished he could be seeing what was going on, but they didn't have a TV set. His father was too stingy to buy one. Only that wasn't true, Alan had to admit to himself. It was just that his father had once been in television up to his neck, and then when he broke with it he refused to have a set in the house. Afraid it might seduce him or something, Alan thought, a little contemptuous of his father.

His mother's voice behind him, exasperated, shrill. "For God's sake, please turn that thing *down!*"

Irritated, Alan turned the radio off and stalked out of the room. Anita looked after him. "Alan . . . you didn't have to turn it off completely." No reply; only his door slamming shut.

Oh, Frank, Anita thought. Your son needs you. And I need you so. She had found her husband again in that one long passionate night at the Plaza. It was as if all their differences, all their frustrations, had been wiped clean away in one great explosion of final compatibility. Oh, if it could only be like that again between them, again and always, Anita thought, her heart filled with longing.

Alan's door opened. He went down the hall to the bathroom, and she heard him running water in the basin, and all she could think of was Frank coming out of the bathroom that night at the Plaza. I've got to see you, Frank, she said to herself. I've just got to be with you tonight.

Only he was busy rehearsing that old bag, Edith Parkes. Even so, if she drove in now, at nine-fifteen, she could be there before midnight. Frank would be pleased—she knew it; she was sure of it—he would be delighted to find her in his room, waiting for him in her black nightgown.

Anita dialed the hotel, but there was no answer from Frank's room. No, she would not leave a message. He was rehearsing Edith Parkes, so naturally he wouldn't be in his room. Why shouldn't she drive in anyway, without calling him first?

Alan came out of the bathroom, went to his room, emerged, putting on a sport jacket.

"Where are you going?" Anita asked. "Isn't it getting a little late?"

"Out."

"Out where?"

"Just out. What's the difference?"

"You're taking Christina to the graduation dance tomorrow night, aren't you? Nobody's stopping you from seeing her."

"Thank you . . . thank you for nothing," Alan said, unhappiness masking as sarcasm in his voice.

"Oh, Alan . . . Alan . . ."

"Alan, Alan," he echoed derisively. "There's no need to wring your hands, Mother. Just tell me what you're trying to *say*."

"Nothing." Anita turned away, pained by her son's hostility to her. "Only, if I'm not here when you get back, you'll know I've gone to New York to see your father."

"Well, give him my best," Alan said, and closed the door behind him with a bang.

Anita walked back and forth in the empty room. Would Frank be angry if she came in now to see him? All she wanted was to be with him, to share the happiness they had experienced

244

that one unforgettable night. But no, it would not do for her to take him by surprise. He might think she was spying on him. She must get in touch with him first, feel out his reaction before she drove in.

She looked up Edith Parkes' number, dialed and waited. The phone rang, and rang, and rang again. But they couldn't be rehearsing at the Central Plaza, not just a line rehearsal. They weren't in Frank's room, and they wouldn't be at the studio. Where were they then?

At last there was a click at the other end of the wire, and she heard Edith Parkes' hoarse, husky drawl. "Hello."

"Oh, hello, Edith. This is Anita . . . Anita Gattone."

"Well, what a surprise, dear," Edith said.

"I'm trying to locate Frank. He told me he was giving you a line rehearsal, and I assumed he would be at your place."

"No, Pumpkin. There must be some mistake."

"But he told me . . . just a little while ago."

"Sorry, Pumpkin." A small, tinkling, teasing laugh.

"Well . . . I mean you did rehearse, didn't you? Or you're going to, aren't you?"

That irritating laugh again. "Sorry, Pumpkin. You'd better look somewhere else."

The phone clicked down. Anita thought, Frank, you lied to me again. And then, not thinking at all, she opened the liquor cabinet and poured herself a straight shot of bourbon. It was not until she'd finished that she realized she'd taken a drink at all. Well, what of it? There was no reason not to have another.

The gnawing doubts and jealousy came during the second drink; the rage came with the third. Frank was with that Joan Leonard, of course. She should have known it, goddamn stupid as she was. But he wouldn't get away with it this time. This time or ever again.

There were four Joan Leonards in the phone book. The first

two did not answer. The third said, "Who? No, there's no Amanda here. . . . Lady, you're not getting through to me." The fourth call brought Joan Leonard to the phone.

Miss Leonard was very polite, much too polite. "Why no, Mrs. Gattone. I haven't the slightest idea where he could be." In the background Anita could hear flamenco music. Joan raised her voice. "Yes, perhaps he is giving Edith a line rehearsal. She does need one, you know and . . ."

But Anita was not listening. Somehow the music seemed to grow louder and louder, drowning out the girl's voice. She shook her head sharply, hung up, and sat there holding her head while the music roared on inside her brain. Perhaps she was going crazy after all. The screaming sound again, flamenco, castanets, guitars . . . Somewhere back in the Slayton family a cousin had been born an idiot. . . .

The music stopped abruptly. The room was a tomb, sealed off from the world outside. She remembered the slip of paper Frank had given her. "Call me here," he'd said, pointing to the telephone number he'd jotted down, "if there's any emergency."

Anita found the paper tucked in the drawer of the telephone stand beneath an unpaid bill from the drugstore. GR 4-2286. A TD, Frank had said that first night he'd stayed in town. "You don't know him," he'd said. "Just a friend."

She placed the slip of paper under the Joan Leonard number in the telephone book. Leonard, Joan, 14 Waverly Place, GR 4-2286, the book said.

Another drink, Anita letting it all settle slow inside her, the liquor and the final bit of proof, the honest passion in the Plaza not honest, but guilty perhaps, an effort on his part to seem honest. What a fool she had been not to see through his pretense. . . . He was having an affair with Joan Leonard . . . sleeping with Joan Leonard. . . . So very tired, of course, and what an effort, trying to keep two women satisfied. . . . One lousy, faking night! That ought to hold old Anita for a while.

246

She can come in and see the show tomorrow. But not tonight . . . not tonight. Tonight he was rehearsing Edith Parkes. The hell you are! . . . I'm very tired, Anita. . . . I'll bet!

Furious, she sat motionless in her chair. She would fix Frank Gattone. Once and for all, she would fix that lying, no-good, two-timing bastard of a husband of hers.

She got up and went over to the cabinet to make herself another drink. Then impulsively she returned to the telephone and called Paul Barker.

"Paul Barker talking," she heard him say when he picked up the phone, and she thought how like good old self-righteous Paul it sounded, always so correct and formal. She was a little tight, she knew, and tried to speak slowly, so as not to slur her words.

"Hello, Paul. You 'member, Paul? Way back . . . way back, back, back in your cottage . . . I said, sometime, and you said sure, sometime . . . So I thought maybe tomorrow night it might be sometime . . ."

"What are you talking about?" Paul said.

"Well, you know, Paul. Tomorrow night, at nine, Frank puts on his show . . . Frank the great . . . the TV boy wonder. . . . And I thought, Anita, you've got to see that show."

"Of course. I understand."

"Good boy, Paul. Good old understanding Paul. Only you've got a portable TV at the cottage, and I haven't, so I thought tomorrow night at nine . . . just you and me . . . at the cottage . . ."

"I don't know, Anita. We have to chaperone the dance, you know."

"Say hello to Batty-ass Bullock. . . . Meet all the nice boys and girls . . . and then leave, scram. . . . It'll only take a little while and then you can get back to the party. . . . Okay, Paul? Is it a date or isn't it?"

"Anita, you're drunk," Paul said.

"So what's a little drink between friends? I'll be seeing you, Paul. Must see little old Frank's big show . . ."

Anita hung up slowly, and slowly left the telephone stand and went over to the sofa and sat down. For some moments she continued to sit there rigidly, staring out into the room. Until suddenly, with an almost animal cry of rage and frustration and hurt, she flung herself full length on the sofa and buried her head in the cushions and sobbed as if her heart were breaking.

Frank sat on the gold-braided couch, watching Edith Parkes at the telephone. She was wearing a black negligee with gold trim at the neck and sleeves. Her laughter tinkled like the ice in the gold-leaf highball glasses. She hung up the telephone and, still laughing secretly, went over to the phonograph, where she selected a long-playing record from the cabinet beneath the machine. "*Music to Sleep By,*" she said, reading the title from the record's jacket. She chose another. "Ah, this is better. *Music for Lovers.*"

"Edith, who was that on the telephone?" Frank said.

"Normally, it would be loving before sleeping, except you're not staying the night, are you?"

"Who was it, Edith?"

"I'll play the sleeping first. It's about an hour's worth of music altogether, which ought to be plenty of time. Unless you're a very great lover, Pumpkin."

"Edith, I asked you . . ."

"Your wife," she said unconcernedly as she put the records on the turnstile and started the music playing.

"What did she want?"

"In the still of the night," Edith sang, "my heart goes out to you . . ."

"What did she *want?*"

248

"Oh, she had some idea you were giving me a line rehearsal."

"Goddamn it!" Frank swore, and went to the bar and poured himself a stiff drink.

"Now don't blame me, Pumpkin. After all, you could have told her the truth, you know."

"Very funny." He was angry, but not so much with Edith as with himself for not having warned her about their supposed rehearsal. If she'd told Anita it was a rehearsal, if he'd spoken to Anita himself, then she would have no reason to become suspicious. Now there was no telling what she might think—worst of all, what she might do.

Edith said, "Don't drink too much, Pumpkin."

"I should have warned you. I should have *warned* you."

She came over and took the glass from his hand. "Because too much is going to make you impotent, and frankly, I don't think you're too much of a man anyway. Frankly, Frank. Could I be wrong, frankly Frank?"

He gritted his teeth and kept his mouth shut, trying to wipe out from his thoughts the image of Anita betrayed, Anita resorting to drinking again, Anita in a towering, destructive rage. Edith was loosening her negligee, and he could not afford to be angry with himself now, or afraid for Anita, any more than he could afford to be drunk. He sat back on the sofa and watched Edith swaying to the music, watched her bare shoulders emerge, and her small firm breasts as she coyly let the negligee slide down about her waist. He said, "God, yes, you do have a body, Edith," and tried to believe he wanted her and to make his face register some expression of desire. He wet his lips, leaned forward, elbows on knees, and thought perhaps he might get her drunk and end the evening that way. But there was only one way to end the evening—Edith's way. Unless he wanted to go on the air tomorrow night without his star.

The song ended. Edith said, "Come along, Pumpkin," and

went into the bedroom. He hesitated, finished the half-empty glass she had taken from him, poured himself another drink and took it into the bedroom with him.

She was lying seductively, ridiculously posed on a huge circular bed with gold pillows on a black bedspread. The room smelled of expensive perfume. The lights were pink and low, and he supposed that in the old days there must have been French whorehouses like this, although he'd never been to France—or to a whorehouse either, for that matter. He put the glass on the table, said "Well," and wondered whether he should undress or simply start making love to her the way he was. Whichever would insult her the least; whichever would arouse her the most. He sat on the bed, touched her shoulder, looked into her lustful, enigmatic eyes, then suddenly pulled her close and lay down beside her.

"Aren't you going to take off your clothes, Pumpkin?" Edith laughed. "The etiquette book says the gentleman always removes his clothes first."

Angry, Frank obeyed, keeping his back turned to her, feeling her laughing at him behind his back. Then he lay down beside her again. His heart began pounding as her experienced hands moved over him, and he realized, with enormous relief, that he actually wanted her after all.

"Stewart, Edgar, Percy, Norman, Felix," Edith said. "All my darling Pumpkiny husbands . . . all in one with frankly Frank."

His passion grew. He forgot about Edith's age and about contraceptives, about Anita and the purpose of what he was doing. His breath came faster now and he began mumbling the meaningless words of passion. Until abruptly, at the most agonizing moment of all, she pushed him away, sat up, pulled the negligee about her shoulders and said icily, "And now, will you please get the hell out of here."

250

He stared at her, unbelieving, still breathing hard.

"Go ahead, scram, get out," she said. "I've had my part of the bargain."

"Edith . . ."

She laughed sarcastically. "Don't tell me you really want to stay."

He would stay. Because he could not leave now, had not the will. She'd known he would stay, and he understood now how well she had planned her little revenge, planned it so he would lose pride not once but twice, and could never claim afterward, not even to himself, that she'd blackmailed him.

Oh, she understood men well. He'd stay because now he felt too driven by desire to do otherwise. And yet, once interrupted, passion rises more slowly, and in the end his mind groped for other women to substitute behind the darkness of his tightly closed eyes. And just as once with Bubbles, the Mammary Marvel, he had conjured the likeness of a still-unknown Anita, so now he thought of Joan Leonard as he had seen her in the early morning of the day after the night he'd slept on her uncomfortable sofa. She'd been sitting naked in the claw-legged bathtub in the middle of her ramshackle kitchen. She'd slipped into the soapy water and said, "Pardon me. You might as well use the john while I finish here."

He'd gone into the windowless bathroom, stood silently listening to the water splashing in the tub, picturing her nude body encased in the soapy water. When he came out into the kitchen later, she was there making coffee, completely dressed.

He said, "Oh, God! . . . God!" and Edith said, "Now, Pumpkin, now!" and he said, "Yes, yes," and he could see clearly under the soapy water and the woman was young and dark, with long smooth limbs, and firm round breasts, and the blackest eyes he had ever seen.

"That was a very nice line rehearsal," Edith said afterward, getting out of bed and going into the living room to fix herself a drink. "Perhaps you'd better go now before your wife takes a notion to call you again."

Chapter Twenty-Seven

SUMMER was officially two days old, so in keeping with years of personal tradition Mr. Beatty donned his "summer uniform" on that morning of the twenty-third of June, his summer uniform being the same as his winter one, except that now in the warm weather he could go without his coat on the long, familiar route through Plimpton Ridge. Neither rain nor hail, sleet, snow, rheumatism or a bad cold ever kept Mr. Beatty from his appointed rounds, though he did prefer a day like this—sunny, warm, the grass still damp from the morning dew. It was the kind of day to go out into the world, and although Mr. Beatty's world was small in area, it contained, he believed, all there was to know in any larger world outside. He knew the people behind each curtained window—from a "good morning" over the years, from the postmarks on their letters, from the postcards which he read unabashedly and often discussed quite openly with their legal recipients. Mrs. Crossworth's son was coming home from Alaska. The Stuterfield girl had broken her engagement. Mrs. Thelp, a widow, was carrying on a lonely-heart correspondence with a man from Tulsa.

"Hear the sun hardly ever comes up in Alaska," said Mr. Beatty. And "You know how girls are," said Mr. Beatty.

"Never can make up their minds. Why, my own daughter, Millie, married to Roy Slayton . . ." And "Tulsa's a long way away," said Mr. Beatty. "If he's coming all the way from Tulsa just to meet up with you, then he must mean business, Mrs. Thelp. Serious marriage business."

Mr. Beatty shuffled under the trees along the green, past the bandstand, up the small incline along the edge of the campus. The chapel bell tolled and the boys spilled out to the gravel walks. Today they were laughing, pushing, playing, because today was the last day of school. Tonight was the graduation dance, and after that lay the long, lazy summer—and they were young, thought Mr. Beatty, they were young.

He left two circulars at the stucco house of the Paul Barkers, where pretty, young Christina said, "Good morning, Mr. Beatty," and "Yes, I'm going to the dance," with her eyes fixed beyond him—somewhere far away on a child's dream he supposed. And then three bills at the Frank Gattones' dormitory apartment, where Mrs. Gattone looked red-eyed and troubled, her hand shaking as she took the bills. "Yes, the show's tonight, Mr. Beatty. Nine o'clock."

The bag was lighter after he left Dr. Bullock's office. His step was lighter, too, and his heart lighter, because he was going homeward now, downhill all the way. He went up the long walk to the Plimpton place and wondered why Mr. Slayton didn't get after those formal gardens of his. He said, "Good morning, Mrs. Mauldin," shouting at the deaf woman, who stood in the doorway holding that big cat, Mattykins, all that was left of Lottie Slayton. "Yes, Mr. Slayton will probably be back to attend the Academy dance," Mrs. Mauldin shouted back at him.

Some day, Mr. Beatty thought, he might have a drink with Mr. Slayton—after all, weren't they kind of related?—and tell Mitchel how to turn over the soil behind the house and how to grow the largest strawberries in Connecticut.

At home once more in the early afternoon, Mr. Beatty hurried into the back yard and studied the green shoots that would be tomatoes some day. He put his ear to the ground and was certain he could hear the roots stirring. Then, satisfied that all was well, he sat on his porch with his high black shoes on the rail, drinking lemonade and watching the world go by his door.

It was a good life, Mr. Beatty always said.

Mildred Slayton found the tie clip quite by accident that afternoon. She had been lying down in the bedroom, taking a short rest after the morning's work and wondering where Roy might be. He had been acting so strangely since he returned home the night before. Not suspicious; he didn't seem to be suspicious in the least. But somehow remote, as if his mind was far away, and he became irritated when she questioned him.

Mildred sighed, and swung off the bed. She smoothed out her skirt, brushed out her red hair, then searched absently for a bobby pin. Usually she kept them in a small bone-china dish on her vanity. But the dish was empty; she would have to buy a fresh supply at the drugstore.

There were none to be found in the bathroom, nor in her sewing box. Idly she looked along the vanity once more, the night table, the ashtrays, the top drawer of Roy's dresser, and then, last of all, in the little white box where Roy kept all his unused tie clips and cuff links. She decided to sort out all his odds and ends. Some of it was just junk, some sentimental like the little campaign ribbons and battle stars he'd worn during the war, some quite valuable, like the gold links his father had once given him for Christmas. And then, not quite grasping her own discovery, she found the tie clip—Matt Barlow's tie clip.

For a long moment she stood stock-still, holding the bit of silver in her hand, realizing that the clip must have been the other thing Anita had found in the back seat of the car that day, along with the zipper. And then, as panic engulfed her, she cried "Oh, my God!" and rushed down the stairs to the telephone in the living room.

She dialed, waited, turning the clip over and over between her fingers, dialed again, waited impatiently, until finally she heard Matt Barlow's lazy voice come over the wire. "Oh, hello, there, Millie. How's tricks?"

"Matt, your tie clip," she said tensely. "The one with your initials on it."

"What about it?"

"You know, the one you lost when . . . You remember. You even called me about it."

"Sure I remember. Want to give it back to me the same way I lost it?"

"Matt! Listen to me." She was almost screaming.

"All right, Millie, I'm listening. No need to get so excited. After all, it's only a lousy tie clip."

"But I found it in Roy's dresser. Anita found it in the car and gave it to Roy and he hid it in the box with his cuff links and things. Don't you see? . . . I mean, can't you understand?"

"So Roy put it away with his other junk. So what?"

"Roy's not stupid, Matt," Mildred said. "The tab on my zipper, and now this, both in the same back seat. And he didn't throw it away. He kept it, Matt, and he's not stupid."

"So . . . let him divorce you, then."

"I don't want a divorce."

"I'd still take you after all these years," Matt said, and she felt that he was laughing at her at the other end of the wire.

"Oh Matt, will you be sensible! Roy's been acting funny lately, sort of avoiding me, and now he must know . . . I'm sure he knows, Matt. Oh why, why did it have to happen?"

"Because it had to happen," he said unconcernedly. "That's the way things usually do. Shall I come over, Millie?"

255

"Oh, God, no! No, Matt, *no!*" She slammed down the receiver and continued to stand there, trembling, hating Matt Barlow, hating herself for having called him. Matt didn't care what Roy thought. It was all a big joke to him, even if it meant the end of her marriage. In fact, he might have placed the clip there deliberately. He was probably laughing at her this very minute.

What in the world was she going to tell Roy? Mildred thought, wringing her hands in anguish. How was she ever going to be able to explain?

"Will that be all, Mr. Slayton?" Miss Calhoun said.

Mitchel looked up from the papers on his desk, saw the girl's averted face, and said absently, "What?" as he returned to his papers.

"I said will that be all?"

"Yes, thank you, Miss Calhoun. You may go now."

"I hope you have a pleasant weekend, Mr. Slayton."

"The same to you," Mitchel said, without looking up.

Miss Calhoun hesitated. He could sense her thoughts, even without looking at her. He hoped she was not going to make a scene, begin to cry or anything stupid like that. After all, what was past was past; there was no point in remembering.

"Do you want me to quit, Mr. Slayton?" Miss Calhoun said softly.

"Do you want to?"

"No . . . But ever since . . . well, you've acted as if nothing happened. Every day I've wanted to talk to you about it, but I thought I'd only be annoying you, and . . ."

Mitchel looked up at her and she lowered her eyes. "And what, Miss Calhoun?" he said.

"It's just that I . . . well, I don't understand you, Mr. Slayton. I mean I know I made a fool of myself . . . and . . . well, I just can't go on working here day after day as if nothing

256

at all had happened. I hope you don't think I'm that insensitive."

"I don't think anything, Miss Calhoun." He gave her a warm, honest smile. "I just think we understand each other, that's all. You're quite an ambitious girl, and there seemed to be an opportunity for advancement with me, only it didn't work out. I don't think it ever will. So there you are. You may, if you wish, continue as my secretary. I have no complaints, or you would have heard about them if I had. On the other hand, you may want to find another position, where there's more opportunity for you. That's entirely up to you."

He saw that she was blushing, and he said, "No irony intended."

"I'd prefer staying with you. Mr. Slayton . . . if you can forgive me . . . and forget . . ."

"There's nothing to forgive, and I've forgotten long ago. I think that will be all, Miss Calhoun."

She left the office, and after a while he heard the outer door close behind her and he sighed, feeling the silence close in around him. And the loneliness, like the walls of a solid, inviolable cell.

He was expected at the graduation dance at the Academy that night. He supposed he ought to attend, even though Roberta would be there and he would rather not see her just now. Only that wasn't true; just the opposite was true, and he knew it. He wanted more than anything in the world to be with Roberta, would marry her gladly if she would have him. But why should she? At his age, and considering he had just about ruined her life. It was ridiculous even to think of it. And yet the need to love, the need to be loved, remained unchanged despite the advancing years. And love and Roberta were for him now one and the same.

But what was the use of his thinking such thoughts, sitting alone here in his office in the silence, mooning about himself as if he were some schoolboy instead of an elderly man? All he should be wanting at his age was . . . well, there was that portrait of Siras Plimpton in Dr. Bullock's office, for instance. The picture would look good in his living room, even though he would hardly ever be home to look at it. The notion of his wanting an old picture instead of love was sufficiently absurd to make him laugh aloud. But there was no happiness in his laughter.

And suddenly, for no reason that he could think of, he remembered a prostitute he'd picked up in Soho on that long-ago trip to London.

"Do you want to go home with me?" the girl had said from the doorway where she'd been standing, perhaps to keep out of the rain.

They'd gone to her room off a small courtyard, and he'd paid her five pounds for a half hour. "I want to talk with someone, I'm lonely," he'd said impulsively, and so they'd talked, and she'd been very intelligent about most everything. She'd proudly showed him a simple Christmas card she'd received from a sentimental client. She'd explained that no, she never kissed a client because, after all, that was a bit personal, wasn't it?

"Now what the hell!" Mitchel Slayton swore aloud in the quiet office. That was so long ago. Why should he be thinking of it now? He shook his head, got up to take his hat and walked, heels clicking, down the empty corridor to the elevator. Whatever had happened to that girl in London? he wondered as he waited for the car to take him to the basement garage. He hoped she had found someone she could kiss and feel personal about.

Slipping behind the wheel, he drove the black Cadillac up the winding ramp, west on 53rd Street, and then north on Fifth Avenue. His thoughts kept returning to Roberta. If, as seemed almost certain now, she and Paul were to be divorced, why shouldn't he make amends for the past and marry the girl he had never ceased to love, acknowledge the child who was his? Only it wouldn't work. Roberta was too proud. She would think he was being sorry for her, pitied her because she was being rejected by her husband. She could never understand how much he needed her.

No, you could never go back, never go home again, he thought as he turned into the Hudson River Parkway. You could never turn back the clock, he thought despondently, staring gloomily through the windshield at the winding road ahead.

Chapter Twenty-Eight

FRANK said he would strike the shrubbery. He told Mike Purdue to set up a hand cue for Edith's last entrance. He told Joan Leonard that the last scene should be played slower. He told the sponsor's advertising manager that women in love did not always act with neatly defined motivations.

The talk swirled around him. The control room was filled with smoke, and it was already ten after seven, the dress rehearsal over, and still Anita had not arrived, and women in love did not always act with neatly defined motivations.

"You want to give your notes now?" Les said. "Then we'll have dinner—just the two of us."

"Five minutes," Frank said.

Les spoke into the microphone. "Actors' notes in five minutes." He disappeared down the iron steps to the studio below. Mike Purdue followed, taking the advertising manager with him.

"I think it's going to be all right," Joan Leonard said. "You know what they say about a bad dress."

"I know what they say," Frank said.

She looked at him, frowned, then picked up her notes and left.

Of course, Anita could have been delayed in the traffic, Frank thought. Or perhaps she called, but was not put through to the control room. The important thing was to stop worrying about her.

Joan returned. Leaning against the rail behind the row of monitors, she said, "Your wife was supposed to be here for the dress, wasn't she?"

"Yes . . ."

"You're worried."

"Yes, I am."

"I didn't want to tell you this, but she called me last night."

"So?"

"So I was just thinking. You gave your wife my number that night you slept on the sofa. I was just thinking."

"I see."

"I'm sorry. Maybe I shouldn't have told you."

"No," Frank said. "It's all right," and waited until she'd left before he drew in his breath and lifted the phone. His hand shook, and he could not keep his voice level when Anita finally answered.

"No, I'm not coming in," Anita said. "Yes, I called your Miss Leonard's place last night, and I realized you lied to me and I know where you were last night— No, don't lie again, not again." And then the most incredible of all, "I want you to come home this very minute."

The horrifying part of it was that she seemed perfectly sober. "Home?" Frank said unbelieving. "*Home!*"

"The show's all done, isn't it? From now on it's just a question of people pushing buttons. You don't push the buttons, so there's not a thing Les Garret can't do in your place."

He laughed, incredulous. "Are you serious, Anita?"

"I was never more serious in my life."

"But I have to be here. Everything depends on my being here. Besides, I have to appear for a quick interview at the end of the show."

"You don't *have* to do anything."

"Anita . . ." He felt suddenly chilled. He wished she was drunk. He wished she was not quite so calm, as though she actually meant every word she was saying. "Listen, Anita . . ."

"If you love me, Frank, you'll come home immediately. If you don't love me . . . if you've slept with that Joan Leonard . . . if you value your lousy television show more than you do our marriage, I'll not be held responsible for anything I do."

"Three hours," Frank groaned. "My God, Anita, that's all I'm asking. It'll all be over in three little hours."

"So will we, Frank, unless you start home immediately. Take your choice."

He heard a click. The phone was dead. Les Garret's voice echoed through the speaker. "Actors are waiting, Frank." He pressed the button. "Coming," then went down the iron ladder. All the way down he kept thinking that of course it was all a ridiculous joke or something, except that it was not a joke at all. *I'll not be held responsible . . . take your choice . . . take your choice. . . .*

The actors were waiting, more or less patiently, lounging on the chairs in the classroom set. He gave them his notes, mechanically, speaking to faces he did not see. Edith asked questions. She was polite, co-operative. And sardonic, too, damn her! She had placed the guilt inside him, and she knew that one way or another he would use it to destroy himself.

"That's all," he said. "Have a good dinner, and if we're all on our toes, it'll be a hell of a show." He kept staring at Edith, who smiled back at him sweetly, knowingly, almost pityingly, he thought. Damn her!

Les said, "The English Grill?" and he nodded and went down with Les in the elevator. In the restaurant they sat near the windows, inside where it was air-conditioned.

"You know your own lines for that interview bit at the end?" Les said.

Frank nodded, hearing Anita's voice again: *I'll not be held responsible* . . .

"Nothing to it, really," Les said. "Not even a particularly good idea. But the sponsor seems to think the audience likes to feel they're on the inside of the show. So if they get a chance to see the director . . ."

Frank nodded again. *Take your choice*, Anita said. *Take your choice* . . .

"Something eating you?" Les said.

"No," looking out the window at the lighted umbrellas, beneath which people drank and ate and gossiped in the summer evening.

"Frank." Les leaned forward across the table. He took off his horn-rimmed glasses, wiped them, put them on again, ran a hand over his close-cropped hair. "Frank, I know how you're counting on this Hollywood thing. They'll be watching the show, and I've made them promise to give an immediate decision. They'll call me as soon as the show's off the air."

"I see."

"But don't count on it, Frank. Don't count on it."

"I won't." But he was. Now more than ever before. He'd gone this far, was risking this much—his own personal integrity, his own wife, his own marriage—and if a man risked that much, he deserved a great deal in return.

"I mean doing a movie isn't everything," Les said.

"Isn't it?"

"Hell, you might not even like Hollywood."

"I'd like it." He'd like it, with Anita or without Anita. You're off to market to buy a fat pig, Edith had said. She was right. He was going to market, and he'd buy that pig, in a poke or not in a poke—he would not go back to teaching in that deadly little prep school—would not take orders from Anita or anyone else. He'd jumped headfirst into this long, costly gamble, and goddamnit, he was going to win.

"I want Hollywood, Les. You understand that? This show is going to be *good*. It has to be good. It *has* to be."

Les frowned, poked at his kidney pie. "There's not that much at stake, Frank."

"No?" He was grim, almost angry, and the words came out slowly one by one. "I'll tell you this much, Les. If they don't hire me to do this picture, then I haven't got one single goddamn thing worth working for—even *living* for."

"Don't be so intense, fella," laughing nervously.

"I mean it, Les."

"Look . . . it's a cornball . . . you said it yourself."

"I *mean* it."

Les stared down at his plate. He poked at another piece of meat, gulped a long drink of water from the large goblet, then began talking slowly, softly, like a father giving hard learned advice to an impulsive son. "Frank . . . let me tell you something. You've never been on the Coast. So all right, I understand how it seems like the end-all for a director. I understand that. But don't forget. I worked there once, and I know something about it. *Something*. And I know it may be all right to work there, but you've got to *live* there, too, and it just isn't worth it. I mean even Plimpton Ridge is better . . . I mean how the hell can I explain it? Hollywood isn't a place . . . it's a warped attitude, a set of contradictions. Everyone's unemployed, yet everybody drives Cadillacs and sports cars. . . . So they need them. All right, in Hollywood you spend half your life in an automobile . . . no taxis, no buses, no subways, no center of anything, and to prove it, they even name this place the 'City Center' just to give themselves confidence. You drive around and around, passing all these handsome, tanned fellows in Corvettes, with beautiful ash-blondes leaning on their shoulders. Every one of them looks exactly like Kim Novak, and you wonder where the hell they're driving *to*, but you never find out. . . . You never even know where *you're* going. . . . Everyone lives east or west or north or south, and you have to watch the sun, or carry a compass, and even then you haven't got a chance. The pedestrian's always right. You even have to *stop* for him at certain crosswalks. Can you imagine stopping for a pedestrian in New York?

"And that Hollywood Freeway! You get on that, you have to go all the way to the end, up in Azuza or Anaheim or someplace in Death Valley, because you can't get off it unless you want to get killed. . . . So all right, you take a chance . . . all right. You even learn to orient yourself in some vague way with Hollywood, Sunset, Wilshire, and Olympic, and a couple of cross streets like La Brea or Highland or Western Avenue. All right, now you can't make a left turn without being in a very special lane, except why do you want to make a left turn anyway? . . . Where are you going? . . . To your home in Beverly Hills? . . . Very nice. You've got a heated swimming pool. It's one hundred and ten in the shade—still you heat the swimming pool. Stay in the pool, stay in the house, and drink yourself silly and die of loneliness. . . . Or go out on the town? Fine. . . . They pull in the sidewalks at half past ten. . . . Go to a special showing of *The Son of Dracula's First Cousin*. Everybody's there. Everybody claps like hell, and after that, you go have a malted milk or a Coke in Schwab's drugstore, and that's it—you've had it.

"Hollywood, for Christ's sake, Frank. . . . There's one bookstore in the whole town. . . . It's impossible to get a shoeshine.

264

. . . You can get your Cadillac washed automatically on any corner, buy gas in the biggest goddamn stations in the world, but you have to drive five miles one way for a haircut, then five another way to buy a pound of hamburger. Everyone claims they don't drink. You can't even get a beer in the studio commissary—but there's a liquor store on every corner. Half delicatessen, too, except all they sell is canned peas and bottled orange juice and Maxwell House Coffee. . . . Frank, in Hollywood you *have* to drink Maxwell House Coffee. . . . And it's got to be liquor or coffee because the water tastes terrible, and it's so goddamn hard you can't get a decent shave without cutting yourself to ribbons."

Les stopped talking. He said, "Well, you get the point?"

"I wasn't even listening."

"So I was just making conversation."

"You don't know, Les. The point is, you don't understand at all."

"No, I guess I don't," Les said.

Chapter Twenty-Nine

TONIGHT, of all nights, Millie was so terribly nice, knocking herself out for him when all he wanted was to be left alone. It made Roy feel guiltier than ever. She talked about attending the graduation dance at the Academy as if it was her girlhood dream. The graduation dance, for God's sake! Roy thought. He had no intention of going.

She was wearing a sexy black cocktail dress, cut low in front, and she seemed so eager to please . . . like a hostess, maybe, or a mistress, instead of a wife. She said, "All right, darling, if you want to see Paul first . . . before the dance. I mean, whatever you want to do. But just one cocktail first with me."

Roy sank nervous and exhausted into a chair. She brought him the cocktail. He sipped at it and looked dully over the rim of the glass at the red-haired stranger who sat across from him talking about a lot of meaningless, irrelevant things in which he wasn't even remotely interested. Things like, "Did you know I spoke to Matt Barlow on the phone today? The first time in ages. Because I happened to give him a lift the other day. He sat in back, you see, and he dropped his tie clip in the back of the car."

"Did he?" Roy said, wondering why this, why is she telling me this? And what the hell's Matt Barlow got to do with it, and who cares about his goddamn tie clip?

"Yes, I found it among your cuff links and I'll mail it back to him, because of course I don't want to see him. I never do see him except to pass him on the street or something."

"Well," Roy said, "well," wishing she'd stop talking about Matt Barlow, of all the stupid, uninteresting people.

"Oh Roy, darling . . . darling." She was on her knees now, her head in his lap, saying, "Believe me, believe me."

Believe me what? What was there to believe, except that he loved an almond-eyed girl in Hawaii, and she was bearing his child, the child of his passion, and now he would never, never see her again.

Millie's body was trembling. "I wore this dress just for you," she whispered. "I thought maybe . . . before you go looking for Paul . . . right now, darling, if you want to come upstairs . . ."

"For God's sake, Millie," he said, and got up from the chair

266

and stood looking down at her, wondering why she was crying, what there was to cry about. What was worse, he didn't even care. He wanted to say, "Can't you see, Millie, I don't love you? Can't you see it? I was planning on a divorce. I was counting on Luanai. Now there's no Luanai, but still I don't love you." He wanted to say it, but could not, could only put down his drink and go up the stairs, feeling unutterably weary and indifferent to the woman who was crying her heart out for some reason he could not fathom.

He took three aspirins and then, on a sudden impulse, he reached under the bed for the box where Big Roo still lay hidden after all these years. For a long moment he remained there by the bed on his knees, staring down at the toy stuffed animal, surprised that he had forgotten Big Roo had only one eye. Then he rose to his feet, and carrying the toy in his arms the way he used to when he was a little boy, he went downstairs again.

Millie was still in the living room, still sobbing for some strange reason of her own. He went through the hallway to the kitchen, took a fifth of bourbon from the cabinet over the sink, opened the back door quietly and went out to his car. He propped Big Roo on the seat beside him, placed the bottle in the kangaroo's lap, and backed out of the drive. As he passed the buttonwood trees the front door opened and Millie stood there, framed black in the yellow light.

"Roy!" she screamed. "Come back, come back!" until he'd left the drive and her voice was drowned by the engine's purr.

"What's got into her tonight?" he said to Big Roo as he sped recklessly down the road. "What the hell's the matter with her?"

He drove past the Academy. There were no lights in the Barker house. Roberta was probably at the dance and poor old Paul was probably hiding out, sulking in the cottage. There were Japanese lanterns strung along the walk in front of the gymnasium. The orchestra was playing, and all the nice young kids were having themselves a hell of a nice time, only to hell with them!

He drove past his father's house. The porch light was on, though the Cadillac was not in the driveway. Dear old Daddy was at the dear little dance, too, no doubt, giving the shaft to dear old Batty-ass Bullock. To hell with both of them! He stopped the car, took a long pull at the bottle, then drove on.

"To hell with everybody!" Roy said drunkenly to the one-eyed kangaroo sitting solemnly beside him, and he drove fast through the town, under the black trees toward the cottage where probably poor old Paul was hiding out, licking his wounds inflicted by his goddamn deceiving little wife.

"To hell with everybody but poor old Paul!"

Though it was only six months old, Alan's tuxedo was already too small for him. The sleeves were too short, the pants tight at the crotch, and his widening shoulders threatened to split the seams each time he swung his arms.

"We'll have to get you a new one," his mother said. "You'll be needing it for college, anyway."

"If I go to college, that is," Alan said, straightening his bow tie before the small mirror in the hallway.

"Now why wouldn't you go to college?"

Alan shrugged, tightening the narrow coat across his back. "Maybe I just don't want to go."

"You'll change your mind."

"I know what you mean. Say good-by to Christina like a good little boy, cry the sad little tears of youth, and then forget her. Isn't that what you mean, Mother?"

"You look very nice," Anita said, "except your handkerchief needs straightening." She reached for the handkerchief in his breast pocket, started to draw it out, when he jerked away from her, his face suddenly white.

268

"Don't touch it!"

"But why?"

"I like it the way it is," Alan said, patting his breast pocket as if to make sure everything was intact. If his mother ever knew what he had there, wrapped up in the handkerchief, she'd have a fit, he thought.

"Well, have a good time," Anita said, hurt by his behavior.

"What about you?" Alan said. "I thought you were going to the studio."

"I changed my mind."

"I should think, with Dad in the television business, we'd break down and get a set of our own."

"He's not in the business, Alan. It's just this one shot."

"I thought we were going to Hollywood afterwards."

"We're not going to any Hollywood," Anita said determinedly.

"Very mysterious," Alan said. He patted his breast pocket again, kissed his mother a quick good night, and left the house.

She heard his feet on the gravel path, and felt a quick rush of sympathy for her son. Before, her sympathy had been smothered by her fear that Alan and Christina might marry against her protests and Roberta's—or even because of them. But now that the Barkers were splitting up, moving away, she was free to care about her son's emotional life in the same way that any mother might show concern and interest.

It was almost nine o'clock. If Frank had left the studio immediately after she had told him to come home at once, he should be here at any moment now. She heard a car approaching, and stood rigid, her heart beating faster as she listened for it to slow down. But then the car went on, and she knew that Frank would not be coming. There was no use deluding herself any more. It was odd, though, how calm she felt. Not hoping any longer, and not crushed, either. There was the liquor cabinet, so handy, such an easy way to let her emotions go. But she did not want a drink. She wanted only to understand herself very clearly, and what she was going to do, and why.

Frank had slept with that pseudo-sophisticated beatnik, Joan Leonard, and more than once, probably. Very well; she accepted the fact. She had warned him that his return to television would ruin their marriage, but no, he had insisted on going through with it. It was still not too late, if he would come back to her as she asked and show her that his marriage meant more to him than a television show.

Only he wouldn't. She was sure of it. Nevertheless, she would call again. Maybe he actually had left for home and was delayed. Maybe he had missed the train . . . the train was late . . . he could not get a taxi from Bridgeport . . .

When she got through to the studio, a girl's voice answered. It was Joan Leonard. Anita said, "Miss Leonard, this is Mrs. Gattone. Could you please tell me—is my husband still in the studio?"

"Why, of course, Mrs. Gattone." She seemed surprised, Anita thought, as if it was somehow unnatural for a wife to be asking for her husband.

"Then would you give him a message, please?" Anita said.

"Just a moment, Mrs. Gattone."

Silence, then Frank's voice, hoarse, desperate. "Anita . . . listen, Anita."

"I'm leaving, Frank."

"Leaving? . . . What? . . . Where? . . ."

"Oh, I'm going to see your great show, Frank. And at the end, when you come on for your interview, when you look into the camera and think of all those millions of people looking back at you, then think of me, Frank. Because I'll be there, looking back at you, and I won't be knitting, and I won't be alone."

"Anita, what are you talking about?"

"An eye for an eye, a roll in the hay for a roll in the hay."

"For Christ's sake, Anita."

270

"You've made your bed and now you can lie in it. I'll make my own, thank you."

"For *Christ's sake!*"

She slammed the receiver down, went into the bedroom, and calmly went about making up her face. Frank would not call back. He'd made his decision, and time and television waited for no man. She brushed out her hair, moved toward the door, hesitated for a long moment, giving the phone a final last chance to ring. Then she walked out into the night, got into her car, and drove slowly toward Paul Barker's cottage.

All the way there she wondered how much of what she was doing was simply calculated revenge, and how much was purely selfish. Hadn't she really counted on Frank's not coming home —counted on the opportunity, the chance, without guilt, of going to bed with a man as deceived and disillusioned as herself, who happened also to be the most attractive man in Plimpton Ridge?

"What if I did?" Anita said aloud, recklessly. "What difference does it make?" But she could not rid herself of her guilty thoughts so easily, could not so easily blind herself to the fact that she was hurting Frank because she loved him, was going to Paul because she could not escape from her need for Frank. "Oh Frank, Frank," she whispered, feeling the hot tears come to her eyes. "I'm so mixed up."

Chapter Thirty

THE band played softly and under the Japanese lanterns in the gymnasium that had been converted into a ballroom the young couples swayed and swirled—the girls in white and pink, in blue and orange, in an occasional bright red, smiling and radiant as they moved on enchanted feet, while the boys shuffled awkwardly in their tight black shoes, their starched white shirts, some barely recognizable in their unfamiliar formal garb and formal manners.

A few latecomers arrived. They bowed and shook hands with Roberta and Paul Barker, with Dr. and Mrs. Bullock. "How-do-you-do? . . . How-do-you-do? . . . So very nice to see you." Paul knew most of the boys by sight, many by name. He'd taught them history, coached them in tennis. The girls, except for a scattering from out of town, were friends of Christina's from the local high school. Finally the last couple had arrived. They could sit down now. Roberta tucked her skirt under her as she eased onto the bench.

She was wearing the same dress she had worn that fateful evening at Dr. Bullock's. How long ago it seemed, although actually it was only a matter of some weeks. But then, time was not measured in hours, but in the number and importance of the events that filled it. A few weeks ago . . . a hundred years ago . . . She touched Paul's arm, nodded her head. "Doesn't Christina look lovely?" she whispered.

Paul felt a pang of love—or was it jealousy? He could not tell which it was, except that it seemed to pierce him to the heart as he watched his daughter—*his* daughter?—in virgin white, swaying happily in Alan's arms, her head resting lightly on his shoulder, their faces close, tender with the sweet solemnity of youth. Who could blame the boy for being in love with her? Paul thought. She looked so secure in his arms.

Poor innocents, Paul said to himself. God keep them from ever having to know the truth.

He could feel Roberta's thigh touching his, and he remembered the previous night when she'd invited him to use her in any way he pleased, whether he cared for her or not. He stole a glance at her face, beautiful under the many colored lights, and his whole being yearned for her.

Dr. Bullock was glancing at his watch. "I guess he's not coming," he said.

"Who?" his wife asked.

"Mitchel Slayton, of course."

Of course, Mitchel Slayton, Paul thought bitterly. "You didn't tell me he'd be here," he whispered to Roberta.

"I didn't know."

"If he's coming, we can't stay."

"Paul." She covered his hand with hers. "We have to stay. Think what it would look like if we were to go now."

"I cannot face that man again."

"Paul . . . please." Her hand moved up his arm, and involuntarily he pulled away from her. He saw Christina leaving the dance floor with Alan. Somebody ought to be keeping an eye on them tonight, he thought, and because he was worried he became angry.

"I told you I'm getting out of here," he said tensely. "Are you coming with me or not?"

"But dear," Roberta pleaded, "we can't leave just yet. What will people say?"

He didn't care what anybody said. He remembered that Anita was expecting him at the cottage so she could catch Frank's television show. Devil take Anita and the show! He wanted to be alone with his wife, now, before Mitchel Slayton could come between them again, wanted her with a sudden passion that was overwhelming. Last night she had said, "Whenever you want me," and he wanted her now, right now, wanted her with all his being. Urgently he whispered in her ear, "I want you . . . Let's go home."

She turned to him, thrilled by the passion in his voice, and looked into his eyes and knew that he desired her. "You know how much I want to, darling . . ."

"Then just for a few minutes . . . in the car. . . . We never have, in the car."

"My dress, Paul—"

"Goddamn your dress!"

"Paul, it's crazy. . . . After we get home . . . then, anything. But not now. . . . Don't you see, Paul?"

"No, I don't see." He turned from her and saw Mitchel Slayton coming into the room. He felt Roberta's hand tighten on his arm, and then, in the swirling lights, it was not a dance at all he saw before him but that evening at Dr. Bullock's, and Anita had just told him the numbing truth, and there was nothing to do, nowhere to go, but away, away—Paul jerked to his feet and strode fast across the gymnasium floor, under the basketball net, and out into the night and his car parked nearby.

The night was clear, warm, the stars bright overhead, and he was driving the same road he had driven that night, in the same blind way. Roberta didn't want him back, not the way she pretended, or she would have left with him when he asked her. *What will people say? . . . My dress?* . . . What could such things matter if a woman really wanted her husband? She'd never wanted him, only married him to save herself. And

274

now Mitchel Slayton was talking to her, and everything was right back to where it had started.

Bouncing down the dirt road to the cottage, he saw Anita's car. He drew up beside it, sat staring at her figure behind the wheel. Anita got out. "For a while I thought you wouldn't come," she said softly, smiling at him through the open window, and from the sound of her voice he knew it was not of her husband's television show she was thinking.

He hesitated, but then remembering Roberta's refusal to leave with him, her insistence on staying to see Mitchel Slayton, all his anger and jealousy surged up in him anew and he got out of the car.

Let her have the father, he thought bitterly. I'll take the daughter.

Mitchel said, "Good evening, Roberta," holding her hand overlong. Then taking the seat beside her so abruptly vacated by Paul, he added gallantly, "You look particularly charming tonight, my dear."

Concerned as she was about Paul's angry departure, she still did not miss the special tone of Mitchel Slayton's voice. It reminded her of those days long ago when she had thought she was so much in love with him. Now, while she kept glancing anxiously toward the doorway, he sat stiffly beside her, one hand fidgeting with his mustache as he tried to make conversation.

"So Paul has taken that post in Pennyslvania . . . and you'll be leaving soon with Christina."

"Yes," Roberta said absently. "As soon as the dance is over . . . tomorrow, probably . . . everything's over now." Oh Paul, she thought unhappily, why didn't I go with you when you asked me? Now it's too late. . . . Where are you, Paul?

"You wouldn't have to go away," Mitchel was saying. "I

275

mean after you get your divorce. I was thinking only this afternoon . . . I'm a very lonely man, my dear . . . it occurred to me that perhaps you would let me make amends."

The music was playing softly. Roberta watched the young dancers swaying under the lanterns, and worried about Paul, and thought—half listening to what Mitchel was saying beside her—what in the world was the man talking about, why was he sitting so close to her? She edged away from him.

"It's a lovely dance, isn't it?" she said. "Would you like to dance, Mitchel?" Anything to make her stop thinking so desperately about Paul.

"Roberta," Mitchel said sharply. "You're not listening to me."

She turned, surprised, to look into his troubled eyes.

"I'm sorry, Mitchel. I guess my mind was wandering."

"I was saying"—he cleared his throat nervously—"I was saying . . . after you get your divorce . . . it would make me very happy— Oh my God!" he broke off abruptly. "Why is it so hard for me to ask you?"

"Ask me what, Mitchel?" she said, questioningly.

"Marry me, Roberta," he blurted out, seizing her hand. "Be my wife. Let me make up for all the unhappiness I have brought you. Marry me. Let me live with you the way I should have before Christina was born. . . ."

"You don't have to feel sorry for me, Mitchel," she said softly, proudly.

"It's not that, my dear. It's not that at all. If I feel sorry for anyone, it's myself. Believe me. Believe me, my child. It's not pity I'm giving but asking . . ." His voice broke.

"Oh, Mitchel!" Roberta said, overwhelmed by the old feeling of tenderness for him. She laid her hand on his arm. "I do believe you, Mitchel. But don't you see, it's not possible. I still love Paul. I'll always love him no matter what happens."

"But you are going to be divorced."

276

"That won't matter. Divorce can't change my feelings any."

"No, I suppose not," he muttered. "We can't turn back the clock, can we?" He smiled sadly into her eyes. "I know you think I'm being ridiculous. After all, I'm old enough to be your father. You must forgive an old man's folly."

"Oh no, please, Mitchel, don't say that. I don't feel that way about you at all."

Roberta felt that in another moment she would be crying. "Excuse me," she said, rising hurriedly from the bench. "Don't get up. I'll be back in a moment." And weaving in and out among the dancing couples she left the room.

Mitchel Slayton wiped the perspiration from his brow. "Warm in here," he said lamely, going over to Dr. Bullock, who was sitting nearby on his right.

"Umm," Dr. Bullock said, looking at him curiously. "Anything wrong, Mitchel? Would you like a cigarette?" He snapped open his cigarette case.

"No, thank you." Mitchel fingered his mustache nervously. "Well, maybe I will have one after all." His hand shook as he took a cigarette from the case. "A lovely dance," he murmured. He lit his cigarette. "A very fine group of young people."

"Ummm," said Dr. Bullock.

Christina's dress had a full skirt that swung gently as she walked, so that she seemed to float beneath the dark shadows of the tall elms that lined the campus path. Alan's feet made crunching, heavy sounds on the gravel path, and he tried to walk more lightly but found it impossible. He wondered if Christina felt as strange and tense as he did. He wondered if she regretted her passionate promise. He was not so sure he didn't regret it himself. Now that this thing between them was going to happen, he was afraid.

"It was awfully warm in there," Christina said, and he had a feeling that she'd read his thoughts.

He slipped his hand under her bare elbow. Her skin was cool, and he thought that she was probably cool all over her entire body, and soon now he would know for certain. He wished he did not feel so warm himself. He wished he could tell Christina that he'd taken care of everything, though it had been difficult and embarrassing. He'd gone to all three of the town's drugstores. Twice a woman had waited on him and he'd left in near panic. In the third, he had started to say, "I'd like to buy . . ." and then had forgotten the technical name for what the boys called merely "safes." Finally he'd bought one for fifty cents from a classmate named Harry Sudergill, who was always boasting about the way he had with women. "A girl from the other side of town," Alan had explained with a show of casualness, and Harry had only winked slyly and said it was about time he lost his virginity. He'd said, "Hell, I lost it two years ago," though it had been a lie. But then, perhaps all those times—perhaps Harry had been lying, too.

"What are you thinking about?" Christina said.

"Nothing, particularly," though he was thinking how his mother had almost found it there in the breast pocket of his tuxedo, tucked away in his handkerchief.

"Where are we going?"

"I don't know. I borrowed a car from this fellow I know. We can go anywhere we like."

"Won't they miss us at the dance?"

"Who cares?"

"Even so, Alan . . ."

She was trying to put him off now. He was angry, and when they reached the car behind the dormitory, when he opened the door for her, after she'd slid into the front seat he slammed the door hard to let her know.

Christina sat away from him, in the corner, leaning against the door, her eyes fixed straight ahead. All right, if that was the

278

way she felt. He stepped hard on the accelerator, swung out of town, driving very fast.

"Alan," Christina said timidly, coming closer to him. "I didn't mean what you thought. I just meant—well, maybe my parents will worry about me."

"You don't owe them anything. And I don't owe anything to mine, either."

"I know. They've made things hard for us."

"You're damn right they have!" He pulled up at the side of the road, flung an arm around her shoulders. He was surprised to find her skin so warm, almost as warm as his own hand. He kissed her hard on the mouth. "I love you, Christy," he murmured, his lips upon hers. "I love you . . . the only person in the whole world." And she answered, holding him close to her, "Me, too, Alan . . . me, too." And then, as the passion grew within him and feverishly his hands began to explore her body under her dress, she whispered, "Not now, Alan . . . not here. Please, dear, darling, not here," and pulled away from him.

Alan drew back, panting. "All right," he said, "all right," starting the car again. If not here, where? he wondered. And even, how? And suddenly he was very much afraid.

Roy Slayton had managed to finish most of the bottle of bourbon deposited in Big Roo's lap for safekeeping by the time he approached Paul Barker's cottage. He had not come there directly, by any means. As he explained seriously to Big Roo sitting beside him, "Sometimes the longest distance around is the shortest distance between two points. Right, Big Roo?" Now he had arrived at last, and bumping down the rutted road toward the lighted window he saw two cars parked side by side, and recognized Paul's station wagon and—by God!— his sister Anita's car. "Well, what do you know?" Roy said to Big Roo.

He stopped the car, the better to think about the situation. "I'll be damned," he swore softly. Anita here at Paul's cottage. His own bitchy sister. And what were they doing in there, behind the lighted window? And why bother even to ask the question? How could you ever know what was going on in this crazy, mixed-up world?

So leave them alone, to do whatever they were going to do anyway. . . . Drive back up the road . . . find a turn-off in the woods . . . drive along the overgrown path . . . a deer staring into the headlights . . . a skunk scurrying off into the bush . . . pull the car to one side . . . turn off the lights . . . open the bottle again and take a good long drink . . . for Luanai and for Millie . . . for Anita and Paul . . . and one more for Big Roo. . . . "Would you like a drink, Big Roo? . . . No drink for Big Roo. Pure, decent, wise Big Roo. In the whole rotten world, the only real friend. . . . He didn't deceive you, didn't love you too much, didn't go rolling in the hay with your nymphomaniac sister. No, sir, a friend is a friend is a friend, and another drink to you, big friendly Roo.

Headlights . . . a rattling car, stopping, two figures inside . . . a boy in tuxedo . . . a girl in white.

The boy said, "Mr. Slayton." It was Alan Gattone and Alan's mother was down in the cottage rolling in the hay with Paul Barker, and the girl was Christina Barker, and her father was down in the cottage rolling in the hay with Anita Gattone . . . and you two kids better look out, Roy thought fuzzily. Because if you two kids ever get an idea to roll in the hay too, that's going to be just too awful bad.

The car doors opened. Alan got out one side, Christina the other. They came closer and looked at the almost empty bottle, and saw the big toy kangaroo, and looked at each other in wonder. The girl said, "Are you all right, Mr. Slayton?" and he said, "I'm fine, I'm feeling no pain, and would you like a drink?" They both said no. The girl was very young and very beautiful, and it was a damn shame. . . . His goddamn father's child, and God it was a shame and he felt like crying about it.

"Are you sure you're all right, Uncle Roy?" the boy said.

"Fine, fine."

"Mr. Slayton . . . please," the girl said.

"Anything for a poor little child."

"Well, my mother and father . . . I . . . I wish you wouldn't tell them you saw us here."

"Not a word, you poor little child." And God, he did want to cry, want to save the poor little child as he'd saved Big Roo and Luanai, hold her close as he'd held Big Roo and Luanai. "Not your fault not your fault . . . your mother's fault . . . but you've got to understand. Lots of good girls get in trouble . . . have to marry the first man who'll have 'em. Happens all the time. . . . So don't cry, little girl, don't cry . . ."

He talked on drunkenly, comforting the little girl. The little girl backed away, climbed into the car. The boy got into the car. The engine started, the car backed up, turned around, disappeared. . . . Something moved in the bushes. That old skunk, probably. . . . Where did the little girl go, all dressed in white, leaving him alone again, alone with Big Roo, all, all alone?

He took another drink, the last in the bottle . . . "to you, forlorn little girl in white . . . to you, Big Roo . . ." and flung the bottle into the woods. Very drunk . . . very . . . drunk . . . very lonesome in the dark woods. Start the engine, drive through the dark, dark woods, faster and faster, bumping, bouncing, jouncing on the overgrown path, fenders scraping trees, rocks scraping the low-slung body . . . down and down we go . . .

And there was the lake, and the small wooden dock, and there, beyond the dock, a float, only yards away. . . . An island in the black water, and now he wanted an island for himself and Big Roo. They were the ones who deserved an island, where they could sit alone together . . . Christopher Roy Robin, and his great friend, Big Roo. . . .

The car was doing fifty when it sailed off the end of the dock. The front wheels grabbed at the float, missed, and hit the water with a hard smack. "Hold on!" Roy cried to the kangaroo, and clutched it to him as the car sank slowly beneath the water. He was saving Big Roo from the cold, indifferent world, rushing him home to hide in a big box under his bed. He was saving Luanai now, rushing her down the dock away from the strafing planes. He was holding Big Roo, soft and furry, holding Luanai, smooth and cool. But both were cold now, drowning now. And he realized dimly at the very end that there was still time to save them both all over again, even time to save himself . . . if he really wanted to . . . if he really . . . if . . .

Chapter Thirty-One

AT QUARTER to nine the T.D. had gone back to his panel to match cameras and check the tapes, video, music, lights, film studio levels and master control. Ten minutes later Frank Gattone called, "Positions, please." Four minutes later he called, "One minute, and good luck to everyone." Sixty seconds later, as the red second hand on the big clock above the monitors moved to exactly 9:00 P.M. Eastern Daylight Time, he ordered, "Up on One and cue the boys!" Then, turning to Joan

Leonard, who sat close behind him on a folding metal chair, "Here goes everything or nothing."

The commercial . . . the slow dissolve to the children fooling around in the classroom . . . titles over . . . "Slow pan to the doorway," Frank said into the microphone . . . "Cue Miss Parkes . . . Go in . . . *in* . . . Fishpole, I can see you, dammit . . ."

The show went on. Good? Bad? You could never tell from the control room. You gave the orders and tried not to think of anything except what was on the screen right now and what would be there next.

To the children, Edith said, "I'm leaving for a short vacation."

On that last, threatening call from Plimpton Ridge, Anita had said, *I'm leaving, Frank.*

Edith laughed, said to the inquiring children, "I need a rest. Catch up on my knitting."

Anita had said, *I will not be knitting.*

Don't think of Anita. Don't think about Anita.

"Number two, you're hitting Edith with the camera . . . Now there's a big boom shadow on the kids' faces . . . All right, pan up . . . slower, *slower* . . . Now, slow dissolve . . . Close-up on resort sign . . . Pull back . . . Pull *back* . . . All right, cue her . . . But hold it until she's there . . . It's a fast change, so give her time . . . Good . . . She made it . . ."

He kept talking. First act over. Commercial. "Roll the film . . . *Roll it.*" Then two minutes of relief and two minutes to remember. Roll it, roll it. A *roll in the hay for a roll in the hay.*

What the hell had Anita been talking about? A roll in the hay with whom? . . . Whom? . . . When, where?

Joan Leonard nudged his arm. "Yes . . . All right . . . Dissolve . . . Keep the music down . . . Now the crickets are too loud . . . Calm down those goddamn crickets . . . All right, it's a love scene . . . Who the hell is sneaking around the bushes? . . . Keep that stage hand out of the bushes . . . Slow . . . It's a *love* scene . . . Fine . . . We're right on time, so relax, relax . . . Now dissolve . . . Dissolve . . . Easy there on One . . . Relax, relax . . ."

The second commercial. Another two minutes, and time now to relax, relax.

Anita hadn't been drunk, either. So where was she, doing what, with whom? "Oh, I'm going to see your great show," she had said. "And at the end, when you come in for your interview, when you look into the camera and think of all those millions of people looking back at you, then think of me, Frank. Because I'll be looking back at you, too—and I will not be alone—and I will not be knitting."

"Not be alone," Frank said aloud.

Joan said, "What?"

"Nothing."

Joan said, "Five seconds."

The commercial ended. Act Three. "Slow dissolve from titles . . . Number two, you're getting shadows again . . . Pan the kids' faces . . . Slowly . . . Slowly . . . Who the hell told that kid he could chew gum? . . . Pan him off . . . All right, cut to Edith . . . She's crying . . . Let her cry . . . Closer . . . They're real tears . . . let me see the tears . . . And dissolve to resort . . ." His fingers snapped with each new shot. "Cut to lover at window," snap. "Cut to two shot," snap . . . "Pull back," snap . . . "Cut to camera four," snap . . . "Number four, get the hell into position," snap, "position," snap . . . It's a short scene," snap . . . "Get into position." Snap, snap, snap.

Behind him, Les Garret said, "One minute to get down there, Frank."

Frank nodded. "Ready to dissolve to black . . . black . . .

And out!" He ripped off his headset, raced for the iron stairway, shouting back to Mike Purdue, "Get in all the credits, Mike . . . There's plenty of time," and raced down the narrow stairs, picked his way among the sets, around the long cables, through the waiting actors, toward the small library set where the announcer would interview this week's great director.

"Don't look at the camera," Les had told him. "Talk to the announcer, not to the audience." He tried to remember. He sat beside the announcer in a leather chair. The camera moved in closer, closer . . . The cue, and the red light blinked on and he was on the air.

"Ladies and gentlemen," the announcer was saying, "each week, as you know, we introduce the director of the Electro Theatre. . . . This week, it is our privilege to introduce Mr. Frank Gattone. . . ."

The camera moved. A two shot, himself and the announcer, and he was supposed to say, "It was an honor . . . working with such fine talent" . . . something like that, and he was not supposed to look at the camera, only he was looking at the camera, trying to see behind it, through its cables, through the air to Anita, somewhere, with someone. . . .

"It must be a great strain," said the announcer.

"Yes," remembering his lines now. "Because you can't ever correct the mistakes. Once the mistake is made, there's nothing that can be done about it. So you must not make a mistake. You can't make a mistake. . . . Please, please . . ." The sweat running down his face, talking to Anita, straight into the red light, begging her, pleading with her, "Please don't make a mistake."

The camera moved, leaving him out of the picture. Les's orders, of course. "Get the camera off Frank. He's gone nuts." Something like that, only it didn't matter. The announcer was saying good night. The red light blinked off. On a monitor across the floor, he saw the credits roll and thought that Mike

Purdue had got them all in and now the monitor went black and they were off the air.

He sat dumbly in the leather chair. The announcer looked at him curiously. "You all right, Frank?"

He nodded.

Les appeared as the sets were already being struck around him. "Are you all right?" Les asked.

He nodded.

"You almost blew it there at the end. I had to take the camera off you."

He nodded.

"You don't have to worry," Les said. "Nobody made any mistakes."

"Nobody?" he said.

Les frowned. "You going straight home?"

"Yes."

"Don't care for a drink?"

"No."

"Well." Les's hand touched his shoulder. "I'll be hearing from Hollywood in a couple of hours. I'll call you at home as soon as I get the verdict."

"All right."

"And like I told you, Hollywood isn't the end-all. And even if you don't get the job, it was a great show. Nobody made a mistake."

Les walked off across the floor, picked his way through the stage hands who swarmed everywhere, taking the whole make-believe world to pieces, leaving nothing at all to remind anyone of this agonizing, this triumphant hour. Edith Parkes came near and said, "Good night, Pumpkin. . . . Hope you get your fat pig, Pumpkin," and smiled her witch's smile and left.

A fat stage hand said, "Can I take the chair, Mr. Gattone?"

He stood up, moved blindly toward the big black double doors. Joan Leonard waited, her weight on one flat-shoed foot,

286

her elbow propped against the wall. She smiled faintly. "It was good, Frank, and I hope it was worth it."

"For you," he said, "it would have been worth it. You'd have understood . . . You even said so . . . Compromise . . . You don't make it without compromise . . ."

"I'd have understood."

"But Anita . . ." He shook his head, ran a nervous hand through the black waves of his hair. "I wish I were ten years younger. I wish I loved you. And you loved me. I hope you never see that doctor friend again."

"I haven't. I don't see anyone."

"You will."

"I know."

"I wish . . . what my wife thinks about us . . . I wish it were true."

"So do I," she said.

He said "Well," and touched her arm. "Good night, Joan. . . . Good luck, Joan." Her eyes, he knew, her black eyes were on his back as he walked down to the row of elevators, and he was glad when the door sighed shut, when he was walking out the door at 30 Rockefeller. "No mistakes," Les had said. "It was a great show." A great show. And he thought of all those millions of people who had sat spellbound before their sets to see this great show, directed by the great Frank Gattone. So it had been worth it. All of the deception, the groveling, the lying, the compromising—it had all been worth it after all.

But then, crossing the street, he saw the long line of people waiting patiently for seats in the Music Hall; he saw the late eaters sitting under the umbrellas by the skating rink below; he saw the boys and girls, arm in arm; the old men, the young men, the New Yorkers and the tourists, strolling the night as always, and none of them, not one of them, had seen the show at all.

He hailed a cab. "Plimpton Ridge, Connecticut. Eight miles from Danbury."

287

"That's a hell of a ride, Mac."

"So long as you make it fast."

"Cost you damn near fifty bucks."

"Just keep going."

The cab swung west. Through the window he saw all the traffic, all the people, everything unchanged, as though the show had never been on the air. He looked at the picture of the cab driver, fastened to the rear of the front seat. His name was Hermann Klaffner.

Frank said, "Hermann . . ."

"Yeah?"

"What do you think of the Electro Television Theatre?"

"Think of it!" said Hermann. "I never even heard of it."

Anita could actually see the perspiration running down Frank's face, see how his black hair had fallen in a mop over his forehead, the way it always did when he was upset about something. He was looking directly at her, and at no one else in the entire television audience across the entire country. "You can't make a mistake . . . Please, please . . ." So he was pleading with her now, begging now, after the show was all over, of course, and he had nothing of that to lose any more.

"Please don't make a mistake!" He almost said her name, Anita, at the end. And then the camera lost him and the announcer was saying good night and the credits rolled and it was all over.

"What was the matter with Frank?" Paul said. He was sitting hunched over on the wicker chair, his frowning eyes fixed on the portable television set.

"I don't know." She shrugged her shoulders. "Worried, I guess."

"But I didn't notice any mistakes, did you?"

"You're not one of the keen-eyed boys from Hollywood."

"No, I guess not."

288

Paul got up from his chair and turned off the set. He'd taken off his coat when the show began, and now he stood in his shirt sleeves, still nursing the same drink he'd poured an hour ago. He was nervous, she knew, although she felt little nervousness herself. She had hurt Frank with good reason, stabbed at his manly ego where it would hurt the most, and she meant to hurt him still more. Earlier in the evening she had rather doubted that Paul would meet her at the cottage. But he had, and he was nervous, and she supposed, considering the kind of man he was, that she would have to take the initiative.

He finished his drink, looked at her briefly, ran a hand through his close-cropped hair. "You sure you don't want a drink, Anita?"

"Quite sure," she said, watching him, figuring it would take Frank two hours to reach Plimpton Ridge, and two hours was a very long time.

"Well . . . I'll have another myself, I guess."

"Go right ahead."

He mixed the drink and sat down again, cupping the glass between his big palms, his long, narrow fingers.

"You're angry with Roberta," Anita said.

"Angry?" He laughed shortly. "That's an odd word for the way I feel."

"I mean tonight."

"Yes," he admitted slowly. "Yes, I am."

"Why?"

"The truth?"

"The truth."

"In the middle of the dance, I wanted her to come home with me. I mean I wanted her. But she wouldn't."

"And if she had, you wouldn't be here now."

"That's right." He looked up at Anita, studying her quite openly now. "And I suppose you're here . . . I suppose the whole idea came from much the same sort of reason."

She smiled admission and they were being terribly honest now and that was probably the best way to be. He sipped his drink and she watched him in the dim light of the cottage. She thought how this, tonight, would be the first time she had slept with any man except Frank since their marriage, and only the fourth man she had ever slept with her entire life. Wild, her father called her, and Roy called her a nymphomaniac. But besides the young tennis player on the cot beneath the Plimpton banner, and then that one drunken night at a Dartmouth house-party, when she'd let a member of the ski team practically rape her in the back of a horse-drawn sleigh in the cold of a winter's night, she had never slept with any other men. She'd had her share of drinks of course—alone though, and that had probably made most of the difference.

"What are you thinking?" Paul asked finally.

"The same thing you are."

"Are you sure it is the same?"

"Isn't it?"

"I don't know," rising, moving about in that same nervous way.

"I didn't drink," she explained after a moment, "because I didn't want it to be like the last time we were here together."

"I remember."

"I told you then there'd be a sometime."

"Yes."

A pause. She rose. His back was to her. "Paul . . ."

He did not answer.

"Do you want me to get undressed? Do you want it deliberate or shall we build up to it? Do you want to make love to me or shall we simply crawl into the bunk and get it over with or what?"

Still he did not answer.

"All right, Paul." It was her move. She pulled the green sweater over her head, took off her brassière, started to drop her

290

skirt, then decided it was necessary to make absolutely sure before she went any further. "Paul . . . turn around, Paul."

He turned slowly. His gray eyes moved up and down her body. Excitement was clear behind the eyes, yet still he did not move, merely wet his lips and took a short quick drink.

"What do you think, Paul?"

"I think," he said carefully, "that you have beautiful high breasts. I think that sleeping with you would be as exciting as anything that ever happened to me."

"But?" seeing her mistake now, involuntarily holding the sweater across her naked breasts.

"But I think the 'sometime' was last time. It almost happened then. And if it was ever going to happen, it would have been then instead of now. It was too late at the 'sometime,' and a 'sometime thing' only comes once to all of us."

He turned away again, giving her time to dress, and she put on the brassière but could not fasten the hooks because she was crying and her hands were shaking. "Paul . . . please help me. . . . Please, Paul."

He moved toward her, easily now, and fastened her brassière as though she were a young girl struggling with her first bra, then stayed behind her while she pulled the sweater over her head. "You have lovely hair"—the voice still behind her while she was straightening the sweater. "And I guess you understand why it's like this, don't you, Anita? Because you and I, we're the possessed people in the world. We love someone, and no matter what that person does to us, no matter how we twist and turn, fight and revolt, thrash out at them and at ourselves—still we love them, and there's nothing, absolutely nothing we can ever do about it."

She heard his words over her shoulder, while the tears kept running down her face.

"Frank will be home soon, won't he?"

She nodded, unable to speak.

"Tell him it was a good show. Congratulate him."

Again she nodded, then swung around to him and clung to him, crying into the white cool of his shirt. When she had mastered herself she pulled away, and smiling through her tears, she said, "Good night, possessed."

"Good night, Anita."

"We'll survive, Paul."

"I hope so."

"Yes, we'll survive." And she left him and went out into the dark, the waiting car, and drove home.

The apron no longer hung on the kitchen door—red, with *Roberta* stitched in white—but he could still see it there. The picture was no longer Scotch-taped to the wooden wall—*To Daddy from Christina*—but it seemed to him still to be there.

Outside there were sounds of a summer night—tree frogs and crickets, moths thumping against the screens, the larger thumps of June bugs, a fish jumping in the lake, a small animal scurrying through the brush. But here, in the cottage, there was only himself, and the long thoughts and the memories that could not be changed. "We are the possessed," he had told Anita. So, possessed, realizing it, accepting it, there was no anger left inside him. Only a great weariness, almost a peaceful thing, in which he could light his pipe and close his eyes, lean back in the wicker chair, remember odd, disconnected emotions and events: his mother's funeral services, held in the Congregational Church of Fremont; selfish sister Lucille with her gray-brown hair, her black-black dress, the tears of self-pity streaming along the lines of her face; big, bumbling husband Richard, suffering, worrying through Lucille's exaggerated menopause, going impotent, he thought, red-faced in the unaccustomed stiff white shirt, the too-tight suit, his calloused hands sticking out like huge lobster claws from the short black sleeves; and Jean McElroy Stutgard, paying her respects to a dead woman she had

292

scarcely known. Plump, black-haired and dry-eyed, one hand on her husband's arm, attending the funeral for one reason only—to prove that her husband had come home last night after all, to say "Yes, I made a fool of myself, Paul Barker, but it was all very silly, of course, because here he is, my faithful husband, standing right here beside me where you can see him with your very own eyes." Chester Stutgard, salesman of Odor Out disinfectant for the toilets of New England's gasoline stations. A thin, dapper, mustached man, with a disinfected look, a man possessed, and a possessor, too—possessor of one frame house, one middle-aged, discontented wife, two older boys, a small girl with a runny nose, and many whitewashed stones that must some day be placed in even rows along the driveway.

The funeral was over. The school year was over. His years at Plimpton were over. Even his marriage was over. Sometimes things happened that way. You moved ahead, unthinking, enjoying your work, your family, enjoying life without quite knowing it, cutting your lawn, paying your taxes, painting the dining room ceiling, planning only for tomorrow, next week, next month, knowing the long run would some day become the short run, and why worry about it now? Your life was in motion until a point was reached, a turning point, a climax, if you will, when it stopped, teetered, then all crashed down at once like a pile of carefully laid matchsticks, like a half-finished jigsaw puzzle suddenly kicked into meaningless pieces that would not fit back together. It was over and you were just reaching forty. And it was not, as people claimed, that forty was the age at which you became aware that life was past its halfway point, but rather the age at which you looked ahead at thirty years to go and wondered how you would ever get through such a hell of a long time at all.

Chapter Thirty-Two

THEY sat on the soft grass at the water's edge. A fish jumped in the long, shimmering path of the moon. It looked cool out there. The grass was cool, though grass could stain her white dress, and the air was cool. Only Alan's hand was warm on the bare skin of her shoulder. His hand caressed her neck, then moved down, warm, slow, unbuttoned the top white button, then the second. Christina was fully aware of what Alan was doing, and another time her whole body would have been trembling in anticipation. But tonight it didn't seem very important. She was thinking of Mr. Roy Slayton, Alan's Uncle Roy, trying to fathom what he meant when he said *"You poor child . . . not your fault."* Mr. Slayton had been very drunk, but he was trying to say something to her, she felt certain. Something about her mother making a mistake. Something about having illegitimate children and having to get married.

Alan's fingers were unhooking her bra, and still she sat thinking, hands hugging her knees, while her dress fell half away from her shoulders.

"Christie," Alan whispered. "Christie . . . Oh, Christie."

"Yes, Alan?"

"You're still thinking about what Uncle Roy said."

"Yes."

"But I told you what he meant. First you asked him not to tell your parents we were here, and he could guess what we were doing, of course. So he was telling us to be careful. That's all he

294

was saying. To be careful. I told you not to worry because I got one of those things like I promised. Please, Christie, please don't be so far away . . ."

"I'm not far away, Alan." Though she was, the dress slipping down, Alan's hand warm, hot on her back.

"Christie . . . Christie . . ." He was kissing her now, pushing her back and down, the grass cool on her skin, the dress down to her waist, his mouth pressing down against hers, his hand trembling hot on her naked breast.

That was not what Alan's uncle had meant. Not at all what he'd meant. But she had promised Alan because she loved him and she wanted him and might never see him again all her life. His hand caressing her leg, her thigh, his lips tenderly kissing the nipple of her breast. She was so deliciously warm now, feeling the passion growing and growing inside herself, her mind all on Alan now and what he was doing to her, wondering what it would be like, if it would hurt, afraid, yet wanting him to go on.

But what had Mr. Slayton meant? Why was her own father leaving them? What had happened that night at Dr. Bullock's to send him away so suddenly the next morning? And why had he pulled away when she'd kissed him? Why had he said "Don't call me that" when she'd called him "Daddy"? Why, ever since, had he treated her so differently, as though they were no longer father and daughter? So careful with her, almost too nice. And why, and why, and why?

"Oh, God, Christie . . . Oh, my God!"

And Mr. Slayton had said *"Not your fault . . . your mother's fault."*

Alan's body was all trembling and she was trembling herself, terribly frightened, realizing that he was fumbling now, trying to prepare himself for something he had never experienced before, frightened as much as she was, maybe even more. "Christie," he whispered hoarsely, "Christie . . . I love you, Christie." And then she felt his weight on her, while she lay there with her heart beating, thumping in her breast, her eyes tightly closed, seeing all kinds of colors, reds and oranges, remembering words, faces, meaningless phrases, everything mixed up, disconnected, like the hundreds of pieces that make up a watch or an engine, each piece useless in itself until all the pieces were put together. Alan cried, "Christie!" and she thought, Oh God! he's trying to find me, and then in a flash all the pieces seemed to come together and in that one blinding flash of recognition she knew what Roy Slayton had been trying to say.

"No, Alan, no!" she screamed. "No!" She pushed him away from her, scraping her fingernails across his face. He cried out, "Christie, what are you doing?" seeing her stumble to her feet. Now she was fastening her bra, sobbing as she pulled up her dress and buttoned it. "No, Alan, don't touch me any more."

"But Christie, what is it?" Alan said, forgetting his own hurt in his concern for her. "I told you not to worry. I told you it'll be all right."

"That's not what your Uncle Roy meant at all."

"For God's sake, Christie."

"Not what he meant at all!" The words screamed out across the lake, echoed on the far shore, then crashed back into her own ears, so that she heard them and understood her own final understanding. She turned then and ran, ran, ran headlong through the woods, stumbling, falling, rising to run again, while Alan shouted after her. But she no longer heard him, because her own words were still echoing back, following her, pursuing her, on and on into the woods. She was running from her own words, from herself, on and on to somewhere, to nowhere, in a mad, wild, futile race toward the forgetting peace of oblivion.

Mildred told herself she must stop this ridiculous worrying about Roy. So he'd found Matt Barlow's tie clip. So what! She'd jumped to conclusions, made a fool of herself out of her own feelings of guilt. Roy understood nothing about her and Matt. He was just in one of his dangerous moods, wanted to be alone a while and drink himself stupid, the way he did sometimes when he got fed up with things. He'd be back again soon. This time, when he walked in the door, she would act casual, as though nothing unusual had happened.

She put water on the stove, turned up the gas jet. She took down a jar of instant coffee from the cupboard over the sink and made herself a cup of it. It was only when she was returning the jar to the cupboard that she noticed the missing bottle of whisky. A whole bottle! She hoped he would be careful about driving. She shrugged off her anxiety and returned to the living room. Roy said he was going to see Paul Barker. If he wanted to share a bottle with Paul, there was no harm in that, was there?

She sipped her coffee, watching Edith Parkes waxing emotional on the TV screen. It was a very sad play about a schoolteacher who could not decide who needed her most—the children or a lonely man. In the end, she chose the lonely man. The play was over then, and there was Frank Gattone on the screen acting very peculiar, as if he did not understand what the announcer was saying to him, pleading "Don't make a mistake . . . Don't make a mistake," while the sweat ran down his face. It was almost frightening.

She turned off the set. Don't make a mistake. She'd made a mistake, damn Matt Barlow, and damn herself, too. But Roy didn't suspect, she was sure of it. Only then why did he go off like that with a full bottle of whisky if he wasn't trying to knock himself out about something?

A car passed on the road outside. Not Roy. His Austin Healey had a very special sound. Should she sit here and wait in this ridiculous sexy black dress, or go upstairs to bed as if everything was all right? Lie there in bed and wait, and when he finally came home, make love to him so he could never suspect she'd ever had anything to do with Matt. If she tried hard enough, she might even find some enjoyment in it for herself.

The door to the bedroom was open, and when she put on the light the first thing she saw was the empty box where Roy kept that foolish one-eyed toy kangaroo of his. Only the kangaroo was missing . . . like the bottle of whisky. There was something eerie about the whole thing. A grown man running off with a bottle of whisky and a toy kangaroo. She was beginning to feel really frightened. Where had he gone with the kangaroo? And why wasn't he back? Even if he had gone to see Paul Barker, that was hours ago. . . . Her fright began to possess her now, mounting steadily into panic.

Running downstairs she called Paul Barker, but he said no, he had not seen Roy all evening. Then she phoned Roberta, and Anita, but neither of them was at home. When she called her father, he said, "I swear I don't understand you, Millie. Just because Roy went out for a little drive."

"You don't understand."

"So calm down, Millie."

"You just don't *understand*." She slammed down the phone. Of course he didn't understand. Matt Barlow would, but he would only laugh at her and tell her not to get so excited. No, she could not call Matt, and there was nobody else to call. She could only wait. Just wait.

But she could not wait. The panic was all through her now. She had to find Roy. Somebody had to help her. Somebody . . . And then, in desperation, she picked up the phone and dialed the Slayton home, even though she had never called Mitchel Slayton before in her life.

The phone rang a long time before Mrs. Mauldin answered. She'd seen Mrs. Mauldin only once, at her mother-in-law's funeral. The woman was so deaf Mildred had to shout everything over and over again. "Mr. Slayton!" she shouted. "I have to talk to Mr. Slayton."

298

Mrs. Mauldin said "What?" and "Who?" screaming her questions into the phone, until finally she explained that Mr. Slayton was at the Academy's graduation dance.

"Oh, damn, damn!" Mildred hung up. Outside a car passed. Not Roy. From far off, a dog wailed. She stood close to the phone, shaking, listening to the dog wailing again. Cars passed. Not Roy, not Roy. And why the liquor and the kangaroo? Why, why? Until she could not remain there any longer, alone, could not stand it another moment, and she rushed out to the garage and drove toward the Academy with her high heel shaking on the accelerator.

Mitchel Slayton thought she was out of her mind. He stood there in the gymnasium, under the Japanese lanterns, tall, silver-haired, gray-mustached, immaculate in his perfectly tailored tuxedo, looking down at her with the distant eyes of an adult listening to a hysterical child. "Simply because Roy went for a drive . . . Simply because he took along some liquor and that fool kangaroo . . ."

"But you don't understand, Mr. Slayton."

"No, I'm afraid I don't."

Roberta was there, wearing the white and black dress she'd admired so much at Dr. Bullock's that evening. "I can't explain," Mildred said to Roberta. "But I've just got to find Roy before it's too late."

"Too late for what?" asked Mitchel Slayton.

"I don't know. Something. I don't know what." She began to cry, going all to pieces.

Roberta's arm was around her. "Perhaps Roy has found Paul," she said, trying to soothe the hysterical woman. "Perhaps they're only having a drink together."

"No, no," Mildred wailed, wringing her hands. "I called Paul at the cottage. He said he hadn't seen Roy all evening."

Mr. Slayton sighed and said, "All right, come along,

299

Mildred. I'll take the car and we'll look for Roy, if it will make you feel any better."

Roberta hesitated. Then she said, "If you find Roy with Paul —I mean, if you see Paul—will you please tell him that I'm going home now. Tell him I'm . . . I'm waiting for him."

Mitchel looked at Roberta and his whole body seemed to sag and grow older. "Yes, I'll tell him," he said. Then his hand was firm on Mildred's arm as he led her out to his car. He said, "Please stop sniffling," and she said, "I can't, I can't," and kept crying while they drove off.

When they reached the woods they saw a car coming toward them up the rutted dirt road. "There," Mr. Slayton said, "that's probably Roy now." But it wasn't. It was young Alan Slayton, in a rattling old jalopy. Mr. Slayton stopped him and asked what he was doing there.

"I'm on my way home," Alan mumbled.

"Where's Christina Barker?"

"Home," Alan said.

"Hmmm," Mitchel Slayton said. "There's something funny going on here, and your father's going to hear about this. Have you seen your Uncle Roy?"

"Well . . ."

"Answer me. I asked if you'd seen your Uncle Roy." The big voice was hard, demanding an answer.

"Well, all right . . . yes, I saw him. He was sitting in his Austin Healey down that narrow path that leads to the dock. He was alone and he was drunk."

"Very well," Mitchel said. "Now go on home. You have no business being out here in the woods alone at this hour."

Mildred had stopped crying now, aware that her father-in-law was trying to hide his apprehension behind a show of anger. "I can't understand such nonsense," he muttered, and turned the Cadillac down the narrow path. After a few yards the car

300

could go no further. He took a flashlight from the glove compartment and said they'd have to walk.

The ground was uneven and she stumbled on her high heels. The flashlight picked out trees, rocks, a startled rabbit. Someone, some thing, was rushing through the woods. "Roy!" Mitchel Slayton called. "Is that you, Roy?" No answer. The flashlight swung, caught something white disappearing fast into the thicker woods. "What the hell is going on?"

Mr. Slayton was really worried now. Mildred could tell by the way he spoke. He was not disgusted with her any more. Something strange was happening and even Mr. Slayton could be disturbed by what he did not understand.

They moved on down the path. There were narrow zigzagging tire marks on the soft earth. A tree showed a fresh open wound; a rock had been scraped clean. "He had a few drinks, all right," Mr. Slayton muttered. "I suppose you two had a fight over something."

"No . . . " Mildred could hear the guilt in her own voice.

"Well, something made him do it."

"Yes, I did . . . I did," Mildred cried hysterically.

The light swung to her face, blinding her. "What are you talking about?" he said harshly. Then, "Never mind."

He walked on down the path. She followed, stumbling. A heel broke off, but she did not even notice it as she continued to hobble toward the dock that lay clear and bare in the moonlight. Mr. Slayton stepped onto the dock, turned the light on the boards. There were tire marks all the way to the end. The end. The water beyond. There was no need to say anything. It was too late to ask questions.

For a long time he stood there, saying nothing at all, staring at the tire marks picked out by the flashlight. Then his voice came very low and hoarse, the voice of a man who speaks without knowing it. "He must have been going like hell." The light faltered and went out. He lowered his big, sagging body to a wooden bench and, elbows on knees, covered his face with his hands.

"Mr. Slayton," Mildred said faintly, too numb to think, too numb to weep.

She went over to the end of the dock and looked down into the water. At first she could see nothing at all, but then, looking closer, she saw something dark and lumpy floating into view, and she leaned over and lifted Big Roo from the lake. He was soggy wet. His one eye gleamed in the moonlight. Roy had always claimed that Big Roo could see out of that one eye. But it was no longer true. The eye was staring, sightless. Big Roo was dead.

She sat on the bench beside her father-in-law, holding the dead kangaroo against her breast. Water soaked through her dress, ran down the low neck, cold between her breasts.

"I killed him," she said dully. "I killed Roy."

"An accident," said Mr. Slayton, his head still sunk in his hands. "He was drunk."

"No, no," Mildred sobbed. "I killed him."

What is she crying about? Mitchel Slayton thought hopelessly. As if she could kill my son. It was I who did it. Just as I killed his mother, and ruined Roberta's life, and hurt my daughter all these years. The sin is mine. . . . He groaned, then seemed to collapse within. His big frame was racked with sobs.

It was terrible to see a strong man weep like that—frightening. But Mildred was no longer afraid of her father-in-law now, and she stroked his head and spoke softly to him as to a child, until the sobs passed and he grew silent.

Water dripped rhythmically from Big Roo to the wooden boards of the dock. Big Roo was cold against her breast. And as she looked at the bent body of her father-in-law, and stroked his old head bowed in grief, it occurred to Mildred that only

302

now, in this agonizing moment, had she finally made contact with Roy's disapproving father. She had become a Slayton at last.

Chapter Thirty-Three

YOUNG couples walked arm in arm along the campus. Sometimes they stopped in the shadows of the great elms, and there was silence, then giggling from the girl before they walked on again, arm in arm, their hips touching, until they disappeared in darkness.

"Having a dance?" said the cab driver.

"Graduation." Frank gave him an even fifty dollars, then added another five as a tip. "Thanks, and I hope you get a fare back to New York."

"I won't."

"Well, good night, Hermann."

Hermann said good night, and backed out the gravel drive and drove off toward Danbury.

Frank stood hesitant by the neat hedges at his apartment doorway. The school clock tolled the hour of twelve. Midnight. Music sounded faintly from the gymnasium. They were playing a waltz, probably the final dance of the evening, he thought, and in his mind's eye he could see the swaying couples, sentimental, filled with youthful desire, loath to part and say good night, good-by.

He noticed the car in its regular parking place. There was a light in the living room window. "I will not be home," Anita

303

had said. Yet there was the car, there was the light. Perhaps, after all . . .

He drew a deep breath, climbed the three steps, and pushed open the door, closed it carefully, and moved slowly into the living room.

Anita was sitting on the sofa, her legs curled under her. She was wearing a gray skirt and a green sweater. She was reading a magazine and did not seem to be aware of his presence. Then finally she glanced up from the magazine and said calmly, "I thought you'd be on the twelve-thirty-two at Bridgeport."

"I took a cab."

"Very expensive."

"Yes, it was."

She closed the magazine, laid it carefully on a table. "Can I make you some coffee? . . . A drink?"

"I'll do it." He opened the cupboard, poured whisky into a glass, squirted in a splash of soda from the syphon. "Was there a call . . . from Les Garret?" he said.

"Not since I've been back," Anita said, still surprisingly calm.

He sipped his whisky, painfully aware of the silence in the room. She was waiting, he thought, playing with him, ready to pounce, ready to lash out with accusations, to boast of whatever she had done to pay him off. "Alan's at the dance, I suppose," he said.

"Yes . . ." Then, after a long pause, "The show came off pretty well, I thought."

He turned, looked at her, then sat down in an armless chair and turned the glass slowly between his hands. Where had she seen the show? Where and with whom? He would wait for her to tell him, let her play her game. He could not worry about that now. The telephone was there, only a few feet away, and soon it would ring, and perhaps after that it would not matter what she thought or said.

"Why?" Anita said suddenly. "Why did you sleep with that Joan Leonard girl?"

"I didn't," he said wearily, still listening for the phone to ring.

"Don't lie, Frank. Please don't lie to me any more."

"I'm not lying," he said quietly. "Are you sure Les Garret didn't phone me?"

"I've only been here since eleven," Anita said, still not saying where she had been until then, still playing with him. To hell with her.

He finished his drink, poured another. Behind him Anita said, "You lied about rehearsing with Edith Parkes, didn't you?"

"Yes."

"Why then, if you weren't with Joan Leonard?"

"Just because." He turned to her now, looked directly at her, and said it all calmly, straight out, so that she would know, and understand, and then do exactly as she pleased. "Because I was with Edith, in her apartment, when you called that night. I don't expect you to understand. But Edith agreed to do the show on one condition—that I be unfaithful to you. She wanted to humiliate me, get back at me for rejecting her back there after *The Letter*. . . ."

Anita was looking at him curiously, still without any sign of shock or hysteria. That will come later, he thought, feeling relieved that he was telling the truth at last, wondering at the lack of fear in himself.

"Well," he continued, "it was my choice and I made it. Because I needed Edith to make the show a success, and I needed that success because I can't live here any longer. I don't want to teach any longer. I've got to get back into what I like. If they want me to do the picture in Hollywood, I'm going. You choose not to go with me? All right, that's entirely up to you. But it's

305

my last chance, and I'm going to take it. I don't think I'll ever come back here again."

"I see," Anita said. "First Edith over me. Then, tonight, the show over me."

"Yes. That's about it."

"And suppose they don't want you in Hollywood?"

"They will."

"But suppose—"

"I said they *will*. They absolutely *have to*," Frank said, his voice rising as if he wasn't sure himself, was trying to convince himself.

Anita laughed. It was a strange laugh, half aloud, half smothered in her throat. Then the phone rang. Frank snatched up the receiver.

It was Les Garret. He said, "I told you they were idiots out there . . . The way the ball bounces . . . The way the cookie crumbles . . . You'd have hated it anyway . . . Don't know how lucky you are."

He hung up slowly, finished his drink, took the glass into the kitchen and washed it carefully under the faucet. Then he came back into the living room, sank despondently into a chair and sat with his head resting in his hands, too tired to fight any more, and besides what was there left to fight for anyway?

"I'm sorry," Anita said.

"The hell you are," he said bitterly.

"Three hours ago I would have been glad. Now I'm sorry." Then, slowly, "I went down to Paul Barker's cottage. I saw the show there. I was going to sleep with him . . . in pure revenge. No, not entirely revenge. I think he's attractive, always have thought so. But then . . . nothing happened. He made me realize that I'm stuck with you. And now you're stuck with me. Maybe I'm just a neurotic, a drunk. Maybe it isn't love I feel for you at all—only need. I don't know any more. I guess I'm just a second-class person—like you."

"Don't worry, you're first class," he said, still bitter.

"No . . . I would have slept with Paul if he'd have had me. I'd have cheapened myself for revenge as much as you cheapened yourself for success. . . . I'm afraid, Frank. I'm afraid we're two lousy people who don't understand each other, don't understand ourselves, don't understand our own son, don't understand anything at all. I messed up your first try at success. You messed up your second. So . . . well . . . where do we go from here?"

"I don't know. I just don't know."

Silence. No hatred, no games, no jealousy. Only weariness of body and soul. Only the exact truth of what Anita had said. They needed each other. Two sadder and perhaps wiser people needed each other. They had gone this far together, and it was too late, it would take too much effort to begin again at anything, to begin a new life alone, or with anyone else.

The door opened, and Alan came into the room. "What happened to your face?" Anita said.

"Just a scratch. . . . Did Grandfather Slayton call?"

"No."

"He will."

"Why?"

"He just will." As if in answer to his statement, the phone rang. Alan snatched up the receiver. His voice rang in high, fierce defiance. "All right, Grandfather, they're both here. You can tell them what you like. Any damn thing you like." He dropped the receiver on the desk and rushed down the hall to his room.

"What in God's name . . ." Anita said as she picked up the phone. Then, speaking into the mouthpiece, "I don't understand," and then a low, "No . . . No . . ." and "Oh, God . . . oh, my God!"

Frank looked up. Anita was sitting rigid, still holding the phone in her hand although she was no longer talking or listening. "Roy," she said finally. "He went over in his car . . . in the lake."

"Roy?" Frank said, unbelieving. "Roy? Drowned?"

"He was drunk. An accident. Or maybe on purpose. We'll never know."

"Then you'll be going to your father. Shall I take you?"

"He doesn't want me."

"You ought to go."

"Mildred's there and he doesn't want me. He never did. That's always been my trouble, hasn't it? The poor little girl without a father." She rose, swaying, ran a hand across her eyes, then moved slowly, crying silently, out of sight down the hall.

Frank continued to sit alone in the quiet room. Roy was dead. Death by water. First Anita's mother, and now her brother. And the worst part for her, he knew, was that she couldn't feel her loss deeply, could feel neither loss nor grief, so that if she was crying now it was not so much because Roy was dead as that he had died, like her mother, before she had ever had a chance to know him. She was crying because of her own lack of tears.

She had called him a second-class person. Well, it was true. Frank Gattone, mama's boy Frankie . . . not tough like his brothers, not the strong man like his father . . . ambitious little Frankie . . . from burlesque to television, from The Mammary Marvel to Edith Parkes . . . from there to eternity, obscurity, destroyed by a woman he had married for selfish reasons. No, not destroyed by her. Destroyed, rather, by his own lack of integrity.

Feeling infinitely weary, bearing the weight of his failure on his bowed shoulders, Frank moved about the room, putting out the lights. He went down the hall. Alan's door was closed, but a light showed through the crack at the bottom. Poor Alan . . . poor son . . . Was he, too, only the result of one night's passion without precaution? He had not asked to be born. Life

308

had been thrust upon him, and he, like the rest of them, could only make the best of it.

Frank knocked twice, then pushed open the door. Alan was in his pajamas. He was sitting on the edge of his bed, staring absently out the window at the dark trees. "So all right," he said. "So Grandfather Slayton saw me. So he told you about it."

"No, Alan. Mr. Slayton called to tell your mother that your Uncle Roy was drowned in the lake."

"Drowned?" Head turning, eyes widening in shock. "But I saw him myself. Drunk. Sitting in his car."

"It must have been after that."

The boy turned away again. His face, reflected in the dark window, was expressionless while he tried to understand his own emotions. "It was in the woods," he said. "I didn't see your show. I didn't want to. Instead I went down to the lake with Christina."

"I see."

"No, you don't see. I thought I loved Christina. But I only wanted to hurt her, just like I wanted to hurt Grandfather Slayton on the phone just now."

"Why are you telling me this, Alan?" Frank said gently.

"Now Uncle Roy is dead, and I'll never see Christina again. . . . Nothing is the way it seems to be."

"No, nothing is."

"Christina and I . . . well, I got one of those things, you know, and we were going to . . . well, you know . . . because we didn't have anyone but each other. Then we saw Uncle Roy and he was drunk and he said something I didn't understand. . . . But later, just when we were going to do it . . . go all the way, I mean . . . then suddenly Christina must have understood what he meant, and she screamed, and pushed me away, and ran into the woods."

Alan was crying silently, and Frank felt his heart going out to the boy. "Her father isn't really her father," Alan whispered, his head bowed to hide his emotions.

Frank sat on the other side of the bed, his back to his son. "I know, Alan," he sighed.

"I couldn't find her. I ran all through the woods looking for her. And then I saw the light in Mr. Barker's cottage. I went in and told him exactly what Uncle Roy and Christina had said. I wanted to stay with him and look for her, but he wouldn't let me. And then on the road I saw Grandfather and he was angry with me and said he would tell you, but he won't have to now."

"No, he won't have to," Frank said, getting up from the bed. "There's nothing for him to say." He walked toward the door.

"Aren't you even mad at me?" Alan said behind him. "I mean, my taking Christina to the woods and all that."

"I'm not mad. I understand," Frank said, pausing at the door, his hand on the knob.

"I wonder if you really do," Alan said. "I just wonder."

Frank didn't say anything. It was so hard for a boy, he thought, to understand that his father might have been through the same thing so many times himself. And he thought, too, that he envied the boy, for whom the experience was so new, so fresh, so painful—as if nothing like it had ever happened before on God's green earth.

"I'm glad it never happened," Alan said. "All the time I was trying to think of some way for it not to happen. I'm not much of a man, I guess."

"Don't say that," Frank said. He went over to his son and put his hand on the boy's shoulder. "You're a lot of man, Alan. I wish I were half that much myself."

"I'm sorry I didn't see your show," Alan said, looking up at his father.

"Don't be sorry. It was no good anyway."

"I've got so much to think about."

310

"So have I." Frank looked his son straight in the eye for the first time, it seemed to him, since God knew when. Some day they would have a long talk. Not now, but soon. He'd never thought it would happen, but he was sure of it now, and so, he felt, was Alan.

"Good night," they both said, and then Frank went out and closed the door behind him, and went into the bedroom. Anita lay on her side with her back to him, and did not turn when he came into the room.

"I've just had a talk with Alan," he said. "I know it's late, but I'm going to try very hard to be a decent father to him."

When Anita didn't say anything but still kept her face averted, he continued, "And since we're stuck with each other, as you say, since you and I are stuck with each other, I guess it would be more pleasant for both of us if I tried to be a decent husband, too."

Anita remained silent, but he had the feeling that she was listening to every word he was saying, listening not so much to his words as to his intention behind the words. "Anita . . . that night in the Plaza. No matter what you may think now, for a moment there we were very close. It's always hard to be really close to someone, and the longer you're married the harder it becomes."

"I know." Her voice was muffled deep in the pillow.

"I'm sorry about Roy. About everything. I don't have to tell you that. . . . I'm going to take a bath, try to wash all the crumminess away. I wish, while I'm bathing, I wish you'd put on your black nightgown, the same one you wore the other night. Maybe we don't love one another the way we should. But I'd like to try. . . . We have to *try*." He waved his hands, took his pajamas into the bathroom, and closed the door.

When he came back to the bedroom he found Anita sitting upright in bed. Her bare shoulders, emerging from the black, filmy gown, gleamed in the lamplight, her yellow hair was

311

freshly brushed, and she was looking at him as if somehow he was different from the man she had been talking to in the living room a short time before.

"You look so young," Frank said, smiling, "so . . . well . . . kind of new." He sat beside her. "Tomorrow will be better," he said softly, "even for a couple of mixed-up people like us."

"Oh Frank, Frank, let's make it better," she said, and the tears came to her eyes, only they were different tears, tears of happiness and of hope, and she hid her face in his shoulder as he drew her close to him.

Chapter Thirty-Four

FOR the past hour Paul had driven every road in the vicinity, walked up every path he knew. He had shouted and waited, waited and shouted again, made wild dashes at the sound of frightened animals, returned to his car and driven the same roads over again, walked the same paths, shouted the same words, rushed hopefully at the same sounds.

"Christina!" he cried desperately into the night. "Christina, where are you?"

Suddenly the headlights picked out a patch of white in a small stand of scrub pine along a back road two miles from the cottage. Paul leaped out of the car, stumbled in the gulley alongside the road, fought his way through wild blackberry bushes toward the unmoving blob of white. An old rag, probably, a rabbit, nothing, nothing at all. But the patch of white grew larger as he came closer. It became a cloth, a dress, a form, the body of a young girl, exhausted, curled up like a baby on the bed of pine needles.

"Oh my God!" he sobbed with relief. "Christina! Baby!"

He knelt beside her. She was half asleep, trembling, shivering although the night was warm. "Christina . . . honey . . ." She did not move. "It's Daddy, honey . . ."

"No . . . No," she whispered into the ground.

"Don't be afraid. It's Daddy, honey." He gathered her into his arms. She did not resist, only said "No," over and over, "No, no, you're not my Daddy, not my Daddy."

"Yes, honey," he said soothingly as he walked slowly back to the car, bearing her in his arms as if she were a little child. "I remember when you were born, honey. I was so very proud. You were my little daughter. And now you're my big daughter, and it's never been anything different. Can you remember when it was different? . . . Ever? . . . When I didn't love you? Haven't I always been your Daddy? . . . Always, always?"

"But Mr. Slayton said . . . Alan's uncle . . ."

"Mr. Slayton was drunk, baby. You'll see. Tomorrow, in the morning, we'll ask Mr. Slayton what he meant, and then you'll see."

"You're sure?" she said, looking up searchingly into his eyes. "You promise?"

"Yes, honey . . . I promise."

He'd reached the car. He placed her tenderly in the front seat, then went around the car and slipped in beside her. She sat motionless, disheveled, staring through the windshield as he started the motor. He touched her arm. "You'll see, honey . . . I love you, Christie." The car moved on down the road.

After a while, Christina said, "I know it was a crazy idea,

running away like that. But you don't love Mother any more, and you're going to leave us, and . . ." Her voice broke, and she was crying bitterly.

"There, there, baby, don't cry," he said, putting his arm around her shoulders and drawing her close to him. "I've always loved your mother."

"But you don't act as if you do. And now you're going to be divorced . . ."

"I love your mother and I love you, and you must never think anything else."

Ahead was the dirt road that led down to the cottage. A state police car stood at the entrance. Searchlights shone bright through the trees at the water's edge. All Alan's doing, Paul thought. He'd called the police and they were searching for Christina. He stopped the car, leaned out the window. "Officer, I'm Paul Barker. If you're looking for my daughter . . ."

"Your daughter?" The man was young. His badge shone in the moonlight. "No, it's an accident, Mr. Barker. Roy Slayton. His car went into the lake."

"Roy Slayton?"

"Drowned."

"Drowned? . . . Oh my God! Poor Roy!"

An ambulance moved up the dirt road, the red light blinking on its roof. "Mr. Slayton," Christina whispered in a hushed, awed voice, "Mr. Slayton . . ."

They drove off in silence, too shocked to say anything. Behind him, Paul could hear the wailing of the ambulance. After a while, Christina said quietly, "I can't ask Mr. Slayton after all."

"No."

"I'll just have to believe you."

"Yes, honey . . . yes, you will." Then, as they entered town and drove past the lighted windows of Mitchel Slayton's house, past the bandstand and the ivy-colored buildings of the Acad-

314

emy, "Of course, Christie . . . of course, you must never let your mother know that you ever thought such a ridiculous thing . . . about my not loving her . . . about anybody but me being your Daddy. I mean, you can imagine how she'd feel."

"Yes, I know, Daddy."

"Say it again."

"I know, Daddy . . . Daddy, Daddy, Daddy, Daddy," the words growing softer and softer as she fell off to sleep, breathing gently now, a small child safe, a small child going home.

Roberta looked at the clock on the mantel, then continued to pace the room in an agony of suspense. More than an hour ago Paul had called to say that Christina and Alan had been walking in the woods, had become separated. Christina was lost. He was going out to look for her. No, don't call the police, Paul said. He would find her himself. But that was more than an hour ago, and still no word of them.

Why didn't Paul call again? Why hadn't she notified the police instead of waiting like this, pacing up and down in her dressing room, listening to the ticking of the clock, unable to do anything at all but wait and walk, wait and walk.

Then the car in the driveway. Roberta rushed out to the porch. Paul was getting out of the car. "Thank God, you're here," she cried. "I was so frightened." He was carrying Christina in his arms. She was scratched and bruised. Her dress was torn. But she was alive, thank God! Alive and unharmed. She was sound asleep in Paul's arms.

Paul carried the sleeping girl through the doorway, up the stairs to her room, with Roberta following close behind. He laid her gently on the bed. Christina's eyes opened sleepily. "Good night, Daddy," she whispered.

"Good night, honey." He kissed her, and she sighed and her eyes closed again. "You'll have to undress her," he said to Roberta, and left the room.

Roberta prepared her daughter for bed, washed the scratches and applied antiseptic, then helped her, half asleep, half awake, under the covers. "Good night, baby . . . Good night . . ."

Christina's eyes fluttered open. "Daddy loves you," she said. "Christina . . ."

"I know, because he told me. And I believe anything, *everything* my Daddy says . . . Oh, I'm so sleepy, so sleepy . . ."

Roberta kissed the eyes closed now in sleep, put out the light and tiptoed from the room. In the living room she found Paul drinking a cup of black coffee. Around him were boxes of books, barrels of china, rolled-up rugs, all waiting to be shipped away, some to Pennsylvania and some to California.

She said, "Christina's not hurt. Just dirt and scratches."

"That's good."

"I suppose you've heard about Roy."

"Yes."

"Mildred called me. Poor Mildred. Poor Mitchel."

"We should stay for the funeral," Paul said.

She looked at him surprised. "But I thought you were leaving."

"No hurry." He reached for his pipe, filled it with tobacco.

"I thought you hated Mitchel. You wouldn't go to his wife's funeral. Why is this any different?"

"Roy was a friend of mine," Paul said, striking a match to his pipe. Then, puffing slowly, "And besides, I don't hate Mitchel Slayton any more. In fact, I feel terribly sorry for him. That's an odd thing, isn't it? But tonight, when I was looking for Christina, I was searching for *my* daughter. Not *his*, but *mine*. I wanted to find her safe, and I wanted to bring my daughter home to my wife. Then I found her. I felt so relieved, so happy. I see now it doesn't really matter who conceived her. What's important is that she's grown up with me, she's mine. What's important is I'm so damn grateful she was born at all."

Roberta remained silent, her heart too full for words. She

316

heard the clock ticking, and it seemed to her like the beating of her own heart. She watched him put down his coffee cup, and wondered if he could read in her face how much she adored him.

"All I ever wanted," Paul was saying, "was a small measure of happiness. I never had Roy's dreams or Frank's ambitions. It's always been enough for me to love and be loved. And I think perhaps Mitchel wanted the same thing, only he's lost everything now because he didn't know how to treasure the little happiness he had."

Silence. Only the silence was no longer empty and menacing. Instead, it seemed to Roberta that the silence was warm and pulsing and alive, surrounding Paul and herself with a loving embrace and bringing them closer and closer together.

"Yes, I've learned something tonight," Paul said thoughtfully. "I learned how close I came to being God's biggest fool. Now I think I know better, and I don't intend to lose the happiness of sixteen years, just throw it away as if it's nothing, when it's all I have."

Roberta came over to him and took his hands in hers and put his arms around her. "Oh Paul," she said, looking up at him happily, "I've waited so long for you to talk to me like this. I knew . . . I was confident, but I had to wait. And now . . ."

"As long as you love me," he said. She could only weep for the joy welling up in her. "I love you, I love you, Roberta," Paul said, kissing the tears from her eyes. And then, their arms around each other, they went slowly up the stairs to their room.